Rise of the Abrogators

The Rune Fire Cycle, Volume 3

Lance VanGundy

Published by Lance VanGundy, 2023.

This is a work of fiction. Similarities to real people, places, or events are entirely coincidental.

RISE OF THE ABROGATORS

First edition. September 14, 2023.

Copyright © 2023 Lance VanGundy.

ISBN: 978-1735427294

Written by Lance VanGundy.

Table of Contents

Chapter One: The How and Why of Things.............................1

Chapter Two: The Taker's Gamble.............................. 13

Chapter Three: Like Snow Down a Mountain 24

Chapter Four: A Hole in the Darkness.............................. 33

Chapter Five: Bartusk on the Borderlands 38

Chapter Six: A Question of History 44

Chapter Seven: Princely Impulses.............................. 51

Chapter Eight: The Aspect's Last Motivation 58

Chapter Nine: Gifted, Not Cursed 65

Chapter Ten: Through the Pillars of Eldrek 74

Chapter Eleven: Ill Omens at the Pillars 83

Chapter Twelve: The King's Respite.............................. 89

Chapter Thirteen: Finding the Right Path.............................. 95

Chapter Fourteen: Pulling Weeds and Planting Seeds.............................. 102

Chapter Fifteen: Safe Passage in the Dark 110

Chapter Sixteen: Shadowed Secrets 123

Chapter Seventeen: The Path the Taker Laid 132

Chapter Eighteen: Nothing and Everything 137

Chapter Nineteen: An Audience of One 151

Chapter Twenty: Second Chances 158

Chapter Twenty-One: Tapping the Leech.............................. 169

Chapter Twenty-Two: The Source and the Pack 176

Chapter Twenty-Three: Venlith's Last Stand.............................. 182

Chapter Twenty-Four: Colors in the Valley 195

Chapter Twenty-Five: A Sympath on the Run.............................. 204

Chapter Twenty-Six: Wrong Place, Wrong Time 209

Chapter Twenty-Seven: The Vessel.............................. 220

Chapter Twenty-Eight: Company in the High Country.............................. 225

Chapter Twenty-Nine: The Source of the Regent's Folly 231

Chapter Thirty: A Story for a Story 242

Chapter Thirty-One: Keeping Pace with the Old Man 254

Chapter Thirty-Two: Scars from the Past.............................. 262

Chapter Thirty-Three: The Power of True Belief.............................. 268

Chapter Thirty-Four: Mingling with the Unsuspecting 276
Chapter Thirty-Five: Perfect Timing 281
Chapter Thirty-Six: Something Dark Stirs in the East................ 288
Chapter Thirty-Seven: Releasing the Reins 296
Chapter Thirty-Eight: Searching for the Source.......................... 303
Chapter Thirty-Nine: Beyond Suspicion 310
Chapter Forty: The Luna Rova.. 316
Chapter Forty-One: The Winnowing of the Shades 325
Chapter Forty-Two: Mixed Blessing in the Wolf's Maw 330
Chapter Forty-Three: Spun Glass and Dragonflies 339
Chapter Forty-Four: The Giver's Rare Touch 345
Chapter Forty-Five: Dangerous Missions 351
Chapter Forty-Six: The Giver's Last Breath............................ 356
Chapter Forty-Seven: Following Their Nature 364
Chapter Forty-Eight: The Killing Field 372
Chapter Forty-Nine: All About the Details 382
Chapter Fifty: Joy and Pain 390
Chapter Fifty-One: A Passage in Stone 399
Chapter Fifty-Two: Confronting the Past................................ 406
Chapter Fifty-Three: The Rite of Sundering 412
Chapter Fifty-Four: The Taker's Run 417
Chapter Fifty-Five: Trading One Evil for Another 425
Chapter Fifty-Six: The Ascent 434
Chapter Fifty-Seven: Rise of the Abrogator 440
Chapter Fifty-Eight: The Sons of Japheth and Nebrine 445
Chapter Fifty-Nine: Abrogator Interrupted............................. 462
Chapter Sixty: More with Less.. 467

My brother, Jason, keeps my story and its characters honest.

My wife, Kristin, makes me want to be a better man and inspires me to create.

My hope is that all readers will dive into Karsk with the same reckless abandon as my daughter, Madisun. The simple observation of her joy at being swept up in the adventures herein is all that ever matters. With that, turn the page and keep your eyes to the horizon!

Preface: Synopsis of *Runes of the Prime*, Book 2 of the Rune Fire Cycle.

In *Runes of the Prime*, Laryn rescues Kaellor and the brothers, delivering them to the safety of the Valley of the Cloud Walkers. They immediately discover that Lluthean's festering wound, the result of an attack by a shadow chaser, has placed him near death. With Kaellor lending the strength of his gift, Laryn is able to heal Lluthean, but the effort throws them both into the malady called the draft, and it takes days for them to recover.

The group learns that travel over the Korjinth Mountains is extremely dangerous due to the storms of zenith and nadir that collide in dreadful eruptions among the peaks, a result of the cataclysm that raised the mountains hundreds of years ago. They are effectively trapped in the valley until a ceremony can be performed in which ancestral spirits can provide them with a safe path forward. The brothers use the time to train with the wolvryn, and Kaellor teaches them sword forms.

Kaellor and Laryn rekindle their love after a twelve-year hiatus. Kaellor learns the strengths and limitations of his gift, including how the guardian sword seems to magnify his combat prowess. Laryn uses her skills in healing on more than one occasion throughout their adventures.

The abrogator Volencia survives a disfiguring wound and is tasked by Tarkannen with finding a new clan of grotvonen called the Brognaus. They reside under a mountain range in the far northwest regions of Karsk and use shamans to perform rituals powered by nadir. With the added guidance of umbral, the shamans create a portal to allow Volencia to travel to Callinora and retrieve "the vessel," a living person to whom Tarkannen is tethered, thereby allowing him to remain connected to the world of the living. She fails in the initial attempt.

Elder Miljin of the Cloud Walkers learns from the ancestral spirits that Tarkannen is close to returning to the world of the living and advises that Laryn, Kaellor, and the boys must risk crossing the Korjinth Mountains if they hope to thwart him. Using the sight of the wolvryn, the brothers can identify the dangerous cyclones of zenith and nadir before they erupt. The family makes a harrowing trek, surviving sinister dangers and the elements. After crossing the Korjinth, they recover on the slopes in the Northlands.

Karragin's quad returns to base camp, and she is drawn into combat with a grondle. The beast nearly kills her, and afterward, she is tasked with a distant assignment in the Great Crown, Warden Elbiona's attempt to keep the Lefledge children out of harm's way. While ranging the Great Crown, they discover strange trails that turn out to be umbral tracks, and when investigating the grotvonen warren, Amniah is captured. Karragin recruits a quad led by the Prime Savnah, and the group of them make the descent to find Amniah. Inside the warrens, they are met with significant resistance.

The underground journey leads them deep into grotvonen territory. They encounter the umbral, and the demolitions expert, Argul, blows up a narrow land bridge, killing the umbral but trapping the rest of them until they find a way out through old grotvonen tunnels. They emerge outside the Great Crown mountains only to battle a crush of grondle. The skirmish leads to the discovery of embertang as a possible weapon against the beasts.

Amniah, Karragin's guster, incurs battle shock and requires a reprieve from the Outriders. Savnah and Dexxin join Karragin's group, increasing their collective battle prowess. They travel on a diplomatic mission to Voruden, deep in the Borderlands.

Ksenia Balladuren is a sympath gifted with the ability to communicate with animals. Thanks to her mother's meddling, she is coerced into taking an assignment in the regent's court as a scribe. She feels displaced, isolated, and frustrated by the way her life has been controlled. She is attracted to the sense of community among the Lacuna, a growing political group that seems to support the poor and disenfranchised, like orphaned children and the runeless. She befriends Therek Lefledge with genuine empathy, and he leads her to phrases in the Founders' Memorial that allow her to begin to unravel High Aarindorian, a long-dead language.

Reddevek, the warden, was injured at the end of book one and recovers in Journey's Bend. As the winter unfolds, he befriends Ranika, the street orphan who followed him from Callish. He begins to teach her woodcraft, and a game develops in which he attempts to track her with his gift. When he fails to do so, she reveals to him her secret: that she can bend nadir to her will and hide inside shadows. He realizes that she is an abrogator. The two of them escape Journey's Bend, as representatives of the Immaculine had begun seeking out anyone capable of wielding zenith or nadir. They head to Aarindorn.

Runes of the Prime culminates with Kaellor and his family traveling across the Borderlands, pursued by two crush of grondle. They defeat the first group and engage the second only to be rescued by Karragin's Outriders on their mission to Voruden. In the chaos of battle, Karragin's rune of premonition, a typically frustrating gift that defies her control, surges with a prophetic vision. She becomes aware that Savnah and Dexxin are members of the Lacuna and will act to assassinate Kaellor and his family unless Karragin can reshape the future events. Using her gifts to first communicate with the wolvryn and then engage the grondle, she alters the events just enough to allow a peaceful resolution to the conflict.

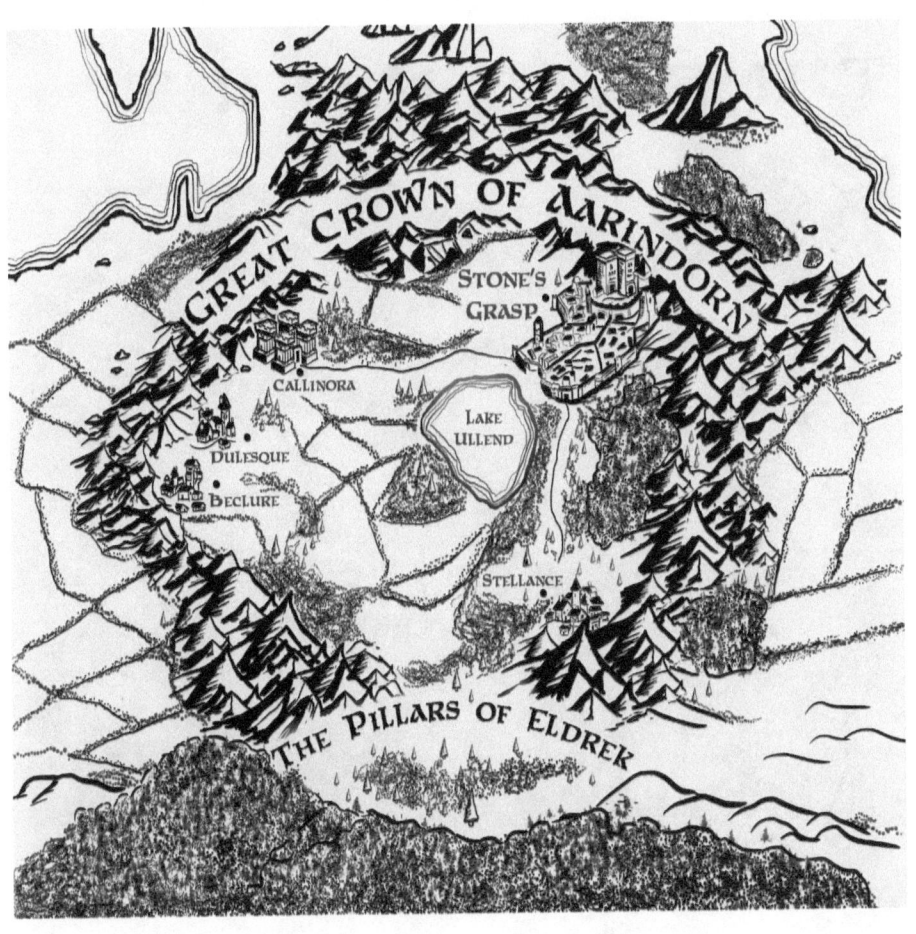

THE
RODENDIAN
SEA

DERNEGIA

KREEG

FALTUSCH

GREAT CROWN OF AARINDOR

STONE'S GRASP

BESKEN

MILLSTONE

NORFOLD

THE PILLARS
OF ELDREK

THE

THE RODEMAR RIVER

VARGAST

VORUDEN

THE VALLEY OF THE CLOUD WALKERS

KORJINTH MOUNTAINS

THE MOORLOE WOOD

THE SOUTH

RIVERTON

LAKE AVORELL

JOURNEY'S
BEND

Prologue: A Rent in Space

In the high places of the Great Crown, snow fluttered to the ground. A mountain hare, completely invisible when sleeping, opened its dark eyes. Its pink nose twitched, searching for the scent of fresh pine. Oversized back feet carried it lightly over the drifts.

Something caused the side of the mountain to tremble, and the creature froze, training all its senses to identify the source of the disturbance. A harsh clang, like stone splitting apart, preceded a ripping, tearing sound that echoed over the canyon.

A black, serrated rent appeared directly overhead, and something from another world fell through the breach before it sealed back up, leaving placid blue skies.

The hare watched, instinct keeping it rooted in place. The creature that fell into the world smelled of things long dead and only discovered when the summer sun melted the snow. The amorphous ball of black jelly wriggled, its surface rippling and morphing. The mass of tissue grew in height, extending first as a column, then sprouting appendages. In moments, a humanoid with great wings stood only a few feet away.

Vertical rows of black eyes on a rounded head twitched and searched the horizon. The hare felt its unnatural gaze and remained as still as the surrounding snow. Clawed feet stepped forward, and the beast screeched in surprise when it sank several feet into the drift. Now was the chance. The hare bounded away, its great padded feet propelling it down the snowbank.

The action, timed perfectly and executed with instinctive precision, would have evaded normal mountain predators. But the thing standing in the snow was anything but normal. Faster than the twitch of a bowstring, a black appendage shot out, impaling the hare with a hooked tip. The otherworldly thing retrieved the body, holding up the limp form as drops of bright red blood stained the snow.

It pulled the hare to its torso and flowed around the carcass, enveloping it, probing it, then finally consuming it whole. The first change took a few minutes. Slowly and with tedious effort, delicate white hairs sprouted across the creature's surface. Moments later, it collapsed into an amorphous jelly again as it labored to produce the new form.

Bones stretched out inside the substance, a leg here, a shorter delicate arm there. A spine and skull lifted from the surface, and eventually, a flawless mimic of the mountain hare emerged.

It hopped in a hesitant circle, expecting to sink beneath the snow. Learning new body mechanics was the specialty of greater feigns. It allowed them to thrive, masquerading as one of the far more formidable predators in certain currents in the Drift. And so, after a few moments of experimentation, it effortlessly bounded down the slope to investigate the shadows on the horizon.

Trees came into view, but the feign had never seen trees before, so it stopped and studied the protrusions erupting through the snow. Wind caused the trees to lean and creak, snow spilling from branches. Not perfectly still, then.

It could digest and assimilate something that large over time, but the things appeared more structural and relatively immobile. And if the feign had learned anything in its long life, it knew that mobility and the ability to change was its purpose . . . its instinct.

The hare turned to hop away when the fangs of a wolf savaged into its side. The feign screeched once, allowing the bones and sinews, all the tissues, to deconstruct, reducing back to its amorphous, globular form. The wolf shook its head violently, then sat back on its haunches, overwhelmed with curiosity and confusion at the strange turn of events. Eventually, the predator crept forward, sniffing at the otherworldly substance that wriggled on the ground.

A thin, black tentacle speared forward into the wolf's snout. The wolf staggered back, but the feign had the purchase it required and pulled itself into the wolf's nose and mouth before flowing into its eyes and ears. In seconds, the feign had poured into the predator, suffocating it from the inside.

This digestion and transformation took longer. But within the hour, a grey wolf, smelling perhaps less like a wolf and more like a discarded carcass, loped off into the timber in search of other forms to possess.

Chapter One: The How and Why of Things

SILVY DECHANCE PULLED her daughter, Ranika, down a narrow hall in the center of Felpinge House. Sconces with rose-colored glass cast soft shadows by their dusky illumination and made it seem like twilight regardless of the time of day. Their feet tread silently over an ornate red and black runner with gold tasseled fringes at the sides. Ranika ran her fingers along the textured wallpaper and wondered, not for the first time, who the pretty naked women were whose silhouettes adorned the walls.

"Mama, where's your picture?" she asked.

Silvy ignored her question and pulled on Ranika's wrist with more insistence. "Not now, Nika. We need to get you sorted. Into your burrow, my little mouse."

Silvy stopped near the end of the hall and looked up the long set of stairs to ensure that no patrons were descending. Assured of their privacy, she pressed on a recessed panel hidden by the heavy wallpaper. A small door popped open, revealing Ranika's room for the night. After kissing her daughter on the top of the head, Silvy nudged her forward. "In you go. You can watch the clients when they leave, but you have to stay down here and don't let any of them see or hear you. Understand?"

Felpinge House sat on a bluff overlooking Foden's Wharf on the northeastern shore of the Port of Callish. Affectionately referred to as "the Pinch," the house catered to discerning clients interested in more than a messy grind offered by common street whores. The courtesans of Felpinge House excelled in music, poetry, and all manner of high arts, and the clientele visiting the Pinch spent high sums for an evening of culture and fine dining on balconies overlooking the sunset across the Port of Callish. They paid more for the subsequent festivities behind the gilded doors.

Ranika stepped inside her recessed alcove under the stairs, turned, and nodded once, then waited for her mother to close the door. Alone in the darkness, she held both hands up and walked forward until her palms rested flat against the back edge of the fourth step. She felt along the side until she found the familiar edge of a defect in the wood.

Squeezing until the tips of her fingers burned, she eventually popped a knot out of its hole, and a shaft of rose-tinted light spilled into her hideout. She turned to the side, allowing the pale beam to fall behind her and onto the handle of a broken comb inlaid with mother of pearl. A muted kaleidoscope of color reflected up onto the backside of the stairs.

The effect reminded her of the night sky with faint stars twinkling in the darkness. She focused on the most prominent spot and forced her eyes to relax. After a moment, a tingling cold sensation, as if the winter wind was streaming in through the knothole, rippled across her cheeks. In that instant, all of the shadows evaporated, and the interior of her cubby revealed its secrets to her.

Her eyes adjusted, and she turned to inspect her belongings. A stained and threadbare sheet covered the thin mat she used for sleeping when her mother entertained clients late into the night. She pulled back the corner of the mat and inspected a few items: a single black garter adorned with delicate sequins, an empty weathered coin pouch with gold filigree, and finally, a small paring knife with a cracked ivory handle.

Satisfied that her treasures remained untouched, she dismissed the cold, vaporous current that clarified her night vision, and the cubby's shadows surged back into place. She yawned and lay down on the mat. The familiar heavy scent of incense wafted in through the knothole. She sat up more than once over the next few hours to watch clients depart down the back stairs, but in her boredom, sleep overtook her easily enough.

"Nika, Nika wake up," said Silvy.

Ranika stretched and turned to squint at her mother. Silvy pulled a light blue silk shawl over her shoulders. The garment complimented a cream-colored dress embroidered with delicate blue flowers. Her yellow hair was swept over one ear in an intricate braid, then draped down her shoulder. She only wore the ensemble for one person.

Ranika rubbed at her eyes. "You look pretty tonight, Mamma. Is the man with the fancy boots coming to see you?"

"Lord Drassle is coming to see me soon, but someone is here to see you first. Come with me, child, and be quick about it."

Ranika stepped out of the cubby without giving the odd hour much thought. Such visitations were not unusual at Felpinge House. Silvy led her back down the hallway and through the kitchen to the steps reserved for servants. After climbing to the second floor, they entered a side parlor.

Ranika peered under her mother's arm when the door swung open. A burly man with a thick, wiry beard leaned against the window, looking out across the harbor. He turned to reveal a ruddy scar running from forehead to chin. The injury had obviously claimed the milky eye set in the middle of the angry wound.

The man glared at Silvy and her daughter for a moment, then growled and displayed a gap-toothed grin. He knelt and held his arms open wide. "Well, don't make me chase you all the way over there. Get over here and give ol' Jorund a squeeze, lass."

Ranika skipped into the room, giggling, and tumbled into the man's arms. After they shared a familiar embrace, she stepped back, waiting. Jorund held two meaty fists forward, and Ranika tapped his left hand. He turned his hand, palm up, and uncurled his fingers to reveal a small chunk of crystal. Ranika reached a hesitant hand forward to retrieve the bauble.

The strange rock weighed more than she would have guessed, with its tiny grey crystals jutting out at random angles. She looked up in question.

"That, lass, is a rare moonstone, taken from corsairs off the eastern coast. Hold it by the windowsill so it can collect the light of the moon and see what happens."

Ranika did as she was instructed and kept her eyes locked on the strange crystal but remained aware of the conversation in the room.

Jorund stood to his full height and nodded at her mother. "She's never really been the talkative type, aye? No matter. Silvy, you look well."

Silvy tilted her head. "The blessings of the seven fall upon us from time to time."

"Good. That's good. Well, I won't keep you long. He . . . he sent me to check on things, on her, if you have my meaning," said Jorund.

"I know well enough why you're here, Jorund. Why doesn't Mallic come here himself? His daughter doesn't bite."

Jorund splayed out meaty fingers in a gesture of innocence. "Who can say, Silvy? I only do as I'm paid. I would sooner blind my good eye than cross Lord Shawlin or his wife. That's one woman who can cut ice with a glare."

The two considered one another for long moments. A bell tolled from across the harbor announcing the encroaching hour. "Tell Lord Shawlin I've seen nothing unusual. She's like any other girl but smarter. You're right, she doesn't talk overmuch, but she understands more than most her age. Beyond a sharp eye and keen ears, she's a normal ten-year-old girl. But if anything changes, I know how to reach you. Ranika, come. We need to get you situated for the night."

Ranika pocketed the small gemstone from the windowsill and followed her mother. Silvy returned her to the hideout under the steps. Before pressing the door closed, her mother bent down, holding out a parcel wrapped in cheesecloth. A savory aroma drew an involuntary gurgle from Ranika's stomach.

Silvy smiled. "Take it, silly. There was plenty left over this evening. There's a sweet butter roll, some cheese, dried fruit, and roasted nuts. That should be more than enough to hold you until I return."

Ranika placed the food on her mat, then turned and held out her hands. They shared a firm embrace that lasted only a few seconds. Without words, she retreated to her mat and unwrapped her dinner while her mother closed the door.

After eating, she fell fast asleep but awoke some time later from an ache pressing into her thigh. She sat up and retrieved the moonstone from her pocket. Pale light flooded her cubby, streaming from the gem facets. She stared in wonder. The individual gem shards varied with intensity and emitted light in a slow rhythm that reminded Ranika of the tides.

The discovery felt too wonderful to keep to herself. Without giving voice to her plan, she replaced the knothole, opened the panel door, then pocketed the moonstone and her other treasures. She climbed the back stairs to the third floor, where her mother kept a room. Her progress slowed when she allowed her bare feet to squish into the plush carpeting of the third-floor hallway. Finally, she made her way to her mother's door.

She waited outside and listened. Sometimes her mother had visitors late into the night, and Silvy deChance had made it clear that Ranika was not to enter if she heard voices or noises. What she did hear was neither of those things. Not really. From beyond the door, something crashed to the ground, something heavy enough to make the floorboards vibrate under Ranika's feet. The strange sensation was followed by heavy thuds . . . one . . . two . . . then three.

Ranika grasped the handle and pushed the door open, holding the glimmering moonstone in her hand. Her mother lay face down on the floor, her yellow dress torn and hanging off the shoulder. A strange bloody cavity marred the back of Silvy's skull, and something glistening mushroomed out of the wound. The man with the fancy boots stood over her, naked, panting, and holding a blood-smeared tankard with a wild look in his eyes.

They stared at one another a moment, and Lord Drassle took a step forward. Ranika threw the moonstone at his head, then turned and bolted down the hall. She bounced over the plush carpet, her feet barely leaving an imprint, then reached the back stairs.

At the bottom, she pushed open the back door before turning to catch a glimpse of a disheveled Lord Drassle stumbling forward in nothing more than his breeches. Ranika ran out into the night and crossed a cobblestone street.

She stopped at a stone wall only four feet high and looked down on the Callish harbor. The blue moon, Voshna, sat full and proud, and she could see the waves crashing far below. Ranika considered climbing over the wall but instead pushed back and sprinted until her legs ached, then turned and looked over her shoulder to see Drassle only a few blocks back.

She veered down a dark alley, passed by a few doors and a hawker's cart, then found herself at a dead end. She scurried back under the cart, pulled her knees to her chest, and waited.

Her heart thrummed in her ears, and she struggled to control her panting. Moments later, Drassle staggered into the entrance to the alley. Moonlight outlined his silhouette. The man clutched at his knees, panting, for over a minute. When he stood, Ranika could see that he still held the bloody tankard in one hand and her moonstone in the other.

Drassle walked slowly down the alley, ambling from side to side in a shuffling gait, holding the moonstone up to chase away the shadows. Alone in the darkness, she had no trouble understanding his slurred speech. "Where did you get off to, little mouse? Your mother would be pretty worried if she knew you were out here all alone."

She watched him search two different doorways. He kicked through a pile of straw and upended a basket full of potatoes. She crowded against the back wheel of the cart and could just make out his feet as they turned and began to walk toward her. As his plodding steps approached, Ranika reached out as if to grab the shadows. If she could just pull them to her and wrap them around her like a blanket, the man might not even see her.

As suddenly as she had the thought, Drassle stood barefoot in front of the cart. "You wouldn't be hiding under here, would you?"

With a frantic effort, she clutched at the shadows, and a cool wave tingled over her skin. Drassle crouched down and held the moonstone forward. He peered first one way, then the next, appearing to look through Ranika. He was close enough that she could smell the sour tang of ale on his breath. She held her breath and waited, clutching at the blanket of shadows that she imagined around her. Eventually, the drunkard stood. She watched his feet as he turned to inspect the dead end, then paced a lazy circle before walking out of the alley.

She watched as he leaned against the short wall on the far side of the cobblestone street. He lingered there in the moonlight for what felt like a long time, and Ranika's feet fell asleep. She crawled out from under the cart on legs that should have been wobbly, but instead, she felt oddly invigorated.

A nervous tingling feeling cascaded across her body, and she found herself making small, rapid jumps in place. She must have made a noise because Drassle turned and stared back into the alley.

Ranika froze. In her strange excitement, she had wandered out into the moonlight to stand at the edge of the cobblestone street. Once again, the drunkard looked right past her. The man set the moonstone on the ledge of the stone wall, then climbed up and began to urinate off the cliffside.

With an impulse she had never felt before, she surged across the street directly at Drassle's backside. Her hand found the cracked ivory-handled paring knife in her pocket, and she plunged the small blade down on top of the man's bare foot.

A pitiful cry of surprise, more than pain, escaped the man's mouth, and he hopped away. He seemed to hang in midair a moment, confusion painted on his face. Pale moonlight glinted off the oversized whites of his eyes. Then he plunged into darkness, taking the small blade with him.

$$\times\!\!\!\times$$

RANIKA AWOKE, AND HER head was buzzing. She surrendered her hold of nadir and shook her hands as if she could get the tingling feeling to dissipate faster. *Mogdure's bite.*

She really hated that dream. Every time she relived that night, her gift triggered while she slept, leaving her to awaken feeling restless and edgy.

Reddevek lay not far off, his breaths slow and steady. She lifted a lock of hair from his face and studied the cobblestone scar on his cheek and forehead. Someday she would have to pepper him with questions about how he got the scar. He didn't like to talk much about it, but she thought it rather distinctive. In some ways, it reminded her of Jorund's marred face—not as disfiguring, but there was definitely a story there.

She gazed across their camp on the Borderlands. Pale blue moonlight spilled over the remnants of an abandoned farmstead. She considered shifting her eyes; she understood now that nadir allowed her to see through the shadows. But if she channeled more, she would never get back to sleep. So, instead, she removed the moonstone from her pocket. In only a few minutes, the blue moon charged the stone, and she had enough light to safely navigate through their camp.

She walked a lazy circle. Two of the Outriders, Savnah, and Dexxin, if she remembered right, lay in what appeared to be uncomfortable positions, their hands and wrists bound to the base of a stone monument. A thick pedestal rose to support a shallow basin. Reddevek called it a Giver's Stone and said it was used to hold the ashes of the dead. It seemed to Ranika that any gentle gust of wind would carry ashes away, but maybe that was the point. Regardless, she figured is was heavy enough to anchor the prisoners in place.

Something stirred in the shadows nearby, and she stepped back. Neska padded forward. The wolvryn walked right up to her, nose to nose, licked her forehead, then settled back to the ground, keeping a vigil over the captives. Ranika scratched behind the wolvryn's ear. "Can I tell you a secret?" she whispered to the wolvryn. "I can see in the dark too when I want, so if these two cause trouble, come wake me first."

Neska sniffed once at the air and lifted her nose high and to the side.

Ranika stifled a giggle. "I know you don't *need* anyone's help. That's the way it is with us women. But still, I'm always ready if you want some company."

Ranika continued her stroll in silence past the others. The ginger-haired medic, Tovnik, slept easily while smacking his lips and mumbling something about crown beetles. *Whatever those are.* Karragin rolled to her side and adjusted a blanket over her shoulder. Ranika shoved the moonstone into her pocket, but the woman seemed none the wiser.

A short distance away, the Baellentrell brothers lay on bedrolls on either side of the larger wolvryn. A veil of long, dark hair covered Bryndor's eyes. She waited a moment to see if he would awaken but lost herself in the way the moonlight accentuated his jawline. He had filled out in the year or so since she last saw them in the Bend. His shirt stretched over a broad chest, and even in the dim light, she could tell that his shoulders barely fit into his outer coat.

His brother, Lluthean, lay on his side, turned into the wolvryn's flank. He had matured as well, but neither of them so much as the wolvryn.

For his part, Boru snored louder than anyone in camp. The great creature slept on his back and looked more like a giant overturned turtle. From nose to rump, he stretched well beyond either brother. His thick purple tongue hung from the side of his mouth, and all four limbs jerked randomly into the air as he dreamed.

She left them each to their nocturnal adventures and walked around what remained of a partially collapsed barn. Once again, she removed her moonstone to better survey the structure. The lady, Laryn, lay recovering inside. Ranika saw her stumble out the day before, assisted by the medic. She had little idea what "the draft" was but steered clear in case it was contagious.

So everyone's asleep except Neska and me. She glanced back over the silhouettes of the sleeping captives. *How is that a smart idea?*

Kaellor's deep voice startled her, disarming her assumption. The wonder in his tone gave her ease. "Is that a moonstone, child? I haven't seen one in an age."

She turned, holding the stone high. Kaellor stepped out of the shadows of the barn. He looked over her head, inspecting the perimeter for several moments, then drew his gaze down to her.

"It's from Callish. A friend of my mother gave it to me." She brought the stone down, holding it at her waist so it illuminated her face, then lost herself for a moment staring at the slow wave of light rippling across the glimmering crystals.

"Your mother had rare friends," said Kaellor. "I'll show you mine if you let me see yours." He took a knee and reached into his pocket. Something solid clacked in his palm. She watched as two crystalline orbs began to glow with a faint blue hue. Over the next few moments, their intensity blossomed, and the light they emitted eclipsed that of her moonstone.

"Yours are polished! Where did you get polished moonstones?" she asked.

He scratched at his beard and held his hand forward. She took one of the orbs and placed her moonstone in his hand. The orb filled her palm, and she ran a finger over its flawless surface. Blue light twinkled from deep inside the structure.

"Fascinating," said Kaellor as he stared into the depths of her moonstone. He then handed the moonstone back, and she deposited the glowing orb in his palm. "The older I get, the more keenly I understand how much there is in the world that I don't understand."

A distant expression occupied his face for a time. Eventually, he drew his focus back to her. "Back in the Moorlok outside the Bend, Bryndor and Lluthean tangled with a feral wolvryn. I can't say I understand the how or why of it, but when a wolvryn dies, at least the one I'm talking about, its eyes become these." He rattled the orbs in his palm and then pocketed them. "They absorb the light of Baellen the same as your moonstone."

She wrinkled her nose. "Those were the eyes of a wolvryn? Why would you collect them in the first place?"

Kaellor shifted his gaze back across the camp. "We were trying to maintain a very low profile back in the Bend. You know what the people there were like. I could sell a tale about an alpha wolf coming down from the Korjinth, but not if its glowing eyes were discovered. Explaining that particular miracle would draw too much attention."

She tried to imagine the act of enucleating the globe even from a dead creature, and the thought gave her pause. He must have sensed something in her unease because he cleared his throat.

"Nobody was more surprised than I. The wolvryn was several hours dead when I inspected its corpse, and these orbs had already . . . well, crystallized, I guess. Anyway, they popped out without fuss or mess."

"How come they shine in the moonlight? How does it even happen, for that matter?" she asked.

"Like I said, the how and why of it all still remains a mystery to me." He stretched his arms overhead, rolled his shoulders, and yawned. "You can either let it keep you up at night or just wonder at all the miracles the Giver created."

"Hmm . . . I like that. I already have enough trouble sleeping some nights. I don't need anything else causing my head to buzz."

He smiled at that. "If you can, you should get some rest. As soon as Laryn is able, we will push hard into Aarindorn. Reddevek will need you fresh. We all will."

"What about you? When will you sleep?"

"In another hour, I'll awaken one of the boys or Karragin. There's more than enough to take a turn keeping watch."

"No offense, but that sounds kind of silly. I mean, I'm awake, and I don't think I'll find sleep tonight."

"Rough dreams?" he asked.

"Something like that. Anyway, if you like, I can keep a watch. If anything strange happens, I'll come get you straightaway."

He considered her proposal. "You sure? I won't turn down the chance to get another hour of rest."

She jostled the hand holding the moonstone. "I'm sure. Besides, Neska is probably more than enough to guard the entire camp."

"That's true enough. Alright. You have the watch, Nika. Wake one of the boys if you get tired. Until then, keep your eyes to the horizon."

She nodded as he turned and retreated under the lopsided roof of the dilapidated barn. After pocketing her moonstone, she waited for her eyes to adjust, then allowed a trickle of nadir to sift across her face. Under the influence of her gift, moonlight, bright and cheery, seemed to flood the camp as the shadows receded. Bryndor stirred in his sleep, and Karragin sat up to rub at her eyes. Ranika sucked in a breath and closed herself to the flow of nadir, allowing the natural shadows to return.

They may not know the how and why of everything, but if you're not careful, they'll mark you an abrogator for sure.

She walked a brisk perimeter about the camp, allowing her mind to wander, too distracted to dissect everything that she felt at that moment. She remained in that frenzied state until clear into the afternoon of the following day. And the next night, as sleep claimed her, she wondered fleetingly if her dreams would trigger her gift once again.

Chapter Two: The Taker's Gamble

The smell of moldering hay and fermented grain lifted Laryn from the depths of sleep. The sickeningly sweet odor lingered on the back of her tongue, and she tried to swallow but found her mouth too dry to manage the simple task. Something prickled the back of her neck, and she lifted a hand to investigate the nuisance.

Her fingers discovered a bit of straw, and she might have puzzled out her surroundings from that, but the joints of her arm flared with a sharp pain matched only by the aching fatigue in her muscles. Her eyes cracked open against the stinging burn of daylight, and orientation finally settled upon her.

Giver's last tear, climbing out of the draft again . . . at least I don't have a headache anymore.

Grunting through the pain, she sat forward to consider her surroundings. Her legs sprawled out on a meager amount of hay pushed into the corner of an animal stall. Sunlight cast irregular shadows off the splintered rafters and two of the walls of the small barn listed at odd angles. She searched a dark corner where something stirred in the shadows.

Her hand found the small knife at her hip but released it just as easily when the dirt-smudged face of the young medic appeared.

"Your Radiance, you're awake! Giver, that's a relief. Here, water first." The young man handed her a skin of water, and she drained half the contents.

"Tovnik, right?" she asked. "How long?"

"Your Radiance?"

Laryn held up a weary hand. "Your name, it's Tovnik? And please drop the title. We're not in Callinora or at court, and I'll not have the healer bringing me back from the worst case of the draft concerning himself with such . . . needless details. Now, how long have I been like this?"

Tovnik sat back on his heels and nodded. "Yes, of course, your . . . well then, how should I address you?"

"By my name, I expect. Laryn is fine. When we reach Stone's Grasp, we can fall back into official titles. But something about sleeping in the remnants of an abandoned barn sort of undermines the credibility of all that nonsense."

"I understand," said Tovnik. "This is the third morning we've been at this camp. It's what's left of an abandoned farm. You've been up several times a day to attend to the call of nature, but you don't remember any of that?"

Laryn squinted her eyes and searched her memory. She vaguely recalled Kaellor assisting her to her feet a few times but could not orient herself more than those fleeting memories.

Tovnik handed her a smaller flask. "This should ease your pains without making you tired. It's a tincture of spiritwort, my own blend. But just a swallow, it's fairly potent."

She swapped the water for the flask and sniffed once at the rim. An acrid scent filtered into her nose and opened her sinuses. She took a breath, then tipped the flask back. The tincture smelled worse than it tasted and puckered her cheeks as if consuming a very dry wine. She smacked her tongue on the roof of her mouth and, frowning, handed the flask back.

Tovnik dipped his head in apology. "I know, I know, it's truly awful, but follow with these, lammen berries."

He opened a cloth full of dark red berries. She took one, more out of caution than curiosity, and crushed it in the back of her mouth. The inside of the fruit released a refreshing jelly that immediately dissipated the astringency of the tincture. "Tovnik, where did you find these? They're like concentrated kevash." She continued to eat the lammen berries one at a time, savoring the intense flavor.

"High up in the Great Crown a while back. We were lucky to find a clutch of them at the end of a very long crawl through the grot warrens. They won't eliminate the draft, but I've always found them restorative. I recommend you save some. The spiritwort tincture can be taken about three times a day, and those berries are the only thing I've ever found to make the medicine more palatable."

She heeded his words and folded the cloth back over the rest of the berries. The pains in her muscles and joints seemed to subside. "I've been away too long. I think . . . I think I used to know that, but in the valley, on the other side of the Korjinth, we didn't have access to the same herbs from home. Isn't spiritwort usually brewed as a weak tea?"

Tovnik secured the flask and berries in a satchel. "Yes, but it's only by the Giver's smile that one ever finds the berries, and, well, you looked like you could use the stronger variety of the brew." He dipped his head in a gesture of submission, then stood. "I beg your pardon, but I'm under strict orders from your husband to let him know when you awoke. I also have some Veramanth's decoction to prepare. If you'll excuse me."

The medic stepped out of the barn and disappeared through a bramble of weeds. A moment later, Kaellor stepped into view. The tension in his shoulders eased when their eyes met. He cocked his head to the side and took a knee before her, then reached forward to remove an errant bit of straw from the hair at the side of her head.

She dipped her head forward in a giggle of self-deprecation, then divided the white locks of hair that framed her face. Tucking the strands back behind her ears, she searched for any more offending bits of hay. "I must be quite the sight if you've yet to find the words."

Kaellor inhaled a deep breath. "You look like . . . the woman I love, and that's all that really matters to me. How do you feel this morning?"

"Thanks to Tovnik, I do feel better. I think I could ride tomorrow. Sooner if need be."

"There's no rush. The Lefledge boy is a scout. I have him assisting Bryn and Llu. With the wolvryn, they sweep the area three times a day. They have yet to find any sign of danger. We seem to have pushed far enough to the north to avoid any more grondle."

"Lefledge boy? Tovnik said we've been here three days, but I don't remember . . . How is everyone else?"

"They're fine. Do you remember much about the grondle attack and what happened after?" he asked.

"Not really. I barely remembered Tovnik's name, and he's apparently been ministering to my needs for several days now."

His brow bunched in a frown of concern. "You pushed too far, I think, and gave too much of yourself."

"Perhaps, but it's no less than you gave when we healed Lluthean back in the valley. Besides, did you manage to fend off the grondle or not?" she challenged.

A sigh and nod of agreement were all he offered in response.

"Help me to my feet." She held her hands forward.

He grasped them firmly, then pulled her up and into an embrace. She leaned into his warmth and his strength. Eventually, he ushered her under a splintered beam and out the entrance. They stepped through and around clumps of grasses and weeds, then onto the remnants of a pasture.

To the side, their four common horses nibbled at grasses alongside five Aarindin. In front of her, a group of eight sat around a stone hearth. The structure rose from the rubble of a burned-out home. A stone chimney belched smoke into the sky.

Bryndor stood over a kettle, stirring something savory that caused her stomach to cinch like an empty sack. Some distance off, Lluthean led Neska and Boru in a game of chase.

Kaellor pointed to the group gathered around the hearth. "The young woman sitting on the rubble with the serious look about her and slate and silver-streaked hair is Karragin, the daughter to Therek Lefledge. She's a prime in the Outriders."

Kaellor searched the horizon and pointed to a lone young man walking a perimeter on the crest of a hill. "That ginger-haired lad is her younger brother, Nolan, a scout by his gifts. You already know Tovnik."

She watched the medic administer what appeared to be tea to two more sitting off to the side. Thick ropes around ankles and wrists constricted their movements and tethered them to the pedestal of a Giver's Stone.

"That's Savnah, another prime, and Dexxin, her sender," said Kaellor.

"It appears I missed something significant. Why are two Outriders tied up like common criminals?"

A growl escaped Kaellor's throat. "Because they're with the Lacuna."

The words cut through any lingering haze of the draft. "What . . . what happened?"

"It's a long story, but Karragin has something of her father's gift of premonition and prevented those two from carrying out our assassination."

She puzzled over his words for a time, initially thinking he meant them as a jest. His stern expression and constant glare disabused her of the notion. "Oh . . . that's . . . oh . . ."

"I know what you mean," said Kaellor.

"Have you decided their fate?"

"Not yet. For now, our medic is stilling them with doses of Veramanth's decoction. He has enough for the journey back to Aarindorn."

"What about those other two? The other man and that skinny girl?" she asked.

A smile split Kaellor's beard. "That is an old friend, Reddevek, and his little shadow, Ranika. They're the ones I told you about from back in the Bend. He made it back to Aarindorn while we were with the Cloud Walkers. Anyway, the regent sent him to escort us home, but things are a bit more complicated now."

They stood together for several minutes as she studied the faces of the newcomers. Eventually, she turned to him. "Sort it out for me, Kae."

"Well, first, there is our mission to return to Callinora with some urgency. Before we can even consider returning to Stone's Grasp, we have to see if there is a way to sever Tarkannen's connection to this world. In that effort, the last thing we need is any delay or resistance. Keeping that sender separated from his gift is just one piece of that problem."

Laryn nodded in agreement. "If word gets out ahead of us, our countrymen will certainly delay our progress, and that assumes they are friendly. Have you learned anything about how extensive the Lacuna are?"

"Some, but not from our two prisoners. Reddevek believes they must have members spread across the kingdom," said Kaellor. "He's concerned that they have become pretty established in our absence."

"I see."

"And then there is the diplomatic mission to Voruden," said Kaellor. "Therek charged his daughter's group to initiate negotiations for an alliance and possible future trade. That's why they were in the Borderlands in the first place."

She turned to him. "So then, you've had several days to sort out a plan."

Kaellor blew warm air into cupped hands, then palmed the side of his cheek. "I thought I might send the Lefledge group on their way to finish their original mission and rely on Reddevek to guide us to Callinora."

"What about the two from the Lacuna?" she asked.

"I don't have an easy answer. At the moment, I'm not even sure what crime they can be charged with. Savnah, the prime, admitted to her involvement with the Lacuna, but she didn't actually do anything."

"Is conspiracy against the crown still a treasonous offense?" asked Laryn.

"I suppose it is, but Taker's spit . . . I wanted to have time to establish our presence, our authority first, not rule against a prime in the Outriders who might have committed an offense. The whole thing just feels messy. Anyway, Reddevek says we are three days' ride from the Pillars of Eldrek. There is an Outrider staging area there. We could hand them over to Elbiona, who is in charge, but making our way past in secrecy would be a challenge."

"Mmm, messy indeed," said Laryn. "You say the young man is a sender? What's Savnah's talent?"

"She's a deadener and a minor nascent, though her ability to project herself is apparently not something she's worked on."

"She has the ability to ignore pain? That's an unusual gift," said Laryn.

"And dangerous. I knew a deadener when we were younger. His career was short-lived because he incurred too many injuries," said Kaellor.

"Kae, you're missing an opportunity, I think," said Laryn. He stood beside her in silence, appearing to study the group before them.

"I welcome your counsel."

Laryn watched as the Lefledge woman listened to something Savnah said. The two stared at one another a long moment, and finally, Karragin shook her head as a half-smile blossomed on her lips.

"Forgo the mission to Voruden. I know you can protect us, but our mission, with everything that's happened . . . there is too much at stake. Keep this group here together for now. We could use the security and expertise of the Outriders. Once we succeed, we can explain everything to Therek."

Kaellor humphed in agreement. "Pull the weeds in our own garden first, then worry about our neighbors.'"

She gave him a quizzical look. "That another expression from Journey's Bend?"

Kaellor nodded. "I get the feeling you see us traveling with the traitors. Why exactly would we do that?"

"Think about it. You've been gone over twelve years, and I've been away for almost half that time. That's plenty of time for people to make up all kinds of things about us. If we can't learn something about the Lacuna, then maybe we can teach them about the truth of who we are through this sender."

"Why not just let Karragin continue on her mission, recruit Reddevek to our cause, and make for Callinora?" he asked.

"Something tells me we'll be more successful turning the hearts of those two if we keep them with their peers."

He stood, shifting his weight from foot to foot, considering her words. "That's either brilliant or risky. I'm not sure I can decide. What made you think of it?"

"Mmm. First, I do trust your ability to protect us. But more . . . I suppose it's the healer in me. If the Lacuna is the disease, I would rather try to treat it instead of waiting for it to wash over the kingdom.

Speaking our truth, if even through that young man, seems like one way to start."

"Giver help us. I do love your instincts. I considered sending Reddevek to Voruden, but he doesn't exactly have the skills of a politician," said Kaellor.

She couldn't help but giggle. "I don't know; maybe he could scare them into submission."

Lluthean led the wolvryn back toward the camp, and Nolan returned from his patrol. Laryn felt their eyes as everyone that had gathered around the hearth turned their attention to them both. Kaellor turned to her. "Do you feel up to formal introductions?" he asked.

"The sooner begun, the sooner done. Lead on."

She let him lead her forward, and Karragin stood up from her seat on a stone beside the hearth. "Your Radiance, please, take my seat."

Laryn thought about remaining standing, but the draft eroded her sense of decorum. She nodded and felt relief once seated. "My thanks. The draft still has my legs, I fear. Karragin, is it?"

"Yes, Your Radiance," said the prime. "We met a long time ago. I saw you in my father's chambers before you left."

"I remember," said Laryn. "Those were dark days. How is your father?"

"Well enough. He'll be glad of your return, to be sure," said Karragin.

She studied the stern face of the Lefledge woman. She errantly sucked at a thin scar that grooved her upper lip. *So much like your mother. There is cunning and drive behind that calm expression.*

Kaellor cleared his throat to address the group before she could respond further. His baritone voice commanded their attention. "Everyone, this is my wife, Her Radiance Laryn Lellendule. Laryn, this is . . . everyone."

Kaellor paused a moment, attentive to something internal, and she spied the flicker of zenith as it played across the runes visible at his wrist. He grunted once, a sound of surprise, then turned and lifted penetrating eyes to hers. He pitched his voice low. "It still feels like the Taker's gamble."

She lifted her chin. "Better to swing the sword than watch it rust in the scabbard."

He leaned closer. "The phrase is, better to *die* swinging the sword than watch it rust in the scabbard. But your point is well made."

"What did your gift tell you?" she asked.

"There is a fair bargain to be struck, but the balance is precarious." Kaellor turned back to the group. "Bring Savnah and Dexxin over here. They're part of this now whether they like it or not."

Without question, Karragin and Tovnik released the ankle bindings, then assisted the two members of the Lacuna to their feet. Together, the four of them joined the gathering, and Kaellor continued.

"I'm about to tell you all something that nobody in Aarindorn knows, so listen to me like the welfare of the kingdom depends on you, because it does. It's not fame or power or greed that draws Laryn, the princes, and I back to Aarindorn. It's the abrogator Tarkannen. In our travels, we discovered that he remains tied to this world. The answer to his final demise might lay within the halls of Callinora, of all places. So before we even think about returning to Stone's Grasp, we make straight for the healers."

He turned to address the Lefledge woman. "Karragin, I'm overriding your father's orders. I want your quad to accompany me secretly to Callinora. I will describe in more detail our mission as we go. Reddevek, I need you to accompany us as well. We could use the security and expertise of the Outriders."

Laryn studied the group as Kaellor spoke. Blood welled in Nolan's cheeks, and the young scout stared for long moments at his sister. To her credit, Karragin restrained any response while Kaellor spoke. At last, she dipped her chin in a gesture of acceptance.

The thin girl at Reddevek's side whispered something in his ear, and the warden rolled his eyes to the sky. The two of them entered a conversation marked by his grumbles and her protests.

"Red, is everything alright?" asked Kaellor.

"I'm . . . more than able to accompany you," he glared at the girl. "And it seems Ranika would like to come along as well, if that is acceptable."

Kaellor's shoulders relaxed. "She's your ward and not subject to my rule." He stepped forward to address Savnah and Dexxin.

"I have a proposal for you both. I—"

Savnah dramatically hocked a glob of spit on the ground. "We've already sworn oaths to the Lacuna, and they work to see a free and prosperous Aarindorn, so shove your proposals right up the Taker's blighted—"

Before she could finish her taunt, Kaellor unsheathed his guardian sword and slashed a tight circle, bringing the tip to rest under the woman's chin. He held the weapon with both hands, arms cocked, prepared to deliver a plunging thrust. Laryn noticed his jaw muscles clench, but otherwise, he remained still.

Giver, grant him peace.

Slowly, Kaellor dipped the point of the sword to the ground inside Savnah's forearms. With a fluid slice, he pulled through the bindings at her wrist.

"We don't know each other, not yet. It's by the softest breath of the Giver that I don't cast judgment on you both in this moment, right here and now. But . . . if I do that, with the limited information that I know about you, then I'm everything the Lacuna have said about me and worse. And yet . . . if you two hold on to your venom without even beginning to understand who it is you stand against, then you are both even less than I. My wife thinks there is a better pathway forward, and she usually has the right of things. Ride with us as part of our group but betray nothing of our arrival to anyone. Not your family, your countrymen, and especially not the Lacuna. See us past Callinora so that we can show you who the real enemy is. And after that, you're free to go."

Savnah rubbed at the rope burns on her wrists. "What makes you think we can trust each other?"

"Oh, I don't trust either of you, not yet," said Kaellor. "But I have two pieces of leverage to tip the scales. Reddevek and Karragin know full well the identity of your families." Kaellor made quick work of Dexxin's bindings. "Whether by design or the Taker's bad luck, if you or any member of the Lacuna interrupt our progress, then the full wrath of the kingdom will fall on your entire extended families."

Dexxin swallowed hard and paled. "What if . . . what if I can't keep them out? They're always in my head. Maybe . . . maybe I should stay on the veramanth."

Reddevek charged into their circle, inserting himself in the conversation, barely constraining his rage. White knuckles gripped the haft of his axe. "You're Outriders, Redd Riders, my riders! If I had my way, I would put an axe between your eyes and be done with it! Do not fail in your duties to the prince. If you do, it won't be royal justice that you and your families have to worry about."

Kaellor placed a hand on the warden's shoulder. Reddevek stared down his Outriders until even Savnah appeared cowed. Then he snorted in disgust and stalked back to stand by the thin girl who was his constant shadow.

"What's the other piece?" asked Savnah.

Kaellor sheathed the guardian sword, but Laryn heard the creak of leather as his fingers gripped the hilt. Color flared across his cheeks, and she placed a restraining hand on his forearm. Kaellor sighed and, with considerable effort, relaxed his posture. "In Karragin's premonition, you surprised us. I'm the first highborn guardian in an age in full command of my gift. Surprise is not something you will ever accomplish now that I know something of your true nature."

Laryn tried to soften the temper of the conversation. "Savnah, it's the Giver's providence that Karragin had a glimpse of a *possible* bloody future, and that has set us on a divergent path which you never saw coming, one that has joined us all in this struggle for survival against the one who threatens to cast a shadow across all of Karsk. You may not know him, but Tarkannen is coming, and you can choose to stand with us or burn under his foot."

Something in her words caused a shift in the Outrider's bearing, so Laryn pressed on. "People are always better when they come together. I trust the gift the Giver bestowed on me to see us all through to better days. So, what do you say?"

Chapter Three: Like Snow Down a Mountain

The light of dawn fell anemic and sterile across the city of Aarindorn. The moon of Baellen hovered full just above the western horizon, reflecting the morning sun in shafts of pale blue. The phenomenon lasted only a few minutes every two weeks, magnified this spring morning by the eclipse of the red moon of Lellen.

Chancle Lellendule, vice regent of Aarindorn, stood alone in the antechamber used to receive petitioners to the regent. From his vantage point in Stone's Grasp, he watched and waited for the full color of the sun's light to enrich the panorama.

He popped the last bit of a crownberry muffin into his mouth, then pressed his thumb across the small plate, collecting the last few crumbs. Something about the offseason crownberry left him wanting. The expected tang failed to draw at the sides of his tongue. He placed the plate to the side with a sigh and waited.

Over the next few minutes, the forest beyond the Timber Gate transitioned from muted shadows of slate and grey to their natural appearance. Delicate wildflowers of pink and blue accompanied the fresh yellow-green buds of the stark canopy. Farther out, the rich pine and conifer groves shadowed the curtain wall.

In moments, the city blossomed to life. White stone foundations supported timber framing that bleached from russet to tan depending on their orientation to the sun. Blue-domed roofs topped the villas of the homes in affluent neighborhoods. Farther away in the commons and the Sprawl, thin trails of smoke rose from slate and timber shake roofs. Those neighborhoods appeared as a disheveled, checkered pattern across the city. While he would have appreciated a more orderly appearance to the cityscape, something about taking in the full measure of Stone's Grasp as it pushed through the hollow zenith-laden light gave him a sense of peace.

He studied his reflection in the window, assessing how the trim of his beard framed his jawline. With a swivel to the left, he inspected the cut and tailoring of his uniform. The latest fashion cut the outercoat flush to the waist and emphasized the gold stitching along the pockets and seams of the pants.

Satisfied with the new attire, he drew his attention to the list of petitioners for the morning. Captain Oren of the city watch was first on the list. *He'll likely have a report on the activities in the Sprawl. The Spicer gang holds sway there now. Such a tangled issue. While the murder rate is down, the vivith trade swells, not to be outdone by the addition of another brothel, two gambling houses, and only the Giver knows how many taverns. Still . . . there is stability at a time when we need it most.*

Distracted by inner thoughts, he lifted his gaze briefly to stare at the road winding out of Stone's Grasp to the southern horizon and toward the Pillars of Eldrek. He wondered, if he employed the full measure of his arca prime, could he alter the weather pattern that far away? *Focus, old boy.*

He ran his fingers down the list, spending a significant amount of time delegating numerous minor requests to the magistrates. Next, he grouped similar petitioners where appropriate, slated in those with more pressing concerns, and shuffled others of lower priority to the bottom of the morning.

He turned over a simple folded note, sealed shut with the stamp of Callinora, and broke the blue wax as he shook his head. Few people utilized the archaic wax seals when a zenith-stained thumbprint over the envelope offered a far more efficient means to secure a letter's legitimacy. Only the ungifted relied on wax seals, and very few of them had reason to send written communication. He could only imagine one person who still employed the practice.

The Docent Venlith. I wonder what that old crone wants now. She's likely going to complain about the stockpiling of embertang by the Outriders.

25

The sooner begun, the sooner done; might as well place her early in the lineup. But the overwarden should likely be the last order of business Therek attends to this morning.

Chancle placed the petition from Overwarden Kaldera at the bottom of the pile. Kaldera commanded not just the respect of the Outriders but of the regent as well. He had a tactician's mind, and Therek respected the way he dissected complex issues and offered austere solutions.

Chancle imagined how the conversation might play out. Kaldera would discuss the practical limitations of waiting for a Baellentrell heir to materialize at a time when the kingdom required clear guidance. The overwarden would list off the pressing issues at hand: the apparent resurgence of grondle and grotvonen, an umbral sighting, and proposed trade alliances with the border kingdoms. Those truths would weigh heavy on the regent's mind and prevent him from making progress with the other decisions of the morning.

Ahh, my friend. How will you weigh those facts against the convictions brought on by your gift? Premonition, like the Giver, can be a tricky bitch. We'll see which way Kaldera's arguments sway you when we need you the most.

Satisfied with the order of petitioners, Chancle drafted a formal roster, then asked a scribe to make copies of the list and post it in the receiving chamber. He made the rounds, ensuring that the royal guard stood prepared to receive the petitioners. A trio of butlers with refreshments ready appeared, and the scribe was seated in the regent's hall.

A resonant gong echoed up from a tower on the lower level, signaling the first bell of the morning and the routine start of business.

Where are you, Therek? You're never late.

Chancle walked toward the back of the room with the intention of checking on the regent. Therek burst through the door, crossed the room in four long strides, and assumed his position.

"Good morning, Regent," said Chancle.

Therek's eyebrows swept up to his grey hairline, then settled back, adorning his keen eyes like the tufted fur of a lynx. A smile graced his face, and he nodded once. "It is a fine morning, isn't it," he replied, more as an observation than a question. "Apologies for my late arrival. I lost track of time in the Founder's Memorial. Master Hoff keeps an amazing garden."

"Is everything well with you? Do you need more time before we begin?" asked Chancle.

"Hmm? Oh yes, everything is fine. Let's see what the day has in store for us," said the regent.

"As you wish, Your Grace. Our first petitioner is Captain Oren of the city watch," said Chancle.

"See him in," said Therek.

Chancle opened the door to the receiving area and waved in the captain. A bald man with a salt-and-pepper beard, Oren stood politely and delivered his report with brevity.

"And so, murders are down, and commerce is up. There seems to be a genuine enthusiasm in the capital ever since you opened the way through the Pillars, Your Grace," Oren finished.

"Your report a few weeks ago mentioned an organized element in the Sprawl. Can you speak to that, Captain?" asked the regent.

Oren clasped hands behind his back and bowed his head once with deference. "Certainly, Your Grace. The Spicers are a local gang, miscreants and the like. They've organized most of the significant criminal elements into what we would consider something of a syndicate, I suppose? We haven't been able to get anyone on the inside yet to understand their motives, but we will. For now, our patrols manage quiet streets, and I'll count that a blessing of the Giver."

"What counsel would you give regarding the Spicers, Captain?" asked Chancle.

The captain nodded, understanding flavoring his expression. "Diligent surveillance is all that's needed at the moment. When times are lean, I expect we'll have to raise a heavy hand to address their activities. But times are good."

"And prosperity is the soothing voice of the Giver quieting the restless mob," said Therek. "I understand, Captain. Do continue to work to insert someone on the inside and keep me informed of any new threats."

"Of course, Your Grace. Will there be anything else?" asked the bald man.

Chancle turned to Therek, gauging his friend's body language. The regent pursed his lips. "No, Captain. Thank you for your time this morning. We'll leave you to your duties. You have the gratitude of the capital city for your role in our security."

"Your Grace," the man bowed.

Chancle escorted him out and searched the antechamber. Several petitioners stood in small groups engaged in polite conversation over tea. His eyes fell on the docent. Venlith stood alone, leaning a bony shoulder against the window frame. He approached and cleared his throat. "Docent Venlith, the regent will see you now."

Venlith grunted once, then hobbled through the doorway. She stopped two steps in and surveyed the room. "It's bad enough you make us wait without proper seating, but I have to stand in here as well?"

Therek cocked his head to the side, appearing irritated. "When petitioners stand, they conclude their business with efficiency. You are the second of roughly twenty such appointments this morning. I should think you would be more grateful that you were not last on the list. As I recall, you are quite accustomed to the practice of . . . hurry up and wait," said Therek.

The two considered one another for a moment. Then a knowing smile flared his eyebrows. The regent stood and crossed the room. With a lanky arm draped around the woman, he ushered her to his chair.

"Ven, my chair is yours. Please sit and tell me what brings you here in person," said Therek.

The docent situated herself as if she expected nothing less. She wriggled her shoulders against the high back of the chair and turned to consider the young scribe to the side. "Does he record everything we discuss in here?"

"If it pertains to official business of the kingdom, yes," said Therek. "But you already know that."

Venlith leaned into the arm of the chair, scrutinizing the young man. "Nope. Not today. Be off with you. Take a break."

The young man turned to the regent, then Chancle. "Best to do as the docent directs. I'll find you in the receiving hall later," said Chancle.

The scribe gathered his papers and zeniscrawl, then retreated through a side door at the back of the room.

"So then, let's have it," said Therek.

"Three, no . . . four things," said the woman, holding up four knobby fingers. "First, before I forget, my nephew and his gilders in Callinora finished your order early."

She leaned to the side and tossed a small velvet satchel to the regent. Therek caught the pouch and opened it, removing a small delicate stickpin with blue and red gems sitting on top of a tiny marble of polished white stone. A miniature gold staff with silver veining supported the marble and jewels.

Therek held the jewelry between thumb and forefinger, inspecting the work. "These are magnificent . . . and early."

"Did you really expect anything less?" asked the docent.

"In truth, no," Therek replied. He walked over to Chancle. "My friend, would you accept this gift as a sign of your position in the kingdom? I had several made in anticipation of the spring assembly. I thought, with so many attending this year, that our most essential dignitaries should be both recognized and easy to identify."

"Of course, Your Grace," said Chancle.

The regent nodded once and applied the stickpin to Chancle's left breast, then stepped back. "Hmm, should have done that years ago. What do you think? Be honest."

Chancle looked down at the sparkling gemstones and intricate gild work. *These must have cost a small fortune.* "The gemstones, they represent the twin moons?"

Therek touched a finger to his nose, then pointed at Chancle. "Yes, just so. And the marble is crafted from polished mountain stone, representing Stone's Grasp."

Chancle fingered the stickpin. "I'm honored, Your Grace. It's truly lovely."

Therek exhaled in relief and placed one of the stickpins on the outside of his robe, then handed another one to Chancle. "Would you see that Captain Oren receives this one? I can see to the others. Make sure to wear them whenever acting in any official capacity. I think they add a flare of the distinguished, not that you needed much help with that, my friend."

"Yes, of course," said Chancle.

"Now then, Ven, I believe you had three other items to contend with this morning?" asked Therek.

Venlith leaned an elbow on the chair. "Yes, we need to invest in a better way to send cross-kingdom communications. Carrier pigeons can be unreliable in the best of times. Next, we need to address the Lacuna. And lastly, what have you done with all my embertang?"

At the mention of the Lacuna, Therek cast a sidelong glance to Chancle. "We can certainly discuss investing in research for a better means of communication, and you know well enough why we requisitioned the embertang. You facilitated the development of the brittle amber as a weapon against the grondle. All of this is preamble. Ven, what's the real reason you are here?"

Venlith mimed Therek, touched a finger to the side of her nose, then brushed it forward. "Still the same old lynx, sharp as ever. Alright then, here it is. Last night, I received a communication from the Sanitorium in Callinora . . . by carrier pigeon." She drew out the last words. "Several days ago, there was an attack, a breach, really. A woman, an abrogator, opened some kind of portal into the hall and was searching for something, or maybe someone. I can't be sure."

The three of them remained silent for long moments. "And here I assumed that your knowledge of the Lacuna was going to be of great import. How can they be sure it was an abrogator?" asked Therek.

Venlith sighed. "Because Veldrek Lellendule, a healer of the third order, sent the message. The woman was his sister, Volencia."

Chancle shivered in recognition of the name and became aware of a heavy silence settling in the room. The vice regent paced in a slow circle, processing the docent's revelations. He pulled errantly at the high collar of his uniform, finding something about the restrictive clothing suddenly offensive.

"Can you be certain?" asked Therek.

"Yes, she can," said Chancle. "That's a . . . dark page in the Lellendule histories. I don't think Veldrek would make up a tale like that. Docent Venlith, what else did you learn?"

"Not much, which is why we need a better method of communication. I leave in a few hours to learn what I can, but I knew this couldn't wait."

"I'm to meet with Overwarden Kaldera later this morning. We could arrange for Outriders to bolster your security until you learn more," said Therek.

"The Outriders are garrisoned at the forward base camp between the Pillars. It would take longer than a week to get word to them and have them ride to Callinora. Send me with a royal guard if you want, but I don't think we should wait so long." The docent stood with a grunt.

"Yes, of course, Ven, anything you need," said Therek. "I do, however, have the means to report to Warden Elbiona. We have been using a trio of senders, though one of them, Dexxin I believe, is out of service. Regardless, I have the means to reach Elbiona promptly. I'll dispatch a few quads immediately. They could reach Callinora just a few days after you return, I imagine."

Venlith hobbled a few steps from the chair. "A sender? Too bad we don't have more of those, but that's a rare gift of the Giver. If you can manage it, we could use the assistance."

"Docent Venlith, before you go, you mentioned being concerned about the Lacuna. Can you elaborate on that?" asked Chancle.

The docent grunted. "I've known for some time that the group holds gatherings in Callinora. They seemed harmless at first, but I've reason to believe otherwise. You see—"

A clamor of angry voices preceded the eruption of the back door as Ksenia Balladuren pushed her way into the room. Her brother, Rugen if Chancle recalled correctly, strong-armed the scribe, who had failed in his attempt to bar their entry. Rugen tossed the slight man back and closed the door, stepping into the chamber. Ksenia stood breathless and wide-eyed.

"My sincere apologies, Your Grace . . . Vice Regent. I'll accept any punishment you find appropriate for the intrusion, but I have information vital to the welfare of the kingdom, and it can't wait." The woman's earnest expression gave Chancle pause for the second time that morning.

He turned to Therek. The regent lifted his chin in recitation. "Ill news tumbles like snow down a mountain. Whatever you have to say is safe before Docent Venlith and Vice Regent Lellendule. Please . . ."

"Your daughter, Karragin, sent me a private message through an Aarindin. Your senders might be compromised, so she used a mount to communicate with me. The royals, the Baellentrells, return in secrecy. I don't know how many, but they are close, and Karragin thinks the Lacuna will work to prevent their return."

Chapter Four: A Hole in the Darkness

A stream of irregular clicks and rasps trilled about the caverns deep under the Torgrend Range. The Consort of umbral crouched over a focus of concentrated nadir. The steady drone of their cadence had echoed about the cavern for two days, and all they had to show for their efforts was a pinch of onyx powder. The ritual required to open another stable portal to Callinora would consume far more crystallized nadir than what they had.

Volencia rose to her tiptoes and held up a torch to peer into the center of their circle. Long shadows cast off the rounded head plate of the closest umbral. Sigils adorned the bony ridges, and she lost herself for a few moments studying the unique shapes, then drew her attention to their work. Each umbral held forth gnarled hands. Some of them looked burn-scarred, others were wrapped in desiccated, leathery flesh the color of bleached bones. From each, thin rivulets of power streamed into the gathered focus of nadir that hovered between them all in a twisted knot. The flatheads crouched together without complaint and continued the laborious process.

"I suppose if I didn't need to eat or sleep, I wouldn't complain much either," said Volencia.

"Mistress?" asked Eguma. The lithe grotvonen turned large, luminous eyes to her.

"Nothing, Eguma. How long will this process take?"

The grotvonen shrugged bony shoulders. "Mine not knowing because they not knowing."

"At this rate, it's going to be weeks. I'm going to join Grasdok on the surface and begin construction of the chute we'll need for the Rite of Sundering. I'll come back in a week, but if they look ready to open another portal to Callinora, send word for me immediately."

Eguma dipped his head in a gesture of submission.

"And Eguma, send me a Brognaus to guide me to the surface. I plan to leave as soon as one is ready."

With a web of nadir, she snuffed out the torch. She left the chattering echoes of the umbral behind and walked the familiar paths to her chamber. The humid air, thick with the reek of sulfur, washed over her, but she had long ago become numb to the odor. A school of tiny fish darted about in the canal of water along the footpath. The creatures emitted a faint green and yellow light. When she stamped her foot hard, they flared to pink and blue, racing ahead and illuminating her path.

The dancing light of a candle spilled out of the private cave that served as her chamber. She entered to find a parcel of spiced, dried mushroom sitting on her bedroll. She removed a thick slice and chewed the meaty wedge. The fibers stuck to her teeth. She washed them down with fresh water, then stored the extra in a rucksack.

She gathered a few extra torches and turned at the sound of padded feet to see Eguma. He stepped to just the edge of the light.

"Mistress, this is Mawg. She will take you up top to Grasdok. I will also send her to you when the Consort be ready to open the portal." The little grotvonen screwed his face in painful grimaces as he produced a crude reproduction of the Kindred tongue.

Volencia inspected Mawg. The grotvonen leaned forward on muscled forearms. Mawg lifted her head, and the saucers of her eyes squinted into the room a moment. She turned to face the darkness and waited for Volencia, who reignited a torch and held it high. "Good. Let's be off then."

Mawg seemed to understand and loped ahead on all fours, keeping just at the leading edge of the torchlight. The climb back to the surface took most of the day. Mawg led her through caverns so massive the torchlight failed to reveal the ceiling and others so narrow she coughed on the fumes from her torch. Eventually, Volencia turned to nadir to dissipate the aching fatigue in her muscles.

As they approached the surface, currents of fresh air caused her torch to gutter. She snuffed out the flame and waited for her eyes to adjust. Light filtered in from a crevice high overhead. Mawg must have sensed something in her bearing because the grotvonen picked up the pace, and Volencia followed.

They walked out of a cave to stare east across a mountain valley. A warm spring breeze lifted the smell of damp soil and wet leaves from the forested basin. She didn't realize until just that moment how much she missed the simple ability to see beyond the limitation of torchlight and couldn't help but stand in place for long moments, drinking in the sight.

"If I didn't know better, this could pass for the western slopes in Aarindorn. Don't you think, Mawg?"

Hearing nothing, she turned to search for Mawg, but the grotvonen had already scurried back into the edge of the darkness.

"Right, you likely hate the open sky as much as I hate being underground."

Volencia used the time to sit and rest, freed from the oppressive confinement of the caverns below. She lingered for a time, watching as the setting sun cast long shadows across the valley. Eventually, the grotvonen loped forward, and they watched in silence as a sliver of the red moon and the half-moon of Baellen took their places.

She stood, and Mawg led her out into the night. They walked around the side of the mountain and dropped into a long canyon. By moonlight, she could make out the shadows as a steady stream of grotvonen excavators removed stone and mud by the basketful. In the distance, flickering lights revealed farmsteads and villages. *Let's hope there's at least a thousand of you. We'll know soon enough.*

Volencia followed Mawg down to the floor where the canyon narrowed to a ravine only fifty feet wide. They passed a continuous train of grotvonen laborers, each one hoisting heavy baskets of stone. At last, they arrived at the end of the ravine. A dark, unnatural hole dropped at a steep angle. Volencia stepped close, but the odor of so many toiling grotvonen caused her to draw back. In the few hours of walking under an open sky, she had already become accustomed to fresh air.

She cast a thin web of nadir before her and temporarily dissipated the reek. With torch held high, she stepped close to the dark opening. A chain of luminous eyes peered back at her from the depths. One at a time, in monotonous succession, grotvonen laborers departed the hole hauling baskets and small wagons of stone.

The opening to the chute was perhaps six feet in diameter. She leaned in to get a sense of their progress when something large stirred in the shadowed corner of her vision. Her torchlight fell on the brutish face of Grasdok. The Brognaus chieftain retracted plump, bloodless lips behind oversized jagged teeth that resembled tusks. She knew it was his attempt at a smile, but the gesture provoked anything but friendship.

He spat out a greeting, laboring over the words. "Dark lady, come to check on Grasdok? See what Brognaus can do!" The grotvonen chieftain pointed toward the hole with the massive double-bladed axe that was his constant companion.

"How deep does it run?" she asked.

Grasdok relaxed his features in a look of stupefied confusion. The two stared at one another a moment, the torchlight reflecting off his vacant eyes.

Volencia cleared her throat, speaking slowly with exaggerated enunciation. "How many days before you reach the bottom?"

Muscles strained Grasdok's face back into a smile. "When next the blue moon is full. Grotvonen work under the moon. Death's Mistress work under the sun."

She nodded with understanding. "Yes, good. I can manage that. Once I start smoothing out the chute, any grotvonen in the channel will be killed. Make sure that once the sun is out, none remain."

She continued to watch the procession of excavators exit the channel. "Where do they all come from if you haven't reached the bottom?" She asked the question more to herself than to the chieftain.

"Chute runs . . . close to other caves. Brognaus dig, make new way in, get into chute, bring rock up!"

"Then why don't you just dispose of the rubble down below? Why go to all the work to carry it out?" she asked.

Grasdok stared at her slack-jawed another moment, then massaged the base of a tusk between grubby fingers. "Because is . . . rubble. Death's Mistress put shit in her house? No. Grotvonen not drop . . . rubble in their home."

"I see." But she really didn't. "Once I make the chute smooth, will the grotvonen be able to climb out? Maybe I should wait until you are done."

"Chute is for many human go down. Brognaus have no trouble climbing back up. Dark lady not wait, she see, we be climbing out fine." The chieftain knuckled a meaty fist into his jaw muscles.

Volencia cocked her head to the side, considering his words and calculating the task ahead. "Grasdok, have you sent scouts to find a thousand people?" *Taker's spit, can you even count to a thousand?*

Grasdok puffed out his chest and clanged the side of the axe blade against a shoulder pauldron. "Might be . . . problem. Eguma count . . . almost a thousand in Torgrend valley."

"I'll leave you to this and see what I can find out. Be sure to clear out everyone before I start. Once I release the globes of nadir down the chute, I won't call them back."

She turned and began the trek back to the cave at the entrance to the ravine. Fatigue sapped her focus, and she allowed her mind to drift. She thought about the chance to return to Callinora and whether she would encounter her brother again.

Two weeks at least to create another portal to Callinora, then who knows how long in preparations for the sundering. Maybe then I'll have my answers.

Chapter Five: Bartusk on the Borderlands

L luthean took a knee. His breeches crunched into a thin crust of ice and snow. The transition from winter to spring had begun, but a bitter wind swept across the Borderlands, numbing his lips and nose. He buried his face in the fur at Neska's neck, stealing some of her warmth.

"There's a bite in the wind this morning, but it's nothing like the Korjinth," he muttered to the wolvryn.

Neska sat beside him in a valley on the rolling hills of the Borderlands. Fresh sprigs of green undergrowth erupted on the crests of the hills and south-facing slopes, but winter's grip held firm in the shadowed depressions. He punched through the iced crust to find fresh snow underneath. From this, he scooped a fistful, molding the crystals into a single clod of ice that he sucked on. For a moment, he recalled the Cloud Walker children as they discovered the wonder of water becoming ice, then water again as it melted on their tongues.

"That was the day you and Boru taught Kae something about the nature of our bond," he spoke softly in her ear. Neska twitched her head and leaned into him, so he rubbed the side of her cheek with affection.

Footsteps crunched in the snow behind them. Lluthean looked down the short hillside to see the Lefledge siblings approach with the woman named Savnah. Karragin, the older and far more aloof one, led her younger brother. For his part, Nolan appeared preoccupied, studying something about the tracks in the snow. The crass Outrider woman walked between them both, keeping her own company.

Lluthean waved as they approached. Nolan waved back, and Karragin nodded once. Savnah seemed to consider the Lefledge siblings, then gave a begrudging nod. The morning sun glinted off the twin moonblade axes that hung, one on each of Karragin's hips. Apparently, she had appropriated them from Savnah, replacing the blade she'd lost in their defense against the grondle.

"Fair morning for a hunt," said Lluthean.

"Prince Lluthean, it might be . . . unwise to wander so far from the group without protection," said Karragin.

The title and deference she used felt like sliding his fingers into a new set of leather gloves. He understood that everything fit, but it still felt more than a little rigid.

He studied the woman, not for the first time that week. Something in her bearing intrigued him. She was often reserved, except when she stole away for private conversations with her brother. On those few occasions, her stiff veil lifted, and something resembling a genuine smile touched the corners of her eyes.

At all other times, she addressed the group with stiff professionalism. Though her demeanor left something to be desired, her input summarized the dangers before them and offered the best course of action with efficient military precision.

Lluthean had met plenty of dignitaries, soldiers, and members of the various courts of the Southlands. The brief and novel nature of those interactions had always involved a certain formality. But eventually, most monarchs allowed the genuine side of their nature to grace the conversation. Several days ago, he had challenged himself to try to wrench a smile from the woman at least once a day.

I'm glad that wasn't a formal bet, or I would be out a fair bit of coin.

"I appreciate the concern," said Lluthean. "I think we're safe for the moment. Nolan swept the area twice in the past few days. Neither he nor the wolvryn have caught sign of any more grondle. Besides, Bryndor is the one you should worry about, and he's already circled upwind to drive a herd this way."

Karragin looked back at him with a stolid expression and sucked on the scar of her upper lip. A strange moment of silence unfolded between them all until Nolan cleared his throat.

"Your Highness, your brother said that you both trained with an expert in your travels. A wolvryn handler, I believe he said?" asked the tracker.

"We did. Mahkeel spends his days and most of his nights among a pack south of the Korjinth," explained Lluthean. "He taught us hand signals, how to recognize signs of illness, all kinds of . . . things."

Lluthean's words trailed off as Neska turned to consider Nolan's sister. The wolvryn took three deliberate steps forward and stared at the Outrider not more than a foot away. Their strange trance lasted an unusually long time. Lluthean had never seen Neska react in such a way with anyone and began to wonder if he needed to redirect Neska's attention when Karragin bowed her head and stepped back.

Neska seemed to consider the woman a moment longer, huffed once, then turned her nose into the wind and sat at Lluthean's side. "Sorry about that, Karragin. She's never behaved that way before," said Lluthean.

"No, Your Highness, the fault is mine. We have an understanding, she and I. I've just never had anyone ask me to get out of their head before," said Karragin.

"You spoke to her? With your gift?" Lluthean asked. "What's it—what is she like? What kind of . . . voice does she have? What did she say?"

A shallow furrow gathered between Karragin's brow. "So complex . . . her phrasing is like nothing I've ever encountered. It's layered with emotion, and imagery, and so much sensory information. Sounds, even taste and smell, weave into even her most basic thoughts. I don't think I followed all of it, but she definitely let me know I was . . . intrusive."

"Is that bad?" asked Lluthean.

"No, Your Highness, it's quite the opposite, I think," said Karragin. Something in her reserved posture changed. "Prince Lluthean, can you . . . would you show us how you commune with her?"

Lluthean ran his fingers through Neska's fur and massaged the muscles over her shoulders. "Sure, but from what Kae tells me, there isn't much for anyone else to see. When I am attuned to her senses, the whole world opens up. It's not just how far they see. It's how they . . . sense everything around them. It's like you said, all of their senses are mashed together."

"I think I understand. It's like the difference between one person singing a tune and an entire chorus performing the same song," said Karragin.

"Yes, if the choral performance smells as good as it sounds, I suppose that's a good way to think about it," said Lluthean. "Give me a moment."

He settled his mind and focused on Neska's breathing. In moments, his awareness shifted. The cold sensations of the wind on his face and his knee pressing into the hillside vanished. Vivid smells flooded his perception: new shoots of grass pushing through moldering stalks left from the prior season, the fresh and sharp tang of a badger in heat. Spring melt layered over everything as water vapor rose from the thawing ground, creating a tangible quality to the aromas. And yet, cutting through it all, a heady, musky scent carried on the wind. He tracked the odor upwind to the west and sensed something vibrating across the plains. Something surged over the horizon, and Lluthean sucked in his breath.

"What have you done, brother?" he muttered.

"What is it?" asked Karragin. The prime stepped forward with her hands gripped on the axe hilts.

Lluthean lifted his awareness from the rich submersion of Neska's attunement. "I've never seen anything like it. There's a small herd of something that looks a bit like a massive boar, only they have multiple sets of tusks and look as big as the Aarindin. There's only perhaps six of them, but they're headed this way."

"Well, there's the Giver sending us on our way," said Savnah. "Last one in the trees is a nadir lover."

Karragin shared a look with Savnah and then her brother. Nolan nodded once and trotted up to the crest of the hill. After a minute, he returned. "He's right, a herd of bartusk. The same ones that left the tracks at the bottom of the valley. I give us about one minute before they arrive."

Karragin nodded once. "Grind it. Can we make that stand of timber to the south?"

"It will be close," said Nolan.

The prime turned her gaze back to Lluthean. "I need you to trust me and do everything that I ask."

Though her expression did not appear any different, something in the direct way she engaged him sent a cold tingle down his neck. "Alright."

She pointed to Savnah and Nolan. Clods of mud and snow lifted from the back of their feet as they ran down the rolling hillside toward the stand of timber. "Run like your life depends on it because it does! Go!"

Lluthean jumped to his feet, Logrend bow in hand, and signaled Neska to follow. The wolvryn loped along with ease as they sprinted in Nolan's trail. Karragin caught up and matched his pace.

"Why the trees?" he gasped.

"Save it. Put everything into making the timber, then I'll explain," said Karragin.

A part of his awareness puzzled at how she was keeping an easy pace with him and still managed to speak as if completely unlabored. He saved his questions and focused on lengthening his stride. As they raced down the valley, his thigh and shoulder muscles burned, and the mud collecting on his boots began to feel heavy.

Twenty yards from the tree line, he chanced a glance over his shoulder. The first bartusk crested the hill, followed by several more. Lluthean startled at the size and girth of the beasts and plowed ahead with renewed vigor. Nolan ran ten feet into the trees and began to climb. Savnah nimbly picked her way into another.

Without needing direction, Lluthean veered to the side, looped the bow over one arm, hopped off a trunk, and swung high into an adjacent tree. He picked his way to a comfortable fork in the branches, then turned his attention back to Neska.

"*Hide,*" he signed. The wolvryn huffed once, a sound of discontent, then trotted deeper into the timber.

Karragin climbed into a similar perch to his left, and Nolan adjusted something in his pack to the right. Farther away, Savnah settled on a high branch. Lluthean peered back across the valley, where the bartusk surged into the area they were resting only moments ago.

Sun glinted through coarse tufts of hair covering thickly muscled shoulders, and the wind carried a sour and musky odor. Sprouting from the broad neck of each bartusk, a set of black horns rested like two great sickles. Other smaller tusks erupted from their jaw and shoulders. The beasts spread out, searching the ground and using their tusks and hooves to churn up the snow. In less than a minute, they followed the tracks through the snow toward the timber.

Lluthean considered climbing higher into the tree as the herd prowled closer. They communicated in low-pitched grunts and fanned out in a semicircle as they approached the tree line.

Karragin's voice broke through the trance of his fascination. "When you linked to Neska, did you sense your brother or the other wolvryn?"

Lluthean turned to consider the prime. "Now that you mention it, no."

Karragin nodded once. "Nolan tracked him off to the north, not the west. Bryndor didn't drive the bartusk toward us."

"Then what did?" asked Lluthean.

The prime turned a passive face in his direction, and he wasn't sure if she was serious or mocking him, though he thought the muscles around her eyes tightened ever so slightly. "Nothing. You weren't hunting the bartusk. They were hunting you," said Karragin.

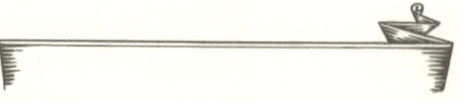

Chapter Six: A Question of History

Ksenia leaned forward, placing her palms on a rail at the edge of the upper bailey overlooking Stone's Grasp and the lower city. The royal plaza stretched out in a semicircular stone patio more than fifty yards to each side. She and Rugen had retreated to the private setting after the impromptu meeting with the regent. On their way out, he remained guarded until they walked far enough away to avoid anyone who might eavesdrop.

A warm breeze, rich with the moisture of melted snow, gusted from the city below. An unpleasant mix of faint alpine and chimney smoke carried on the wind. The gutters of the Sprawl melted as well, tainting the air with the unmistakable reek of human excrement. The conflicted scents mirrored her mood.

Rugen brooded beside her. He looked so much like her father when he took a serious tone. "Kess, that might not have been the best move. You should have waited for me to check in."

"Not the best move for who? I had no choice but to inform the regent about the secret message that his daughter sent me, the one sympath she felt that she could trust."

He turned away from her and rested his elbows on the rail. "I know, I know. It's just that . . . this could jeopardize everything the Lacuna are working for. There could be . . . consequences."

Her big brother looked concerned, and that alone caused something in her stomach to flutter. "I didn't do anything wrong, Rugen. What do you think would happen to me if I never shared the information and Karragin returned to discover the fact? All she would have to do is communicate with Tacit or Winter and learn of my deception. If Mother

44

and Father found out, or the regent . . ." She interlocked her fingers overhead, straining to take a relaxed breath against the tight sensation rising in her chest.

Rugen hung his head a moment, then looked up. "This movement, the Lacuna? It's not just a club, Kess. These people . . . they're serious about changing the kingdom." He walked a slow circle, coming to rest beside her again. "Whether it was the right thing or not, I'm glad you brought me along. That was clever, and I'll pass on the information. You should get out of the city for a while. Go home to see Mother as you planned."

The thought of escaping to the countryside with Winter allowed her to relax. "Walk me to the stables?"

"Sure thing. Give me your travel pack." Rugen held out his hands, gesturing her forward.

She unshouldered the pack, and he hoisted it over an arm, leading her down a broad set of curved steps to the next tier of Stone's Grasp. Over the next half hour, they made steady progress down to the street level of the city.

Outside the front gates, they turned toward the stables. The aroma of manure and hay overpowered other smells. Though off-putting to some, Ksenia felt lighter knowing she and Winter would be well out of the capital city within the hour.

As they approached, a young man sitting on a hay bale stood. He wore ordinary grey trousers worn thin at the knees and elbows. Ksenia guessed him to be several years her junior.

The teen cast a nervous look around, then flashed the symbol of the Lacuna, hands formed in a broken circle. Rugen closed the distance, nodding, and held up a hand, acknowledging the teen's purpose.

"Master Rugen," he spoke in a hushed voice.

"You found me. What can I do for you?" asked Rugen.

"Kunzie sent me. He wants a meetup at Bekson's. You know the place?"

"I do," said Rugen. "When does he need me there?"

"Now, if you can manage it, and you're supposed to bring her," said the teen, lifting his chin to Ksenia.

Rugen flipped the messenger a coin. "Thanks for the information. May the Giver break the circle."

"Why am I needed at Bekson's?" asked Ksenia.

The youth scratched behind an ear and shrugged his shoulders. "I don't know. I don't ask. But if you're his sister, you're supposed to come." With his message delivered, the teen pushed his hands into pockets, turning to leave.

"That's it?" Ksenia pressed.

"That's it," he said over his shoulder.

"Can I interest you in a walk to the Delve? We could grab a bite at Bekson's," Rugen asked Ksenia.

"Don't you have responsibilities as a subcaptain in the city watch?"

"I do, but they can wait. Kunzie doesn't ask for me often, so it must be important." Rugen turned on a heel and held his elbow out as an invitation. "How about it? Put off returning home a bit longer?"

Ksenia imagined herself pulling open the stable door and stepping inside. Winter was so close, and she hadn't been riding in days. With an effort, she squashed the desire to escape the city.

"Fine, but you're buying," she said.

She sulked, wringing one hand around her opposite wrist as they backtracked to the front gates and then around the inner curtain wall to the Delve. Shop owners burned survivor's essence in oil lamps, and the crisp pine scent lifted her spirits. They passed by the bakery she loved and several artisan shops, finally arriving at Bekson's Fine Restoratives.

Inside the lobby, several patrons sat and stood clustered in small groups waiting to be seated. The amount of them made the spacious entrance feel congested. The aroma of baked bread and fried vegetables drew a gurgle from her stomach.

Rugen stepped to the manager and said something Ksenia couldn't understand. The man glanced up, making brief eye contact with Ksenia, then nodded once. Rugen turned and waved her forward to follow the manager. They walked past the ornate shelving of resco and other rare liquors, past the polished wood bar displaying the dishes offered for the day, down one hallway, and turned to a closed door.

The manager unlocked the door, revealing a small room with a circular table and four cushion-padded chairs. A similar door, located on the opposite side of the room, remained closed.

He stepped forward and tapped a finger on the outer edge of a chandelier of crystals. From deep within the spiral of crystals, a pale light source appeared.

"Nice trick," said Ksenia.

The manager pulled a chair back and indicated that she should sit. Once seated, the man poured each of them a cup of water from a glass decanter. "The private suites offer security and anonymity for discerning customers, but are far too small to accommodate the smoke of a lantern. Lord Kunzie was able to procure the last three zendoliers in the kingdom." The manager sighed. "So much was lost in the Abrogator's War."

The man seemed to withdraw into himself a moment, then returned his attention to the room. "My apologies. Lord Kunzie should be along shortly. My staff will see to your needs." Without further word, he left from the same door.

Ksenia found the chair more than comfortable and was beginning to relax into the high back when she heard the manager lock the door behind them. She gave Rugen a look of surprise.

"Relax, Kess. We can leave any time. It's a one-way lock, for privacy," said Rugen.

Before she could ask any further questions, two servants entered from the far door with plates of dried fruit, a bowl of spiced bulgur pilaf, bread, and sliced marbled cheese. They set the table and departed as a middle-aged man entered from the opposite door. He wore a tailored suit, similar to the vice regent's fashionable attire, and trimmed his mustache and beard to accentuate the sharp angles of his chin and jaw.

"Lord Kunzie," said Rugen as he stood.

Kunzie took a seat on the opposite side of the table. His nasal voice cut through the room. "Please, remain seated, friends. I appreciate your prompt arrival. I don't know about you, but I'm famished, and my kitchen has prepared this spiced pilaf just for us today. Let's eat, and then we can get down to business."

Ksenia studied the man. He appeared at ease and comfortable, even genuine in his desire to keep the tone friendly. Kunzie spooned a large helping of the pilaf onto his plate, then pushed the bowl to Ksenia. She removed a small portion and grabbed a slice of bread and dried fruit.

After they each had a few bites, the man purred. "Mmm, there's diced pine nut and a hint of mountain basil in the pilaf."

"My compliments to the kitchen," said Rugen.

Kunzie blotted a napkin at the corners of his mouth, then tilted his head to look directly at Ksenia. "Well, let me get right to it. The Aspect appreciates the difficult situation you were in this morning."

Ksenia swallowed hard on a bite of bread that stuck in her throat. Heat blossomed around her collar and cheeks.

"Regarding the message sent by the regent's daughter . . . and the future arrival of the royals," Kunzie clarified. "Anyway, the Aspect finds the strategic involvement of your brother a very clever means to ensure that the Lacuna received the information as well. Job well done."

"But, we only just left the meeting, and Rugen hasn't had a chance to relay the information yet. How could you possibly know already?" she asked.

Kunzie nodded in understanding as he popped a slice of cheese into his mouth and chewed. "You have more friends around you than you know." He waved a hand at her as if fanning away any fumes of discontent. "Don't trouble yourself over trivial details. What matters is that the Aspect has been impressed with both of you. I understand that you've made progress in unlocking a historical text written in High Aarindorian. Have you learned anything of value yet?"

The question and abrupt change in topics confused Ksenia. "No, I intended to spend more time on that project when I returned."

"Ahh, well, all in good time," said Kunzie. "And since time is a currency we can ill afford to waste, I'll come right to the point. Rugen, we have been impressed with all your work so far. Your support of Captain Oren in the city watch has been commendable, but your resourceful organization of our interests on the Borderlands has been, frankly, exceptional."

"I'm flattered. Tell me what else I can do for the cause," said Rugen.

"We want you to resign your position in the watch. You'll receive full compensation and an honorable discharge, of course. Instead, the Aspect wants you to lead a team to Norfold. Norfold and Faltusch are border kingdoms we've had favorable trade relations with in the past. Based on our shared history, we assume that an Aarindorn envoy will be well received. We'll set you up with your own offices here in the Delve, and you'll report directly to me. What do you say?"

"I say . . . it beats night patrol and sounds like a fun challenge. Count me in," said Rugen.

Kunzie smiled, then directed his attention to Ksenia. She resisted the urge to wring her hand around her wrist. "I'm afraid that my orders for you, Ms. Balladuren, are not so glamorous but just as important to the cause."

Ksenia made herself look the merchant in the eye, waiting for him to continue.

"First, we want you to postpone your trip home. We are at a critical juncture with the regent and need you to remain in your current position as one of his scribes. Your observations on the job are important, but the man seems to trust you. Find more opportunities to engage him outside of work, in the Founder's Memorial and such."

Ksenia's mind swirled with questions that bled together. *How do they know I've met the regent in the Founder's Memorial? How will I explain this to Winter? Taker's breath; how will Mother react when I don't return home?*

Her mouth felt suddenly very dry.

Kunzie tilted his head and considered her through squinted eyes. "Is your sister unwell, Master Rugen? A pallor seems to have stricken her face."

"I'm quite fine. I just . . . don't like being ordered about or told what to do, especially on such short notice and by a man I've never met before." Ksenia realized that irritation had flavored her tone with more venom than she intended. She struggled to master her frustration. "Apologies, Lord Kunzie, I meant no disrespect. This is all rather sudden. I mean, I'm just a scribe and nobody special in the Lacuna."

Kunzie leaned forward on elbows, fingers interlocked. "Everyone has a role to play if we are to free the kingdom from the relentless control of the royal families. Whether great or small, the time for you to step forward and be counted among those who would shape our history has arrived. The question is, Ms. Balladuren, will you remain in the stables with that albino mount you are so fond of, or will you ride out at the head of our great movement?"

Chapter Seven: Princely Impulses

KARRAGIN TILTED HER head to better view the bartusk herd. The matriarch, the largest of the group, snorted commands and lifted dark, beady eyes to the trees where they perched. Appearing to follow her orders, the other bartusk fanned out in a wide semicircle, then began a cautious approach.

Clever girl. Let's hope we can convince you to take your leave.

"How did they track us when we were downwind the whole time?" asked the prince. Lluthean sat in an adjacent tree not ten feet away.

"They are crafty," said Karragin. "Maybe they see the world more like Neska and less like you and me. Anyway, it's the Giver's blessing that we have the trees. They'll follow our trail here and not back to camp. Once they get here, we only need to subdue one of them. The rest will see we're nothing to trifle with and move off. Savnah, can you project an image of yourself to draw them in? Right under Nolan if you can manage it."

"You know, Lefledge, it might be a fun muddle to see if you and I could take them head-on," said Savnah.

Karragin turned to regard the woman. Savnah stood casually on one branch, leaning forward and suspending her weight from an overhead limb. She winked once, twitching her scarred eyebrow. Karragin felt the side of her mouth start to draw up into a smile but shook her head. "Just the apparition, if you please. Then Nolan's embertang, combined with my warning, might do the trick. Get ready; they're close now."

Savnah wedged herself in the fork of two sturdy limbs and withdrew into her gift. Her likeness appeared at the base of Nolan's tree, leaning back against the trunk. The apparition of Savnah kicked at the dirt in a gesture of challenge, and the bartusk herd responded.

Five of the six beasts charged to surround the woman. One rammed directly into the trunk. A loud crack echoed across the Borderlands. Tufts of coarse hair puffed into the air, and the bartusk staggered back. Nolan tossed two embertang eggs into the fray; one broke over the snout of the staggered beast, and the other splashed at the base of the tree. The injured bartusk squealed in pain, the sound sending shivers up Karragin's spine.

Two others sniffed at the ground where the other egg broke, and soon, a chorus of wailing broke out. The beasts thrashed about and swept their snouts into the ground with violent, reckless abandon, trying to dislodge the painful substance.

Karragin channeled zenith into her sympath rune and focused on the matriarch. She assumed the intention of a predator and filtered in images of gore, pain, and blood. The sow emitted a strange bellow and turned to withdraw. From the corner of Karragin's vision, something streaked out of the trees.

The bloodied fletching of a broadhead arrow, one that had passed clean through the chest of one of the bartusk, quivered as it embedded in the ground. The wounded bartusk squealed and ran back toward its leader, then fell dead.

Karragin watched as something sharpened in the eyes of the matriarch; she sensed the sow's rage and severed their connection. "Taker's bite, why did you do that?"

Lluthean didn't answer her. Instead, the prince had already nocked a second arrow and trained it on another bartusk as it thrashed about. Before she could warn him, he loosed the shot, but it struck over the front shoulder blade, and the beast only seemed all the more enraged.

The sow charged directly at the trunk of Lluthean's tree, lowered her head, and rammed. The jarring force caused the young man to lose his footing. She watched in shock as he windmilled his arms, then surrendered to the fall. Instead of dropping to the ground, he leaped out, catching an overhead branch and swinging his legs up even higher into the canopy.

The sow watched her quarry a moment, then snorted in rage. She began swinging her broad tusks in massive swipes that cleaved into the trunk of Lluthean's tree like broad axes. Wood chips littered the ground as another bartusk joined the matriarch, attacking the trunk from the opposite side.

"Grind it. Nolan, use all your eggs. Savnah, you might get your wish; be ready!" yelled Karragin.

Karragin lifted the moonblade axes and engaged her arca prime. In a fluid motion, she flung one of the weapons at the base of Savnah's tree. Karragin crouched back and leaped out, bringing all her weight down with an overhead, two-handed strike. The crescent blade cleaved through the massive left tusk of the matriarch, and the sow roared.

It surged forward and caught Karragin with a shoulder, but she pivoted and shoved, causing the beast to stagger to the side. The sow charged again, and Karragin sidestepped, keeping to the beast's left side. They battled back and forth, the sow trying to gore Karragin, who nimbly darted to the side. Sometimes Karragin chipped away at the smaller tusks, but the lone unfamiliar axe seemed an imperfect weapon for the fight.

The struggle brought Karragin in a wide circle as she retreated to the beast's left side. In frustration, the sow snorted once, summoning the other bartusk from the base of Lluthean's tree. Together, the two prowled forward, intending to surround her.

With uncanny intelligence, the other bartusk swept wide to Karragin's right, preventing her circular retreat. They eventually corralled her to a clearing, separating her from the group. She spun the moonblade axe in a wide arc, but the weapon only clanged off the tusk of the matriarch. The beast recoiled, snorted a derisive sound, and pawed at the ground.

"Grind it," she hissed.

From her side, something silver and grey slashed in, colliding with the bartusk on her right. One wolvryn latched onto the beast's throat, and the other took a rear leg, incapacitating the animal. In the distance, at least two of the other bartusk continued their tortured attempt to escape the embertang, and Savnah harried another from behind the trunk of a tree.

Karragin drew her attention back to the matriarch just as the fletching of one arrow and then another sprouted on the sow's hip and shoulder. She diverted zenith to her sympath rune a final time. "*Stay here and die, or take your herd and go.*"

The glaze of rage fell from the beast's eyes, and it turned to consider the battle. The harsh bellow lifted once again from its throat, and the sow trotted out of the clearing, taking the remaining three bartusk.

The last bartusk surrendered its final gasp under the combined assault of arrow fire and Boru's suffocating bite. Bryndor walked forward, bow in hand, his brow knitted together. He called the wolvryn to his side, then set them on what appeared to be a patrol with only a few hand gestures. Neska led Boru, loping off and disappearing behind the undergrowth.

The dark-haired prince finger-combed errant strands behind his ears and surveyed the scene. "Are you injured? Is everyone alright?" he asked.

"We're fine, but thanks for the assist all the same," said Karragin. "How did you know to come when you did?"

Bryndor shouldered his bow. "It wasn't me. It was Boru. He sensed something fell on the wind, and we thought to come warn you. What were those things?"

She watched him work to retrieve his arrows from the hide of the bartusk. Bryndor sucked on his teeth and seemed to be studying the creature as much as collecting the arrows. He had to use a skinning knife to cut them free. "Is everything up here made of thick muscle and hide? First the grondle and now these?"

"Bartusk," said Karragin, "and no, you've just had a rather unpleasant introduction into a few of the more dangerous elements, I think."

"I'll take your word for it. Where's Llu?" he asked.

She lifted her chin toward the tree in which Lluthean perched. They watched him descend as Nolan joined them. Something in Lluthean's carefree, easy manner niggled at the edge of her awareness, like an irritating gnat. She couldn't decide if she was frustrated with him or impressed that neither prince took to bragging about the encounter.

One brother is a planner, the other a gambler, and neither one has enough common sense to know what's at stake when they wander off.

"Taker's eye teeth, that bow shot clean through!" Savnah crouched just up the hill, probing at the corpse of the bartusk felled by Lluthean's arrow. She hocked a glob of spit and jogged to join them. "That's some kind of draw."

"Logrend recurves," said Lluthean, as if that explained everything.

Karragin did not recognize the term, but anyone with a passing familiarity with bows could see that the caliber of the weapons exceeded anything crafted in Aarindorn. "Logrend? Is that something you could share with the artisans at Stone's Grasp?"

"The bows were gifts from King Vendal Braveska of Hammond. It's a kingdom on the southwest coast in the Southlands. Anyway, the Logrend were their trading partners," Bryndor explained.

From the corner of her eye, the younger prince's fidgeting caught her attention as he twirled a lone arrow about his fingers before replacing it in the quiver. "I believe I owe you an apology," said Lluthean.

Karragin found the admission more than a little surprising and realized a moment too late that an awkward silence had fallen over the group. She cleared her throat. "How so, Your Highness?"

"I didn't realize you had a plan to deal with the bartusk until after I shot the first one. Better to beg forgiveness than linger as the ghost of regret over your own corpse, right?" asked Lluthean.

"That sounds like something a Derrigand would say," said Savnah.

"Well, your father and my uncle Kae," said Lluthean. "Anyway, my apologies. I didn't mean for anyone to be put in danger. I never imagined those things could fell a tree."

"That's . . . gracious and understandable. You're still learning about the Northlands, Your Highness," said Karragin.

Lluthean squinted at her, then smiled. "I don't think I'm speaking out of turn when I tell you that all the formal titles feel rather strange."

Karragin considered them both. Eventually, Bryndor cleared his throat. "Our experience with royals boils down to taking their contracts in cartography and paying our taxes to the margrave in Riverton. I know we have to get used to the titles, but . . . maybe when it's just us, you can use our first names?"

"Bryndorllean and Llutheandellen, as you wish," said Karragin.

Lluthean wrinkled his nose. "It's Llu or Lluthean if you prefer."

"And Bryn or Bryndor is how our friends know us back home, I mean . . . in the Southlands," said Bryndor.

"I'll try to remember that," said Karragin. "But only when it's just us. You both should become accustomed to the new titles. I know you've traveled a long way, but Stone's Grasp is closer than you think," said Karragin.

She handed the lone moonblade axe to Savnah, who took the weapon cautiously as if waiting for a trick. "Kaellor said to return them to you when it felt right. They aren't meant to be wielded as a lone weapon. The reach is . . . off. To be effective, you need to wield both, and I'm not familiar with them. You keep them. I'll get my own when we return."

Savnah holstered the axes, then tucked a thumb behind her belt. Karragin looked long into Savnah's eyes. *Don't make me regret this.*

Something in Savnah's edgy gaze softened, and the woman's cheeks flushed. For the first time since they had met, the woman from Midrock seemed at a loss for words. She gave a curt nod of understanding.

"Llu, give me a hand. We can field dress at least one of these and take a portion back to camp," said Bryndor.

Karragin watched in puzzled amazement as the brothers worked together to situate the carcass for butchering. Lluthean wrapped both hands around a hind leg and leaned back with all his weight, exposing the underside of the bartusk. Bryndor rolled up his sleeves, preparing for the gruesome work.

"Moons, you're not joking," said Karragin. "Even with ten of us, we can't possibly consume but a portion of the meat."

The older prince chewed on his lip, surveying the bartusk corpse. "You haven't seen Boru eat yet, and Neska's not much better. The wolvryn will eat the organ meat, and that will likely last them about three days. I would prefer to carve out a loin before they have their way."

"At least let us tend to the work," said Karragin.

Lluthean looked over his shoulder. "Care to make a friendly wager? You three take that one up the hill, and we'll take this one. The last group to finish field dressing their carcass has to cook dinner."

Karragin looked to her brother, then Savnah, for some confirmation that she heard the prince correctly. His proposal struck her as both absurd and completely incongruous to the behavior of any member of the royal class. Nolan shrugged his shoulders and followed the other prime.

"Come on, Lefledge," said Savnah. "I've tasted what passes for your cooking, and it's nothing compared to the royal stew he cooked up yesterday."

Chapter Eight: The Aspect's Last Motivation

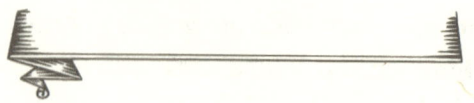

The Aspect of the Lacuna waited for his inner council to gather through the zenith seeds. Always the punctual one, Inasia of Callinora waited with him in silence. In minutes, the shadowed outlines of Burl, the merchant Kunzie, and the brothel owner Valdesta joined the conversation.

The Aspect relaxed the muscles in his throat, adjusting his pitch, then addressed the group. His shadowed silhouette appeared through the zenith seeds. "Welcome all, and thank you for attending on short notice. We have several actionable items to discuss today, so let's begin. First, let's hear a report on the latest conversations with the Dedicant. Have we been able to secure the trust of the ungifted, or at least ascertain his or her identity?"

Kunzie's angular and sharp edges appeared in the nimbus of the zenith seeds. "I believe the Dedicant is a he, though his specific identity remains a closely guarded secret. Nonetheless, it looks like we have won him over. Our work with the orphanages and resources for the poor in the Sprawl made all the difference. While he will never be able to use the zenith seeds, he has expressed a desire to join our next conversation."

"Excellent," replied the Aspect. "Since you have already revealed yourself to him, secure his attendance at a meeting. Perhaps he could join you in a cloistered room."

"As you wish, Aspect," said Kunzie. The image of his face persisted inside the cloud of the zenith seed, and the Aspect could see the man wrestling with ill news.

"What is it, Kunzie?" asked the Aspect.

Kunzie's eyes lifted, and he sighed. "It's the Spicers. They manage the Sprawl with efficiency and continue to coordinate with us on most things."

"Most . . . but not all things, then?" asked the Aspect.

"I might be reading too much into the situation," said Kunzie. "Since they've come to power, crime in the Sprawl has dropped, and we continue to receive a more than equitable cut of their management of the brothels, gaming houses, and vivith trade, which makes sense since the Lacuna own the properties leased by those businesses."

"I sense a but in your preamble. Get on with it," prodded the Aspect.

"Well, my recent attempts to engage their leadership in matters of strategy, even a review of the books, have met with either a strange quirk of circumstance or outright resistance. Salveen, their current leader, canceled three of the last four meetings due to some urgent situation requiring her presence. As I said, I might be overly worried."

"But the suspicious mind is the one least likely to be caught off guard when the Taker turns the Giver's blessing into dirt," said the Aspect.

Valdesta broke into the conversation. "You're both chasing alley cats. The Spicers mingle with my girls on a daily basis. Business has been up and without the usual hassle of a mark becoming violent or trying to, shall we say, dine and dash? If anything were amiss with the gang, I would surely know it. You might not see a lot in my small world, but what you hear certainly makes up for it. Let me handle the Spicers, and I'll let you know if anything seems to change."

Kunzie acquiesced. "As you say, you are the one best suited to interact with Salveen. I appreciate your expertise, Val. That will allow me to focus on our other endeavors."

"Moving on to other matters. Tell me about your work with the Balladurens. Where do we stand?" asked the Aspect.

Kunzie tipped his face such that his pointy nose dipped up and down. "The oldest son, Rugen, has a sharp mind and will organize a trade envoy to Norfold with subsequent plans to meet the nobility at Faltusch. Neither kingdom has the benefit of skilled healers, and both suffer the ravages of a minor flux. We'll introduce ourselves under the guise of a humanitarian mission. Inasia secured the service of a healer of the second order from Callinora. The acolyte is a breaker and is willing to serve in Norfold as a gesture of goodwill in exchange for favorable terms. The plan is to trade our mined goods and casks of resco in exchange for grain and beef.

"The Balladuren daughter, Ksenia, accepted the mark of the circle breakers last week. She has agreed to remain at her post as the regent's scribe and continues to garner his favor. I understand she has managed to decipher the basics of High Aarindorian, but as of yet, her studies have not revealed anything meaningful to our cause."

"What of our efforts to invest in the Balladuren Aarindin franchise? A foothold in something as legitimate and well-respected as the Aarindin trade could bolster our reputation," said the Aspect.

The side of Kunzie's nose sneered back. "Alas, their patriarch, Elbend, has not been willing to discuss the matter further. If we have a serious desire to obtain even a partial interest in the Aarindin trade, we will either have to wait for one of his children to inherit the family business or arrange for a more . . . timely passage, shall we say?"

The blue aura of the zenith seed remained still for long moments. The Aspect reviewed several scenarios and their possible implications. *Too many variables to predict whether we or even the kingdom would benefit from Elbend's untimely demise.* "Let's continue to engage him in friendly conversation when we have the chance, but in the meantime . . . find out if their ranch relies on any specific materials. If we can identify where they incur most of their expenses and obtain a monopoly of, say, the grain they use or—"

Inasia's crisp voice entered the conversation. "Water rights. We might be able to hold water over their heads, so to speak,"

"Alright, I'm interested. Tell me more," said the Aspect.

Inasia tilted her head. "In the reparation years, Callinora stood alone as the neutral part of the kingdom, serving the needs of rebels and loyalists alike. But we still had our own set of struggles, and one of them pertained to securing the water supply for the aqueduct that provides our water. The hill people dammed up three mountain streams, all tributaries to the Callinoran aqueduct. The regent himself had to attend a delegation to get them to come to an agreement. We now staff a House of the Blue Moon in the high country and offer care free of charge in exchange for keeping the waterways open. Anyway, the Balladurens must rely on some water source to irrigate their expansive grasslands and water the herd."

The Aspect trilled his fingers on the table. "That angle holds promise. Why haven't I heard of this conflict until now?"

"I imagine that a disagreement over water rights made for relatively boring dinner conversation in those dark days, Aspect," said Inasia.

"Yes, just so," said the Aspect. "Burl, your people are the closest to that part of the kingdom. See if there is any way the Lacuna can use Inasia's angle to press an advantage."

"Your words, my deeds, Aspect," said Burl.

"Turning to other matters, the auger's predictions . . . recite that reference to the nobles again, would you, Burl?" asked the Aspect.

The pitmaster's face appeared in the swirling blue nimbus of the zenith seeds, and the sound of shuffled papers carried across the communication. Eventually, Burl cleared his throat. "The sons of the blue moon ride like wolves for vengeance in the west, and the radiant daughter of the red moon eases their pain. As resco calms the nerves, so does the regent placate the masses."

The Aspect nodded, recalling the prophecy and puzzling over its meanings. "So . . . it seems likely that they ride in the west, but to what purpose?"

Burl grunted. "Would they seek to broker an alliance with Faltusch or Norfold? That could disrupt our plans. Perhaps they want to arrive in strength with the backing of an outside kingdom."

"Kaellor's been gone a long time, but his wife . . . Laryn Lellendule has not been absent so long as to forget how many in the kingdom would resist the influence of an outside force. Still . . . desperate times might draw them to desperate measures," said the Aspect.

"What do you think about that last part involving the regent?" asked Valdesta.

Kunzie sighed with theatrical drama. "Despite the whispers of my little mice in Stone's Grasp, we've been unable to tell who the old lynx favors. Some days he seems receptive to overtures for a kingdom free from the nobility. But then he casts judgments in support of the old laws. I've . . . manufactured a few recent domestic squabbles . . . some over land, others over the expansion of this business or that into spaces held aside for the kingdom's welfare."

"To what end? That sounds like roasting sparrows . . . all feathers and no meat," said Burl.

"The specific consequences of his decisions matter little," said Kunzie. "We reimburse both parties for their efforts. But his rulings might give us insight into his state of mind. Do his rulings favor kingdom-first strategies, or does he look to more progressive notions?"

The Aspect nodded. "I asked Kunzie to engage the regent's court in such matters. If nothing else, it keeps the old lynx and that vice regent of his busy attending to the mundane details of governing the kingdom without giving our activities much scrutiny."

Inasia's porcelain face broke into the conversation. "It's not Faltusch or Norfold," she said thoughtfully. "I'll wager that they're here, the royals are here, in Aarindorn. We know from the Balladuren girl's message that the royals are returning to the kingdom. We must assume that means they make a westerly approach. They likely skirt the western duchies."

"I agree," said the Aspect. "What assets do we have in the field? We'll need at least a few Outriders."

Burl and Kunzie both began to speak, but the pitmaster deferred to the merchant. "I think Overwarden Kaldera grows suspicious of our influence in the Outriders. He's kept nearly all available troops garrisoned at the forward base camp or on special assignment. However, a quad led by a glider just returned from diplomatic travel."

"This quad, are they loyal to the breakers?" asked the Aspect.

"Indeed," said Kunzie.

"Could we not engage them on another mission, say to one of the western duchies?" suggested the Aspect.

"It's possible," said Kunzie.

"Make it happen," said the Aspect. "And recruit extra muscle for the job. Desperate types only, those willing to spill blood to better their own lot. We don't want to encounter the royals with anything less than overwhelming force, after all."

"I think we can attract the right types. We've built enough goodwill with the common people to tap into the resource," said Kunzie.

"If we commission Aarindorians for murder, we need to take steps to ensure that the nature of the mission is kept secret. No loose ends. You should choose capable but expendable resources, Kunzie," said Valdesta.

Burl's bearded chin lifted into the zenith cloud. "Does it really have to be so? I understand that we don't want any backwash, but let me speak plainly. Valdesta just suggested that we kill the young people we send out to do our dirty work. It feels less than honorable and more than extreme. Is this what we've become?"

A long and rather pregnant pause settled across the zenith seeds. The Aspect recoiled from the truth of Burl's words and withdrew into contemplation. He swallowed once and pitched his voice low. "Burl speaks caution and wisdom. Better to talk about the Taker's work from a distance than actually embrace his grip. We don't want to blacken our palms so much that we can't wash them clean when this is all over. Kunzie, work to keep the identities of our royal quarry obscured, even from those pursuing them. If the truth of the mission comes out, we can deal with that at a later time."

"Your words, my deeds, Aspect," said Kunzie.

"Now then, let's discuss our strategy to build goodwill with those who worship at the Church of the Giver. And before you voice your opposition, Burl, I know your concerns on this front. Rest assured that we are only discussing how to make introductions. We're not talking about altering their canon," said the Aspect.

Inasia and Kunzie offered different opportunities to engage congregations scattered throughout the kingdom. In the end, they settled for a formal donation to the church located in Stone's Grasp and the placement of a few healers loyal to the breakers in the more remote congregations. With all of the business settled, the Aspect drew the meeting to a close.

He replaced the zenith seed in the snuff box and secured them both in the secret compartment of his lockbox, then poured himself a glass of resco. The amber liquid swirled in his glass, and volatile aromas tickled his nose. He withdrew a silver oval pendant from a front breast pocket and gazed at it. Preserved inside were the images of his last motivation.

A young woman held one child on her hip, and her hand rested on a toddler's head standing at her side. Their silhouettes shimmered with traces of zenith, which the artist had used to capture their likeness. As one, they turned and smiled, the little boy waving, the daughter resting her head on her mother's breast. He stared overlong at the last record he had of the wife and children he lost in the Abrogator's War.

He rubbed a forefinger around the edge of the pendant, willing their spirits to sense something of his need, his urgency, and his love.

I do it all for you.

Chapter Nine: Gifted, Not Cursed

"NIKA. NIKA, WAKE UP." Reddevek's voice cut through the fog of sleep, and Ranika startled awake. Foden's Crown, a bright constellation overhead, illuminated the warden's silhouette. He crouched next to her, eyes squinting as he stared into the darkness.

"What is it . . . did I siphon nadir in my sleep again?" she asked.

The warden fixed his gaze on her with a curious expression. "What? No . . . wait, has that been happening?"

She flexed the muscles in her legs, narrowly avoiding a cramp in her calf muscle, then bolted upright and pulled back on the ball of her foot. "Only a few times," she spoke through a yawn. "What is it then?"

"I need your help. Something's not right. It might be a large predator. A bear maybe, except I don't sense any fresh signs. Something lurks in the shadows just west of camp. It passed by earlier in the night, but it's returned."

She rubbed at her eye grounds and stared out into the night. "How can you tell?"

"Crickets and other night critters . . . they stop singing when whatever it is passes by. Ten minutes ago, they ran quiet. I'm going to check it out. I want you to drop into the shadows with your gift and follow behind me; see if we can determine what might be out there."

She frowned. "Should we wake the others? Maybe get one of the boys to link with a wolvryn. Maybe grab Neska herself?"

Reddevek tilted his head and ruffled her hair with affection. "I did already. Bryndor has the watch. He says he can't sense anything through the wolvryn but agrees that something is off. I'm going to have him stay back here on guard while you and I wander out there to get a closer look. What do you say?"

She pulled on her boots and stomped her heels into place. "What do you really think we're going to find out there?"

"Can't say. Might be something, might be nothing. The hill folk talk of creatures left over from the Abrogator's War, umbral, hounds of shadow, and things that take to wing on the darkest nights."

"That sounds like something a drunk sailor from Callish would brag about to one of the painted ladies."

Reddevek grunted. "Swish a little resco around the mind of a young man, and they'll come up with all sorts of stories to explain the sounds in the night. Still, this can be dangerous country. Most days, I'm grateful to wake up on this side of the dirt. I just want to keep it that way."

"I'm ready."

Reddevek nodded. "Wait a little bit before using your gift. There's only a crescent moon to see by, so you should be safe after thirty paces."

They walked through grasses and approached a stand of trees. Her fingers rubbed over the top of the ruby-hilted dagger and gently lifted the blade in the sheath. Reddevek stopped and turned to look back in the direction of the camp.

"Should be safe enough here. Go ahead and hide yourself, then follow behind me, maybe thirty or forty paces." Faint blue light rose from his collar as he activated his arca prime.

"I can see your light, Redd, your zenith. Maybe you should pull the collar tight."

"I know. If something is out there, we'll either scare it off, or it will see me and . . ." He shrugged.

"So you're bait? How much resco have you had tonight?"

His head dipped once and gestured back toward camp. "Look, there's none of them, not Karragin, the wolvryn, or even Kaellor, who can protect me in the dark like you. I'll be fine. Just watch my back." The warden withdrew a short sword and axe, then crept forward.

She stood in place, watching his shoulders weave in and out of briars and undergrowth. When his silhouette was finally obscured, she siphoned nadir. In tandem, she pulled the flow across her eyes and covered herself in shadow. Reddevek appeared more than thirty paces ahead, a silvery figure with a nimbus of zenith lighting him up like a beacon to her vision.

She followed him in and out of stands of timber, across open meadows, and around rocky outcroppings at the foothills of the Great Crown. Something did feel strange as they carried out the nocturnal patrol, and it was more than the absence of night sounds. The muscles between her shoulder blades tightened. She felt like something watched her as she, in turn, watched the warden.

Ranika turned a slow circle, scanning high and low, searching for the source of her unease. Nothing unusual revealed itself to her senses, and she stepped fast and light to catch up to the warden, who was walking into another stand of trees.

A breeze from the south gusted, causing the trunks to creak and sway. Reddevek pulled back as a rabbit darted out from underfoot. Instead of tracking the animal, the warden's attention seemed distracted by something overhead. He crouched and let the haft of his axe slide silently into his palm.

Something in the trees was holding his attention. She scanned the canopy but found nothing unusual. The warden jerked his forearm forward, and the axe whipped up from an underhand throw, spinning into the trees. Instead of thunking into wood, the blade pitched into something soft and unseen that perched in the branches.

A harsh, rasping screech of surprise split the night as the shadowy outline of a great, muscular cat dropped to the ground. The creature wavered in her vision, an indistinct and muted shape. Dagger in hand, she circled around and crept forward, struggling to see the beast. It shifted in and out of the shadows, rippling in her perception.

It howled again, a growl that conveyed more anger than fear, and crouched as if to pounce. In seconds, the shadowy cat compressed into a formless shadow, mercurial slicks of color and light sliding over its amorphous surface. Reddevek's axe fell to the ground, and something resembling an oversized weasel scurried forward. It leaped onto another tree trunk, chattering at the warden as it scurried out of reach.

Now that she understood what to search for, Ranika watched as the creature became another formless slick of color before shifting into a thick snake. It slithered higher into the trees, and she lost sight of it once again in the canopy.

Reddevek prowled under the tree, short sword in one hand and a dagger in the other. He rasped the edges of the two weapons together in a challenge. "I thought we sent the last feign to the Drift years ago," he growled.

The branches rustled overhead, but Ranika's vision caught up with the feign only as it crashed down onto the warden. He grunted and collapsed under the massive weight of a bear. She sprinted forward, dagger in hand, and skidded to a halt as the beast bellowed. Both the sound of its roar and its shape shifted. The growl of a bear morphed into the original raspy screech, and the body altered into a muscled humanoid with great leathery wings.

Reddevek struggled to roll free, but the feign enveloped him in its grip and began to constrict. The blades of his weapons punctured through the backside of the leathered skin more than once, but the creature stood its ground.

Ranika wasted no time and dashed forward. She jumped up, plunged her dagger into the beast's shoulder, and held on with both hands, allowing all her weight to hang on the hilt. Prickly tufts of hair rasped against her hand, and the beast exuded an oily, rancid odor she hadn't noticed before.

The feign screeched in surprise and shivered muscular shoulders, trying to shake her loose. Ranika held fast, but the hilt slid down its backside with no more resistance than thick mud.

She stumbled back, dumbfounded, as the dagger lost its purchase. Even more discouraging, the serrated wound her attack had created along the leathery wing sealed back up. The warden's pained grunt spurred her to action. She slashed once, twice, and a third time, pulling the blade through the muscled fibers of the beast only to find that its tissues parted and then sealed back up.

In a panic, she hopped onto its back and climbed up to its shoulders. A thick neck supported a bald head, so she plunged the dagger into where she thought an ear should be, then reached one hand forward, grabbing what felt like the depression of an eye. Her fingers pulled across the area, and the side of the beast's face peeled back, only to knit together when she reached for another handful.

The feign's muscled wings undulated, and she looked down to see Reddevek's face. The veins of his neck swelled, and a ruddy unnatural tint flared on his cheeks. The warden groaned, and the hand holding his dagger erupted again beside her. It pulled a slashing rent clean through one wing. The beast cackled, rippled its shoulders, and Reddevek's hand dropped the dagger.

Ranika continued to rake her fingers over the feign's face while plunging her dagger in and out of its head. She watched, feeling helpless, as the warden's face took on a mottled blue hue. He gasped once before his eyes rolled back, and his head flopped down. Attacking with nothing but base instinct, she wrapped her arms around the beast and tried to peel it off the warden. She strained with all her might, first sliding her hands around the creature's neck, interlocking her fingers, then squeezing.

She pulled until her muscles began to fatigue, and in the desperate moment when she felt her grip weaken, she siphoned more nadir. The force, both cooling and nourishing, seethed across her aching shoulders and down her arms, where it responded to her will. Ranika renewed her grip and sent tendrils of nadir coiling around the beast, inserting the extension of her will between Reddevek and the feign.

The beast arched its neck, emitting a roar of anger. Its thick, muscled arms reached up, trying to break free of the new bindings, and the warden slumped to the ground. The wings flexed against her bonds, but Ranika siphoned more nadir, reinforcing the coils, and began to constrict them.

Unlike her knife attacks, the creature's flesh remained something of substance, resisting and struggling against the onyx ropes. She felt the lashing begin to weaken, and the feign wriggled, craning its head to look at her with a vertical row of three bulbous black eyes that reminded Ranika of a giant spider.

A buzzing feeling swelled in her head, and her heart thrummed in her chest. She had never pulled on so much nadir before. Fueled with a mixture of terror and rage, Ranika yelled and tugged on the nadir coils, heaving one last time. The eyes of the feign bulged out a moment, and the two of them struggled. Twenty heartbeats. The beast shuddered under her tenacious grip. Forty heartbeats. Finally, she felt something pop under the constricting tentacles of nadir.

All at once, the feign burst like a wine sack, rupturing into a formless slick on the forest floor. Ranika fell back, gasping and choking on the nadir still surging through her body. She rolled to the side and retched violently for several seconds, then rose to all fours. She watched in fascinated horror as the bits of the feign attempted to fuse back together like slicks of hot candle wax.

A rabbit's leg appeared, kicked, and spasmed, then melted into the congealed mass of the thing. A thick cat's paw stretched out once, and a brown tail whipped about. The broad snout of a bear began to coalesce on the surface of the blob; then, all at once, the pieces fell apart.

The tissues liquefied and seeped into the ground. Ranika ran her hands through the leaves and dug her fingers into the dirt, searching for any sign of the creature, but found nothing. The soil didn't even seem saturated with blood.

She rose to her feet and panted, awash in a sea of frantic confusion. She turned in a clumsy circle, expecting another attack. Her mind reeled, unfocused. She sifted through the leaves, finding her dagger, and her fingers ran over the cold butt of Reddevek's axe. "Oh, I've got your axe here, Redd."

The warden lay on his side, lifeless. A terror-filled scream filled her throat. *Laryn, get Laryn, she can help.*

She began to run back in the direction of the camp only to realize she was utterly lost. Her addled mind couldn't recall the steps they had taken. She had just enough awareness to turn in a half circle and run back to the warden.

What do I do? What do I do? I'm all buzzing. I can't think. I can't think!

She pushed the warden over onto his back, straddled him, and lifted an eyelid, willing him to awaken. The lone eye drifted to the side without focus. She slapped his scarred cheek and punched his shoulder, crying in an agitated mixture of panic and loss.

She didn't know how long they sat there, the warden lifeless and her mind racing. *They're going to think it was me. I'm an abrogator in a group of zeniphiles. I should run, run far away now before they send the wolvryn after me.*

She imagined where she might go and how she might get there. Perhaps she could hide in some dark alley of Callish or find her way to Miss Della at the Bashing Ram in Journey's Bend.

I'm a monk twice over, and Lutney's fool for sure. I don't even know the way back to camp. Why did you leave me, Redd? You can't leave me. "Don't you leave me, Redd!" she cried.

In the periphery of her awareness, she heard the warden cough. "I'm trying not to. But you sitting on my chest ... makes it ... hard to breathe."

Her sobs renewed with unbridled emotion and relief, magnified by the need to release the tempest of emotions swirling in her head. "Grind you, Reddevek Taim, grind you for a monk and me for listening to you! Now I'm buzzing, buzzing like never before, and ... Maedra ... I thought you were dead! I thought you were dead!"

She fell onto his chest, sobbing hysterically. He shifted his hips back and reclined against the trunk of a tree. Ranika clung to his tunic and wept so long that she soaked his front. Her sobs eased to involuntary gasping spasms as the predawn light dispersed the stars overhead.

"Nika, can you tell me what happened? Where did that creature go?"

She lifted her head back, a long line of drool and snot clinging to his tunic. She wiped her nose on her sleeve and stifled a laugh. "Sorry, Redd."

"I'm sorry too. I shouldn't have put us in danger like that. I figured we would find . . ." He sighed. "I don't know what I thought we would find, but I didn't imagine anything like that."

"You called it a feign?" she asked.

"Feigns are shapeshifters. Tarkannen pulled a few over from the Drift and used them in the Abrogator's War. But that was no feign. That was something else altogether. Our weapons didn't seem to damage the creature at all."

"I couldn't see it, not until after you hit it with your axe. How did you know it was there?"

"I didn't really, but I knew something was out here. I got lucky. It took the form of a cave lark, but it left no trail of zenith, and cave larks never venture far from water. Looking up in time to see it perched there was the Giver's good fortune."

They sat in companionable silence, watching the sunrise. "Nika, you still haven't told me what happened. Where did that thing go? Are the others in danger?"

She wrapped her arms across her abdomen, warding off a chill as she thought back to the moment she felt nadir bend to her will. She wasn't sure she wanted to confide in him, but at the same time, it was Redd. There were no secrets between them.

"I tried to kill it with my dagger, but the cuts healed up as fast as I wounded it. The thing was suffocating you. Somehow I used nadir and made these . . . ropes, I guess? I was just trying to get that thing away from you, so I strangled it so hard with the ropes that it burst apart. I think it tried to put itself back together, but then it sort of melted into the dirt."

She searched his face for any expression of judgment or disappointment, but he tilted his head with unusual empathy. "Nika, I told you a long time ago that you're gifted, not cursed. You're learning to use your gift, and tonight, you used it to save my life."

"That may be the case, but don't count on that again. The way I felt after was . . . the worst. I couldn't think straight. I must have made a dozen different plans to find you help and run away all at the same time. The buzzing, Redd . . . it was like an entire hornet's nest in my head. I don't think I'll be able to sleep for days."

Reddevek grunted. "Huh. You know, if I channel too much zenith, I drop into the draft. It's a sickness. I get dizzy, nauseated . . . and if I push on, it gets worse. I pass out, have to hibernate like a bear to recover. You must get something like that if you channel too much nadir."

"Maybe, but instead of slowing down, everything inside speeds up. I get—" She shook her head, trying to find the words to describe the complete inability to ground herself in rational thought.

"Buzzed," he said.

She smiled at that. "Should we tell the others about me?"

"We should, and we will, when the time is right. For now, let's keep it between you and me?"

She sighed with relief, stood up, and dusted her leggings off. He held up a hand, and she stepped on his feet for leverage, then heaved him to a standing position. Before she could step back, he hugged her tight and kissed the top of her head. "Always remember, Nika. Gifted, not cursed."

Chapter Ten: Through the Pillars of Eldrek

Karragin pulled her gaze across the northern horizon, where broad tracts of conifer crowded at the base of the Great Crown. Her mount, commandeered from Nolan, flared his nostrils, and she channeled into her sympath rune.

"What do you smell?"

A myriad of images flooded her awareness. *"The forest holds many scents."*

"Giver's tears," she muttered. *"Do you sense any danger, anything unusual?"*

"Just your brother and the man. They are close now."

"My thanks." She suspended further communication.

Savnah fell in beside her as their mounts wandered up a broad hill. "The sun is out, the path is clear, and we ain't seen a grondle in days. So what's got you mumbling to yourself, Lefledge?"

"I asked this Aarindin a stupid question and got a stupid answer."

"He's not Tacit, then? All the same, anything useful?" asked Savnah.

"Reddevek and Nolan are on their way back. They should be here soon."

Savnah turned to look back at their small company. Dexxin rode directly behind them, with Kaellor and Laryn farther back, and the brothers, Bryndor and Lluthean, last. The wolvryn loped alongside the boys with the strange girl, Ranika, riding Reddevek's Aarindin.

The woman from Midrock scratched errantly at her belly as she sat on her Aarindin. "What do you think our chances are of slipping past the sentries at the forward base camp?"

"As we have the only gifted scouts in the Outriders, good. Sentries will be on the lookout for grot sign and grondle tracks. The passage of a few common horses and Aarindin shouldn't give anyone much concern, and if we hug the west pillar, the ground is rocky."

They rode on in silence for a few more minutes. "I've been meaning to ask you something, Karra. Why did you give me a second chance?"

The question, dropped onto her lap without segue or warning, caused Karragin to shift her weight. The Aarindin huffed a grunt and regripped her. She turned to regard the woman. "You didn't actually do anything."

Savnah laughed. "I don't think the infamous Lefledge gift of premonition lies." She hocked spit off to the side and sighed. "But all the same, my thanks. I never knew if I was capable of doing it. Now I don't really have to wonder, I suppose."

Karragin studied her friend. They had survived some extremely unpleasant things in the past, but none of that had made Savnah's expression darken like the current inner turmoil that played across her face. "What do they have over you, Savnah?"

"How did the Giver put that particular notion in your head?"

"Because, the Savnah Derrigand I know is too street smart to be duped by Lacuna propaganda."

Their mounts climbed several paces before she answered. "It's my older brother, Kovesk. The Giver cursed him, and the Lacuna use him."

They rode on, and Karragin held space for Savnah to continue. Either she would explain herself further or wait for another time, but that she was willing to talk about it at all was a good step, and the first meaningful conversation they had shared since joining up with the Baellentrells.

"Kovesk is a dream augur. After he sat for his Rite of Revealing, his arca prime remained dormant for years. Everyone thought his gift must be something like your father's, triggered by some random act of the Giver. But he was betrayed."

"How so?" asked Karragin, now invested in her friend's story.

"Kovesk dreams premonitions every night. Some of the things he talks about happen to people and in places I've never heard of. Others describe mundane events in the lives of Aarindorians, but they always ring true."

"How was he betrayed?" she pressed.

Savnah picked at the long hairs of her Aarindin's mane. "The gift causes Kovesk to talk in his sleep. After years of watching things he rambled about come true, I took advantage of his predictions, showing up in the nick of time to save some poor merchant from being gored by a bull or a toddler from falling down a well. I even roused the local healers to attend to a woman who wasn't in labor yet but who nearly died shortly after they arrived."

"It doesn't sound like you took advantage of his premonitions at all but that you used the information for the greater good," said Karragin.

Savnah bobbed her head side to side, considering Karragin's words. "I try to tell myself that. But one of the healers caught on to my unusual timely interventions. I was just a girl, barely into my first rune, when Inasia weaseled the information from me. After that, she got a promotion with the Lacuna, and Kovesk disappeared. That was over six years ago. And the worst part is, he whispered about all of that in his sleep."

"If Kovesk knew he was going to be discovered, why didn't he do something to prevent it?"

"Like I said, he was cursed." Savnah's speech became pressured, heated with emotion. "He never remembers anything of the visions he dreams. When he sleeps, he's like some battle-shocked soldier at the Sanitorium, babbling about nonsense only . . . it's never nonsense. It's all about things that haven't happened yet."

They rode on for a time as Karragin considered her friend's revelations. "And now they have him, don't they? The Lacuna must keep him under lock and key, learning what they can. Is that it?"

Savnah sagged on her mount. "You have the right of things."

"Have you ever tried to break him out, to rescue him?" asked Karragin.

"No, but apparently someday I will, and I'll come to a messy end of it."

"What do you mean?" asked Karragin.

"Kovesk predicted an attempt to break him free, but that particular endeavor ends with me pincushioned with crossbow bolts."

"And you believe them? The Lacuna? Maybe they just told you that to control you, to use you like they're using your brother."

Savnah shook her head. "Nobody told me. I read it for myself. They have people who scribe everything Kovesk utters, and I recognized myself in one of his ramblings."

"Let me hear it?" asked Karragin.

Savnah cleared her throat but spoke the words with exhaustion rather than passion. "'Threefold are the bolts that will find purchase in the chest, with two more striking mortal blows to the deadener who comes to rescue the augur.' But I altered the record to read, 'the bolts will find purchase in the chest and deaden the one who comes to rescue the augur.'"

"Clever enough. Are you sure the Lacuna don't know about the alteration?"

"Pretty sure. That particular line of phrasing was wedged in between random forecasts for a drought in the west and heavy snows in the Great Crown. None of that matters. They made it clear that the only way I would ever see Kovesk alive again was to cooperate from within the Outriders."

Karragin nibbled at the firm edge of the scar on her upper lip. *How would I react if someone made that kind of threat against Nolan?*

"What about Dexxin and his siblings? What's the angle there?" asked Karragin.

Savnah puffed out her lips and raised her eyebrows. "Those three are true believers in the cause. At least, they think they believe in something righteous."

"That makes sense," said Karragin.

"How so?" asked Savnah.

"In my vision, you were necessarily efficient, but Dexxin was ruthless. He shot Lluthean with arrows, three times if I recall, then gave Nolan a gut wound and stuck a dagger in Tovnik's eye. I mean, I think can sort of understand the motivation to take out the royals but not members of your own team."

"Except we weren't really part of your original team, were we?" asked Savnah.

Karragin left the question unanswered, turning the conversation over in her mind for a time. Without breaking her gaze from the trail ahead, a question of her own bubbled forth. "So, you don't believe that the Lacuna are righteous?"

Savnah cocked her head to the side. "Not when they sequester my brother for his insights and threaten me with his death. And that's just the beginning. They have their hands in everything from legal trade to black market vivith, brothels, and gaming houses. If there was profit to be made in mining the Taker's asshole, you can be sure that the Lacuna would roll up their sleeves and brown their elbows to find it."

"What about the famous Derrigand family? Do they know about your brother's confinement?" asked Karragin.

"No, and I need to keep it that way. If he found out, my father would burn the world to find Ko'. But in the end, I would only lose a brother and make enemies of the largest political group outside of the noble families."

The defeatism in Savnah's tone surprised Karragin more than she expected. *But can I blame her, really? The question now is, how do we get you out? Maybe with Nolan's gift, we could start, but would she even go for that? Would I, if it meant walking into certain death?*

"Karra, this is the part where I wait for you to offer some of that straight-as-an-arrow advice with no grinding whinging about."

"I was just . . . thinking. It's a lot to take in," said Karragin. "Thanks for telling me. Does Dexxin know about your brother?"

"No, he thinks I'm as moonstruck for the Lacuna as he is. It's his brother, Craxton, really. You see, there's two sides to the Lacuna: the orphanage-sponsoring, proper guild hall side, and then . . . the rest of it. Craxton is involved with the first part and keeps Dexx informed of all the things the Lacuna do to 'raise the standard' among the common folk of the kingdom." She hocked another glob of spit to the side.

"Has Dexx been able to keep his siblings fooled about accompanying us back?" asked Karragin.

"He doesn't trust himself, so he has Tovnik dosing him with veramanth tea every other morning." Savnah shivered at the thought and shook her head. "I know most medicines and tonics taste awful, but that stuff is so bad that I . . ."

Karragin failed to stifle a shudder as laughter escaped her lips. "I know. I wasn't truthful before when I told you I had never taken Veramanth's decoction. A long time ago, my father 'ranthed me when I got this." She tongued the scar on her upper lip.

"You were 'ranthed for a simple cut? That's crazy," said Savnah.

Karragin shook her head. "No, the night my mother died during the Abrogator's War, I was badly injured. I needed the art of the healers at Callinora to reconstruct the delicate bones under my eye, and my jaw was shattered. Since I had to travel, he made me take the decoction until we reached the Sanitorium to prevent any fragments from setting."

"By all the dead in the Drift, what happened?' asked Savnah.

Just then, Nolan and the warden trotted forward on foot, emerging out of the thick timber along a game trail. They stopped on the far side of a stream. Karra and Savnah crossed the stream to join them, and the four waited for the rest of the group to gather.

"Report, Nolan. Terrain and traffic," said Reddevek.

Nolan smiled and followed the warden's directive. "Ahead is a gradual climb through timber. The ground becomes rocky and favors our passing. I found no grot sign, nothing of the grondle or umbral. Benyon Garr is a taskmaster. While we've been gone, he's erected a defensible palisade with walking ramparts almost the entire distance between the Pillars. There's still a half-mile gap left open on this side and only scattered foot patrols. The moon of Lellen cuts before Baellen tonight. That should give us more than enough cover to slip by."

Karragin turned to regard the rest of the group. In the last several days of travel, Laryn's color and vigor had improved. That she weathered the journey without so much as a complaint was no small wonder. She was, after all, a royal. *Giver, is she Queen Laryn now? Tovnik refers to her as Your Radiance because of her station among the healers, but where does the line of succession go now? Is Bryndor the heir to the throne?*

Kaellor and the boys looked surprisingly fresh, given the long day of travel. Only Dexxin appeared weary, and she guessed that had more to do with the effects of the veramanth.

Reddevek walked over to his mount and stroked the Aarindin on the muzzle, then assisted Ranika down to the ground. "I suggest that we hold here. Rest up and wait two hours until the sun passes, then try our chances skirting the Pillars. Once we are farther into Aarindorn, we can camp in the foothills with relative anonymity, then make our way along the roads to Callinora. If anyone stops to inquire, you four are dignitaries from Stellance being escorted to Callinora." He nodded to Kaellor, Laryn, and the brothers. "Does that sound agreeable?"

Kaellor tipped his chin. "Far be it from me to second guess one of Aarindorn's finest. You heard the warden, lads."

Kaellor dismounted and walked his horse to the stream. Karragin watched as the brothers methodically dismounted and unsaddled their horses. The older one, Bryndor, began to brush the mounts. Lluthean strung a bow, issued hand gestures to the wolvryn, and the three loped off into the woods before she could think to rein them in.

She watched the wolvryn weave into the timber without so much as a broken twig and shook her head at their silent passage.

Karragin walked over to Bryndor. "Prince Bryndor, if I might suggest, we can't make a fire until after we cross into Aarindorn. May I inquire as to why your brother is hunting for game?"

Bryndor looked at her over the flank of his horse and continued brushing. His flat grey eyes held a look of curiosity. "I'm still not used to that title, so maybe . . . never mind. It's not for us. The wolvryn haven't had game since the bartusk three days ago. They get some of their sustenance from zenith but still need to eat."

"There's nothing inside the Great Crown as formidable as those creatures. Why is Prince Lluthean going with them?" she asked.

Bryndor smiled and patted his mount on the flank. "You don't miss much, do you? He's going to link with Neska."

"What for? Reddevek and Nolan already surveyed the area," said Karragin.

"It's not that we don't trust them. Llu's not looking for grondle. He's looking for any sign of abrogators or anything from the Drift, really. Kae's orders. We're sort of used to seeing to our own security," said Bryndor.

"That makes sense. Will you let me—let all of us—know if he finds anything?"

"Surely," said Bryndor. "Can you keep the horses close by, or do we need to tie them out?"

"The Aarindin won't stray, and the horses you ride should remain close, but I'll keep an eye out," she said.

"A kindness, my thanks then," he said, then began grooming Laryn's mount.

Karragin studied the group. It felt strange traveling in such company. Riding with the warden was one thing, but riding in the company of royals who acted more like seasoned Outriders was surreal.

Reddevek grumbled something gruff, but the girl who was ever his shadow giggled and poked him with a pine needle. Kaellor worked with Tovnik, gathering pine boughs for bedding. Laryn approached Dexxin with a water flask and engaged the sender in quiet conversation.

Taker's twisted bits, I'm literally riding with two potential traitors to the crown and the nobles who will likely wear it. Who is even in charge of this mess? If things grind sideways, who gives the orders?

She walked over to her brother, who sat on the bank tossing pebbles into the stream. "Can you range a bit longer yet?"

"Yes, what do you have in mind?" he asked and rose to his feet.

"I need you to follow Prince Lluthean; see that he stays out of trouble," Karragin ordered.

"I'll do my best," he said, then turned and climbed back into the tree line.

Karragin turned back to the group and caught Reddevek's eye. The warden lifted his gaze to Nolan, then dropped his focus back to her and nodded approval.

Savnah leaned in and pitched her voice low. "Maybe you should go. That one's been making eyes at you, Karra. He always saves the best cut of meat for you too, in case you hadn't noticed. You could do a lot worse than a prince, and he's a looker."

Karragin gave her a sidelong glare. "We're all just novelties. I'm sure that once he is established at court, there will be plenty of pretty girls vying for his attention, and I won't be one of them."

"What do you suppose the prince will find that the warden and your brother didn't already suss out?" she asked.

"Hopefully nothing, but if we're going up against the Usurper, I would rather have as much warning as possible."

"You really believe all that?" asked Savnah.

"We've had firsthand contact with an umbral, grondle, and more grotvonen than I can count. It's not such a stretch to consider that something must be behind all of that. Better to plan with the Giver's blessing than wait for the Taker's desire."

Chapter Eleven: Ill Omens at the Pillars

L luthean perched on a rocky ledge as the sun fell below the horizon. He sent the wolvryn off to hunt, knowing they were more efficient together. Within two hours, they returned, and Boru gnawed at the marrow of a leg bone from what he guessed to be some type of deer while Neska sat beside him. Lluthean used the opportunity to merge into her senses. He directed his attention to the north, where Kaellor had told him they needed to travel.

The world took on a zenith-laden hue: amber light bent to shades of blue punctuated with the iridescence of other life forms. Sleeping birds and burrowing creatures huddled in place, while the aura's of night creatures in search of food migrated across his field of vision. A chorus of aromas and sounds mingled and rose up from the forest floor.

Within moments, Neska made him aware of Nolan sitting just above and behind him. The tracker smelled of Aarindin, wet leather, oiled steel, and some kind of herb he couldn't place. Lluthean withdrew his focus and returned his awareness to a muted human experience.

"Was it Reddevek or your sister who sent you to look after me?" he asked. He craned his neck around in time to see Nolan stand up. The tracker smiled ruefully through messy, tumbling cinnamon curls, shrugged an apology, and approached.

"How do you know it wasn't your uncle, my prince?" asked Nolan.

A smile erupted on Lluthean's face, and he couldn't stifle a giggle. "Alright, first, you can join me as long as you drop all the princely talk. I mean, I do kind of like it when your sister calls me that, but only because it sounds so silly. I keep thinking it's bound to make her burst out laughing. And second, I know it wasn't Kae because he asked Bryn and me to take turns surveying the area every night, and tonight is my night. Have a seat," said Lluthean.

Nolan plopped down beside him. "Well, in answer to your question, it was Karra. She's all business when we range."

Lluthean tilted his head to the side and squinted. "Is that an Outrider thing?"

"Ranging? Yes, I suppose. We use it to describe most of the activities when we travel on mission in service to the Outriders." The scout plucked a seed head from a cluster of dried grasses, rubbed the grains between his palms, then inhaled. Lluthean saw the play of zenith across the runes on Nolan's wrist.

"What does your gift tell you when you do that?" asked Lluthean.

"Sorry, it's more habit than anything else. I can sense whether a plant is toxic, or . . . get an idea if it might be useful in baking. Once in a while, I can tell if there's a medicinal component. Before I sat for my Rite of Revealing, I thought I was sure to be a healer."

"Why is that?"

"Well, lots of medics and healers are gifted with lesser runes that enable them to discern such things. It's like the Giver clusters certain runes together. So, healers are often gifted with understanding things about the natural world around them."

"From the campfire talk, I gather your father is able to forecast the future?"

"Only sometimes, and not at command. When a vision comes upon him, it arrives unbidden and completely overtakes his senses. His other gifts enable him to understand when someone is duplicitous or untruthful."

"Kae wears the guardian rune as his arca prime but has lesser runes of judgment and perception. Are there lots of guardians in Aarindorn?" asked Lluthean.

The whites of Nolan's eyes flared. "Giver, no, that's a martial talent. Only the high families of Baellentrell or Lellendule inherit those kinds of gifts."

Lluthean frowned. "Your sister's arca prime endows her with raw strength. Isn't that a martial power?"

"Only in the way that she has trained to use it," said Nolan. "Histories show that only direct descendants of the two high families inherit gifts that allow the manipulation of zenith for the defense of the kingdom. Think of rune fire or your uncle's ability to create wards of pure zenith, things like that."

That information gave him pause, and Lluthean wondered, not for the first time, what abilities he might inherit. His only experience with zenith amounted to an uncontrolled surge of power that erupted between him and Bruug Hawklin in the Southlands. Otherwise, the mantle stifled any connection to his supposed gifts.

He imagined he would be impressed with any ability to shape zenith, and thought more about the members of their party. It sure seemed to him like Karragin's gift, more than the others, fit into a martial skill. Then he wondered if inheriting the gift changed someone or altered their personality.

"Is your sister always on point? Does she ever relax?" asked Lluthean.

"In the field? Not often, but give her time. Once she gets to know you, to trust you, she opens up. It took us weeks of hard travel before she began to joke around with Savnah, and then . . . Karra has always been slow to trust, but what she saw in her premonition . . ." Nolan shook his head in disbelief.

Lluthean nodded, trying to understand the depth of Nolan's bewilderment. "It's strange that they are getting along at all. I mean, can Karragin trust Savnah or Dexxin? Can any of you?"

Nolan puffed his cheeks out. "The truth is, I don't know for sure. By my count, Savnah saved my sister's life at least twice. Moons, she even saved my life, if I'm honest. Before we met you, I nearly dropped down into a grotvonen cave without the proper rigging and harness. Savnah called me a few choice names, then basically kept me from becoming a Nolan pancake."

Lluthean huffed a laugh. "I can imagine. Savnah swears like a Callishite sailor. Is she as tough as her talk?" asked Lluthean.

"You don't know the half of it. And to see those two in combat? Makes me glad I hang back with the bow, so I'm not measured against them."

"I suppose if she saved your sister twice over and you once, then it seems fitting to give them a chance to be better people. In the end, we have to trust what Kae and Laryn are trying to do. For now, I'll step lightly around Karragin, but give Savnah a return jibe when she throws down the gauntlet?"

"You don't have to step lightly around Karra. You just have to do what you say you're going to do. Don't break her trust, and you'll be fine. And as for Savnah, you have the right of it, I think."

"I think I can do that," said Lluthean.

"And if you ever see either of them light up their arca prime in anger, just run."

The two of them shared a brief laugh. "What's it like when you . . . channel? How does it feel?" asked Lluthean.

Nolan sat silent a moment, and Lluthean began to wonder if his question gave offense. At last, the scout cleared his throat. "Zenith is basically all around us, just . . . waiting to seep in. I can feel it like floating in warm water. When I have need, I sort of . . . open myself to it. It courses through the runes the Giver granted, and I can direct the flows to activate one or all the runes at once. After that, it's all about the unique gifts you inherit."

Lluthean juggled a few pebbles in his hand, losing himself once again in the future possibilities of what shape his gifts might take. They sat in companionable silence, and he considered the stars, finding them no different than the ones in Journey's Bend. Though his mind felt unsettled by the unknown future, something about the familiar constellations gave him a measure of peace. Eventually, he tossed the stones one at a time down to the forest floor. "Let me finish with Neska, and we can head back."

He rekindled his connection to the wolvryn, searching the far horizon for anything that reminded him of the hounds from the Drift. Sensing nothing out of the usual, he began to pull his attention back to their surroundings. Directly overhead, a kettle of strange hawks circled on thermals. Lluthean watched as the large birds glided, then blurred and shimmered as if made of blue light. He pulled his hand back from

Neska but couldn't make the birds out in the night sky with his human senses.

"That's something new," he said.

Nolan withdrew an arrow from his quiver. In the darkness, Lluthean could see the upper crescent of the scout's arca prime flicker to life. "What did you see?" he asked in a hushed voice.

Lluthean placed a light hand on Nolan's wrist. "Nothing dangerous, I don't think. High overhead, at least a dozen large hawks were circling. As they climbed higher and higher, they became pure zenith."

Nolan replaced the arrow in his quiver, then interlocked the fingers of his hands in the shape of a basket. "Did they carry their talons together like this, like they carried a parcel?"

"Yes, actually. I don't think I understood how strange that looked, but now that you point it out, I think that's right."

"It sounds like you saw an escort of moonwings. A dozen, you say? That's a bad omen in some parts of Aarindorn. They usually fly solo or, at most, in groups of two to three. Not much is known about them because they vanish after they ascend."

"Do other animals in Aarindorn vanish like that?" asked Lluthean.

"Not that I'm aware of," said Nolan. "A single moonwing is a rare sighting. I wouldn't go telling anyone outside of our group that you saw so many."

"Alright, but why?"

"In the mountains, people call them riftwings and believe they carry the souls of the departed to the Giver, holding them in their talons. So, if you see one, it means one person died or that a person is soon to die. If you see a large number—"

"Then a lot of people die? Twelve, one for every riftwing?" asked Lluthean.

"That's the folk tale," said Nolan. He stood and shouldered his quiver. "We should get back to camp, catch a few hours of sleep before we push through the Pillars."

"Sounds good. You lead. I'll follow." Lluthean fell in behind Nolan, and they picked their way back to camp. As they walked, he realized that

Nolan was perhaps the first person since leaving Journey's Bend that he might consider a friend.

"Nolan," he said.

"Yes?"

"Thanks."

"Just doing my job," said Nolan with a cheery tone.

"Not just that. Bryn and I, we've just had each other all these years. Well, and Kae, of course. Before the mantle frayed, let's just say we had trouble making friends."

Nolan gave him a quizzical look, so Lluthean continued, "When our parents banished Tarkannen, they wove a mantle around Bryndor and me. In addition to separating us from inheriting the ability to use zenith, it basically prevented anyone from remembering who we were unless we invested a lot of time with them."

"That could come in handy once in a while," said the tracker. "I mean, you could get away with all sorts of mischief."

"Oh I did, believe me," said Lluthean. "But in the end, it made for hollow friendships growing up. And sometimes it's hard to know if we are fitting in."

"Well, for what it's worth, you're not doing too bad. My runefather is the vice regent, a Lellendule, so he's a royal. Traveling with him is like a holiday really: fine food, comfortable lodgings. Chancle travels with an entire entourage of servants. I've never met a noble who groomed his own mount, set camp, and prepared a meal. But your whole family could drop into the Outriders as its own quad, and no one would be the wiser."

"Will you hold a spot for us if this thing in Stone's Grasp doesn't work out?"

Nolan laughed. "I would be sorely disappointed."

"Are you afraid we'll sully the Outrider reputation?"

"Nah," said Nolan. "I truly look forward to seeing the faces on some of the stodgy royals from Dulesque or Beclure when your family assumes the throne."

Chapter Twelve: The King's Respite

Volencia summoned thin strands of nadir and draped them as a filter across her body, removing any lingering scent from the grotvonen caves. She had already deployed a similar technique to remove the stains from her clothing but could do little to hide the appearance of wear at the elbows and cuffs of her outer cloak.

She stepped along the only road through a village set high in a mountain valley overlooking Dernegia, the mining kingdom. The path was a crude, rock-scalloped affair free of wagon ruts that bent in a gentle semicircle following a natural bend in the valley. Slabs of stone took the place of a formal wooden boardwalk.

A sour feeling bubbled in the pit of her stomach, created by genuine hunger and a nagging fear.

I should have double-checked Eguma's figures before today. There is simply no way that the valley holds even close to the thousand people required for the Rite of Sundering.

Her gaze passed over the simple dwellings. Stones cleaved from the adjacent mountains had been stacked up to form walls ten to fifteen feet high and were topped by thickly timbered roofs. Several homes crowded together in a manner that suggested they must share interior walls. A few storefronts common to every village lined the road. The familiar ring of hammer on anvil announced a blacksmith shop. A carpenter shop sat next to a beekeeper, of all things. At the end of the row stood a ramshackle pole barn claiming to be a stable. And right next to that, her eyes came to rest on a faded wood sign.

A weathered image of an ale stein tipped to the side and spilling its contents over a small mound of coins indicated the tavern. She stepped onto the front stone slab, kicked mud off her heels, and double-checked the placement of the veil across her scarred face before pushing the front door open. Inside, the steamy aroma of baked bread awakened her senses.

Three long tables with enough bench seating for forty patrons filled the empty room. In the far corner, an elderly man wearing a travel-stained, patchwork cloak sat on a three-legged stool tuning a lute. He looked up and nodded at Volencia.

The gleeman cleared his throat. "Got one out front, Cabe!"

A muted voice from behind a door on the far wall yelled. "Grab a seat, and I'll be right with you!"

Volencia decided to place herself reasonably close to the bard. The man scratched at the grey stubble on his cheek. "You're a month early. The king's entourage won't be here for a moon yet, and only if the weather holds."

"I could say the same of you," said Volencia.

"That's the Giver's truth, it is. I come early every year before the nobles arrive for the annual spring hunt. I like to get a feel for the place, see how the sound bounces off the rafters. And Cabe serves the best fare in the valley."

"I imagine Cabe serves the only fare in the valley," she said in an attempt at playful banter.

The bard slapped his thigh, set his lute in its case, and straddled a bench opposite her. "That's a sad reality. So, what brings a cultured woman up from the kingdom?"

"What makes you think I'm cultured?" she asked. A half-smile played across the unmarred side of her face, and she realized how much she missed human conversation, made all the more entertaining by the adoption of a false persona.

"Oh . . . that fancy veil is a giveaway, and though your clothes have seen better days, one can't mistake the fitted tailoring. Besides that, anyone who walks into Sifter's Valley this time of year carries the stink of the mountain on them."

"Fair enough. I inherited a tract of timber northwest of here. It's been in my family for years. My husband wanted to build something there, but I couldn't stand the notion of leaving the city. I can't say that I have much use for it, really, but my husband died this past winter. I thought I should see what kind of opportunity the valley might hold before I decided to sell," said Volencia.

The bard's shoulders relaxed, and he swiveled on the bench to face her directly. "I'm sorry for your loss. Small talk, right? If you don't want to find a snake, stop picking up rocks. All the same, your reasons set my heart at ease. I thought you might be my competition at first. Is this your first time up the valley then?"

"Yes. I admit that I thought I would find more people here. Is this small village the only settlement?" she asked.

"No. The mountain folk gather in small family groups all over. Nothing as substantial as what you see here, mind you. You should stick around; wait for the Winnowing of the Shades."

"I must admit, I'm not familiar with the term, but I've also led a bit of a sheltered life. Winnowing of the Shades, did you say?" asked Volencia.

"It's an old Dernegian superstition. The mountain folk believe that the unsettled spirits of the dead wander the frigid passes. Their loremasters explain that these ghosts inhabit the animals that live here: the mountain goats, sheep, deer, and the like. The spirits get sort of . . . trapped inside the animals. Dernegians see it as their responsibility to cull the herds, thereby setting free the tormented spirits."

Volencia dipped her head, nodding as if she understood. "That's why my husband would never visit this area. He always was superstitious regarding spirits."

"Well, it's a shame he felt that way. The whole affair is more of a celebration. I like to think of it as the Festival of the Hunt. All kinds of vendors accompany the royal entourage. A tent city springs up every year, and the population swells for several weeks."

"I've heard the same but didn't really believe it to be true. How many people do you think gather here?"

A deeper voice from behind Volencia answered, and a muscled forearm placed small plates and a platter of thick-sliced toasted bread with melted cheese on the table. "We set a record last year at a thousand three hundred. Welcome to the King's Respite. Best tavern in Sifter's

Valley. You've met Gauvin, our perennial troublemaker, I mean, troubadour. I'm Cabe."

Volencia turned to greet their server and, for the first time since entering the small village, felt overwhelmed. Cabe stood with hands clutched over an apron and wearing a white shirt with the sleeves rolled over his muscled arms to the elbows. He was singularly the most handsome man she had ever seen and not what she had expected to find in a remote mountain village.

After an awkward moment, she cleared her throat. "It's a pleasure, Master Cabe. I'm Shalla. What's the story behind the name of the village?"

"Two generations back, someone discovered gold in the streams that run down from the mountains. All sorts came from Dernegia to try their luck, and I'm told there was gold aplenty, until there wasn't," said Cabe. "Nowadays, it's mostly mountain folk passing through until the festival."

"I see. Well, can you . . . recommend something? What's good here?"

Cabe nodded. "Honey-style mead if you have the constitution for it. Otherwise, all that we have to offer is toasted bread with cheese and something that passes for chicken stew. We won't have goat, venison, or boar for another month, when the king's entourage arrives."

"That sounds perfect. I'll have the mead and stew, and one for my friend the . . . troublemaker here," said Volencia.

"Seems like she's already taken your measure, Gauvin," said Cabe.

Gauvin smiled and accepted the jibe. "That she has, my friend. Since we only get one chance at a first impression, maybe tap a fresh keg? None of that stale stuff from last season."

Cabe snorted and tucked his thumbs under the straps of his apron. "If you would bother to pay down your tab, I wouldn't have to offer you what's left from last season. But since you are keeping exceptional company, I'll gladly oblige. Retta will be out with the rest soon."

The bard lifted bright eyes to Volencia. "It would be my honor to serve you, my lady."

Volencia tipped her head, accepting the gesture. Gauvin cut her a generous portion of the toasted bread. "So, Ms. Shalla, what do you think? Fancy sticking around? At least pay us a visit during the festival. It's sure to be a corker this year."

"What's special about this year?"

"Every five or six years, the hunt takes on special significance. The Dernegians believe that the most tortured of souls get trapped inside the elusive crag-horned ram. Any hunter lucky enough to take a ram receives riches the likes of which I've not seen. The chance for that kind of prestige attracts an even larger crowd. With the right kind of introductions, you could likely find a number of buyers for your property if you decide to sell."

Volencia caved to her stomach and took a generous bite. Though simple, the mingling of the salted, aromatic cheese and sweet, toasted bread made her groan. "Oh, Giver's salty tears, that's a blessing on a plate, it is."

Gauvin chewed a bite, swallowed, and nodded. "It beats foraging on the trail, to be sure. You've been away longer than I gathered?"

Volencia politely set the bread down. Inwardly, she admonished herself for the slight divulgence of information. *But it has been a long while since I've had anything that passes for human food.*

"I've been traveling a fair bit, that's true. While the food is good, I think I will pass on the opportunity to visit the festival. I gather it's a collection of ale-soaked soldiers and ill-mannered mountain men all vying for the king's attention. That might be a bit more rowdy company than I desire."

"By rowdy, if you mean all the mountain children, then sure, but soldiers? There might be a handful out of formal deference to whichever royal attends this year, but nothing more. The king himself hasn't attended in over six years. Isn't that right, Retta?" asked Gauvin.

A girl of not more than ten years served two foaming mugs of mead. She wiped her hands on her apron and smiled enough to crease a dimple in her cheek. "Papa says not to agree to much of anything you have to say, Gauvin."

At her teasing, the bard reached out to swat her on the bottom, but she giggled and scurried out of reach. She waggled a finger at him. "Now, you behave, gleeman, or I shall not return with your soup."

Gauvin feigned exasperation, holding hands to his chest. "My fairest lady, if I have given cause for offense to thee, then I am truly most aggrieved. If you could see it in your heart to forgive a wayward bard and offer us your tasty soup, I would labor to honor thy service with a song."

A muscle in the girl's cheek twitched. "Huh?"

Gauvin bowed his head. "A song for thy soup, that is my offer."

Retta squinted her eyes. "Song first! Then soup."

"Very well, my lady," said Gauvin. The bard stood and walked to the three-legged stool. "Horn or lute, my lady?"

"Horn!" said Retta.

"As you wish," said Gauvin. He leaned down, opened a case, and retrieved what appeared to be a long animal horn with a gentle bend. Holes drilled in parallel series ran down the neck of the instrument. Gauvin placed his lips over a fenestration along the wide end and began to play. A haunting, sweet sound resonated in the hall. While the color of the tone lacked any of the sophisticated harmonics of the minstrels in Callish, the bard played the tune with a passion and skill that held her attention nonetheless.

When the last notes sighed away, Gauvin set the horn into his lap, and both Volencia and Retta rapped their hands on the table in applause.

"You're too kind," said Gauvin. He returned to the table as Retta brought forth the steaming bowls of stew. The girl returned to the kitchen, leaving Volencia and the bard to finish.

Volencia held a spoonful, waiting for it to cool. "Is that music a sample of what one could expect at the Winnowing of the Shades?"

"There is that and so much more," said Gauvin.

"Do you suppose that the festival will break another record in attendance this year?" asked Volencia.

"The festival has grown in size every year. With the special reward for a crag-ram, I don't know why this year should be any different. You really should come and see. Spread the word, bring some friends," said Gauvin.

"I think I might just have to do that," said the abrogator.

Chapter Thirteen: Finding the Right Path

On the Founding of Stone's Grasp in Aarindorn

I, Nivosh Baellentrell, youngest daughter to Eldrek Baellentrell Eldrekson and the 'fo, having reached the eighth decade of life, have decided to record my memories of our arrival to Stone's Grasp in the days after the Great War in this, the year 75 post cataclysm.

We arrived, my older brothers and sisters and I, orphaned by the struggle against Mogdurian and his host of abrogators. We survived by the kindness of the other high families, the Endules, Llentrells, and Lellendules. Though we struggled through dark days in the years immediately after the war, I look back on those times and recall the sense of peace and unity. Shared misery does that, I suppose. But those days seem now but a shadow as we struggle to find our way. Some days, I wish for a small war to make us remember our common alliances instead of our differences, as we are always so apt to do. But more on that later.

Ksenia rubbed at the delicate weave of runes on her forearm. She watched the last flicker of zenith pulse across her linguistics gift. An achy feeling settled across her temples, and she pressed her palms against the side of her head to dissipate the bothersome sensation. Translating the ancient text required tedious study and progressed as fast as molasses in winter.

Between her desire to ride Winter and her formal duties as the regent's favored scribe, she had found less time than she imagined with the ancient tome. She flipped back to her notes on the first page. *"An early account of Aarindorn, by Nivosh Baellentrell. Daughter of Eldrek Baellentrell Eldrekson and the 'fo."*

A tangled web of verbs with possible connections to names and places filled the space under the title. She thought back to the line scrawled at the base of the Founder's Memorial. *Channel zenith to save the world, or nadir to destroy it. Channel confluence to become the Eidolon reborn? I wonder what that really means in today's speech. This would be so much easier if I had more context. Taker's breath, I should be a lot farther into this by now.*

Bells gonged, announcing the new hour. Ksenia sighed more out of relief than frustration and closed the ancient tome, returning it to the archivist. She climbed back up through Stone's Grasp, made her way back to the scribes' office, retrieved her folio and zeniscrawl, then shouldered the door open into the regent's chambers.

The vice regent stood speaking with Therek. Ksenia situated herself to the side at the scribe's table, then realized that the nature of their conversation had strayed into something beyond typical small talk. The regent sat forward, elbows on knees, and frowned at Chancle like a hawk sizing up a rodent on the plains. She waited for one of them to glance her way. The vice regent pulled at the waist of his surcoat in a gesture of uncharacteristic frustration. She followed the sharp line of his jaw, accentuated by the well-manicured beard as he turned. "Should I leave? I can certainly come back when the next petitioner is ready," she suggested.

"That's not necessary," said Therek. "You already have complete knowledge of the events pertaining to our predicament. Besides, you might have an interest in the vice regent's report."

At his words, Ksenia placed her hands in her lap and listened with interest. Chancle cleared his throat. "Of course. First, Overwarden Kaldera reports that three separate expeditions into the grotvonen warren show that the creatures have vacated the area. All Outriders returned with no casualties. He ordered the entrance sealed and sent the flank ranging over the southwestern portion of the Great Crown in search of any other exits. So far, there have been no other encounters. Once they finish their sweep, the overwarden intends to place sentries in the area. The rest of the flank will return to the forward base and fortify the remaining area between the Pillars."

Giver's breath, just return in one piece, Kerv.

"Before we admit the first petitioner, I should like to revisit our conversation from this morning, regent," said Chancle.

Therek lifted a hand. "I am more than comfortable with you making a diplomatic visit to Faltusch, but the timing seems . . . risky. So much hangs in the balance. When the Baellentrells finally arrive, I should think that you would want to welcome your cousin, Laryn. But more than that, I need you here to assist in making introductions and soothing certain . . . elements in the noble houses."

"You said that the kingdom needs to move forward, that strong trade relations with the border kingdoms are key to our growth." Chancle rubbed at his temples, appearing uncharacteristically strained. Despite his obvious frustration, he replied with no heat or venom in his tone, ever the polished politician. "I've organized an entire expedition. We had planned to set out immediately to solidify trade with our closest neighbors to the west. Surely those alliances would prove fruitful."

"You know as well as I do that Norfold and Millstone, and even Faltusch, will be more than eager to renew trade relations. We have been turning away their merchants for years now. Those will not be difficult conversations to manage. As soon as Benyon Garr has the last stretch between the Pillars of Eldrek shored up, we can control and manage who enters the kingdom and ensure mutually beneficial trade this time around," said Therek.

Chancle stared at the regent a long moment and shook his head with a rueful smile. "I can see that you've already made up your mind. I don't want to add to your burdens . . . I will be only too happy to cancel the trip and remain here as you wish. What business can I see to at this time?"

Therek's shoulder relaxed, and the hawkish man considered his friend. "I would have you organize the spring assembly festivities. We anticipate one of the largest crowds ever. There are matters of ensuring adequate food and security, especially in the lower commons and the Sprawl. Then there is the not-insignificant matter of entertainment the noble classes demand."

The regent stroked long fingers along his eyebrows. "Your skill and relationships are, frankly, critical to bolstering our alliances inside the kingdom. Troubled times are on the horizon, but once we sail over dark waters, then we can set our sights on a path of expansion."

Chancle's focus drifted, and he seemed to be calculating something. He tilted his head at last and drew back to the room. "We have but a handful of petitioners this afternoon. It would benefit my planning if we began right away."

"I agree. If everyone is ready?" Therek turned to Ksenia with a question on his face. She brandished her zeniscrawl and smoothed the blank parchment on the table, indicating her readiness.

"Let's begin," said Therek.

The next two hours rolled by faster than any of the prior sessions. The last petitioner, a spice merchant with a shop in the Delve, drew out the discussion, lobbying for permission to expand the size of his store by excavating into the Great Crown. The man arrived ill-prepared for the proposal, having no idea about the experts required to survey the site and the possible effects of excavation on the surrounding strata.

Chancle cut him off, much to everyone's relief, just as the merchant pressed with a third rebuttal that sounded more like a bribe than any legitimate business plan. "I think what the regent is trying to politely express, is that you need to hire a certified royal orologist, commission a study on the surrounding stone, and the stability of any changes to the foundation. Then you have to get the blessing of the merchants' guild in the Delve. If you manage to convince that stodgy lot that your plans are sound, then you can approach the regent . . . and only then will your proposal merit serious consideration."

Without waiting for further response, Chancle escorted the merchant back out the front door to the chamber. Though his behavior was uncharacteristically curt, Ksenia puffed out a breath in relief. She set her zeniscrawl down and rubbed at the sore muscles of her hand.

Chancle returned. "Apologies. I should have vetted his petition before allowing him an audience."

"You can't be expected to be everywhere at once, my friend. I think that canceling the trip to Faltusch will allow you a much-needed break from being pulled in too many directions," said Therek.

Chancle nodded and smiled. Something in the light of his soft, downturned eyes gave the indication that he'd genuinely warmed to the opportunity. "I think you might be right. By your leave then, I'll see to the arrangements."

"The Giver smile on you, my friend," said Therek.

Ksenia stood and collected the papers of record from the afternoon's session. She placed them into her folio and thought of what she might do with the rest of her afternoon. *It's always a fine day for riding.*

"Have you made any progress since your discovery at the Founder's Memorial?" asked the regent.

"Yes, some but . . . not as much as I had hoped, Your Grace," she said. "I do know that it's a record of some type started by Nivosh Baellentrell, daughter to Eldrek 'and the 'fo,' whatever that is."

The regent's wispy eyebrows lifted with interest. "I can not say that I have ever heard of that expression. Anything else?"

"No. The phrasing from the Founder's Memorial lacks any significant tense or gender context, making it less helpful than I had hoped, so it's slow going."

"I see," said Therek. "And Low Aarindorian doesn't help clarify those issues?"

"The low dialect was used by artisans and craftsmen as a type of shorthand language for the trade. I don't think it was ever intended for historical prose."

They began to walk to the back door of the regent's chambers.

A strange thought came to her. "Did you know that Eldrek's last name was not Baellentrell? That was his middle name, if I have deciphered everything correctly. His children adopted that as their surname."

"Is that so?" said Therek. "Well, scholars have long argued that our ancestors, the founders of Stone's Grasp, were a melting pot of refugees from the Great War. The Docent Venlith at Callinora certainly falls into that camp. If that's true, we should not be surprised by anything you might discover in your studies."

He opened the door for her to depart. "Ms. Balladuren, your parents are good friends of mine. Without revealing the nature of your brother's mission, you have my permission to write to them."

Ksenia's face flushed as she thought first of Rugen. She searched the regent's sharp eyes, and then realization caught up with her. "Oh, you mean Kervin! That would be . . . Mother would appreciate that."

"I'm sure they would enjoy hearing news of his safe return to the forward base camp," said Therek. "If you don't mind, might I ask why you decided to postpone your trip home? I thought the warm spring weather would see you elbow-deep in Aarindin foals."

"It's lots of things, really, not the least of which is my work with the tome of Nivosh. Besides, Mother and Father will be here at the month's end for spring assembly. While it's nothing I care about, I sort of promised Vennedesme I would go." *And the Lacuna want me here.*

Therek chuckled. "The spring assembly is not that painful, and you never know who you might meet there. I met my wife at my first spring assembly gala."

"I'm pretty sure my brothers would scare off any interested young men, but . . . if I know Mother, she'll try to introduce me to several unsuspecting souls."

"Sometimes, the people who love you the most only desire to put great opportunities in your path," said Therek.

"I know, Your Grace, but would you do that to Karragin?" she asked.

The regent nodded in understanding. "Karra? No. I would never presume, and she would call me out for any such machinations. I just hope she can get out of her own way and let someone love her someday."

"Some of us need to find our own path, I guess." They reached a fork in the hallway. The stairs down to the clerical offices stood to the right, and the regent turned to the left. "Founder's Memorial?" she asked.

"Yes. We all have our escapes, and Gardener Hoff has a new water lily to show off. Care to join me?"

"Thanks for the offer, Your Grace, but I should see to the delivery of the afternoon's records, and then I think I might try to get Winter out for a ride," she said.

"That sounds like the making of a great afternoon. To finding your own path, then. Eyes to the horizon, Ms. Balladuren."

"You as well, Your Grace. Eyes to the horizon." She turned to walk toward the stairs, then reconsidered. Kunzie's directive entered her thoughts. *Look for ways to befriend and engage the regent.*

She stepped lightly to his side. "Actually, if you don't mind, I could spare a few minutes to see the gardener's new lilies. You never know where a fun diversion might lead."

Chapter Fourteen: Pulling Weeds and Planting Seeds

The regent schooled his face to one of neutrality and stifled his gifts of sapience and discernment. "Allow me," he said and swiveled open the thick door, gaining entry to the Founder's Memorial. A rich, sweet fragrance spilled forth as the door opened on silent hinges. *That man is truly gifted beyond measure when it comes to cultivation.* He welcomed his young scribe inside.

"After you. Let's see what Master Hoff has in store for us today," he said.

"Thank you," said Ksenia.

A few steps inside the gardens, she turned with surprise. "Is that winter night's asylum I smell in here? How is that even possible? The vines only flower in the wild in midwinter."

"I suspect Master Hoff might have the answers you seek. Let's give the man his due, shall we?" said Therek.

They walked past shrubs with broad leaves and others with fluted purple flowers to the back of the garden. Fagle Hoff stood knee-deep in the memorial pool, admiring his work. His rough-spun trousers were rolled up just above the waterline, revealing knobby knees. Fagle gathered the wispy strands of beard at his chin and twisted the hair around his index finger.

The memorial, a crescent of stone that defied gravity, towered over vibrant green lily pads. In the center of each nestled a rounded blue fist of tightly closed petals. The dense array of plants eddied about the pool, covering the entire surface.

"Afternoon, Regent, Miss . . . Balladuren, right?" asked the gardener.

"Yes, good afternoon, Master Hoff. It looks like you've been busy," said Ksenia.

"Indeed. I went with a full load of Baellen's eclipse this year," explained the wiry man. He held a fist forward and, with an expression of youthful exuberance, opened his fingers as he spoke. "By week's end, the blue petals will splay open to reveal an orange center. The blooms should last well through the spring assembly, but I intend to harvest them for centerpieces, so be sure to stop back before then."

"I will," said the young woman. "Master Hoff, do I smell winter night's asylum in here?"

The gardener placed a finger to his nose, then pointed directly at Ksenia. "A sharp nose you've got. It's my latest project. Behind the pool on the far wall, I tricked a vine into blooming. If you like, you could pick the flowers today. They aren't likely to last more than a day or two."

"Ms. Balladuren tells me that the vines only grow in the wild and bloom midwinter. How did you manage such a task?" asked Therek.

"She has the right of it, Your Grace. Asylum is a finicky vine. Of the seven samples I procured from the wild, only two survived. Getting this one to bloom was a labor of love. You have to make the vine think it's midwinter by shading the sun's first and last light, then expose the roots to extremes of cold. I don't think I'll likely manage it again, and now I owe a rather large favor to my daughter, who is, among other things, a chiller."

"I've never met anyone with that gift," said Ksenia.

Fagle scratched at the stubble of his beard. "Well, it's a fine enough gift to be sure, and in another month, her skill will be in high demand with the summer heat and all. If you don't mind my asking, how is it you know so much about asylum?"

"It's because of Winter, my Aarindin. She's an albino. Aarindin normally foal in the late spring, but her mare dropped her in midwinter. I was following the fragrance of the wild vines several years back when I found Winter abandoned and shivering, lying on a lush bed of fallen asylum petals."

Fagle smiled. "Giver's truth? Tell me, was the snow all around melted? If the conditions are just right, the petals give off heat when they drop, allowing the roots to spread on the uncontested ground. Is that how your filly survived?"

"Yes, that's likely the only reason she survived until I found her," said Ksenia. "And ever since, it's been my favorite flower."

The gardener looked about the memorial wistfully. "It's one of my favorites too. It's the only flower I've ever seen that pushed its way out into the world for itself. It's not beautiful to attract bees or show off in a garden. Most times, you can't even see the blossoms as they blend in with the snow. They are beautiful . . . just because."

"I never thought of it that way," said Ksenia. "Do you have any plans for the asylum flowers?"

"Not really. Growing them was more of a curious challenge, something to do. You are welcome to them," said Fagle.

"Are you sure? Just a few handfuls steeped in clear resco overnight makes a perfume that sells for a good profit in the Delve," said Ksenia.

"If you can put them to good use, then have at it," said the gardener.

Ksenia turned to Therek, who stood to the side observing the conversation. Something in the young woman's eagerness made him smile. "Don't wait on me."

She pivoted and disappeared to the back of the garden. Therek waited a moment, then turned to Fagle. "It seems you've outdone yourself again, Master Hoff."

The gardener twirled a finger through his beard once more, then tilted his head. "Baellen's eclipse is a tricky species, but why don't you tell me what really brought you here before our young scribe returns?"

"Redleaf and pine resin," said Therek. He waited to see if his friend was still as crafty as he had once been.

The gardener walked a slow circle among the lily pads, then eventually lifted his face. "The redleaf, I understand, seeing as we distill it into embertang. I heard you requisitioned all available stores to the staging area between the Pillars of Eldrek. You still need more?"

"Despite my efforts, another party learned of the kingdom's need and secured a monopoly on the available stores of embertang. They are demanding an exorbitant cost."

"You've got to be talking about the Lacuna. That group is like an invasive weed, popping up uninvited in all the flower beds and choking out the healthy plants for its own purpose." Fagle unwound the finger from his beard and itched his chin in contemplation. "We can help. It might take a few weeks to distill it into embertang, but the Great Crown is flush with wild redleaf this time of year. It's not as potent as the cultivated variety, but in a pinch, you take what the Giver gives. Same goes for the pine resin."

"Good. I've already secured the exclusive services of a local alchemy guild favorable to the crown. They can be placed at your disposal to manage the distillation," said Therek.

"That's even better, and it frees up my people to focus on the harvest."

Therek gazed to the back of the gardens, confirming their continued privacy. Though he doubted the Balladuren woman would undermine his efforts, any slip of the tongue to the wrong person these days seemed to deliver a random state secret to the ears of the Lacuna. "I just have one request. Offer the job only to those you can trust. I would prefer that the Aspect of the Lacuna only learn of our actions at a time when it's . . . unprofitable. It won't hurt the organization much, more of a moral victory really."

"Pulling the shoot is a start, but you've got to get at the roots. Have you any plans in that regard?" asked Fagle.

"A few. I have already placed key stakeholders on alert in Stellance and the major duchies. Venlith has returned to Callinora and intends to clean house. I should not like to be on the receiving end of that woman's wrath. Anyway, when they approach your group again, and they will, go ahead and play along with their movement and let me know how things unfold."

"I can do that, my friend, but it won't be an easy sell. Lots of my people have been damaged by the Lacuna. Their exploitation of the ungifted in the Sprawl is one thing, but the vivith trade . . . it's rotting us from the inside out."

Therek grabbed a towel from a nearby bench and handed it to the gardener as he stepped out of the pool. "I know, my friend, the time is overdue for us to take action." They sat down on the bench, admiring the gardens in companionable silence.

"What do you suppose our wives would make of us if they could see us today?" asked Fagle.

Therek allowed his mind to drift for a moment, and he heard a throaty laugh ripple from the back of his mind. His wife had watched as a young Karragin chased after her brother, who labored to finish the last of a crownberry muffin he had pilfered from her plate. He lingered there, lost in the moment of those happier times when he was but an adviser unfettered by the daily complexities of running the kingdom.

At last, he dismissed the memory and sighed. "Who can say? Yours would be impressed, no doubt, by the way you've stepped up to give a voice to the voiceless. Whereas mine would badger me endlessly about ever accepting this post to the regency."

Fagle dried his feet, then began to slide on his stockings and boots, stamping the heel down for good measure. "You're too hard on yourself, Therek. Your children have turned out better than most, and the kingdom prospers despite these difficult times. That we didn't fall into civil war throughout the reparations is no small miracle, and it's thanks to your leadership."

Therek offered him a smile, but the expression was born more out of unease than any feeling of joy. "I only hope the historians record me as kindly. For now, I need to have faith in the gift the Giver bestowed on me . . . forgive me, poor choice of words there."

Fagle waved a hand, dismissing Therek from his assumed guilt. "No need for any of that talk between friends."

"I appreciate that, old man. What I meant to say is that we need but only hold out a bit longer. Then I should be able to step down and let a Baellentrell usher in a new era of prosperity for the kingdom."

"You don't sound as confident as the last time we spoke," said Fagle.

Therek rubbed a hand over the wispy edges of his eyebrows. "Something happened to the sender who traveled with Karragin, and I haven't had word from her or Reddevek. I can only hope that at least one of them rides with a Baellentrell and the other is on their way to a safe return. Elbiona has yet to send word of any developments."

"Without a sender, how long will it take a message to get here from the forward base camp?" asked Fagle.

"Warden Elbiona took a dozen birds to the Pillars and has only used three. They make the journey in half a day, and she saves them for the exchange of important information," said Therek.

"I see. So no news means either nothing of major import or the warden knows as little as we do of the current whereabouts of our lost family of royals."

"So it would seem," said Therek.

Fagle tapped a stickpin on his left breast. The polished stone marble gleamed under the red and blue gems. "Why haven't you given Elbiona one of these yet?"

"What good would that do, really? It allows me to eavesdrop, but meaningful communication is still not possible, not yet, anyway. But . . . give Venlith and her scholars some time, and I'm sure she will craft a better means of communication."

"People can be resistant to change, but an ability to communicate from a distance? Even one the runeless can use? That would be a true blessing most folks would stand behind," said Fagle.

"I agree. I was hoping that she would have something ready by the time of the spring assembly, but I don't think her artisans will make that particular deadline. And so, I'll leave that discovery to the next generation."

"Are you certain that you can trust the governance of the kingdom to anyone who has been gone for so long? I mean, so much has changed," said Fagle.

"Some things have changed, that's a surety . . . others remain but simply wear a different name. Families struggle for favoritism and power. Men and women alike seek out profit at the expense of not just the kingdom but their neighbors. Our hope to move away from all of that lies in a leader who is committed to serving the people."

"Some would say that's a naïve hope, my friend."

Therek barked an uncharacteristic laugh. "Not just some, but many. Many are the voices who have given up on that ideal." A flicker of motion drew Therek's attention up toward the ceiling of the blue zenith dome where a drab hummingbird, a mother by its lack of color, hovered before a tiny cup of leaf and fiber perched at the end of a branch. The bird zipped back and forth but always returned to the nest. Eventually, as if enticed by her example, a tiny bird half the size of the mother lifted from the edge of the nest and floated a moment then dropped back down. The mother returned once again and bobbed back and forth around the nest until, at last, the baby hummingbird followed it out. Therek lost sight of them after that.

He grunted once. "And yet sometimes we just need an example to inspire us all, to show us a better way."

"You are already that example," said Fagle.

Therek regarded his friend. He knew the words were spoken out of kindness, but they sounded like the flattery offered by affluent members of Stone's Grasp known to carry allegiance with the Lacuna. "You're too kind. But inspiring the masses and leading the kingdom like that was never for me. I am but a placeholder and will be all too happy to step aside when a Baellentrell returns."

He turned at the sound of Ksenia returning from the back of the gardens. Therek pitched his voice low and spoke to Fagle. "Time to take the first step in pulling at the roots."

A fragrant, humid wave of heat preceded her. She had gathered up a large basketful of asylum petals. She set her prize down and stepped back, brushing sweat-matted hair from her forehead.

"Seems you've made quite the haul there, young lady," said Fagle.

"Well, I'm not going to let them go to waste," said Ksenia. She dipped her head to Therek. "Your Grace."

"Ms. Balladuren, I wonder if I could give you a rather unusual assignment. It shouldn't be too much. I've written down the addresses of several key locations scattered throughout Stone's Grasp. I plan to contact the titleholders with a proposition. The next time you are in the archives, see if you can prepare a list of their names."

He retrieved a folded paper and a stickpin and held them out. She pocketed the list and considered the jewelry. "Certainly; how soon do you need it?"

"Just . . . delegate the task on my orders to one of the clerks in the archives the next time you sit down to wrestle with that tome from Nivosh," said Therek. "Wear the stickpin; it reflects your status in the offices of the regent and should grant you more access than those without one."

Ksenia tilted her head and placed the stickpin over her breast pocket. "I don't know what to say, Your Grace, except thank you. It's lovely. I'm honored, really." She reached for her basket once again. "Consider the task done, Your Grace. By your leave, I will get these to my room."

"Of course. I need to take my leave as well. I have a meeting with a group of spice merchants, of all things. Best not to keep eager parties waiting." Therek watched her leave, then turned and nodded once to Fagle.

"I can't tell if you are pulling weeds or planting seeds," said the gardener.

"As I understand it, the best gardeners do both," replied Therek. He winked and strolled out of the Founder's Memorial.

Chapter Fifteen: Safe Passage in the Dark

The pattering chorus of rain muted the sounds of hooves slogging through mud in the predawn hours. Kaellor shook his head, spilling the water that had collected at the chin of his beard, and studied the clever way Reddevek deployed Lluthean and Bryndor with their wolvryn.

The boys' enhanced sight, coupled with the talent of the scouts, had enabled the group to sneak past the sentries at the outskirts of the forward base camp between the Pillars of Eldrek. They rode the entire night, camping by day under the cover of the dense forest along the foothills of the Great Crown. They continued from there in a similar fashion, traveling by the light from the moon of Baellen for three nights and resting during the day.

Reddevek chose a heading tempered by the need for secrecy and expedience. The route, veering slightly to the northwest, kept them isolated in parts of the kingdom sparsely populated and well to the east of the duchies. Occasionally, the first light of day glinted off Lake Ullend far to the east, but this morning the brooding sky did little to remind him of their location.

Kaellor watched the warden disappear with Ranika into the shadows. The other scout, Nolan, had left with Lluthean a short time earlier, veering slightly to the northeast. Reddevek had assumed responsibility for the more difficult terrain to the northwest. The rest of them would wait for at least half an hour, then push on until sunrise.

"Not quite the return home I imagined," said Laryn. She gathered a portion of oiled canvas around her shoulders, and water streamed to the ground. He had procured the canvas from the market outside Voruden and initially questioned the utility of the purchase. After cutting it down into four crude rain ponchos, he felt like the Giver must have steered him to that particular stand in the market.

"It's not the traditional robe of a queen, but you wear it rather well, all things considered." He turned when her hand found his under the folds of his poncho. He searched for the crystalline blue fragments set beside the red ones in her left eye, but in the darkness, all he could make out was her silhouette. Still, even that allowed him to forget how everything felt cold and damp . . . everything except his hand.

Kaellor looked over her shoulder to see Bryndor in friendly conversation with the younger contingent of the group. He kindled zenith through his lesser runes of balance and judgment, assessing the others.

The women, Savnah and Karragin, sat off to the side on their Aarindin. Dexxin and the medic were inspecting Bryndor's Logrend bow. Tovnik pulled on the string, testing the weapon's draw.

Bryndor chuckled. "I know, you wouldn't think it by the draw, but I'm telling you, it shoots farther and drives the arrow with more force than any longbow from the Southlands."

"There is something in its make, I'll give you that. I've never seen different materials grafted together in the limb like this, and the grip has a nice feel," said the healer.

Dexxin inspected the bow in turn, then reached over his shoulder and removed several arrows, handing them and the bow to Bryndor. "You should try it with these, Outrider standard tactical broadheads. They're made for killing but can't fly as far as a bodkin or field point. The tips are filed to a razor's edge to inflict lethal internal bleeding, so leave the cork in place until you're ready to use it for big game or . . . well, whatever we might encounter."

Bryndor pulled off one of the cork plugs and inspected the arrow tip, carefully running a finger along one of the metal edges, then replaced the cork. "Thanks. I can see how these would cause a lot of damage. Any idea how they stack up against grondle?"

"Not as good as you might hope," said Dexxin.

The medic nodded his head in agreement. "My advice? Stay behind your uncle's shield and shoot them in the gill slit, or better yet, dose them with embertang."

Kaellor felt a reassuring resonance pass through his gift and sensed no ulterior motives. He shook his head in wonder and turned to Laryn. "So far, it seems like your plan might be working. Savnah is social enough, but that sender is likely more important when it comes to announcing our arrival. That's the most I've heard him speak since we met on the Borderlands."

"It's a good sign," said Laryn. She yawned and rolled her shoulders. "How much longer before we leave?"

"We can ride out any time now. Reddevek thinks this will be our last night ride. He wants to get us past the territory patrolled by Beclure. There are several obscure villages with taverns and inns along the way. Apparently, on the west side of the kingdom, there are only a few that hold allegiance to the crown first and the duchies later. He plans to navigate us to those places as we make our way north to Callinora."

"That makes sense," said Laryn.

"Still. If we encounter anything that smells of danger—"

"I know, love," she interrupted. "Stay under your shielding or at the back. Find one of the boys and stay close to a wolvryn if possible."

He sensed the exhaustion in her response and softened his words. "Laryn, I know you can handle yourself. But if we encounter real conflict, I can't be the guardian and worry about you too. Just tell yourself that it's really more about me, love."

She turned, and the moonlight reflected on her cheek as it raised in a soft smile. "You, you, you . . . it's always about you."

"I can't help it. I'm a spoiled princeling returning home. But, maybe for a few more nights, indulge me?"

She signaled her mount forward. "Eyes to the horizon, love."

"Eyes? Laryn, that's not exactly the confirmation I was looking for."
She urged her mount to continue a slow walk and left him in silence. He cleared his throat to address the rest of the group. "Alright, it's been long enough. Let's mount up and head north. Karragin and Savnah, you have the lead."

Over the next few hours, they trudged ahead, enduring the drudgery of the spring rain in silence. The only sound of their passage was the occasional clatter of horse hooves over rocky ground. His hips began to feel heavy in the rain-soaked saddle. Zenith thrummed unbidden into his arca prime and startled him to alertness. Something splashed into the mud to his side, and he turned to see Bryndor hop down from his horse, bow in hand. He squatted close to Boru.

"Something has him on edge. Give me a moment," said Bryndor.

A deep rumble vibrated from the wolvryn's throat, and he stood pensive, staring up into the mountains. Bryndor remained still, attentive to things revealed only through the wolvryn's senses. They huddled together for a long, tense moment.

Kaellor gripped the reins in one hand and the hilt of his guardian sword in the other. A feeling of urgency crept over him, though he could not ascertain if it emanated from his arca prime or the raw tension of the moment. He siphoned in the currents of zenith around them and waited, holding the power at bay but prepared for release.

"Bryn, what do you see?" he growled the question in a low voice.

Despite the darkness, Kaellor saw his nephew's hands flash a command, and Boru sprinted off. In a blur of motion, Bryndor stood and nocked an arrow, turning to aim directly at Dexxin, who rode not twenty paces back. "Dexxin, veer to your right!"

Bryndor loosed the arrow into the shadows behind and to the side of the sender. A wet thunk followed by a grunt indicated that his shot was true. A brute of a man wearing dark leather gear stumbled forward to the ground. The steely tip of a great spear glinted in the dim moonlight as it clattered down. Dexxin turned on his Aarindin, loosing one, then two arrows as his mount sauntered a slow retreat. Two more, one man and a woman, cried out in pained alarm.

Bryndor gathered the reins of his horse. "Behind us, to the south, I count at least twenty, maybe more. Boru will get the three to the east, but there are more there, and several others approach from the mountains."

The soft twang of a volley of bow fire erupted from the woods behind them. Kaellor unleashed his stored power into his arca prime and erected a blue half-sphere. He extended the shielding past Dexxin and Tovnik, the brilliant light reflecting in the eyes of their assailants. A flock of arrows clattered against the ward, sparking flickers of zenith before rolling to the ground.

"All of you, get to me!" yelled Kaellor. Bryndor stepped close, nocking another arrow, and the Outriders sprang into action. Savnah and Karragin wheeled their mounts and used the Aarindin to flank either side of the party. Dexxin and Tovnik directed their Aarindin to the front and back of the group, positioning them in a similar fashion.

With the Aarindin circled up, Kaellor released his protective barrier, and they all strained their senses into the darkness. Somewhere in the shadows to the west, a wolvryn howled once, a strange short cry that swept up in pitch.

"Was that Boru?" asked Kaellor.

"Yes. He's calling Neska. If we hold here, reinforcements should arrive. Unless . . . Kae, do you think Llu is safe? Why didn't the others warn us of this attack?" asked Bryndor.

Karragin's calm voice responded from the periphery. "This group follows us. They were not ahead of us. Those on our flank sweep in from the mountains. They pursued us or had warning of our passage. It's not likely that the warden even encountered this lot."

Somewhere out in the darkness, men cried out in surprise and pain. The sounds of rasping metal and of limbs thrashing about through the underbrush were silenced by feral growls. A moment later, Boru trotted back to Bryndor's side. Blood matted the side of one cheek and shoulder, but the wolvryn appeared unharmed.

Without warning, Kaellor's gift beckoned for release, and he erected another zenith-infused dome. The pale light reflected several lone arrow shots. The clatter of the shafts arrived in a random pattern for a minute, then was followed by another coordinated volley. Kaellor maintained the barrier as a swarm of arrows peppered the ward.

Dexxin walked a few steps to the interior edge of the barrier and squatted down a moment, then returned. "Some of those arrows are of Outrider make. That might explain how they've managed to find us."

From the distant shadows, the enemy lit torches and shouted, "For the breakers!" Something streamed through the air, leaving a trail of light as it arced across the distance to land on the guardian dome.

Karragin barked a command and shielded her face. "Munitions! Avert your eyes!"

Kaellor looked away, the flash a sunburst at the edges of his vision. The explosion vibrated through his gift with less intensity than a crush of grondle but with more force than he'd anticipated. Sparking light careened off the outline of the dome, leaving smoldering bits to sizzle in the mud. In the distance, the sounds of hooves and boots slogging through the mud announced the enemy's charge.

Kaellor turned to Bryndor. "Link with Boru again before you set him loose among their ranks. Tell me if any archers hang back."

Bryndor communed with the wolvryn once again, then gave a command, and the wolvryn bounded off into the shadows. "As near as I can tell, they have all committed to the charge, none hang back, and at least half are mounted."

Kaellor nodded grimly. He removed the long knife stowed behind his saddle and handed it to Karragin. "It doesn't replace a sword, but it's better than an empty fist. Will the Aarindin remain here during the battle?"

Karragin took the knife, then knelt forward to arm herself with the great spear dropped by the first man felled by Bryndor. She plunged the spear forward, finding the balance on the shaft, then slashed the knife over, then upward in an uppercut. By the grace of her motions, it seemed pretty clear the woman had trained with the combination of weapons before. She stopped and rested the spear shaft casually on her shoulder. "They will."

Kaellor dismounted and addressed the group. "There are perhaps ten mounted riders, ten or more on foot. Savnah, Karragin, and I will hold the line before the mounts. The rest of you gather here and shoot anything that gets past us. If I sense another munition, I'll try to erect a barrier."

Without waiting, the primes joined him out front, one to each side. In the darkness, the chanting of the enemy grew louder, and they continued to shout, but their battle cries were degrading into bestial yells. Savnah clanged the blades of her axes together and set her feet in the ground to Kaellor's left. Karragin wiped rain from her brow, then crouched with the spear held over the crook of her arm.

Kaellor's gift urged him to action once more, and he erected the protective crescent before them. Again, the light reflected off the eyes of their enemy, yet they seemed no closer. Instead, the entire force milled about in the distance, shouting and pacing back and forth. The random staccato of arrow fire rattled against his ward. "Something's not right, be on guard."

A fluttering vibration rippled overhead, and the Aarindin whinnied. The oncoming men continued to shout in a rage. Adding to the confusion, a harsh voice barked a command from behind them, "That's quite enough, Prince. Drop your weapons and stifle your gift."

They all turned to see a man dressed in well-tailored black silks standing behind Laryn and holding a thin blade across her neck.

"How?" asked Kaellor.

Laryn stood holding the reins of her mount in one hand and an unstrung bow in the other. She shrugged. "He just dropped out of the sky."

The man lifted his blade under Laryn's chin, silencing her explanation. "Enough. Drop the ward. Your weapons on the ground, all of you!"

With concerted effort, Kaellor extinguished his barrier and tossed his guardian sword to the ground. "All of you, do as he says, and we'll sort this out on their terms."

Steel and wood thudded to the ground. Laryn's assailant eyed them warily. "Good, that's good. Now, step back—" His words cut off in a grunt of pain, and the fletching of an arrow sprouted just behind his ear, the shaft and barb punching out the other side of his skull. He made a gasping motion once, then slumped to the ground.

"Don't waste a blessing. Arm yourselves!" growled Laryn.

They had only enough time to find their weapons and form up before the enemy fell upon them. Kaellor rushed to Laryn, picking up the guardian sword. He released a pulse of zenith, and several mounted riders flew back like leaves on the wind. All around them, the sound of battle erupted as the enemy closed.

"Grind it to the Drift," said Kaellor. He took a step to wade into the melee but dared not to go too far from Laryn's side.

"Kae, go," said Bryndor. "I'll stay here with Boru. We'll keep each other safe."

In affirmation of his nephew's words, Neska flashed past them and into the fray. Kaellor looked once to Laryn. She deftly pulled the bow down over a shoulder, strung the weapon, and sighted an arrow into the darkness. After the familiar twang of the string, she nodded in confirmation. "I don't need you to be my husband. We need our guardian. Go."

Kaellor gave over to the full power of his gift. Zenith surged first through his arca prime and then into his runes of balance and perception. He stepped forward between the two Outrider primes and slashed the guardian sword overhead, whipping a lash of zenith out into the night. The crescent of energy pulsed forward five to six feet high and arced across the horizon. The blast unhorsed nearly all of the mounted men, and the mounts whinnied, scattering into the darkness.

The gift warned him of a rush of men from the right, all wielding swords. He parried a swing and stepped in with a thrust, skewering one in the chest. With a pivot, he turned the man's body as a shield in time to deflect the attack of another foe. His opponent's wild swing sliced into the back of the skewered man. Kaellor shifted the tip of his sword, releasing the weight of the dead man, and whipped his blade around, catching the other assailant across the neck.

With no time to rest, he charged at the next wave of enemies running up from the darkness. He pulsed a short burst of zenith, knocking several to the ground. From under the tangle of bodies, he felt the pulse of a munition thump. The scent of sulfur confirmed his suspicions, and none of them rose to challenge him. He shielded the group once again, then waded into the melee, crossing paths with Savnah and taking out a man charging her flank with a spear.

Savnah spun once, an axe blade cleaving into the thigh of an assailant. The man toppled to the ground, and she hacked another blade across his neck before he could cry out. Without pause, she deflected an attack from another foe, then instinctively circled around Kaellor, stepping into the void between him and Karragin.

More than once, he plunged his blade into the belly of an enemy struggling to recover on the ground. Others he blocked, parried, and deftly cut down, maimed, or impaled. With each cut and slice, he sought to kill. The three of them, the prince and two primes, fell into a deadly rhythm, weaving back and forth, assisting each other and always turning the charging enemies. Sometimes he delivered the killing blow; other times, Karragin thrust a weapon, or Savnah spun in with a lethal slash. All around them, bodies accumulated.

Kaellor stumbled over the litter of enemies and backstepped to gain his footing. The din of battle felt softer; the battle cries and challenges came less frequently. A lone arrow materialized from the darkness, and he felt something in the guardian sword ignite his arca prime one last time. He stopped the arrow with a pulse of zenith, then turned to face an onrushing attacker. He stepped in low, under a wild overhead swing, and pulled his blade across and through the flank of the last enemy, then searched for his next opponent.

Seemingly faster than it began, the battle was over. He drew his focus to his gifts, waiting to be led in a different direction. He strained his senses into the darkness, but the countryside fell silent save the moaning of a few wounded enemies and the panting breaths of his companions.

Kaellor looked over to see Karragin withdraw the spear from an opponent on the ground. Savnah wrenched a moonblade axe from the pelvis of another. Reddevek stood not far away, a long knife in one hand and axe in the other. The warden stood over two corpses, the light of his arca prime illuminating his face with feral intensity. The girl who was ever his shadow wiped the blade of a knife clean of blood before searching the pockets of the dead.

He turned to see Laryn standing pensive between Tovnik, Dexxin, and Bryndor. Her hands held a bow with a nocked arrow. Beside them, Boru panted and seemed to smile. Several dead bodies lay at their feet. All sprouted arrows, and at least one wore the evidence of a wolvryn bite by the size of the serrated wound on his shoulder.

"Your quivers are nearly empty; are you well?" asked Kaellor.

Bryndor glanced once at Dexxin and Tovnik, then at Laryn. They gave him a solemn nod.

The sound of approaching feet slogging from the north drew them all to attention until Lluthean's voice cried out, "Hold! It's safe now. Only Nolan, me, and the rain to contend with." He walked beside Neska, his Logrend bow in hand and a clutch of arrows in his other fist. The young Lefledge scout led them forward.

"They had the drop on us for a moment. Do I have you to thank for that timely arrow shot?" Kaellor asked of Nolan.

"Not me, Your Highness. I don't think I could have made that shot in the light of day. It was Lluthean," said Nolan.

For his part, Lluthean remained uncharacteristically still, standing with an odd stiffness as if he expected to be reprimanded. Something inside of Kaellor warmed, and he considered the young man, waving him forward. "Then you have my thanks. You did well, son."

A smile played across Lluthean's face. *I'll have to check in with him later. Nobody's ever the same after taking a life.*

Kaellor cleared his throat. "Is anyone injured? Everyone accounted for? Form up here and let Laryn and Tovnik know about any injuries."

"Neska has a shallow wound on her chest," said Lluthean.

Laryn wasted no time and signed for the wolvryn to approach. The whirring hum of her song spilled into the night as she made quick work of the wound.

One by one, they each sounded off, indicating they'd suffered no serious injuries. Laryn and the medic made rapid assessments, managing minor cuts and bruises. Bryndor and Lluthean linked to the wolvryn and, sensing no other enemies, sent them on patrol.

As the group gathered near Kaellor, Reddevek approached his Outriders. They shared a quiet conversation, and he seemed to nod his approval before walking the perimeter in silence. The warden weaved in and out of the grasses and small trees.

Eventually, Reddevek returned. "With the ones we took out on the flank, including those the wolvryn removed, this was a force of thirty . . . mostly men, a few women. At least two of mine." He growled the last phrase, then handed a sword and axe to Karragin before continuing his appraisal of their fallen enemies.

She considered the weapons, wiped the knife blade clean, and then handed it back to Kaellor. "The axe is one of ours, but I don't recognize the sword."

Kaellor watched their exchange. "It's some kind of cutlass hybrid. I've seen blades of similar make along the coasts in the Southlands."

Karragin strapped the scabbard to her hip and sheathed the weapon. "Well, it's mine now, I guess."

"Did we leave any alive? I should like to know how they found us, or their purpose," said Kaellor. "Who are 'the breakers' anyway?"

Savnah stood with her thumbs hooked over her belt and lifted her chin. "Your Majesty, I think—"

"No. Let's have none of that here, not after we spilled blood together in one another's defense," said Kaellor.

Savnah bowed her head once, then continued. "It stands for the circle breakers, another name for the Lacuna."

"This one's still alive, though just barely." Reddevek pulled the dismembered bodies of two corpses from a pile and pointed at a young man. "Taker's breath, what happened to them?"

In the predawn light, Kaellor approached. "One of them dropped an explosive after I . . ." Kaellor waved his hand, indicating how his barrier had repelled the group. He studied the man's injuries. A singed blast injury had exposed glistening fat and dark purple meat from a rent in his flank. One of the man's legs also bent at an odd angle at the thigh, swelling to unnatural thickness.

Kaellor knelt and slapped the man's cheek until he came around. "Your injuries can be healed if you speak the truth to me. Who are you? Why did you attack us?"

The whites of the wounded man's eyes flared against his soot-stained face. He struggled to draw enough breath to speak. He lifted his head and considered the wreckage of his body. "Oh, grind me through and through . . . there's no amount of healing . . . I told that grinding Outrider to mind the munitions."

"Maybe not, but I have a medic and healer who could ease your pain. Answer my questions."

The man dropped his head back into the mud. "All I know is that our leader was with the Lacuna, and he had some kind of warning you would pass this way. With the support of the Outriders, this was supposed to be easy coin, enough to get us out of the Sprawl."

The man's eyes started to flutter closed. Kaellor shook the man's shoulder and slapped his cheek again. "How many from this group were in the Lacuna? Which one was your leader?"

"Half of us were recruited for the job, those on horseback were . . . circle breakers. The Endule . . . Nagen, the glider, he was . . . the main . . ." The man exhaled one last time, then breathed no more.

Kaellor stood and realized that most of the others had gathered to listen to his interrogation. He turned to Reddevek. "Taker's spit. A garden unattended is fertile ground for invasive weeds, but I didn't imagine we would have this much to contend with."

The warden nodded. "It's pretty clear that they know we were coming. They had time to prepare."

"Still," said Kaellor, "they don't know everything."

He walked around, surveying the landscape of their carnage. "Hiring poorly trained people from the Sprawl means they've underestimated our group. Maybe they don't know as much about us as they assume."

Reddevek grunted. "A few of these were Outriders, and at least one, the glider, was a gifted, which means we'll have to be even more careful than we thought." He shifted his gaze, bringing a menacing glare to bear on Dexxin.

Tovnik cleared his throat. "I can assure you; it wasn't Dexxin. He's faithfully consumed Veramanth's decoction every other morning."

"It's my brother; it has to be," Savnah volunteered. "He's a dream augur, and the Lacuna have him captive."

"It makes a strange kind of sense," said Kaellor.

"I wish they knew why," said Laryn. "If only there were some way to get them to understand Tarkannen's threat, the real reason for our return."

"That will only make a difference to some," said Savnah. "And even then, only if they see it for themselves. The breakers have been spinning their web for years."

Kaellor scratched at his jawline. "I wish we knew how deep the roots of betrayal run."

"One thing's for certain," said Reddevek. "This was an assassination attempt. And thanks to the munitions, anyone within miles will know something happened out here. We need to move out. I'll lead as many horses as I can manage to the west to hide our trail. I can circle around and find you up ahead."

"What about the dead. Should we . . . do something with their bodies?" asked Bryndor.

Kaellor rested a hand on his nephew's shoulder. He looked the young man in the eyes and realized everyone was waiting on his orders. *Oh Bryn, you assume that there was some good in them, but I can't say there wasn't and still show Dexxin or Savnah a different way, can I? Grind it, this path my wife set before us is not an easy one to walk.*

He swallowed his misgivings. "The best parts of them, Bryn, rest with the Giver and the spirits in the Drift now. The valley can take what's left. There might be others coming. Gather any quality mounts and the two Aarindin, then we need to put as much distance between us and this battle as we can. Let's just hope the Giver grants us safe passage in the dark."

Chapter Sixteen: Shadowed Secrets

Bryndor dismounted, stretched his legs, then sent Boru off on a short perimeter patrol. The routine of setting and breaking camp, minding the mounts, and tending to the wolvryn made the urgency and stress of the last several days more manageable. After their battle with the Lacuna, he'd struggled to sleep for the first few nights. His dreams replayed the images of the enemies screaming in rage and falling to bow shots or the ravages of the wolvryn.

He lifted the reins over his mount's head and encouraged the horse to graze. "I wonder if your previous owner never gave you a name because he understood something of the journey ahead?"

"When you speak to the horse, do you think he understands you?"

Bryndor turned to see Dexxin leading his Aarindin down a steep hillside. "I'm no sympath, but horses understand more than we think by our touch and the care we render."

In affirmation of his words, Dexxin's Aarindin approached. The sleek, black creature walked right up to Bryndor, puffed a gentle breath of air in his face, then briefly laid her cheek on his shoulder before grazing near the other horse. "She likes you. You should try riding the Aarindin. With the two we recovered from the Lacuna, I could ride another. You could ride her."

"I already feel like the saddle is trying to split my backside like a wishbone. I can't imagine what riding bareback would feel like."

"It is an adjustment, but if you change your mind, let me know," said the sender.

Dexxin stared with a vacant expression for several moments as if working out a complex navigational computation. Eventually, his focus returned. "I see you recovered the broadheads."

"Two of them need a bit of mending at the fletching, but they proved too valuable to leave behind," said Bryndor.

"I never got the chance to thank you. That first man, the one with the spear that you took out, he was likely enough to loosen my grip."

Bryndor puzzled over the words. "I'm not sure I know that phrase."

"It's an Outrider expression. The Aarindin grip us, holding us in place, but they can't do that if we're dead. Anyway, you have my thanks. Can I ask, how did you manage that shot in the dark?"

"When I separate from Boru, from his perception of the world, the afterimages remain for about four or five seconds, like when you still see the streak of lightning in the night sky. I didn't know the man held a weapon, but he smelled and tasted of something . . . hostile, I suppose. Does that make sense?"

Instead of acknowledging Bryndor's question, Dexxin faded away a second time, retreating into himself. With a sigh, he returned to the conversation. "Actually, no, it does not."

"Were you just talking to your brother and sister?" Bryndor asked.

"Talking? No. Listening. It's only been a day, and I don't trust myself yet to speak to them openly. They've been in my head ever since I can remember. They would know if I held anything back. It's difficult, but not as hard as lying to them would be. And still, it's much better than Veramanth's decoction," said Dexxin. "That has been a difficult way to start the morning."

"I'll have to take your word for it. Back in Journey's Bend, where we came from, medicine always left you wondering if the cure was worse than the illness." They stood in companionable silence, watching the Aarindin and horse graze. Boru returned from his patrol, tongue lolling to the side. The wolvryn walked up from behind them and inserted his massive head under Bryndor's arm, demanding affection.

Bryndor finger-combed the fur under Boru's chin, removing a burr. "Just because you've grown faster than a weed doesn't mean you have to bring them along for the ride."

The wolvryn huffed once, then settled down, belly to the ground.

"Are you sure you're not a sympath?" Dexxin asked. "Giver's right hand, that one understands you word for word."

Bryndor chewed on the inside of his lip. "He does at that. I think he understands a lot more about me, about us, than I do about him. They completely sense the world, whereas we only see parts of it."

Dexxin cocked his head, appearing interested, but asked no question, so Bryndor continued, "When I link to him, it isn't just that their sight is superior. All of the senses run together, so . . . all at once, they see, smell, hear and . . . sense the world around them. And with people, they can often sense what their mindset is, their emotional state even."

Boru turned his head to the north and huffed a greeting.

"Neska comes," Bryndor explained.

Moments later, Neska loped forward, tail wagging, and settled next to her brother. They sniffed at each other for a few seconds, then seemed content to lounge on the grass.

"Does your brother have the same connection with that one?" asked Dexxin, dipping his forehead at Neska.

"He does. It's what allowed him to take out the leader, that glider fella, a few nights back," said Bryndor.

"That was no small blessing of the Giver. I consider myself handy with the bow, but that shot? So close to Laryn and in the dark? That was either some kind of crazy or some kind of luck."

Bryndor grunted a giggle. "Probably a bit of both, but that's Llu for you."

Dexxin smiled for the first time, dimples slashing his cheeks. "Your uncle though, that is a man with a rare gift. There's not been anyone to wield martial talent since the war. Did you see him in that melee? His shielding is one thing, but the way that man can anticipate where he needs to be from moment to moment . . . it makes me glad for second chances."

A question needled its way into Bryndor's thoughts, and his first instinct was to suppress his curiosity out of politeness. But the sender had never been so forthcoming, and the issue felt too important to ignore, so he sucked once at his teeth and blundered ahead. "Can I ask you a strange question, Dexxin?" asked Bryndor.

The sender nodded his consent. "How are you doing with all of this?" asked Bryndor.

"How do you mean?" asked Dexxin.

"You belong to the Lacuna, a group that's set against the return of the noble families. Yet, you've been made to . . . keep our company. You could have left any time or stopped drinking veramanth days ago."

Dexxin stared at his boots for a time. "If I'm honest, I don't know what to think. Before this week, I thought I was ready to do anything to advance the cause. Karragin said she saw as much in her vision. But that kind of violence is easy to imagine against an enemy you don't really know. You and your family are . . . not what they said you are, and not at all what I expected."

Bryndor allowed himself a halfhearted chuckle and realized at that moment why Lluthean might turn to humor so often. It did seem to rescue the conversation from a heavy place. "If it makes you feel better, none of this is what I expected either."

The conversation faded to a silence that some might consider awkward, but Dexxin assumed that far-off expression again, so Bryndor knelt and commingled with Boru's senses. A fast survey revealed Neska's vibrant energy. Tiny life forms meandered just under the soil all around them. A faint aura of zenith huddled a few feet away in the brush, obscured by swirling shadows.

He directed his attention to the sender. A nimbus of zenith flared from the young man's chest, his arca prime, Bryndor guessed. Dexxin sighed once. His pupils dilated, his pulse quickened, and his breath came shallow and rapid, then seemed to pause and fall at ease. He permeated a strange scent that made Bryndor think of longing, of loss, and . . . uncertainty, fear. *That's what you're feeling.*

"You don't know where you will stand with them if you tell them about us," Bryndor muttered. He maintained his enhanced perception through the wolvryn. The blue aura about Dexxin's chest faded, and the sender turned to look at him, exuding curiosity.

"I don't know what to tell them or how to say it," said Dexxin. "Craxton is my brother. He only sees the good in the Lacuna, how they help the poor. Mullayne is a realist. She sees it all. The good and the bad and still . . . she likes the changes they say the Lacuna strive for."

"When you look at me, do you see a friend or a foe?" Bryndor asked.

A swirl of emotion played across the ambiance that was Dexxin's aura, like smoke shifting in the wind. Eventually, something resembling resolution broke through. "I want to believe we can be friends. I want to believe that there is a path forward, but I'm still not sure how."

Bryndor sensed no subterfuge and released his connection to Boru. "Then you should tell them. Confide in your siblings when you are ready."

Dexxin lifted an eyebrow in question, so Bryndor continued, "I mean, let's face it. Not telling them is making you miserable. And the Lacuna already know something about our travels here."

"Your uncle advised me against that a few weeks ago, but I'll think on it," said Dexxin.

Karragin's voice, shouted from the hilltop, broke into their conversation. "Reddevek secured lodging for the night at a tavern up ahead. It's supposed to be safe, and the owner holds fealty to Stone's Grasp. He's trading one of the horses we commandeered. There is a decent stable. It's empty and generous enough for our mounts and the wolvryn. We ride out in fifteen."

She turned without waiting for a response and crested the hill. Dexxin approached his Aarindin and issued a hand signal. The mount dropped its hindquarters to the ground, allowing the sender to throw a leg over. With some signal Bryndor missed, the creature rose to all fours and walked in Karragin's direction.

Dexxin turned to look over his shoulder. "Are you coming?"

"In a bit. Call of nature," said Bryndor.

Dexxin nodded and gave him a bit of privacy. Bryndor waited a moment, then turned to the brush at his side. "He's gone. You can come out now, Nika."

The young girl's outline appeared through a strange shimmer of oily shadows. The edges of her silhouette remained momentarily shrouded by ribbons of dark smoke, but within seconds the strange obscurement vanished. She stood, arms folded, curls of straw-colored hair sprouting from under an oversized hat, head cocked to the side.

"Neat trick," said Bryndor. "What gift of the Giver is that exactly?"

"It's not anyone's business, and I would like to keep it that way," said Ranika.

Bryndor held up his hands in submission. "Alright. Your secret is safe with me."

The girl stepped forward with an even more serious tone and pushed back the brim of her hat. "Don't go making a promise you can't keep. Keeping an oath is hard. Breaking it is easy. Too many people from Callish chose easy."

Something about the intense way the girl regarded him almost caused him to laugh. *So serious already. What happened to you?*

"Does Reddevek know about your talent?" asked Bryndor.

"Red's the only one. He's set me to watch over you and your brother whenever you wander off with Dexxin or Savnah."

"I see. Well, I'm not from Callish. I'm not really from the Southlands, it seems. If you will have it, I give you my word that your secret is safe with me."

The tension in the girl's stance relaxed, and she walked behind Neska and ran her fingers through the wolvryn's coat. "How did you know I was there? Redd can't even see me with his gift."

"If I tell you, you have to keep my secret. But like you said, don't make a promise you can't keep," said Bryndor.

She squinted at him, weighing the nature of his unspoken question. "Can I tell Redd? I don't keep anything from Redd, not nothin."

"That would be fine. I wouldn't want to put you in a difficult position," said Bryndor.

With an exasperated sigh, she flapped her hands in the air once, then allowed them to settle back into Neska's coat. "Alright then, fine, you can tell me your secret."

"I don't know. I'm not sure that you're ready," said Bryndor. "Maybe another time."

A confused look played across her face, one of wounded pride mixed with anger, and again, he resisted an urge to laugh. "I'm ready, really you can tell me, I promise, me and Redd and nobody else. I can even trade you, secret for secret."

He chewed on his lower lip with exaggerated consternation. "Alright then. I didn't see you, not once. But Boru and Neska? They can sense when you are about."

Ranika squinted at him, considering the words as if expecting a trick. "Then how did *you* know I was here?"

Bryndor pulled the reins back to rest on the saddle's pommel, then turned and interlocked his fingers. "Come on. We're overdue to rejoin the others. Up you go, and I'll tell you about it on the way back."

A light in the girl's eyes flickered with enthusiasm. Without waiting for a second invitation, she hopped once into his hands, and he tossed her easily up onto the saddle. After hoisting himself up behind her, he signaled for Boru and Neska to follow.

He placed his arms around her and held the reins, turning the horse back to the north. Over the next several minutes, he explained something of his connection to Boru and the training they received with the handler, Mahkeel of the Cloud Walkers. She listened intently but peppered him with questions about the enhanced wolvryn sight.

"I can tell you another secret, a free one. If . . . if you want," she said.

"Don't tell me anything that puts me at odds with members of our group here," said Bryndor. "I can only keep so many secrets, you know."

"It's nothin' like that. I knew we would see a lot of death on this ride."

Bryndor signaled the horse to draw to a stop. "Can you see the future, Nika?"

"I wish. But it's nothin' like that. I was keeping track of your brother a few nights back. He was talking with Nolan, and just like you, he searched the night sky through Neska." She paused to catch her breath and then continued, "Anyway, he told Nolan he saw a bunch of riftwings, and Nolan said a person only sees one before someone dies on account of the riftwings ferry their souls off to the Drift. But to see a flock of them? Well . . ." She sighed. "That means a whole lot of folks are set to go to the Drift."

Bryndor listened to her words spoken so earnestly. Eventually, he nudged the horse forward. "That's a pretty big secret, Nika. Did you tell all of that to Reddevek?"

"Yes, but he said he doesn't believe in the superstitions of the mountain folk. Say Bryn, you can let me have the reins, you know. Minding a saddled horse is easier than Zippy, Red's Aarindin," she said.

"Alright, but go easy. He's on the bit more than most, and I direct him with my legs," said Bryndor.

The horse began trotting up the steep side of a hill faster than he intended, and the strange way he sat on the saddle with the girl in front of him caused him to slide back, off-balance. He wrapped one arm around her waist, and the other lurched forward to grasp the pommel. Once at the top, the mount returned to a walk, and they both giggled.

He realized how he had misjudged her, assuming she was nothing more substantial than a sparrow. But her frame remained as taut as a bowstring, her legs gripping the horse securely.

He leaned back, placing hands on the horse's back as they continued. "Nika, how old are you anyway?"

The girl shrugged her shoulders. "I can't say as I know exactly. Might be as old as fourteen or fifteen. I've seen girls claim as much on the streets of Callish."

He knew she inflated the number, but his imagination was more preoccupied with wondering what life on the streets might have been like. *At least we had Rona and Kae.*

"What exactly were you going to do if Dexxin intended to cause me harm?" he asked.

She held up a knife, the ruby-hilted dagger gleaming in the sun, then twirled the blade and sheathed the weapon with a deftness he found slightly disconcerting for one so young.

"Do you know what a 'monk' is in Stone's Grasp?" she asked.

Bryndor sighed. "Man of no knowledge, right? Kae uses the term on occasion."

"You remember that I saved your uncle's life back in the Bend, right?"

Now he couldn't help himself and laughed, more at his mental error than anything the girl said. "Yes, as I recall, it was with that blade."

"Right then, well . . . Bryn . . . don't be a monk. That seems to be more Lluthean's thing."

"Maybe some days," said Bryndor. "Other times, I think he throws himself into a situation just to see how he can manage to wriggle out of it. And somehow, he always does."

They rode on, trailed by the wolvryn in the late-day sun. As they approached the group, she lifted a leg forward and dropped to the ground. "Thanks for the ride, Bryn. Do you think I could join you again? I love Zippy, but I'm a stick of butter without a saddle. I forgot how nice the saddle is."

He puzzled over her expression but couldn't suss out what she meant. It didn't matter at the moment, though. Something in the casual way she addressed him and shared her secrets made him feel at ease, so he just tilted his head in agreement. "You're welcome anytime, I'm sure any of us, Llu, Laryn, even Kae—especially Kae—would welcome you."

She nodded once and turned to find Reddevek.

"Hey, Nika? When it's just you two, tell Redd that . . . I appreciate the added security."

Chapter Seventeen: The Path the Taker Laid

The Aspect paced in his room in the midmorning hours. He had yet to receive any news of the successful capture of the Baellentrells. Thoughts of the royals returning to Stone's Grasp had interrupted his sleep of late and weighed heavily on his mind. Restless fingers worked open the lockbox and snuff can in which he stored the zenith seed. He flared zenith into the palm-sized nut, then restricted his flow to a thin stream and waited.

As this would be an unscheduled meeting, the officers of the Lacuna might require a few moments to attend. The zenith seed hovered on the small table in his private study, an empty nimbus of ethereal blue currents eddying within the clouded mass.

Inasia arrived first, announcing her presence and indicating she required a moment to finish an experiment. Burl and Kunzie chimed in, their confusion regarding the abrupt summons evident in their reserved expressions. Valdesta finally joined them. As she kindled her zenith seed, she finished another conversation.

"Kyvon, go check on Marlee in room thirty-three. She should have finished with that mark a while ago. Then call the boys to a private viewing line. Be sure to include that new acquisition from the Sprawl, the one with the skinny arms and high cheekbones. I'm expecting a visit by one of the rectors from the Church of the Giver, and he has unique tastes," said Valdesta.

The sound of her door closing and locking was followed by the appearance of her silhouette in the zenith seed. "Aspect, lady and gentlemen, to what do I owe the pleasure of your summons today?"

"I say," said Kunzie. "Are you really that busy at this hour of the day?"

"What can I say?" said Valdesta. "The Taker doesn't limit the hour of his activities, and neither do the good people of Stone's Grasp. If I'm to turn out a reputable service, then I have to be available at all times of the day."

The Aspect arched an eyebrow but kept his face from the zenith cloud. *I can always count on Val to find more than one way to indebt others to the Lacuna. Rectors have needs as well as any others, I expect. I should have thought of that angle. This business with the royals needs to conclude so I can refocus on moving our agenda forward.*

At last, he assumed control of the zenith seed. "Thank you for taking the time to attend on short notice. I know that you each have other duties to attend to, so I will be brief. The last time we spoke, Burl, you conveyed a reputable forecast from our resident dream augur. Were our agents able to put this to good use?"

Burl's full beard shadowed his wispy silhouette, and the tip of his nose came into view. "As you recall, the details of the boy's vision were . . . vague at best, but we sent a large force, thirty or so, with support from some Outriders loyal to the Lacuna and several gifted. The rest we recruited as foot soldiers."

"Why do I get the feeling that all of this is a prelude for ill news?" asked the Aspect.

A heavy silence settled across the cloud emanating from the zenith seed. At last, Burl cleared his throat and continued. "You are perceptive as ever, Aspect. We have received no word from the patrol since they swept north across the hill country west of Lake Ullend. We know our force passed by the hamlets loyal to Beclure. But after that, they just seemed to disappear into the night. We can't reach them by zenith seed, but at our last communication, they believed they might be on the trail of something unusual."

"Something . . . unusual, you say?" asked the Aspect. "Can you clarify that statement?"

"I'm afraid that I can not, Aspect," said Burl. "We've lost contact with them. I sent scouts from Midrock into the field, but the ride there will take several days, and then we'll have to find our . . . missing party."

The Aspect smacked his palm on the table, causing the integrity of their connection to waver through the zenith seeds. He stared for long moments at the dimming aura, tightened his control, and brought his frowning countenance into focus before continuing. "'The sons of the blue moon ride like wolves for vengeance in the west.' Were those not the exact words the augur spoke? This foretelling, coupled with the Balladuren girl's message, means we know that a royal descendant, a Baellentrell, returns to Aarindorn. We cannot allow this to occur. It will upend everything I have worked for."

Burl cleared his throat. "If it pleases you, Aspect, we have circle breakers embedded from the forward base camp to Callinora and Dulesque to Stone's Grasp. It doesn't make any sense, though. Why would they wander up the west side of the kingdom instead of passing through Stellance and taking the road directly to Stone's Grasp? What we need is more ti—"

"What we need is to find them!" boomed the Aspect. "Must I ride myself as the vanguard of an army of breakers to scour the countryside and find them? I'm frankly tempted to make it happen!"

Silent currents of zenith swirled in lazy patterns within the cloud of the zenith seeds. Kunzie's angular face eventually appeared. "You are right to have concern, Aspect. The return of a Baellentrell would pose . . . new challenges."

The Aspect rubbed at his temples. "The resources we expend to sequester the dream augur don't amount to much if the intelligence doesn't lead to results. It makes me think we should abandon that particular project altogether."

Kunzie continued, "Your frustration is understandable, but the augur has never led us astray. Who can say why they might sneak along the western part of the kingdom? However, I think we can all agree that sending an armed militia roving across the countryside, crossing the territories of more than one duchy, would risk drawing the nobles into the conflict at a time when we have not secured their allegiance."

The Aspect sat in silence, laboring to master his frustration. *So close, we are so close, but our success dangles by threads draped across the Taker's fingers. Why can't the Giver grant us this one last gift?*

At last, Inasia offered a clever solution. "Could we place a well-provisioned group in the field if they were working to protect a valuable donation of embertang to the front lines? We hold a monopoly of the embertang stores and could readily demonstrate the critical value of its safe delivery. Anyone questioning the mission could see the merit of letting them pass."

Valdesta spoke over the healer. "Taker's balls, that sounds like a lot of waste. I secured the monopoly of embertang on the promise of a high dividend. If we hand deliver the product to the front lines, we'll be lucky to recover even half of the cost before it's commissioned for the greater good of the kingdom."

Always the miser, Val, but someone has to keep a shrewd eye on our bottom line. It's no small wonder that you own a quarter of the Sprawl.

"Actually, Val, we would recover none of the monetary cost," said Inasia. "But our ability to send clandestine forces across the kingdom, coupled with the obvious goodwill our donation would impart, are both currencies more valuable than gold, especially if it allows the capture of any Baellentrells."

"I say . . . that's rather brilliant, Inasia. What are you all drinking over there at the Sanitorium? You're rather on point of late," said Kunzie.

"It does sound like a good plan, but are we ready? Are we ready to step out of the shadows and be recognized as a legitimate force in the kingdom? The timing matches with our donations to the Church of the Giver. If we do this, if we send a king's ransom in embertang as a donation, the deed will not go unnoticed. We'll have to lay claim to our actions," said Burl.

"And if we haven't cultivated enough loyal members among the duchies? It will be the Taker's gamble," said Kunzie.

Finally, the Aspect weighed in. "We don't need the noble families, not if we have the Dedicant and the runeless. We are also making . . . friends among certain elements in the Church of the Giver. Taken together, these people populate every corner of every household in the kingdom."

He paused, weighing the options. It felt as if he were standing on the edge of a high bluff overlooking Lake Ullend, and someone threatened to push him off. "Alright, I agree. It's not the timeline we planned for, but it's the path the Taker laid before us."

Valdesta added her thoughts. "Well . . . dammit to the Drift. I suppose I have to be in. If we are going to deliver the embertang, we need to be recognized for our efforts."

The Aspect continued, "Good, it's settled then. We've waited long enough. Inasia, you and Burl send what embertang stores you have to the Outriders garrisoned at the forward base camp. Pad the wagons light and keep the goods on top in case any officials want to check the validity of our transport, but get breakers back into the field immediately to hunt the royals. The royals are most likely gifted, so our agents should have a high suspicion for anyone mingling with Outriders or riding Aarindin.

"Kunzie, you and Val see to a generous embertang donation along the roads through Stellance to the front lines. I'll also need one of you to enter formal notice and obtain writs of origination recognizing the Lacuna as a formal business with the offices of the regent."

"Will you be available to assist in pushing the paperwork through, Aspect?" asked Kunzie.

"I am pressed into service elsewhere, which is why the timing of this is so vexing. But have no fear; you are more than up to the task. Funnel the work through our agents in the regent's offices, and you should meet little resistance. Keep me posted on any developments, but above all, bring me the head of the last Baellentrell. Dismissed."

The Aspect sat back in his chair and retrieved the zenith seed, rubbing a thumb over the smooth shell. He withdrew the pendant holding the memento of his family and stared at the images in his palm. *Giver help me; this is what I've become. Another small sacrifice to protect the greater good.*

Chapter Eighteen: Nothing and Everything

Ksenia slid another place sideways on a bench that ran the length of a long table in the archives. The glare of the late-day sun proved too much for her tired eyes, and she adjusted a large report in the shade afforded by a column of stone between the windows. She looked across the broad table and realized by the trail of papers and records that she had been migrating in this fashion for hours. At last, she had run out of room.

No matter, only these two records are left, and then I can merge the entries into a list for the regent.

She fingered through the property abstract, another parcel in the Sprawl of all places. *The regent certainly has been taking an odd interest in the properties there.*

The record detailed a storefront set against the outer wall of Stone's Grasp. The historical lineage of the property revealed that it had started as a modest stone masonry. *That seems logical enough, given that it originated during the founding of the capital.*

The property had exchanged hands several times, then annexed an adjacent building and became a winery for several generations until yet another building was added to the title, and it transitioned into an inn. Several more generations, different owners, and numerous renamings left the property as it stood now, The Taker's Gambit. She knew of the ill-famed gaming house, though she had never set foot inside.

Two years ago, as she prepared to sit for her Rite of Revealing, two of her classmates ran afoul of the gang that managed the gaming house.

One was dismissed from further training, and the other lost an eye for his troubles.

She followed the abstract to its conclusion and discovered the owner, Tixon B'gin. *Whoever that is.*

Just as she was preparing to add the name to her list, a clerk from the archives approached. The man wore the simple garb of an archivist embroidered with a blue filigree on the left breast, indicating his employment in the offices of the regent. With barely enough meat to fill out the uniform, she thought at first he must be a young page, but on closer inspection, she realized he must be at least a decade her senior; there was something in the weathering of the skin at the edges of his eyes.

He stepped oddly close and looked over her shoulder, his attention confined to the page she was reviewing. A pungent body odor leeched from his clothing, and Ksenia couldn't help but recoil. She leaned back and thought it odd that he rubbed the palms of his hands errantly back and forth over his lower ribcage.

Without asking for permission, the clerk flipped the abstract to the first page, muttered a "hmph" sound, then returned to the last page, where he drew a thin line with a zeniscrawl through the last name and wrote, *"Lacuna Trading Company Incorporated."* Next to this, he placed a legal stamp and date.

The man stepped back and finally acknowledged her presence, bobbing his head at her once with an odd smile of accomplishment that only accentuated his underbite. He spoke at last with a strange monotone and cadence that seemed oddly pressured to her. "Here they are. All these records. I've been searching the archives for hours. How many? How many abstracts are you hoarding here? I have to update at least twenty-nine more properties for the LTCI."

A muscle on the side of her neck tightened, and she tilted her chin to the side. When she spoke, she laced her words with exaggerated emphasis. "Good afternoon. My name is Ksenia Balladuren. What is yours?"

The man's eyes traveled across the scattered pile of abstracts on the table. "Hebben . . . Veeble Hebben, archivist of the first order in the offices of the regent," said the clerk, patting the emblem on the front of his uniform. "What you're doing is weird. What are you doing with all of these records? Am I . . . are you here to take my job? Please don't take my job. I love my job."

She placed a hand across her mouth in astonishment at the odd nature of the man, amused at how she had shifted from annoyance to compassion in the brief moment of their interaction. At last, she held up her hands in a gesture of submission. "I assure you, I am not here to take your job, and I'm not . . . hoarding abstracts. I'm composing a list under the regent's direct request."

The clerk humphed again and considered her with an eye of suspicion. "The regent? That never happens. The regent never busies himself with these records. Nobody ever cares. Well, almost nobody. Are you pulling a Kunzie?"

The name startled her. "A what?"

"Kunzie, a kunzie," said Veeble. "Mother says he comes here to take advantage of someone's misfortune, searching the archives, looking for cheap properties left after someone dies. It's smart, I guess, but it doesn't seem right. Are you going to buy something? If you're going to buy property, why look in the Sprawl?"

Ksenia squinted her eyes and looked back across the scattered piles of abstracts and loose papers until she found her writ of sufferance signed by the regent's own hand and tasking her with the work at hand. First, she tapped the stickpin on her breast, then she held up the writ for the clerk's inspection and waited.

One . . . two . . . three . . . and . . . there it is . . . an ever so slight lifting of the eyebrows.

Veeble leaned back on his heels, then rubbed furiously at the front panel of his uniform. He began to shift his weight from side to side. "I see. I . . . see see see. You have everything in order here."

His eyes drifted to the list of properties she had already identified. He patted at the front panel of his uniform with light, rapid taps. "If you like, I can help you with those. If you are making a list for the regent, I could make sure everything is up to date. At least sixteen other entries on your list now belong to the LTCI. It would only take me a minute to update them all, and then you could, of course, tender an updated list to the regent."

The information caused Ksenia to lean back in her chair. "Sixteen properties, you say? Which ones?"

The clerk held his hand out expectantly. Ksenia handed him her list and watched as he made checkmarks beside nearly all of the properties. He handed the paper back to her. "All of these?" she asked.

Veeble stopped his restless fidgeting and rested his palms flat against his chest. "Yes. The LTCI bought all gaming houses, brothels, and taverns in Stone's Grasp. The majority are held by one of their members, a man named Tixon B'gin. I don't suppose you have reports for any properties in the Delve? Or perhaps Callinora or Stellance? I have to amend a few records in each of those regions as well."

Ksenia shook her head, indicating that she did not. Veeble shrugged and muttered, "Still, this was the Giver's good fortune."

Ksenia shook her head in confusion, trying to suss out his meaning. "What?"

"It's the Giver's good fortune that I found you with all of these abstracts. Makes my job easy. Fast and easy is always best. Are you done? If you are done, could I return the abstracts to the archives after recording the amendments?"

"Yes, I'm done . . . for now," she said. Veeble nodded once and began to collect the documents into a tidy pile, leaving Ksenia with her list and her thoughts. She studied the properties the regent had requested her to identify. There were twenty in all, and Veeble had made checks by all but three. "Orphanages," she said out loud.

Veeble turned his head as he placed the last report onto the leaning tower of records. "Yes, I noticed that as well. But if you think about it, there's no profit to be had in owning an orphanage, is there? Have a nice day, Ms. Balladuren, and please tell the regent that I can accommodate any similar requests in the future. You could mention my name. It's Vee—"

"Veeble Hebben, I got it the first time."

The man smiled so full that the center of his upper lip dropped into a point, once again exaggerating his underbite. The effect made him look more than a little like a frog. She wondered briefly if he was mocking her but saw that the smile reached his eyes. Veeble waited there, palms to chest, rubbing back and forth along the lower edge of his ribs.

She felt suddenly sorry for the odd man, along with a little kinship. *You're no less an outsider in Stone's Grasp than I am, but here in these walls, you're safe.* "Veeble, you have my thanks. It will be my pleasure to convey to the regent how important your timely updates have been. I wonder, could you let me know about the other properties now managed by the LTCI, the ones outside of Stone's Grasp?"

Veeble flushed and nodded, patting his hands in rapid staccato beats on the sides of his uniform. "Yes, I can do that. That . . . I can do. I can do that very fast, very easy because—"

"Fast and easy is always best," she echoed with him. She smiled now and nodded once in agreement.

"Yes. All the records are open to the public. But as archivist of the first order, I can get them for you very fast. Mother will never believe me when I tell her about this. No, she won't."

Veeble pulled back a chair and sat down beside her. He attacked a blank piece of paper with genuine frenzy and composed a list of the properties in question. After more than ten entries, he lifted the zeniscrawl to his lips in contemplation, then set to writing again.

"Taker's breath, Veeble. How many in total?" she asked.

"On my list, over forty, though the task was delegated between myself and one other," said the clerk.

"And you remember them all by name? Is that some part of your gift or something?"

Veeble continued to scribble away. "My gift? No, it's nothing like that. I'm ungifted, but Mother said I've always been very good with lists . . . lists and names, and places, and turnips."

"Did you say turnips?"

"Oh yes, I'm very good with turnips. Mashed turnips, maple-glazed roasted turnips . . . did you know you can substitute turnips for potatoes in just about anything?"

Ksenia felt a genuine smile arch the muscles of her forehead. "I . . . no, I wasn't aware. I'll have to try that sometime."

"Yes. Well, I will retrieve the list for you now." His head dropped down, and he scribbled with furious focus. When he finished, he handed her the tally of properties and stood to collect the tower of abstracts on the table. She skimmed over the entries, finding a pattern of taverns, gaming houses, warehouses, and storefronts scattered across the kingdom. One property at the bottom of the list caught her eye.

"Veeble, this one is different. It's just a number. 1346."

"Yes, that one is strange. It's just land. 1346 is the lot number, somewhere up in the Great Crown northeast of Midrock. They could be your neighbors."

"What?" she asked.

"The LTCI; if they build something there, they could be your neighbors. It's close to your family's ranch." Veeble grunted with the effort of hoisting the abstracts and waddled back to the front desk, leaving her to ponder the list and the regent's motivations for having her assemble the items.

A sour feeling washed across her stomach. *What if the regent assigned this task to me because he already knows about the Lacuna? What if he knows about my involvement, or Rugen's? Taker's breath.*

Her emotion raced ahead of her, and she wrapped trembling fingers around her left wrist, then twisted. She sensed her chest rise and fall in rapid succession, and prickly tingling spread across her mouth and fingers. Before her angst surged even further, she pushed back from the chair, pocketing the lists.

A spiral staircase climbed up two stories. She climbed up and down four times before the aching muscles in her legs dissipated the effects of her rapid breathing. Panting now from mild exertion and not pure anxiety, she walked back to Veeble and tapped him on the shoulder. The archivist turned after shelving one of the abstracts.

He rubbed the flat of his hands across his ribs once again. "I like to climb the stairs too. It's a good way to wake up after midday meal. You don't look more awake, though."

"No? Well, I'll have to try to get more rest then, I suppose. Say, Veeble, can you place lot 1346 on a map so I can see where the property's boundaries lie?"

The archivist stopped palming his robes, and his expression brightened. "Of course. Wait right here."

Veeble turned and disappeared behind a broad desk. A few minutes later, he returned with a conspiratorial look, darting his eyes to the far corners of the room. He stood an awkward moment assessing their surroundings, then handed her a rolled parchment. He pitched his voice in a stage whisper. "Hide that fast. Normally, these cost two days' wages, but for you . . . it's no day's wages." He flared his eyes and dipped his upper lip in the smile that made her think of a frog again, and she stifled a giggle.

She leaned in with exaggerated caution. "Veeble, you are the very best. Thank you so much."

Another archivist walked by, holding several books for return. Veeble turned away, making a pretense of reshelving an already shelved text. Once the other man passed, Veeble looked over his shoulder and winked but also fanned his hand, indicating she should take her leave. Ksenia smiled and bowed her head, tapped the rolled parchment, and left the archives.

She found a private alcove and unrolled the map, making a quick assessment of the territory Veeble indicated. After only a moment's inspection, she collapsed the map. *That isn't just close to the ranch; it runs along the north border.*

Without giving further thought to her fears, she quickstepped outside and down to the lower castle green, taking the steps two and three at a time until her legs burned. The late-day sun cast ribbons of orange and pink across the horizon.

Finally standing outside the main gates to Stone's Grasp, she looked to the west, toward the royal stables. Part of her wanted to retrieve Winter and ride off into the Great Crown, just leave it all behind. Different plans and questions bubbled into her mind; there one moment, then replaced by another. She paced in indecision for several minutes, uncertainty her only compass.

Grind it. What if Mother and Father find out? That thought broke through the turmoil of her agitated thoughts. She ran toward the Delve. *Rugen. Rugen will know what to do. Let's hope he's keeping late hours today.*

The steep stone walls of the elite shopping district cast long shadows in the evening, and a chill permeated her sweat-stained clothing. She maneuvered through the crowds, muttering apologies whenever she jostled someone or cut a person off. At last, she arrived at the alley leading to Bekson's Fine Restoratives.

She ran up to the adjacent storefront where a newly gilded sign hung out front reading, *"LTCI."* A stout wood door with well-oiled iron hinges granted entry into a small sitting room and vacant reception desk. A door at the back stood open a crack, and light spilled into the receiving room. She stepped up to the reception desk and rang a bell with rapid, staccato taps.

"Rugen? Rugen, are you here?"

She sighed in relief when the voice of her brother answered from beyond the door. "Kess? Is that you? I'm in my office. Hang on a moment. I'll be right there."

She collapsed into one of the empty chairs and adjusted the parchment, finding the paper damp from sweat. Voices carried from beyond the door, so she rerolled the map into a tight cylinder and tucked it up a sleeve. A moment later, Kunzie walked out of the office with Rugen behind. Both men considered her haggard appearance.

"Why, Ms. Balladuren, you look absolutely spent. Do you feel unwell?" He held a silk square over his nose. "Nothing contagious, I assume?"

Ksenia nodded her head. "No sir, I'm afraid I overdressed for the fair weather today. I was excited to see Rugen and overextended myself on the way here. It's a longer walk than I allowed time for, and I didn't want to be late."

"Late for what?" asked Kunzie.

"Late for . . . our dinner date. Rugen, did you forget the promise you made me last week?"

Fortunately, Rugen stood behind Kunzie, who remained oblivious to her brother's momentary confusion.

"Well, don't let me stand in the way of your little family reunion," said Kunzie. He stepped through the door into the Delve and paused on the threshold. "If you are looking for something different, the kitchen has lamb chops on special this evening."

Rugen nodded once. "That sounds marvelous. We'll be along in a bit." Rugen closed the door behind Kunzie and turned to consider her with a look of concern darkening his expression.

"Thanks for that," she said.

"Sure, but Kess, what's really going on?"

She stood, and words tumbled out. "I wasn't sure, I . . . everything is so confused with the regent and . . . moons, Rug. I think he knows about me and the Lacuna, and now the property lists. I wasn't sure who to trust or what to do, so I came straight here."

"Woah, woah, woah . . . rein it in Kess, slow down."

She paced back and forth in the small receiving room. "Oh, Giver's tears, what are we going to do? How can I ever look him in the eye when I know that he knows that I . . . grind it all, I hate this place. I never should have let Mother send me here." Hot tears streaked her cheeks.

"Kess, come here. It can't be all that bad. Whatever it is, we can figure it out." He held his arms open, and she stepped into his embrace. They stood for a time, and when she regained control of herself, she inhaled a deep breath and stepped back.

She retrieved the rolled map and lists, pushing both into his hands. "What's this?" he asked.

"I've been in the archives all afternoon. The regent had me prepare a list of title holders for properties. Most of the locations are in the Sprawl—gaming houses, brothels, and a few taverns. All are owned by the LTCI. Kunzie is likely a key stakeholder, and someone named Tixon B'gin. Then I stumbled across this information. It's a list of properties outside Stone's Grasp also recently acquired by the LTCI."

Rugen lifted his eyes from the paper, considered her words, then perused the lists again. At last, he unrolled the map. A tract of land in the shape of a crescent and outlined in red ink designated lot 1346. The region lay immediately north of the Balladuren ranch.

Rugen looked like their father when considering the price of feed. At last, he lifted his eyes. "This is odd. Come back to my office. I have more detailed maps of Stone's Grasp and Aarindorn on the walls. Let me just double-check this."

She followed him back to the office, and they stepped closer to the map of the kingdom. He handed her the paper. "What's that lot number again, the red one on the map?"

"1346. It's supposed to be close to the ranch," she said.

Rugen traced his fingers up the eastern side of the map, then across until he found the parcel in question. He grabbed a zeniscrawl from his desk and outlined the property, then stepped back. Together, they assessed the map for several long moments.

"Taker's bony grip, what are they up to?" Rugen muttered to himself. "Kess, were any of the other properties on your list like this?"

"No. There are holdings in Callinora, Stellance, and some of the other duchies, but all seem to be places of business or warehouses."

Rugen shook his head and looked at the floor for a long moment. His face took on a ruddy hue. "Should have listened to Father. I knew the Lacuna were ambitious, but I didn't think they would make moves to threaten the ranch."

"What?"

"Think about it, Kess. If the LTCI own that property, they control everything there, including any people and all of the potential resources. If Mother and Father ever had plans to expand north, they would have to contend with exorbitant fees." Rugen walked a slow circle around his desk.

"After everything I've done for them, I can't believe they would do this to me, to us," he muttered.

"What do we do now?" she asked.

"Never mind. You mentioned the regent. He's aware of all of this? Does he suspect your involvement with the Lacuna?"

"I don't know, but maybe. He has to, right? Why else would he ask me to collect all of this? I thought I was doing him a favor, but now that I think about it, his scribes never take on such tasks."

"He never asked you about your findings?" asked Rugen.

"No. I came straight here once I realized where that lot's property line lay in relation to the ranch. But it feels like the regent might have had his suspicions."

"I'll bet he did. That clever grinder," said Rugen. A sly smile spread across his face and lifted her spirits.

"You look like you've got a plan, so let's hear it. What's next?"

"Nothing and everything," he said. "Do you remember the barren mare from five years back?" he asked.

The strange turn in conversation gave her pause. "The one who lost her colt but still showed up in the fields reserved for the mares with foals? She blended in and even nursed other mares' foals."

Rugen nodded. "Well, that'll be us. We are going to act as if nothing has changed. It's entirely possible that everything is just as it should be. But to assume coincidence where the Taker casts a shadow is the way of a monk. I have to stay and manage things here, but you are overdue for a holiday. Drop off your findings to the regent, then take Winter and ride hard. Find the property and see why the LTCI might have an interest there. It looks like it's well into the mountains just north of the eastern fields. There's a switchback that winds up near a waterfall that spills down—"

"I know how to reach the area, Rug. We both grew up riding those trails. I'll check it out," she said.

He nodded and chuckled to himself. "Right, sorry. That's the easy part."

"What's the hard part?"

Rugen folded his arms and released a heavy breath. He hung his head a moment. When he looked up, he squinted his eyes in a pained expression. "You need to drop in on Mother and Father. They'll be interested to learn about anything you find. And . . . you should tell them everything, all of it, all of this. Do you think you can do it?"

"I don't know. I'm so angry at Mother right now that I could throw it all in her face. Father is too clever by far. If I start to tell him any of it, he'll likely learn the whole truth. Are we ready for that? Is Kervin?"

"Trust me; Father will go easy. Mother is another story. Just . . . do your best, Kess. Do what feels right. But whatever happens, speak with Mother. She's worried about you."

A wave of heat spread up the back of her neck. "Oh, I'll bet she is. She practically forces me to take this job I never wanted, and that lands me right in the middle of . . . wait. How do you know she's worried?"

Rugen leaned over to retrieve a letter sitting on his desk. Ksenia recognized her mother's handwriting and parchment. "She wrote when you never returned home. She's not . . . unaware of how she boxed you in, Kess. She's worried. Here, you can see for yourself."

Ksenia considered him a moment, then took the letter and began to read.

Rugen my son,

I hope this finds you in happy times. Your father and I plan to return for the spring assembly. We considered forgoing the affair to care for the spring foals, but an invitation from the regent underscores the importance of attending this year. We will take accommodations per our usual, in the manor house in Stone's Grasp.

Ksenia postponed her visit home several weeks back. Can you look in on your younger sister?

The following line was written, crossed out, and rewritten several times. Under the illegible mess, the letter continued.

I know she still harbors anger for the way I pressed her into the regent's service. I saw her missing out on all the opportunities the kingdom offers and didn't want her to make the same mistakes I did. Is she safe? Is she happy? Please find out and write back as soon as you can. The waiting alone is worse than the Taker's grip on my heart.

How is Kervin? Send us any information that you can.

Your father and brothers killed a mountain bear responsible for the loss of three Aarindin. You should have seen the look of pride on their faces. They sent the hide off to the tanners in Midrock.

Know that you are loved, and mind after Kess whether she wants it or not. If we don't hear from you before the assembly, I'll send for you when we arrive at the manor house.

Your great-uncle, Kovle, passed to the Drift last week, may the Giver embrace him. I sat with him through his last night, and in his fever, he kept sliding in and out of different tongues as his arca prime triggered randomly. You likely recall he was a gifted linguist. At the end, he found a few moments of clarity and shared with me that our name, Balladuren, was derived from a High Aarindorian term, balladure, meaning unconditional love, owing to our ancestor's treatment of the Aarindin. So, I'll say goodbye this way from now on, and you'll know what it means.

Balladure is always yours.

Your mother, Madola.

Ksenia wrinkled her face to dissipate a stinging sensation from her nose and eyes, then swallowed hard. She handed the letter back to Rugen, and they considered one another for a while.

Rugen tilted his head to the side. "She's not wrong, you know. In all the best ways, you really are a lot like Mother."

A sarcastic comment crossed her mind, but she resisted the impulse. Eventually, she chose for once not to seek anger, and a smile eased its way onto her face. Something in Rugen's posture shifted, and he seemed encouraged by her response. They shared an embrace, then separated.

"Before we set out, are you sure you are up to the trip? We need to see why the LTCI has a vested interest in such a random property," he asked.

"Yes, and the truth is, Winter and I are overdue for an escape."

"Will the regent excuse you from your duties for a time? You should be back here in plenty of time for preparations for the spring assembly."

"It shouldn't be an issue. I only delayed my holiday at the request of Kunzie. What do you think we should tell him?"

"If Kunzie or anyone from the Lacuna ask, I'll tell them that you needed a break. But he has enough eyes and ears bringing him other reports from around the kingdom that I don't think he'll miss you."

She took a deep breath and allowed her shoulders to relax for the first time since leaving the archives. The notion of taking Winter for an extended ride out of Stone's Grasp lightened her mood. "I need to submit my leave notice and prepare a few things. And deliver the abstract lists to the regent."

"After," he said. She looked at him in question. "First, you and I should walk into Bekson's. I'll order the lamb chop. You can have spiced lentil soup and black bread. Remember, just like the mare, we show up. We act as if nothing has changed."

The thought of stepping into Kunzie's establishment made the hair on the nape of her neck stand up, but she suppressed the feeling. "Alright. One last meal before I go."

Chapter Nineteen: An Audience of One

VOLENCIA RESTED HER chin on her hands and leaned forward on the top of a large boulder, looking down into Sifter's Valley. She counted fifteen large pavilion tents that had sprouted up around the King's Respite. Farther down the valley, a steady stream of travelers migrated from Dernegia for the king's hunt. The main celebration was days away, but preparations were well underway in anticipation of future royal guests.

Servants erected the tents, organized in colored tiers like a rainbow. Purple tents stood closest to the center of activity, then blue, yellow, and so on, with red structures starting to sprout up at the perimeter. The workers had set up a temporary market and constructed what appeared to be an arena with a portable stage. The entire affair had the look of a grand festival. She made a rough head count at six hundred.

That's a good sign. If the event is still days away, the numbers should swell to over a thousand. We'll see your release yet, Master. But how to wrangle one thousand unwilling hosts?

The clatter of loose rock sliding down the mountainside from directly above her announced someone's approach. "Taker's breath, Eguma. If you betray my position here, I'll—"

She turned to observe the herky-jerky descent of an umbral, and the sight gave her pause. The creature clambered down the rocky cliff on not just two legs but four limbs that bent at strange angles and ended as blackened, tapered points. The half-spider creature held two withered upper limbs retracted over its chest. Necrotic, oozing wounds glistened with a black ichor from the useless appendages.

Rather than the flattened saucer head with which she was familiar, this one's top rose up in a broad, ridged carapace adorned with the black sigils of its enslavement. A linear, pale gash ran from side to side across the length of the strange crown. The umbral stopped before her and chattered its teeth with what she thought seemed like excitement. A curved, muscular stinger held under its body contracted, causing the barb to jab at empty air.

Uncertain of the umbral's intent, Volencia channeled a dense tentacle of nadir and whipped it forward. The umbral hopped back up the rocky slope faster than she expected and clacked its teeth in agitation. A middle-aged man dressed in worn leather gear common among the mountain folk walked out from behind a clutch of scrub pine.

"Easy, sister. We're all on the same side here." He stopped several paces away and rolled back his shirt sleeves to reveal onyx sigils similar to hers. "I should not like to be the one to explain to Tarkannen how two of his pupils came to blows over a misunderstanding at their first meeting."

She squinted at the man. His face seemed vaguely familiar, but she couldn't recall his name. Alert eyes darkened with the use of nadir stared back at her over a long, pointy nose and pouty lips. His features seemed far too refined for the simple garb he wore. "You bear the mark of an abrogator. Have you the skill?"

Without warning, she flicked the tentacle of nadir to snap at his face. The man tilted his head and flicked his wrist. A rounded plane of nadir appeared in the air, no larger than a buckler shield. Her whip struck the object, and both dissipated, but not before a burning vibration surged back into her arm.

The man wagged a finger. "Don't do that. I'm not your enemy, and I assure you I'm quite adept with feedback wards. My name is—"

Before he could speak another word, Volencia lashed out with two different tentacles, thrashing them in random, violent attacks. She reinforced her power so that the man couldn't disrupt her channeling, but every time she attempted an attack, he created a small nadir shield and deflected her probing. And every time, she incurred the burning shock of feedback. After the eighth such attack, she stifled her channeling.

The man looked over her head down the valley. "We can keep this up all day, Volencia, but I expect someone will eventually come to investigate the disturbance. What do you say?"

She rubbed at her forearms to dissipate the buzzing, burning sensation. "You're good, I'll give you that. What's your name, and why are you here?"

The man nodded once. "As I tried to explain, I'm Verrador. One of Tarkannen's disciples, like you."

"You're Verrador? Verrador Endule of Dulesque? I thought you died in the Abrogator's War."

"More than a few of us managed to escape. Faking our deaths was not an easy task."

"You're with others? How many and where? Damnit to the Drift, I've been doing all of this alone, when you—why did you never surface to help us find a way to release Tarkannen?"

"I've had a mission of my own all these years. As for the others, I cannot say. I've had little contact locked away in my corner of Karsk."

"If you're here now . . . can Master communicate with you? And how did you find me?"

"I can answer all of your questions if you would follow me. The journey will take us the rest of the day, and I can explain everything as we travel. As for how I found you, well, that was all due to him, our mutual friend." Verrador pointed at the strange four-legged umbral.

Volencia took more time to study the umbral and stepped closer, trying to inspect the arcane sigils on its head. Though they eluded her understanding, something in the wounded upper limbs of the creature niggled at the periphery of her awareness.

She shook her head. "I don't understand, am I supposed to know something of this creature? I've never seen an umbral of its make, and you called it him? All of the creatures I've encountered are sexless."

Verrador began to walk back in the direction from which he had arrived, to the northwest. After several steps, he spoke over his shoulder. "See then what's become of your husband, Mallic. A similar fate awaits should you disappoint Tarkannen and fail to prepare adequately for the Rite of Sundering. To that end, walk with me or don't. The choice is yours."

His words rooted her on the rocky slopes, and she stared at the umbral with new fascination. True to form, the creature bore no eyes with which to see nor ears with which to hear; nothing, in fact, that reminded her of Mallic. *Except for your withered arms. Right before you died, a Baellentrell cut off your arms and cleaved through the top of your skull.*

She chuckled, and it struck her that she'd had no cause to generate such a sound in over a month. "Mallic? Is that really you? Taker's pointy prick, there's still a bit of justice left in the world after all."

The umbral made no gesture of recognition but seemed to wait for her. She looked back to see Verrador disappearing over the northwest horizon. "Grind it to the Drift." She scrambled up and over loose rock, reaching a thin game trail, and followed Verrador, the four-legged umbral in pursuit. Within a few minutes, she caught up with the Dulescan.

She fell in beside him, and after several paces, he handed her a waterskin. With her thirst quenched, she checked over her shoulder to see the umbral keeping pace. "Can you speak with it? With . . . Mallic?"

Verrador kept his eyes trained on the trail before them. "Watch your step; the ground here is deceptive. You've no doubt heard the umbral chatter to the lesser hordes, the grot, and grondle. I can't say that I understand them at all. But when the umbral commune with each other, it's beyond normal speech. They send messages on thin streamers of nadir."

"How did you figure that out?" she asked.

"Happy accident, really. The first time I met our friend here, I was no more hospitable than you. I encased myself in a shield of nadir, and only then, when filtered through the webbing of nadir, could I hear their song."

She continued in step beside him, considering the revelation. *I suppose that makes a strange kind of logic.* "So you can hear their . . . song. How do you communicate back? What's the trick?"

"I don't," said the abrogator. "And *song* might have been the wrong word. Their language is one part tormented rasping, one part angry chatter." Verrador rubbed at his shoulder as if resisting a chill. "Listening to it is frankly painful. Most of the time, I have to break contact before I learn anything meaningful. But sometimes, if I push through the agony, that's when their words come to me, wraith-like, as if hearing waves crash on a far shore. Does that make sense?"

Her foot slipped off the edge of a large, rounded rock, giving her ankle a slight twist. She cursed and stopped to ensure there was no serious injury, but Verrador plodded along the side of the mountain without pausing. She hopped a ginger step to catch up. The umbral that was once Mallic stopped at her side.

Through the lingering pain, a thought came to her. She inspected the creature at her side with renewed fascination. "Verrador, wait . . . is this what becomes of us all when we enter the Drift?"

The Dulescan turned and offered her a soft smile for the first time since their meeting. "I don't believe so. To my understanding, they are enslaved by the sigils as a form of punishment for failure. The umbral, this . . . form that we see, is but a construct fueled by the soul of the abrogator trapped inside. But let's not dwell on such things. We have much to do, you and I, and at least another two hours to reach our destination."

Verrador looked down at her ankle, then lifted his pointy nose. "Broken?"

"No. Just a sprain. Give me a moment." Volencia sat down and removed her boot. A streak of bruising appeared under the bone along the outside of her ankle. She pulled her fingers through the air, drafting a thin webbing of nadir, and settled her intent into the weaving.

"That's an unnecessary gamble. The umbral can carry you the distance," said Verrador.

She stifled a retort and focused her attention on the task, then draped the webbing over her ankle. Ice-cold needles lanced into the joint and down to her toes. Volencia panted several heavy breaths until the swelling and, eventually, most of the pain receded. She pulled on her boot, stomping her heel into place for good measure, then nodded once at her colleague.

Verrador tilted his head but made no further comment. They walked in silence, skirting around the side of the mountain, dropping into a valley, and finally climbing up a steep ridge. All the while, Volencia held further questions in check, but in her mind, she worked over several scenarios.

How many abrogators has Tarkannen organized? Why all the isolation and secrecy? Surely we could have accomplished so much more together. What is this Dulescan dickhead taking me to see that he couldn't just divulge outright? Why do men always think that their grand designs are best held for an audience of one?

The fatigue of the journey, coupled with the renewed throbbing of her ankle, unroofed the lid on her bubbling discontent. The sun dipped below the western ridgeline, and a shiver crossed her shoulders. "Taker's grip. Hold a moment. I need to tend to my ankle again."

"As you wish, but we're so close now. Can't you smell it?"

At first, she thought that Verrador was taunting her, but the abrogator lifted his nose into the air and inhaled. "Smells like . . . raw power, don't you think?"

Now that she gave it her attention, something distinctly fetid and musky carried on the wind. "Verrador, if I didn't know better, I would say it smells like a crush of grondle lay just beyond this ridge. Is that what you brought me all this way to see? A filthy crush? Grind it. I've got too much to accomplish to waste the day out here with you. The Rite of Sundering is so close."

The Dulescan just stared back at her without rising to meet her venom. "See for yourself, Volencia. Ten more steps."

Pain lanced up from her ankle to her knee as she took her first step, but she walked without limping the last ten paces. At the crest of the ridge, the last of the fading sun warmed her face. She shielded her eyes to look down into the valley. It took a moment for her vision to adjust. A flicker of motion drew her focus farther down, where two beasts collided together, bashing into one another with curved horns and fists. A moment later, the resonant clack from their horned impact echoed up the canyon. Meandering along the valley and all across the far mountainside lay more grondle than she ever knew existed. Sprinkled among the herd, like strange vigilant spiders, individual umbral shepherded the mass. She began counting.

"You see, Volencia, you have your task, and I have mine." Verrador glanced back to the umbral, who lingered at her side. "And I don't intend to fail in mine. I've been breeding them for the last decade, sequestered at the far reaches of the northwest coast. We've rounded out the numbers to—"

"Over fifty . . . fifty crush of grondle at least. And more umbral. Tarkannen said he left only twelve, but that was just with the Brognaus." A small amount of wonder flavored her response. "You use the umbral to keep them in check. But Giver's tears, what do you feed such a large force?"

"All in good time. For now, I think we can agree that we possess the means to procure the one thousand souls needed for the Rite of Sundering?"

"Yes . . . this will work. If you can control them, organize them. This will definitely do."

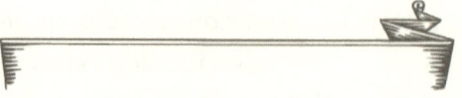

Chapter Twenty: Second Chances

In the short time they had traveled together, everyone from the royals to Reddevek had fallen into a routine for setting and breaking camp. Ranika realized as she groomed Zippy that nobody saddled anyone with specific tasks.

Without any official assignments, camp was set, the perimeter patrolled, and meals prepared. She spoke softly in the Aarindin's ear as she worked to remove a burr from his mane. "Everyone's got a role to play, Mr. Zip. Even me."

She ran a brush across his flank and made a pretense of dropping the tool. When she crouched down to grab it, she watched as Savnah and Dexxin walked together. They strolled in quiet conversation, well out of earshot. She stood up and searched the camp to find Reddevek in conversation with Kaellor. The warden nodded at something the prince suggested, then turned and met her eye. A subtle dip of his chin was all the indication she needed.

She walked to the opposite side of the Aarindin. "Be back in a bit, Zip. Redd might not say it out loud, but he's got a chore for me to do." Once she was sure that nobody was looking in her direction, she pulled the shadows to her, cloaking herself in a veil of nadir.

Moments later, she crept close enough to listen to the Outriders, standing just downwind. Savnah sat on a fallen tree and worked a whetstone over the crescent of a moonblade axe. The rhythmic rasping of her labor was the only sound between them for a long time. Dexxin stood several feet away, transfixed on the eastern horizon. Ranika began to wonder if she had missed the opportunity to glean anything useful.

Savnah paused and fingered the edge of the blade. Appearing satisfied, she placed the weapon in her belt and began working on its twin. "You should at least let them know you're alive, Dexx."

Something in the sender's bearing changed, and it became obvious even to Ranika that for these last several minutes, he had been attentive to some internal conversation.

"I don't know how to explain the secrecy without revealing too much. Craxton would go along with whatever I offer, but not Mullayne . . . she would see through any deception."

"So tell them part of the truth and leave out anything related to—"

"Related to what? Our position? Our status? Our mission? Moons, I don't even know what that is anymore. You know?"

Savnah bobbed her head in agreement. "I know. But, I would lay with the Taker if I knew Kovesk was alright. If I knew he was safe, or happy. All I know is that the Lacuna have my brother quarantined somewhere. Your siblings, they need to know you're alright."

"Do you think he foresaw all of this?" asked Dexxin. He gestured back to camp, back toward the royals.

"Kovesk? Who can say, Dexx? Ko's handlers might not share everything he mumbles in his sleep, and even if they did, it's not as if you and I are privy to the information."

Dexxin sat down beside her and fingered the fletching of a damaged arrow. "That's the Giver's truth, right there. We've already seen the lengths the leaders of the Lacuna will go to see the kingdom transform to their vision. I've tried to broach the issue more than once with Craxton, but he refuses to see it."

"Your sister has always been the brightest of you three. What does she think?" asked Savnah.

"I'm honestly not sure. Sometimes it feels like she's in full support of the Lacuna, but other times I think she's just being the peacekeeper between the two of us and sees alignment with the breakers as the best path forward."

"You make it sound like she's holding back some of her private thoughts. If she can do that, then surely you can protect them and only divulge a small part of the information?"

Dexxin seesawed his head back and forth. "I can, I suppose."

Savnah rasped away a few more strokes, then stopped and pointed the whetstone at him. "You can, but you're not sure that you want to. I get it more than you know, Dexx."

She looked back at her weapon and began sharpening the blade in earnest. "I swallowed the crap the Lacuna shovel and came back for seconds, thirds even. I wasn't just prepared to kill for them; I was going to commit murder, regicide, in fact, when you get right down to it. As if acting in their name somehow absolved me of any consequence. Karra's vision . . . it's my second chance."

Dexxin's usually stoic face flushed. "You believe it then? Everything Karra said about her vision?"

"I do. I know where my head was, and Karra wouldn't lie about something like that. We've been through too much together, you know?"

"I was hoping you were going to tell me that parts of it were exaggerated. How do you . . . get on with them when everyone knows we were set to kill them? I still can't bring myself to speak to Lluthean or Nolan. And Tovnik? Grind me, what Karra said she saw? That's not me on any day of the week."

"Yes, it is, because you followed my lead . . . my *order*, if I understand her vision correctly. And one thing about you, Dexx. You've never disobeyed my order," said Savnah.

The wind shifted, and Ranika marshaled all her focus on remaining preternaturally still. *Mother Maedra or the Giver, whoever you are in these parts, please don't let them notice me. I smell worse than Mogdure's breath.*

Savnah wrinkled her nose and lifted her gaze back to camp, passing right over Ranika where she stood, then shrugged her shoulders. She craned her neck to assess their surroundings, then shrugged once more. "I said it wrong, Dexx. Karra's vision? It's not my second chance. It's ours. Both of us have this rare opportunity to rise up out of the woods and see where our path originated and where it might go. And now we can choose with at least a better understanding of the consequences."

"I can guess which path you are going to take," said Dexxin.

"I'm done taking what the Lacuna give me, if that's what you mean. I'm done looking the other way, convincing myself of the right of their vision just to keep my brother safe. Karra feels like she still owes me twice over for saving her skin. But the way I see it, we're even."

"Isn't your father a supporter of the Lacuna?" he asked.

"He is, but now I have to ask myself if he's motivated by the same fears for my brother that I was."

"How do you imagine you'll tell him that you are not part of the movement anymore?"

"Derrigands don't dance around the truth with each other. It makes us constipated. Some night after we've had our fill of smoked chop and good ale, we'll have a sit-down, and I'll explain everything to him. And then, we'll figure out how to free my brother."

"You make it sound pretty simple."

"The best things in life usually are. So go on. Tell your siblings the truth. Keep it simple. Tell them to trust that you are on a mission and under strict orders from the warden not to betray our progress but that you'll explain it all later. You don't have to confront them about the Lacuna."

A rare smile played across the sender's face. "You make it sound like I plan to leave the circle breakers."

"Leave or stay; that's up to you. But make sure that all three of you understand how dirty the Lacuna play. Your siblings deserve to know the whole truth, not the candy-coated crap Craxton eats every day. Then . . . you just have to trust them with their choice."

Dexxin nodded once, inhaled a deep breath, then sat back to make himself comfortable against the log Savnah was using as a bench.

"Give me your knife before you drop under. I'll sharpen the blade and keep a vigil," said Savnah.

Dexxin handed over the weapon. "Thanks. This might take longer than usual."

"I figured. Just remember. Simple truths. You'll be fine, Dexx."

Ranika watched as all expression vanished from Dexxin's face. His eyes glazed over with an unfocused expression, and occasional flickers of zenith, manifesting as traces of blue light, shimmered at the notch where his neck met his breastbone.

Nearly a half hour passed, and Ranika began to feel restless. Her mind wandered. *Maybe Laryn would like some of the pink flowers scattered among the grasses. Why does the medic insist on calling Laryn Her Radiance? What does that even mean? Radiance. Ray-dee-ence. Dee-ence sounds a bit like dance. I wonder if Laryn is a dancer? Or maybe Kaellor? Now, that would be a sight. I'll bet she could dance like the powdered ladies in Callish. I feel a bit like dancing right now, but my head is starting to buzz.*

The thought startled her back to the surroundings, and she stood as still as a mooring post in the Callishite harbor. She trained all her attention on Savnah, afraid that she might have betrayed herself somehow. But the Outrider was giving all her attention to the detail of sharpening Dexxin's dagger.

At last, Dexxin stretched his arms and arched his back. He wiped away a few tears from his eyes.

"Well, how did it go?" asked Savnah.

"Mullayne called me a few choice names for holding out so long. They both knew I must be alive because no reports to the contrary came through Overwarden Kaldera or the regent."

"Told you, she's smart, that one. Did they press you for anything that might, you know, get us into trouble with the royals?"

"No, but I learned that the Lacuna are wise to the arrival of at least one of the royals in Aarindorn. Their agents search the western duchies believing that a royal might hide among loyalists."

"That matches what the wounded man said before he died. Do they know that we're headed for Callinora or why the royals have returned?"

"I don't think so, but I didn't press. Mullayne would be suspicious if I asked too many questions."

She handed his knife back. "Good as new if you ask me."

"Thanks. We should probably get back before anyone mistakes our isolation for secrecy."

Savnah stood and scratched her butt cheek. "Agreed. Besides, my ass is falling asleep."

Ranika waited for the two of them to wander back toward camp before releasing the shadows. The buzzing sensation in her head settled as she walked back to Zippy, but she spent an extra half hour tending to his grooming while the feeling dissipated.

She walked around the Aarindin's rear and drew up short. Reddevek pushed a waterskin in her face. "You're going to brush all the hair off of him or spoil him, and I'm not sure which is worse."

She drank from the skin and handed it back. "I needed some time to settle myself."

"You were gone longer than I thought. It's getting dark. Did it set your head to . . . you know . . . buzzing?"

"Only a little." A funny thought made her giggle. "Nothing like when I followed you to the Bend. Now *that* was buzzing."

The warden placed his cheek against Zippy's jawline and stroked his mane. "Learn anything useful?"

She nodded her head, then recounted everything she heard from the conversation. When she finished, Reddevek grunted.

"I didn't know that about her brother. I would pity the breakers holding him hostage, except they deserve what they have coming. It's good that Dexxin could break his silence without divulging overmuch. It's a better path forward than I might have chosen. Maybe there's hope for Laryn's plan yet."

"Should we tell Kaellor what we know?" she asked.

"We will, but not in front of everyone. Laryn believes in the power of autonomy." The warden wrinkled his lip as if tasting something unpleasant in the word.

"What does autonomy mean?" she asked.

"It means . . . she believes that if Dexxin comes to trust them enough to share what he knows all by himself, without coercion, then we can count him as a true ally. It's all part of her treatment for the disease that calls itself the Lacuna."

"You don't seem to agree," said Ranika.

The warden glowered at the ground, and menace flavored his tone. "Before I came to the Bend, Savnah and Dexxin were my responsibility. Had I known that two of my charges conspired against the crown . . ."

His expression remained dark until Zippy nickered. He forced a sigh and allowed a grin to spill across his face. "Never could be too mad when you're about, Zip. Anyway, let's just say it's the Giver's will to grant those two a second chance."

"Strange. Savnah said almost those exact same words; only she said Karragin gave them the second chance."

"Well, whether by the Giver's hand, Laryn's wisdom, or Karragin's sharp insight, it's all the same in the end. They have an opportunity to shape the world when I would have likely ended them."

Ranika knew his words would cause some people to feel alarmed. But she took comfort in the feeling that despite all their travels, Reddevek remained Reddevek. He was still the same grizzled acorn with a shaggy cap that she met in Callish. The knowing of that gave her a sense of peace. Without thinking, she wrapped her arms around his waist and hugged him with fierce appreciation.

"What's that for?" he asked.

"You looked like you needed it."

"Hmm . . . maybe I did at that. Don't tell anyone. I'm a warden. Appearances, you know? Come on, let's check in. Bryndor worked his magic with skewered bartusk and wild parsnip stew. The Lacuna might not be able to see much of the cookfire, but those aromas would attract even a highborn from Dulesque."

They joined the others around the campfire, set low near a mountain stream and camouflaged by thick timber stands. As soon as the meal preparation concluded, the embers were scattered. Ranika sensed a tension in the air. At first, she thought it a lingering symptom of the buzzing. But the more she watched everyone, the more it seemed like they all held themselves with strange anticipation.

Bryndor sat down next to her, with Boru his silent, massive shadow. She leaned over and whispered, "If you've prepared the best thing I have tasted since Della's cooking at the Bashing Ram, why is everyone so tense?"

Bryndor thumbed over his shoulder to the north. "Climb that hill, look to the north, and tell me what you see."

More out of curiosity, she made the short hike through the timber. Boru accompanied her, nose to the ground and tail wagging. At the crest of the hill, the timber thinned. In the darkness, twinkling blue lights aligned in a perfect row dotted the north horizon. Ranika searched to be sure that no one was approaching her. She pulled nadir through her eyes and set her focus on the horizon. A city surrounded by tall, polished, white stone walls revealed itself to her senses. Strange lights adorned the walls, emitting light that was not unlike the full moon of Baellen.

She dismissed her hold of nadir and turned to the wolvryn. He cocked his head to the side and stared back, then licked the tip of her nose. She giggled and leaned in close. "If you can smell nadir on me, it's our secret for now, alright?"

Together, they returned to sit near Bryndor.

"Well?" he asked.

"Is that Callinora at last?"

"Laryn and Kae think so, and she would know."

"Finally. I mean, I don't mind the trail myself, but even I could use a bed and change of clothes. What's Callinora like?"

Bryndor finger-combed his bangs back. "I can't say. It's going to be my first time there as well. I've seen most of the different kingdoms throughout the Southlands, so I don't expect to be too surprised."

"Then what's the strange mood everyone seems taken with?"

"Abrogator," he mumbled over a mouthful of stew.

His words triggered a reflex she didn't even know existed. A wave of nausea overwhelmed her, and she smelled her own sour sweat. She looked around their camp for Reddevek's reassuring gaze, but he was off in conversation with Kaellor and Laryn. She wanted to stand, to walk to him, but the muscles in her legs felt floppy, and her head swooned.

She reached out for nadir, thinking to cloak herself in shadows. The cold, tingly sensation seeped into her feet and started to leech up her legs. And there it stopped.

A warm hand grabbed the back of her shoulder, and another slid across her palm. She turned to look into Bryndor's grey eyes, and he stared back with concern. They held one another's gaze for long moments, and she expected him to blink, but he considered her with rapt intensity. His quiet strength grounded her, and she released her hold of nadir. Her breath finally returned to normal. Awkwardly, he released her.

"Ranika? Are you alright? You looked like you were about to faint. I didn't mean to spook you about Tarkannen. You want some water?"

"Water? Yes, please, water would be good," she said.

He returned with haste and offered her a waterskin. She splashed her face and neck, then felt better as the surge of fear subsided. Eventually, she felt confident enough to chance a glance at her feet. *No shadows here, thank the Seven. Get a grip, Ranika. He meant Tarkannen, not you, you silly moon calf.*

"So you expect we'll encounter Tarkannen, even though he's been dead for so long?" she asked.

"I don't know what to expect. When we were stuck for a season in the Korjinth, we stayed with the Damadibo, the Cloud Walkers. They can communicate with their ancestral spirits through rituals. Elder Miljin, a wise man among their people, warned that Tarkannen has only been banished to the Drift, not killed. Somehow, he still clings to the world of the living. Laryn thinks it could have something to do with a practice that the healers at Callinora use to preserve people with severe injuries."

"You don't sound so convinced."

Bryndor chewed on his lower lip. "I've seen enough strange things in the last year to make me realize that I don't have all the answers. And if Kae and Laryn believe we can learn something by going to Calliniora, something that ensures all of our safety? Then I can get behind that."

She leaned her body to the side, shouldering into him playfully, then pitched her voice low to mimic his tone. "'I can get behind that.' Why aren't you more excited to finally see a city in the north?"

He finger-combed his bangs out of his face. "It's just another step on a road that leads to the capital."

"Alright then, how about Stone's Grasp? You've got to be eager to see that place."

A subtle crease played across his forehead, and Bryndor poured some water in his hand, then flicked droplets to the ground. "Let's just say I have mixed feelings about it."

"Reddevek says it dwarfs any of the cities we've seen so far, even Callish. I can't wait to get there and see all it has to offer."

A half-smile played across Bryndor's face, and he rubbed at the back of his neck. "I'm sure it will be as grand as they say it is."

"You still don't sound thrilled."

Boru turned onto his back, rolling his weight against their legs and beckoning for his belly to be rubbed. Bryndor obliged him, scratching along the muscled rib cage. "I imagine that when we arrive, my days will be filled with more than taking in the sights. But . . . don't let me shutter your lantern. I'm just tired, that's all."

Across the camp, Reddevek continued his quiet conversation with the other adults. Savnah and Dexxin approached them and seemed to request an audience. Once granted, the sender stared at his feet as he spoke. Something significant must have passed between them, as Kaellor's commanding posture softened, and he laid a hand on Dexxin's shoulder. The sender looked up, and even Reddevek nodded his approval.

"Autonomy in action right there," said Ranika, trying out the word for the first time.

Bryndor looked sidelong at her.

"It's something Reddevek said about your Aunt Laryn's approach to the Lacuna. She's really something, isn't she? Do you think she always searches for the good in people?"

"I think she probably does, at that. And underneath her good nature is a woman tough enough to walk beside my uncle and brave the peaks of the Korjinth."

"Sounds like someone I should try to get to know better as we travel."

The thump of a stout wood practice sword hitting the ground drew their attention. Lluthean bounced a similar weapon on his shoulder. "Kae says Nolan and the warden have the perimeter patrol tonight, so we should hit the drills before turning in."

Bryndor retrieved his weapon and stood. "You trust me not to crack your head with only moonlight to see by?"

"Stances and foot drills only. Not my idea, by the way," said Lluthean as he stifled a yawn.

Ranika took her cue and pulled her feet out from under Boru's weight. "Don't work too hard. We all need to be fresh for whatever happens in Callinora tomorrow. Good night, Princes Baellentrell."

Bryndor leaned down again and pulled a fistful of reeds, then tossed them at her head. She giggled and dodged. "Sorry. I couldn't resist. Karra is right, though. You should probably get used to the title."

Bryndor sighed and pulled another fistful but let it sprinkle to the ground. "I will try. Good night, Nika."

She found her bedroll and watched as the brothers flowed through stances designed to block and attack imaginary foes. Something in the silent, contemplative nature of their actions gave her comfort. She settled onto her back and took in the stars before sleep claimed her.

Chapter Twenty-One: Tapping the Leech

The Aspect of the Lacuna stared into the hovering zenith seed. A heavy, contemplative silence permeated his rooms. At times, the cloud of unfocused power swirled like a swarm of angry bees, and at other times, gentle currents eddied about the surface. If he held his attention in this manner long enough, perhaps a better solution would rise to his awareness. Perhaps they could find another way. But just as the inevitability of the course they must take made itself clear to him, just as he accepted the decision he would have to pronounce, Kunzie spoke out. "Did we . . . lose you, Aspect? Are you still there?"

The Aspect assumed control of the seed once again. "I'm here. I was just . . . thinking. Are you really so convinced that we can't turn her back to our cause? She could prove a valuable asset. There's not been anyone with her gift in linguistics in a generation, no offense, Valdesta."

"None taken, my lord, and you are correct. My daughter lacks the girl's tenacity," said Valdesta.

"The woman is through and through a Balladuren, my lord . . . strong-willed and independent as the Aarindin they breed. I've had the breakers watch her in a variety of situations, and all report similar suspicions. Her latest independent research in the archives seems to have placed her on a path from which there is no turning back," said Kunzie.

"I agree. If she discovers the strategic importance of our acquisition in the Great Crown, she could jeopardize our entire investment," added Valdesta. "We have worked for years inserting the right people into the regent's offices to manage the legalities of things like this . . . grind it. I personally funded the purchase on the promise of a greater return."

"Peace, sister. The Giver's sweet peace," said the Aspect. "We are all well aware of your commitment and investment. Tell me, if we take definitive action, what of her brother? How would her absence affect him? I understand you've recently tasked him with the oversight of most of our trade and our future plans with the border kingdoms."

"Rugen is well-steeped in our ethos, Aspect. Of late, he labors to see our plans bear fruit. Just this morning, he approached me with an ingenious idea to hide our holdings from the vice regent, thereby avoiding taxation by the crown," explained Kunzie.

"The untimely death of the Balladuren girl could serve our ends," said Burl. "All prior attempts to engage the Balladurens have been met with stiff resistance. This might be one way to soften Elbend's resolve."

"Very well," confirmed the Aspect. "It needs to look like random chance or an accident."

"Perhaps she could simply disappear? The discovery of her body anywhere near our holdings in the Great Crown could undermine our efforts there," said Inasia. "If you like, I could arrange for her to come down with an incurable illness."

"The thought of unleashing a contagion in the kingdom unnerves me no small amount," said the Aspect.

"It need not be an actual infection," said Inasia. "There is an apothecary at the local House of the Moons who can craft an insidious poison. Even if she survived the initial ravages, I could deal with her peacefully once she arrived in Callinora."

"Friends, I fear we are too late for any of that," said Kunzie. "I've just learned that Ksenia was seen riding out of the Timber Gate. She told the groom at the royal stables not to worry about her return for over a week."

"Can she even gain egress out of the kingdom by the Timber Gate?" asked Valdesta.

"Yes, but look, it's a moot point. Even if we found her in the sprawling wood, arranging an accident on short notice in that kind of situation involves too many variables," said Kunzie.

"Then it sounds like we have no choice but to employ the Leech," said Burl. "He's never failed us in the past, and the one time we used another, that Vardell Becks, things didn't exactly go as planned."

"The Leech was unavailable for that assignment. He has become discerning and refuses to consider assignments that take him out of the kingdom," said Kunzie.

"Are we talking about the man behind the regent's folly? Can we find him? I heard he parted company with the Spicer gang," said Valdesta.

"I know how to reach him, but are you sure we want him? He has unsavory predilections and demands a high price," said Kunzie.

"If you can secure his services, I know of no other with a proven record of tracking and eliminating a target with complete discretion. I also agree with Inasia. We need her to disappear. We can't afford the attention her corpse would attract if discovered near any of our projects. The Leech is our only recourse. As for his habits, we can not argue about the results. Perhaps, in the interest of . . . civility . . . demand that he wait until after the target is snuffed before harvesting the eyes. We can afford a higher price if this alters the standard agreement. Does anyone have a better idea?" asked the Aspect.

After a period of silence, Kunzie chimed in. "I shall see to the arrangements immediately."

"Thank you, Kunzie," said the Aspect. "Keep close track of her brother's performance in the coming weeks and report any deviations or concerns to us."

"Your desires, my deeds. Until next time, I'll take my leave," said Kunzie. His image winked out.

"Alright, let us turn to other pressing matters. Burl, have your custodians learned anything new from the dream auger? Anything that might shed light on the return of a Baellentrell to the kingdom?"

"Sadly, no, my lord," said Burl. "I personally review the recordings every morning, and the custodians have strict orders to notify me of anything he says that might relate to the royals."

"What did your scouts learn from the field, Burl?" asked Valdesta.

"Not much there either, I'm afraid," said the gruff man from Midrock. "The grinding reports read more like the ramblings of a drunkard from the Sprawl given to embellishing stories for a free splash of resco. Several of the bodies appeared savaged by beasts. Others received mortal wounds by bow shot, axe, or sword. Some lay in crumpled heaps or burned by their own munitions. Beyond the obvious mess left behind, my people could not determine our quarry's heading."

"Do you have any other Outriders who might be pressed into service?" asked the Aspect.

"Unfortunately, no. All our breakers are garrisoned at the forward base camp between the Pillars or on assignment in the southern parts of the kingdom," said Burl.

Inasia's voice purred into the conversation. "It makes no sense. If they have returned, why haven't they made their presence known? Why the delay?"

Why indeed. What purpose would drive them to risk exposure along the western duchies where the high families might be as likely to skewer them as to welcome them? Then again, what if they know about the Lacuna? Might they be attempting to garner support among the noble houses?

He gave voice to his concern. "That same issue plagues my thoughts of late. Spring assembly is only a few weeks away. They may delay revealing themselves until then."

"I had the same thought," said Valdesta. "What better time to slip into Stone's Grasp than under cover of all the other visitors? Then they could step forward before all the significant houses from across the kingdom. Is it possible that they hide here, in Stone's Grasp, already?"

"Not unless they can fly, and the histories, while flush with accounts of the martial talents of the Baellentrell line, make no mention of that particular gift," said the Aspect. "No, I'm certain that they slipped between our fingers only days ago, but that still places them on the western side of the kingdom."

"Might they be trying to curry favor with any of the noble houses from the western duchies?" asked Burl. "While there was no love lost after the Abrogator's War, I can understand why they might first reach out to some of the older families who might be inclined to resist giving up their claim to power."

"Yes, that rings with a certain logic," answered the Aspect. "I will arrange to have my contacts in Dulesque and Beclure be vigilant for any strangers or travelers. Inasia, you should do the same in Callinora. The queen consort, Laryn, was the radiance of the Sanitorium when she left. Only Venlith held equal status there. If Laryn Lellendule returns with any of the princes, it is possible they would first seek counsel at Callinora . . . find security among familiar faces, so to speak. We should take no chances. If any unexplained guests arrive, they should be secretly detained until we can ascertain any possible relationship to the Baellentrells."

"The old crone is well in hand, and I have breakers in nearly every layer of Callinora watching for the arrival of strangers. I myself have assumed the task of screening any newcomers to the Sanitorium. I can easily quarantine anyone arriving under suspicious circumstances. Thankfully, our census is low. It feels rather like the calm before the storm," said Inasia.

"I understand. When your business is slow, that usually bodes well for the welfare of the kingdom," said the Aspect. *But what does it portend for the Lacuna, I wonder?*

"Speaking of the kingdom's welfare," said Inasia. "Perhaps now is the time to press our open proposal to abandon the monarchy altogether. If we convince enough at the spring assembly to raise the regent as our elected sovereign, it will not matter what the royals do."

"Do you think the old lynx will agree to any of that?" asked Valdesta.

"Possibly," said the Aspect. "Therek Lefledge is well aware of the concept but hasn't been forced to feel the weight of the will of the people." He paused, trying to imagine the best strategy forward. *Close, we are so close. After all these years, why does a Baellentrell have to return at such a time as this? Taker's bitter breath.*

He settled his mind and continued, "Inasia is right. It seems our hand is forced, and I would rather choose from the cards we see than rely upon the king's gambit, to quote an old phrase. This presses our timeline, but imagine . . . if we kindle the message now among the commoners, then allow the idea to take hold . . . by the time the spring assembly arrives, it could burn as the central light of debate in every tavern and house from the Sprawl to the upper tier of Stone's Grasp."

"I like it," said Valdesta. "With our control of the gaming houses and brothels, we could readily begin."

"The illiteracy rate among those neighborhoods undermines the value of the printed word. We want to control the message. The last thing we need is an uneducated, gutterborn mob undermining the legitimacy of our narrative. We need spokesmen and women trained to communicate with accuracy. How much influence do we have in the criers' guild?" asked the Aspect.

"Not as much as we should like," said Valdesta. "That's a group that claims more virtue than those who worship at the Church of the Giver. They receive directives from the offices of the regent and pretty much stay on message."

"How many actually still practice that fading religion?" asked Inasia with genuine curiosity. "I admit we are isolated in Callinora, but the last chapel closed its doors before the Abrogator's War."

"I assure you, the *divine* Church of the Giver is still alive and well in most of the kingdom," said the Aspect.

"We have a small sect here in Midrock," said Burl. "It's a one-room affair, but the rector does well enough holding services for locals and travelers alike. He doles out blessings according to the cycles of the moon. Nice enough, fellow if a bit more . . . righteous than your average Derrigand."

"It's time we lean on the rectors a little bit. Our donations to the local congregations have made a favorable impact," said the Aspect. "If we tap into the absolute conviction of religious belief . . . nothing would give our movement more righteous fervor than entwining our cause with that of the Church of the Giver."

"Now that sounds like the king's gambit," said Inasia. "Moving our agenda forward is one thing, but messing around with people's beliefs? I understand the pressure we are under. But what about after we create a new government? How do we keep those same parishioners from changing everything? We rely on the revenue generated by the brothels and gaming houses. The Spicer gang controls the Sprawl in our name, and we benefit from our control of black market vivith. How do you suppose anyone invested in the Giver's church will see those enterprises once we invite them to the table?"

"You worry overmuch, Inasia," said Valdesta. "I happen to know already that three rectors in Stone's Grasp are loyal customers of our establishments. One likes to gamble, and two prefer the company of boys, if you catch my meaning. The prime rector himself is on a first-name basis with a few of my girls. We'll have no problem controlling those men with our usual means of persuasion."

"I understand Inasia's concerns. The entire affair must be delicately managed. What do you say, Burl?" asked the Aspect.

"I can't say as I like it. The people who attend services here in Midrock are good people. It feels like it . . . crosses a line." Burl sighed. "But it's no worse than anything else we've already done. Just promise me that the end is near."

"How do you think Kunzie will react to involving the church?" asked Inasia.

"Kunzie is a businessman. I think he will be intrigued by the opportunities this new relationship can offer," said the Aspect. "I propose that we move forward on three fronts. I will apply influence in the criers' guild through our connections in the regent's offices. We need to move ahead in the Sprawl and the church as well."

"Leave it to me," said Valdesta. "It will not cost much to incentivize key figures with our message. I will oversee their training myself. As for the church, I think obtaining their participation will be easy enough once I explain to the prime rector how expanding their message will expand their congregation and, in turn, their coffers."

"Alright. You each have your tasks. See it done, and we'll yet lift Aarindorn from the shackles of the monarchy."

Chapter Twenty-Two: The Source and the Pack

THE EARLY MORNING FROST held firm in the shade and made the ground feel stiff, but where sunlight fell in the open spaces, ridges of mud creased up between the pads of Neska's feet as she sauntered forward. A chorus of senses commingled, informing her of the surroundings. In the human camp, all but the small girl slept, announced by the slow cadence of their breathing. Life in all forms, both above and below ground, awakened with the warmth of spring. Birds chatted at their neighbors, claiming territory for their new nests; a rabbit had scampered close to camp just before sunrise, and somewhere to the west, a lone vestek buck left his scent on the wind.

From her side, her brother approached, and she braced herself for his typical greeting. Boru stopped and performed the same assessment of their surroundings before gently leaning a shoulder into her. He sniffed at her ear and then dropped his nose to the ground.

He doesn't seek out my scent anymore. And I already know his. We used to require that information at every moment. When did that change?

Boru lifted his head, and she read his thoughts. *"There's a vestek to the west. A buck. Do you need food? I can run,"* he asked.

"No. Not now. I'm . . . sustained by the current. Zenith, that's what my Lluthean calls it. Somehow, it nourishes me. If you hunger, I can hunt."

"It is the same with me, sister," he replied before craning his head back. Steam billowed forth from his jaw as he yawned, then rocked back to stretch his shoulder muscles. He walked a circle, nose to the ground, then the air, and once more the ground. Finding nothing new of interest, he settled onto his haunches beside her but kept his ears alert and his nose lifted into the breeze.

Eventually, his thoughts interrupted her solitude. *"You are different, my sister. I am . . . different. We have changed. We . . . have become more like Ghetti. Why is that?"*

She sat beside him, considering all that his question implied. That he asked the question at all was no small accomplishment. *When did we start asking questions? When did we, or how did we, awaken to what we are? He is right. Ghetti was . . . aware of herself. Like we are now.*

"Yes. I have sensed it as well. When do you think that happened?" she asked.

"I have memories, dreams from the valley with the pack. Did it start then? I can not . . . remember us before the pack."

A complex tangle of scents, images, and sounds flooded her awareness. *The pack . . . yes, that feels right. Before the pack, and Ghetti, before our time with Mahkeel, we lived only in the moment. Now we live, we think beyond.*

The labor of coming to that realization made something between her ears tingle. She lifted a paw to brush away the strange sensation. *"I felt it first and strongest when we thought the brothers were in danger in the valley. When you separated Kaellor from their play fighting."*

Boru's eyelids dropped once in a slow blink, a gesture of agreement. *"Yes. And later, over the mountains, when the nadir cats attacked. I felt . . . I could not lose any of them, but especially my Bryndor. I stopped being . . . distracted and began . . . this . . . what we are now. Are we damaged like Mother?"*

The question caused an involuntary twist of her head as Neska allowed this new part of herself to ponder that. *"I don't remember her. I remember a scent only. Do you remember Mother?"*

"No, but I remember Mahkeel speaking to our brothers about her. She became wild when she slipped through the mists of the mountains. I . . ." he groaned in mild discomfort, struggling to express himself. *"Something became different with me . . . inside, when we crossed over the mountains, and I have waited to see if we are . . . damaged."*

She huffed a low rumble in contemplative response. *"I felt the same. I knew I would feel pain if my Lluthean felt pain. But we are not like Mother. We are not feral. We are . . . more than we were before. It is the bond. The bond with my Lluthean, your Bryndor. The bond is our source of . . . this . . . of what we are now."*

They sat together in silence, their senses scanning and filtering the environment. In the distance, the girl who cloaked herself in shadows crept back to her bedroll near the large scout. If danger did approach, Neska imagined that Ranika might be one of the first she recruited to their defense. The girl possessed strength underneath that lithe frame. Still, any of the others proved formidable. The woman with the axes reminded her of Boru, capable of extreme violence in the moment but with less forethought in planning the hunt. Two of the others, Kaellor and the woman Karragin, balanced cunning and prowess.

Neska realized a new emotion as she considered these last two: respect. Though she felt secure in having them as part of the pack, she kept a cautious eye on the woman. Something about her ability to invade Neska's thoughts without invitation caused the fur at the back of her neck to stiffen.

She dismissed the feeling and continued her assessment of their pack. She needed to learn more about the aloof warden. He showed an unnatural ability to find their enemy in the dark and proved himself brutally efficient on the hunt. The only time he seemed to display a sense that he belonged to the pack was when he engaged the shadow girl. *He is perhaps the only one as vigilant as me, but he remains aloof, like a displaced alpha.*

Then there were the healers, Laryn and Tovnik. These two seemed to avoid the hunt, but Neska would forever defend Laryn with her last breath. The woman had once returned her Lluthean, made him safe, made him whole when he was drifting away. For that alone, Neska felt sure they would always be pack mates.

Finally, her gaze passed over Nolan and Dexxin. The first lay on his back, snoring as loud as Boru. The other remained silent on his side. Something about this last one puzzled her. He kept so much of himself hidden and withdrawn. In some ways, that resembled the warden. But he smelled different. Something inside of him gave rise to stress or conflict. Neska couldn't be sure. *But none of them is my Lluthean or Boru's Bryndor.*

As she considered Lluthean, a shifting, intermingled array of scents, sounds, and images entered her consciousness: Lluthean laughing and somehow sharing that mirth with her; Lluthean on the hunt demonstrating accuracy with his bow; the peace she felt when their senses commingled or when he ran fingers through her fur.

"We are well beyond what we were. I am . . . more because he is my source."

Boru opened his mouth to taste the air and drew his lips back in that goofy way that made him appear to smile like a human. *"They are the source. We are pack. And you are alpha."*

Neska grunted once and nipped at the steam billowing from Boru's mouth as if she could chase away the feeling, like snatching at an irritating fly. She realized for the first time an awareness of obligation that she had not known before.

Unbidden, thoughts sprang into her mind of responsibility, of keeping track of her Lluthean. She wondered how to keep him safe, how to keep any of them safe. She replayed the battle with the nadir cats, how Boru followed her instruction, and how they dispatched the nadir cats one after another by working in concert to cull the pride one by one. That was the first time she had stepped into her new role as alpha.

Then she considered her brother and what made him content, even happy. She remembered giving him the generous portion of a leg bone full of marrow and how he quivered with eagerness when Bryndor gave him his undivided attention.

And somehow, she realized for the first time what mattered most to her: it was all of them together . . . safe, fed, free from danger. The thoughts blossomed into comprehension, and she remained silent, contemplating her awakening.

"We are both more than Ghetti. And it is right. I am alpha." Then she turned and pressed her cheek and right eye against Boru's, holding him there for a moment until his heartbeat slowed, his scent stilled to peace, and they lingered between a long breath. *"Yes,"* she said. *"We are pack."*

The muffled sound of human voices in conversation brought them both to renewed awareness as the others in their pack rose for the day.

"You run a path to the sun. I will survey the other side. Don't get distracted by random scents. Hunt for danger. Keep the pack safe," she said.

Boru rose to all fours and stretched again. He took a few steps forward but turned before loping off. *"I scent-marked a warning on a tree that way."* His tongue hung out of the side of his mouth, and he panted with playful eagerness.

She waited for him to finish the odd statement, knowing already that he had followed her request to mark their camp the night before. When he didn't answer the obvious question, she stretched and considered the debris in her front paw with indifference.

Boru sucked his tongue back in. *"Right. Well . . . there is a vestek bone by the tree. When I get back—"*

"Yes . . . I will play chase-the-bone with you, but this time I get to start."

She watched him lope off toward the rising sun, then turned to circle in the opposite direction. Part of her awareness coordinated her senses to assess any unusual aromas, the appearance of aberrant motions, or new sounds. She sifted and synthesized the information as she prowled the perimeter. But another part of her awareness thought of her brother and the ridiculous amount of energy he invested in chase-the-bone. And not a moment later, she realized how easy it was for him to goad her into the game even when she preferred to groom her paws.

All of these thoughts created a pleasurable tickle that rumbled somewhere deep inside her. She stopped and turned a tight circle, searching for the source of the odd sensation. Nothing external rose to her awareness, and enlightenment overtook her again as she realized that a simple thought had given rise to the internal feeling. The emotion lingered as contentment despite her attempt to squash it as a distraction. She picked up the pace and continued her patrol.

Keep the pack safe, indeed. No easy task when thoughts of my brother make my belly rumble and cause me to snap at the wind. Still, what we are now . . . is right. We are beyond what we once were. My Lluthean, your Bryndor, our pack . . . we will keep them together, keep them safe.

Chapter Twenty-Three: Venlith's Last Stand

Laryn stood beside her mount. The horse she'd ridden since Voruden had served her well and now nibbled at tender shoots of grass scattered in the timber as they waited for Reddevek's return. She ran a hand over his muscled shoulder. *I could stand to borrow some of your inner peace, my friend. Only the Giver knows what awaits us today.*

She scuffed a boot back and forth, scattering dead leaves from the prior season. Morning dew darkened the toe of her leather riding boots, and as the sun warmed the fields west of Callinora, a thin fog blanketed the ground.

Kaellor walked his mount forward to stand beside her inside the tree line. "It looks like a fine day for Her Radiance to return."

"Mmm. I wish we knew what awaited us. We might have traveled all this way for nothing."

"Or we might discover something vital to preventing Tarkannen's return," he said.

His hand found hers, and he gave a reassuring squeeze. "Whatever awaits, we'll keep our eyes to the horizon and face it together."

She squeezed back in affirmation of his strength and sensed him staring at her from the side, then turned to meet his eyes. "What?"

"You're not worried about what we'll find with the Usurper. You're worried about how you'll be received after being gone for so long."

"I suppose I am at that," she acknowledged. "A lot can change in the time we've been away."

"Tovnik's a medic, and he seemed to have no trouble at all recalling your station at the Sanitorium. From what Karragin told us, your mentor

Venlith still holds the reins, and she was ever a friend. So, what's really bothering you?"

She pulled an errant lock of white hair behind an ear. "My title was a political one. Since I had no access to my gift before, my . . . credibility as Her Radiance was limited to the favor I could curry with the regent. Callinora is not like Stone's Grasp. The people here care more about results and accomplishments than titles."

"Laryn—"

"What do I have to show them that they haven't seen in any random first year in training?"

"Giver's breath, Laryn," Kaellor spoke more forcefully. "Enough. I won't have you casting doubt on the woman I love."

He turned to face her directly, waiting for their eyes to meet. Something in his expression softened. "I want you to think a moment. From what I understand, the scholars at Callinora can be a cloistered lot. I think you might be surprised when they learn of your exploits traveling over the peaks of the Korjinth; once by mystical means and a second time on foot. Then you accompanied an expedition across the Borderlands, through grondle territory. None of this even speaks to your prowess as a healer."

She knew enough to trust her husband's assessment but found it difficult to see herself through his eyes. Still, as he recounted the events of the past year, the feelings of doubt began to melt. She lifted her chin in contemplation.

"Still not convinced? Look back there and tell me what you see," said Kaellor.

She turned to look over her shoulder. The rest of the party was gathered in a half circle, waiting for Reddevek's return. She studied them for a moment, then turned back.

"I see Savnah, Nolan, and Tovnik muttering in quiet conversation. Lluthean is telling Dexxin about the time you unleashed your gift while sparring in the valley of the Cloud Walkers. He must be embellishing a bit because even Karragin seems to have taken an interest. Bryndor stands between the wolvryn, teaching Nika some of the basic hand signs of the Cloud Walkers."

"Yes, there is all of that," said Kaellor. "But I see the future. I see a prime in the Outriders given a second chance by your wise council and who is now making amends with people she might have wronged. In that sender, I see the heart of a believer turned from one cause to consider another. I see two nephews . . . where only one should rightly stand."

That last comment gave her pause.

"Are you aware of anyone, ever, surviving after being wounded by a creature from the Drift? Because I'm not, and Llu is here because of you. We are all here because of what we did together. I don't care how much research a scholar carries out or what accolades they hold behind the polished white walls. I will stack up your accomplishments next to any of theirs anytime and still find them wanting."

She listened to his council and finally set aside her sense of unease. "You're right, Kae. Thanks."

Before he could make further comment, Neska sauntered forward to stand between them. She lifted her nose toward Callinora, studying something on the wind. Laryn signed a question to her. *What do you sense?*

The wolvryn shouldered close to her for a moment, then relaxed belly to the ground. Kaellor turned back to signal Bryndor. "I'm on it, just a moment," he said and linked with Boru. After a short time, he lifted his head, drawing his focus back to the surroundings. "It's Reddevek; he returns."

A few minutes later, the warden approached, and they gathered to hear his report.

The warden accepted a skin of water then cleared his throat. "There is sparse foot traffic, most of which is around the Sanitorium and the south gate. The north gate is closed and unguarded. There are multiple smaller gates on the east and west, all open, all without guards."

"That makes sense. Callinora welcomes all who might need healing any time of the day," said Laryn.

"How do you want to proceed?" asked Kaellor.

"If we can make contact with the Docent Venlith first, she could very likely answer our questions and even escort us past the routine administrative barriers we might otherwise encounter," said Laryn. "She kept a home near the north gate. I think we could make it there with little notice but not with the wolvryn."

"I can stay behind with them," said Bryndor. "We could even skirt around Callinora and wait for you all on the other side."

"That's not the worst idea I've ever heard. If it's all the same, I'll accompany Bryndor," said Reddevek. "We can wait for you in the hills north of the road to Midrock."

"I like the idea of having a scout in each group if we are to separate," said Kaellor. "I don't know what we will find today, but I'd prefer to keep Karragin and Savnah with us inside the walls of Callinora. Does anyone else care to stay behind?"

"I should like to pay a visit to the Sanitorium, if that's alright?" asked Tovnik.

"As well you should," said Laryn. "How about you, Dexxin? Ride in or keep to the hills?"

The sender lifted his eyebrows in an expression of surprise as if he hadn't expected to be consulted. "I've never set foot inside Callinora. Just lucky, I guess. I think I should like to see it as well."

Ranika stepped beside Reddevek, declaring her intention. Laryn shared a glance with Kaellor, who winked back. "That's good, Nika," he said. "Someone has to make sure these two stay out of trouble. Alright, let's form up and ride out.

Bryndor led the wolvryn with Reddevek and Ranika northwest into the foothills of the Great Crown while the rest of them rode forward out of the tree line. Laryn's party encountered no others traveling on the road to the west gates. The solitude gave her time to survey the landscape.

The rolling hills gave way to fields of herbs, the tender green and yellow shoots erupting through the soil in tidy rows like orderly soldiers standing at attention. North of the white walls, other crops stretched off to the horizon with rows of red and purple plants.

"That's new," said Kaellor. "When I think about the scholars in Calliniora, farming is the last thing that I imagine, but those fields would make a Tellend envious."

Laryn shaded her eyes and searched the distant fields. "From what Dexxin learned, the regent requisitioned large crops of embertang. I'm not sure what the others are, but most of that north of us, as far as you can see, is redleaf, for the cultivation of embertang."

Kaellor shaded his eyes from the morning sun as they rode one. "That's a huge investment in embertang."

"I suspect it's as much for the military application as anything medicinal," said Laryn.

They approached the polished white stone walls. Quarried from the Great Crown, the stone showed none of the silver veining in the rocks used to build Stone's Grasp. While lacking in grandeur, the flawless appearance of the thirty-foot-high barrier conveyed a sense of artisan craftsmanship. Beyond the walls, a massive structure cast from the same stone rose into the sky more than five stories.

The Sanitorium dominated the interior of Callinora, occupying a third of the small city. Blue slate shingles covered the conical rooftops of the myriad towers forming the citadel. Outbuildings and offices merged in a complex array of passages and galleries. Laryn recalled how easily she became lost in the Sanitorium in her novice year of training.

Lluthean pulled his horse alongside them. "The outer wall is massive. Is it one endless slab of stone?" he asked. "I don't see any seams, no cracks in the foundation."

"Up close, if you run your hand along the stone, you can find the subtle imperfections where one block was placed on another. But from here, it gives the illusion of a wall of white glass," said Laryn.

Mounted every ten paces on the wall, sconces of silver metal wound around strange globes that emitted blue light, only faintly visible in the bright of day. "And last night, from the distant hills, we could see blue lights outlining the entire city. All that light from those small lamps?" asked Lluthean.

"The secret to forging the sconces outside the walls died with the builders years ago," said Laryn. "The globes inside the sconces hold some kind of crystal that absorbs zenith, or possibly moonlight. They release a continual source of blue light. As the moons vie for dominance in the sky, so does the color change. In time, they will turn purple and eventually red. The craftsmanship allows the walls to magnify the light."

"The sconces could house moonstone crystals or something like the wolvryn eyes," said Kaellor.

A look of wonder played across Lluthean's expression. "We've seen a lot in our travels, but Bryndor should have joined us for this."

The road passed under an arched stone gate peaked at the top, the portcullis open and the way unguarded. They rode in two abreast, Kaellor and Laryn in the lead. She directed them north along a broad paved street, away from the Sanitorium. Tall glass windows dominated most of the storefronts. Inside, groups of locals sat in conversation over tea and rolls or studied books with such rapt attention that nobody bothered to consider their passing.

They continued on, passing the shops and moving into the residential districts. The buildings here lacked the large windows standard in the merchant district, but all appeared relatively uniform: two-story buildings with white stone foundations, timber framing, and slate blue roofs.

"Every single home looks like a copy of the one next to it. How will you find Venlith's residence after all these years?" asked Kaellor.

"She's not so hard to spot. It's just up ahead," said Laryn.

They turned onto a narrow road to discover an abrupt change in the architecture. Kaellor grunted. "Now, this wall looks like something one would see in the Bend. It actually reminds me of the home we left by the river."

Rounded river stones rose only four feet high, but a dense green hedge rose up and prevented them from seeing inside, even on horseback. In the center of the wall, an iron gate with whimsical filigree marked the entrance to the property.

Laryn dismounted and led her horse forward. When she swung the gate open, her mount nickered nervously from the screech of the rusty hinge. The air inside smelled more of the wet, decaying leaves and moldering wood than the sterile paved streets of Callinora.

"Everyone on foot. We can leave the mounts inside the gate. They can nibble the weeds and grasses by the wall here, but mind that they don't trample her private gardens near the house. We need her help, and nothing angers the docent more than disrespecting her herb gardens."

"I can mind the horses," said Nolan.

"I'll stay behind as well," said Dexxin.

"Good. We shouldn't be long," said Laryn.

They walked through a garden crowded with stands of grasses that competed with shrubs and flower beds for habitat. All the plantings appeared to invade the space of one another. Eventually, they passed a small pond shaded by a broad, gnarled tree. A frog leaped from the bank at their approach, but its wake barely rippled, stifled by a thin layer of surface scum.

Bright green buds speckled the ends of the branches of the tree. A stout limb lay near the base, the victim of a stiff winter wind. Passing under the expansive boughs brought them to a covered but warped wooden porch.

Laryn was stepping up to the door to knock when Kaellor placed a hand on her forearm. She turned with surprise to see him holding a finger to his lips to garner her silence. He shook his hand once, then began to sign.

"Look close. Something is wrong. The door is broken. Old leaves gather on the porch. Your friend has not been here in a long time. Step back a moment, and let the others have a look."

She nodded once and silently retreated off the porch. Kaellor drew the sword that was ever at his side and backstepped with caution. Upon seeing the abrupt change in their demeanor, Karragin and Savnah took up defensive positions with weapons drawn.

Llu, retrieve the other two, Kaellor signed.

They continued to retreat several steps back, hypervigilant of the surroundings. Once Nolan and Dexxin returned with Lluthean, Kaellor drew them all into a circle.

"Something is wrong here. The doorframe and lock are broken, and the place appears abandoned," Kaellor explained. "I might be overcautious, but we didn't travel all this way to become careless at the threshold."

"No," said Laryn. "Now that I study it more, you are correct. Venlith is a naturalist, but there was always order to her gardens. We need to see if she . . . if the house is abandoned. The home is simple in design. The main floor opens to an expansive great room. A set of steps lead both up to bedrooms and down to a cellar. A single back door leads to the kitchen."

"Good, that's good," said Kaellor. "Karragin, take a moment and see if your gift of premonition gives you any indication of how we should proceed; I'll try and do the same."

Laryn watched as both of them, her husband and the regent's formidable daughter, lost themselves momentarily in their gifts. Eventually, they both returned their attention to the conversation. "Nothing for me," said Karragin.

"Me either. Sometimes the Giver gives, right? Outriders, favor a breach and reconnaissance?" asked Kaellor.

"It's what we do," said Karragin. "Savnah, take Nolan and Tovnik in the front. Dexx and I will circle around back. I suggest you remain here, with Her Radiance and the prince, Your Grace."

"It's been a while since I covered rear guard, but I think we can manage. Go then and be quick," said Kaellor.

"Savnah, give me a ten count to get set so we can breach together," said Karragin. Savnah nodded once as she unholstered her twin moonblade axes.

Laryn watched as the five of them dashed off without further discussion. Savnah drew her group to a stop on the front steps at the designated time, then burst inside with Nolan and Tovnik fast on her heels. Within a few moments, something blasted out a back window. A loud explosion erupted, followed by a scream of pain or rage. The pounding of footsteps and slamming doors was all that followed for tense moments. Cries of "clear" and "go" rang out. Eventually, Nolan stuck his head out of a window from the upper story.

The scout waved to them, then yelled out, "The main floor and bedrooms are clear. Mind the back door. The docent left an incendiary!"

Karragin walked out the front door, supporting Dexxin. The sender fidgeted, rubbing first one elbow and then another across his eyes. He grunted and moaned with abject misery.

Laryn walked forward, her gift already instinctively ignited by the tension of the moment. "To me, Karra, bring him here."

"Your Radiance, we're covered in embertang, but Dexx got the worst of it. Maybe you should wait for Tov—"

"At once, child. If I know Venlith, she didn't use simple embertang. She likely added something worse."

Tovnik ran forward, unshouldering his medic pack. "I can help. What are we looking at, Your Radiance?"

"You take Karra. Neutralize the embertang with any alcohol, then search within. Make sure there are no penetrating resins and nothing in the lower airways."

Karragin's face flushed; whether from pain, fear, or embarrassment, Laryn didn't have time to tell. The prime deposited Dexxin on the ground with care, then turned to allow Tovnik his ministrations.

Laryn made a fast inspection of the sender. Some unique property of the substance caused it to sizzle and burn into his skin. Thin trailers of acrid smoke rose from the lesions. The young man gasped in pain, appearing pale and sweaty. Closer inspection showed that most of his shirt and the upper portion of his trousers were saturated with whatever substance the docent had added to the incendiary.

With a calm voice, she began, "Dexxin, lay still. This will only take a moment, but whatever you do, do not move. If you do, I can't decontaminate you without getting it on myself."

"I'll try," whimpered Dexxin. "Please, hurry. The pain, Taker's bite, it's worse than anything."

"Tovnik, I need a long pickup, or even a metal clamp. You should use the same," said Laryn. The medic nodded once, slapped a long, thin set of metal tongs into her hand, then resumed his care of Karragin.

Laryn donned leather gloves, used the tong to pull Dexxin's shirt away from his body, and removed his shirt and then his pants in four quick strokes with her herb-cutting knife. "Dexxin, roll to your left once. I'm moving you off the soiled clothing."

The sender cried out in pain, panting and appearing more frantic. Blood started to well from the corners of his eyes, mixing with the tears. "I don't think I can. Oh, Giver!"

"Dexxin! You can do this one last thing for me, son. Do it now, and I can control your pain," she instructed with an intensity in her tone. "Now, roll now!"

Dexxin grunted once, then jerked his body in a clumsy roll to the side to lay prone and naked but for his boots. Thick smoke trailed up from his Outrider fatigues as they continued to dissolve. He held one arm across his eyes and dug his other hand into the soil. Fleetingly, Laryn noticed that the searing rash had migrated down from his face and neck, across his torso, and even beyond.

"Llu, your jacket, it's leather?" she asked.

"Yes," he said, handing the garment over without question.

Laryn knelt behind the sender, making an apron out of Lluthean's jacket, then pulled Dexxin's head onto her lap. The whirring resonance of the healer song droned across the garden as she channeled a soothing web of zenith over his mind. Next, she placed a pain block just above the nub of bone at the bottom of his neck. In an instant, the sender took a deep breath and fell into a dreamless sleep.

Laryn looked up to check on Tovnik. The medic had already completed his assessment and neutralization of the toxin affecting Karragin. The prime looked and smelled utterly marinated in resco but otherwise appeared unharmed. Laryn continued to channel the soothing currents, keeping Dexxin's mind stilled.

"Were you both struck with the same substance?" she asked.

"No, Your Radiance. I'm pretty sure I was only splashed with embertang. The explosive was twofold. An embertang stunner, then a directional blast. It only hit Dexx, some kind of black powder," said Karragin.

Venlith would never unleash such a deterrent without an antidote on site. Giver's breath, that powder could be an acid or a caustic base.

"We need to identify that black powder. I can't leave him. Tovnik, come over here and slow the tissue degradation. Is anyone else gifted with alchemy?" asked Laryn.

"I'm on it!" shouted Nolan from the second-story window.

The tone of Tovnik's gift at work rang slightly lower than Laryn's. "Do you want me to start neutralizing the embertang? I have enough resco left," asked Tovnik as they waited.

"No, just slow the burn process if you can. Let's see what Nolan discovers. We have time now to hurry up and wait," said Laryn. She sent a probing tendril of zenith into Dexxin's airways and was relieved that he hadn't inhaled the substance.

A few minutes later, Nolan sprinted back from the house. A look of pure bewilderment played across his face. He dropped to his knees, shaking his head.

"You're not going to believe this. It's a military-grade alchemic, the stuff only used by munitions experts in the Outriders, ebon balm. But . . . that's monkery. We abandoned its use years ago due to its caustic properties."

"Caustic properties, yes, I get it, Nolan. Think for me now. Does it have an antidote, anything to neutralize it? Is resco the solution?"

A glazed expression fell across the scout as he mumbled a series of limericks to himself. At last, he drew his focus back to her. "Taker's kiss, no. Don't let any resco touch him." Nolan held both hands forward in an exaggerated, pleading gesture. "That would cause an explosion. The antidote is simple! It's clay. We smear him with clay. It should neutralize and remove the residual ebon balm."

With no need for her direction, Nolan, Karragin, Lluthean, and Kaellor ran to the pond basin. Each returned with handfuls of clay. They painted the sender in a thick layer. In seconds, the hissing, smoking flesh sizzled out as the inert clay pack nullified the toxin. Laryn directed Tovnik to gently apply the clay to Dexxin's eyelids and the creases around his mouth and nose. By the time they finished, the only part of him not covered in clay was his feet.

"Does it need to be in contact with the globes?" asked the medic.

Laryn sent her probe into the delicate tissues of his eyes and, finding no injury, smiled. "That's a mercy right there. It only affected his lids. We should be fine with what you've done," said Laryn.

"Grind me, what did I miss?" asked Savnah, returning from her survey of the basement.

"Dexxin and I stumbled into an incendiary at the back door. He caught the worst of it," explained Karragin.

"Grind me with a pitchfork even . . . will he recover?" asked Savnah.

"I think we are past the dangerous part now," said Laryn. She sensed through her gift that Tovnik had already managed to stabilize a significant portion of the burned tissue. "In a moment, I'll attend to Dexxin. Did you find any sign of Venlith? What did you find in the cellar?"

Savnah leaned back and tucked a thumb over her belt. "I don't think this docent is anyone we want to trifle with. There's a similar trap already triggered at the main entrance. I didn't think to search for it until I heard the explosion. Anyway, there are four tripwire traps in the cellar and a series of rooms. There's a typical root cellar. Two other rooms look like something from the medic tent. The last one held munitions and alchemics. But no sign of the docent."

"Alright, Tovnik, stop your channeling before you incur the draft. Give me a moment," said Laryn. The healer song dimmed to her solo resonance, and Tovnik sat back.

Laryn spent the next half hour in concentrated effort, identifying burned tissue, then mending and sealing the wounds. She finally lifted her attention to the group. They all stood around her, even Kaellor, waiting for her prognosis.

"I've done what I can. Let's see what lies underneath all this clay," said Laryn.

Over the next half hour, they made a water train hauling pondwater to liberally wash the sender clean from the clay packing. Most of his front side revealed healthy, unscarred, pink skin.

She expected a wave of dizziness to wash over her, but only mild fatigue indicated the depth of her channeling. "I'd like to be done with this before the draft sets in. Get a fresh shirt and trousers from Kaellor's pack. We'll save him the embarrassment before allowing him to wake."

Several minutes later, Laryn lifted the block in his upper spine and the web covering his mind, allowing him to awaken.

"Dexxin. Time to take a few deep breaths in the light of day. Come back to me now. You're going to be fine," said Laryn.

Dexxin fluttered his eyes open and took in a full, relaxed breath. He smiled briefly, but the edges of his mouth melted into a look of utter horror as he oriented to his surroundings. He began to hyperventilate and sat up, grabbing at his head.

"Dexx, you're fine. Relax, man," said Savnah.

"No, no, no, no, no! How did they get in? I couldn't, I didn't mean to!" Dexxin looked up to Kaellor. "Your Grace, you have to believe me. I didn't mean to, I couldn't control it, and I'm not . . . I'm not on Veramanth's decoction."

Kaellor knelt beside the sender and placed a hand on his shoulder. He looked at Laryn with an expression of genuine concern. "Is it battle shock?"

"I'm not sure. It's possible," said Laryn. She grabbed Dexxin by the chin and gently turned him to hold his attention. "Dexxin, what hurts? If there is more to mend, between Tovnik and I, we can manage."

Tears welled in the sender's eyes, and he shook his head from side to side. "Nothing hurts. I feel better. But when I was under, or whatever you did to mend me . . . I couldn't control my gift. The pain was so intense, I thought . . . I thought I was going to die. I mean, I really thought that was it." He broke down sobbing again.

"That's completely understandable, Dexxin," said Laryn.

Dexxin wiped his nose and looked up with reddened eyes. "No, Your Grace, you don't understand. My siblings sensed all of it, and once you took away my pain, you also took away my ability to keep them out, but by then, we were connected . . . and I think . . . I think they know everything. Where I am, what I'm doing . . . who I'm with."

"Is it really so bad?" asked Kaellor. "Perhaps your siblings will be grateful for your recovery under Laryn's ministrations, son."

Dexxin's shoulders spasmed, and he dropped his head to the ground with silent sobs.

"It's bad, your Grace. Craxton and Mullayne are in deep with the Lacuna. That likely makes our return to Stone's Grasp a bit of a grot-grind, if you'll pardon. Whatever you think we need to do in Callinora, we should get it done immediately, then rejoin the warden and your nephew. We might have a difficult time of it otherwise."

Chapter Twenty-Four: Colors in the Valley

Since her initial visit to the King's Respite, Volencia found herself eager to return and escape the confines of the Bragnaus caverns. Thankfully, her contribution to Tarkannen's Rite of Sundering required her to work from the surface. After stepping out under the starry sky, she dissipated the offensive grotvonen musk by drafting a fine web of nadir. Even then, the sour reek lingered in her nose, an unrelenting scent memory. She stared down into the smooth channel that dropped unnaturally into the shamans' summoning chamber and considered the tasks left to accomplish before initiating the ritual.

The herd of grondle placed at her disposal should make the collection of the human participants a manageable affair. However, she didn't know enough about the Dernegians, and that bothered her. Their reaction to the grondle force involved too many variables. If they proved a stubborn lot or formed a resistance, the grondle's brutal retaliation could lead to countless deaths. She needed at least a thousand to survive for the ritual's success.

How much attrition should I anticipate? One in ten? One in . . . twenty? I can't monitor all of them at once. If only there were some way to draw the people up here without the carnage.

She had lost herself considering the methods she might employ to maintain order among the bestial grondle herd when a strange glowing object meandering down the mountain ravine, making odd progress, caught her attention. She stood and channeled nadir, swirling then folding the substance into two separate globes. Her fists vibrated with the intensity of the gathered power, but the umbral at her side, the remnant of Mallic, remained dormant.

Surely if I can sense whatever approaches, then so can you.

Her fingers began to tingle and numb from the nadir, but she focused on tracking the strange object in its serpentine path. Just when she considered hurtling the globes, Eguma emerged from behind a stand of trees. A green nimbus of light announced his presence from fifty paces away. Volencia grunted once in disappointment as much as relief and hurled the globes down into the chute. A rumbling, hissing echo burped back from the tunnel as the nadir unfolded and discharged.

The lithe grotvonen loped forward on all fours and stopped before her, resting on his haunches. He took a moment to school the muscles in his face in preparation for the Kindred speech. After smacking his lips a few times, he shook his head as if shaking an offensive fly from his ear. "App . . . pologies, Mistress. The Consort will have enough . . . for the making of a portal in two or . . . three nights."

Volencia walked around the small Brognaus, studying the strange illumination emanating from him. "That's good news. I assume they accomplished the task without the loss of any more shamans?"

"Yes, Mistress. All is as it should be."

"Eguma, why are you glowing? Rather, how are you glowing? You've never done that before. None of the grot have."

The creature held out his arms as if inspecting them for the first time, then nodded. "Spores, Mistress."

"Spores? Spores did this? Spores from . . . what, the mushrooms?"

Eguma shrugged his bony shoulders. "Two times a year, we pick. Pick all the food. Spread the spores for next time. The work is . . ." his face contorted in confusion as he searched for the words. "When we do the work, we get . . . this."

"I see. How long will the illumination last?"

"Illu? My not know that word."

"The light, Eguma. How long will the spores cause you to glow?" she pressed.

Eguma dropped his whiskered chin to chest, considering her from the top of his huge eyes. "Too many days, Mistress. Eguma wash for you. Wash it off."

"No, it's . . . it's perfect, you silly little thing," she mumbled more to herself. "Eguma, I need you to collect at least three large sacks of the glowing spores. Bring them up to the surface just before the Rite of Sundering. If you do that, great will be your reward."

Eguma's fur-tufted ears twitched, and his wrinkled nose sniffed eagerly at the air. "My do for you."

He leaned forward on his knuckles and waited for any further commands. She waved him off, and he turned to lope into the chute. "Not that way. Don't use the channel. I need you safe, and it's not ready."

The little grotvonen bobbed his head once, turned, and loped off into the night. Volencia considered the entrance again. The dark orifice sat at the end of a narrow canyon with steep walls. The Brognaus excavators had removed enough stone and rubble to create a steep slope before the twenty-foot-wide opening. She approached and placed a boot on the edge of the incline, finding the surface flawless and slippery, the result of hours of labor working globes of nadir back and forth across the rocky ground.

All we need to do now is smooth out the rest of it.

The muscles in her shoulders gathered in a tight knot, one of the early signs of the frenze. She shook out her hands and cracked her neck to dissipate the sensation. *Small price to pay to avoid Master's wrath.*

The thought made her think again of the umbral at her side. She clacked her teeth together three times in rapid succession, one of the few commands she had learned from Eguma. The umbral command to "come" echoed into the night. In moments, the creature approached on its strange segmented appendages. Moonlight spilled over its pale head, absorbed at the edges by the onyx sigils of its enslavement.

Is any part of you still in there?

Nothing recognizable remained of the man she once knew. The creature never acted with anything resembling familiarity. Instead, it seemed to recognize her prowess in wielding nadir. She'd tried to decipher "the song," as Verrador had explained it. Once, she thought she could understand a hint of the intent of the umbral, but she relied heavily on Eguma's skill as an interpreter and resigned herself to basic commands like "come," "go," and "no."

The umbral squatted beside the opening of the chute, less respectful of the sloping edge that led into a deathly descent. The creature could not command nadir with her finesse or utility.

But no one can discount your brute tolerance for wielding nadir. Do you ever encounter the frenze? What does a paranoid umbral even look like?

Without pause, it gathered dense globes of nadir, then tossed them down into the dark portal. The globes arced along the inside of the chute, leaving hissing echoes whenever they struck resistance from a blemish on the surface of the stone.

The two of them labored in relative silence except for the sporadic clicking and nickering of its otherworldly vocalizations. Together, they melted away the imperfections of the rough-hewn channel and created a slippery tube down to the ritual chamber prepared by the grotvonen shamans.

When the sun edged the eastern horizon, she sensed that she, at least, should stop for the day. Her entire body thrummed with the frenze. Sour water brash bubbled into her chest, and her bowels churned. She paced and shook tremulous hands, trying to bring her thoughts into focus. Curses and swears escaped her control. She strained her vision across the canyon, expecting a revolt from the grotvonen or a raiding party of grondle to ride in.

In a mad attempt to master herself, Volencia dropped to her knees and dug her hands into the rocky ground, struggling to focus her scattered mind. The pain from chipped fingernails and scuffed knuckles barely penetrated the fog of her paranoia. She remained enthralled by the restless sensation for so long that her knees began to feel numb.

Eventually, a rhythmic hiss broke through the haze of her addled thoughts. The umbral continued to toss out globes of nadir, unaffected by the malady.

She shook her head in disbelief and growled. "I'm better than you, Mallic. You hear me, you grinding ass? I'm better!"

Without a formal plan, she pushed herself to her feet and staggered out of the ravine, then down the mountain, making her way to Sifter's Valley. She reached the village by late morning. The labor of the descent dissipated enough of the frenze to give her a clear head. As she paused to catch her breath, the transformation of the mountain community surprised her not a little.

Just as the bard Gauvin had predicted, a colorful tent city had sprouted up. Carts, wagons, and tents crowded into the ordered rows in arches surrounding the central fair like a rainbow. Banners and small flags of similar color fluttered in the breeze, those on the innermost ring stained in deep purple hues. As she watched, more visitors arrived and began setting up their camps at the outer orange and red sections.

The smells of cookfires and grilled vegetables wafted up the canyon, beckoning her onward. Volencia walked among the yellow tents and stumbled back when a patchwork-colored leather ball tumbled over the ground. A rowdy gaggle of children raced after it. She turned and collided with a girl carrying a basketful of baked bread.

The lingering effects of the frenze drew a curse to her lips, but she caught herself when she realized who she had bumped into. "Retta? Aren't you Cabe's daughter, Retta? I'm . . ." Volencia paused, struggling to recall the name she had offered them at her prior visit. She thought of Cabe and his ruggedly handsome features and struggled to reclaim the memories from her previous visit. "Shalla. We met last week. I bought the bard Gauvin drink and stew, and he played a song on his horn."

The girl bent to pick up a few small rolls and tried to dust the dirt off them. Once returned to the basket, however, it seemed obvious that most of them would be unfit to serve at the tavern. A scowl creased Retta's brow, and the girl seemed to have lost some of her exuberance from their last meeting.

Volencia knelt and lifted the girl's chin, forcing eye contact. The frenzied part of her psyche threatened to conjure nadir and crush the child in a dark vice, but she resisted her first inclination and softened her touch. There was still some pleasure to be had in the game.

She drafted filaments of nadir over the rolls, removing the smudges and dirt. "There now, that frown spoils the face of a pretty girl like you.

Besides, I think some of the good spirits of the valley have seen to making things right."

Retta's expression softened, and she inspected her goods, turning a few of the rolls over. "How did you do that?" she asked.

Volencia shook her head. "It wasn't me, dear. Ever since all these people arrived, lots of strange miracles have happened. Some think it's the work of the spirits trying to help out with the Winnowing of the Shades."

The girl seemed placated by her explanation and turned from assessing her goods to inspecting Volencia's appearance. "What happened to you, Ms. Shalla? Did you fall down or something?"

Volencia considered the dried blood on her hands and fingers and her dust-worn clothing. "Something like that. Tell me, Retta, do you know where I might purchase a cloak and fresh attire?"

"How much coin do you want to spend? There are vendors in every rank. The cheapest ones would be from the orange and red vendors, but they haven't arrived yet."

Volencia patted the coin purse at her hip, thankful that she had placed it there out of habit. "I'm able to pay well enough. What would you suggest?"

Retta held the basket on her hip, considering the request. "You want to look like you belong in something green or blue."

Volencia cocked her head to the side. "You didn't buy that bread from a vendor in the blue ranks."

"Just because something costs more doesn't mean it's better, and when it comes to food, Pa insists on the best. These are the best," said Retta, holding out a roll for Volencia to sample.

She bit through the crust, surprised to find a spiced meat and vegetable filling. Retta continued her explanation, "With clothes, it's more about the looks, the color. So if you can afford it, you should buy something in blue. Not purple. That's for the snobby royals or folks pretending to be more than they are. But blue seems right on you. Follow me."

The girl led her down a row of yellow tents to a makeshift road of sorts. They passed numerous vendors and merchants, all eager to peddle wares from their wagons and tent stalls. Customers wandered in and out of the different rows, most holding a myriad of colored packages from the various tiers. A tent stand of baskets stood beside a provisioner selling smoked meats and dried fruit. Next to that, a hawker sold boots and shoes beside a man with crates of liquor crammed in the back of a covered wagon.

This rivals the market in Callish on a busy day.

Retta led them deeper into the tent city, past the yellow and green neighborhoods, before stopping in the middle of the blue rank. She pointed a few wagons down, where blue cloaks fluttered in the breeze from a clever display of ropes tied between two wagons.

"Thank you, Retta. I can manage from here. You run along and tell your father I said hello."

The girl smiled and retreated back to the King's Respite. Volencia walked back to the liquor vendor and purchased a cheap bottle. The vendor seemed not at all surprised when she slid the bottle under her veil and emptied half the contents.

His casual observation of her tolerance seemed odd. "Do . . . many women here command a taste for your spirits?"

The man reached for her bottle, and she obliged. He placed the bottle in a leather satchel with a shoulder harness and handed it back. "I get a few of the blues and yellows, but they don't hold to the drink like you mountain folk."

Mountain folk? I must look a bit rough around the edges at that.

She returned to the blue neighborhood and made her way to the clothier. It took her an hour to assemble an outfit. She emerged wearing a charcoal tunic embellished with light blue threadwork at the neckline, shoulders, and cuffs. The tunic tucked into leggings spun from a lightweight cloth dyed black. To complete the outfit, she chose a blue hooded cape with black embroidery.

After transferring her coins into the pocket of the cape, she made her way toward Cabe's tavern. On the way, she passed a blown glass vendor and caught a glimpse of her image. With her black veil, the entire ensemble blended well with the Dernegians.

Finally, she made her way onto the stone slab boardwalk before Cabe's tavern. A clamor of voices and clattering plates accompanied the vigorous strumming of a lute as she pushed through the doors. Patrons wearing all manner of colors filled the tables of the once-empty taproom.

Gauvin finished his song, strumming the lute high over a shoulder, then dropped it back to his hip to cheers and applause. The bard bowed several times.

"Thank you, friends. You honor me more than you know. Stick around for the afternoon show, a retelling of the tragic love story that began the haunting of the vale. Be sure to tip your hosts, and do try the honey mead. It's the finest around!"

Gauvin placed the lute into a case, then turned and winked once at Volencia. At her smile, he lifted his chin, indicating a set of empty seats not far from the corner stage. She obliged and walked over.

He held back her chair. "I'm glad you could make it, and not a day too soon," said Gauvin.

Volencia took the seat and studied the room. Families sat across from one another, easily grouped by their similarly colored attire. Yet in other places, patrons dressed in various colors intermingled, shared bread and drink, and engaged one another in conversation. Nobody seemed particularly interested in the old bard or with whom he shared a table.

"I suppose I had to see it all for myself. I never imagined that so many would gather."

A young man wearing a stained apron dropped off two foaming mugs of honey mead and a platter with bread and cheese. "My thanks," said Gauvin. "Bring us each whatever Cabe has on special for the day. Put it on my tab if you would be so kind."

The youth eyed Gauvin once and shook his head in what appeared to be disbelief but made no argument.

"None for me, thanks. I can't stay long. I just came to check in on Gauvin here."

"You sure? Cabe took on a pitmaster since you left, a mountain woman from the northeast. I swear she could turn shoe leather into a tender fillet," said Gauvin.

"The mead is more than enough, thanks."

"Suit yourself," said Gauvin. He turned to the young man waiting for their order. "Just the one, then."

"With so many people in attendance, I imagine business has been good?" asked Volencia.

The bard sampled the mead and licked the foam from his greying mustache. "Good? I should say. I've already equaled last year's sum in tips, and there's still another two weeks of reveling. By Cabe's count, the event has already exceeded the numbers from last year. The Winnowing of the Shades always seems to draw the crowds in. Everybody loves a good scare as long as it's all in honest fun, I suppose."

"If I understand things correctly, two entire . . . neighborhoods are still yet to arrive. Will they make it before the big event?"

"As sure as rocks roll downhill. Those who take up residence in the outer rings are the last to arrive and the last to leave. Most of those folk travel from nearby valleys and mountain communities. Some have even been known to take up residence all summer."

Gauvin took another swig, then leaned in conspiratorially. "You'll want to avoid those areas at night, the red zones, as we say. Those folks are superstitious as a tanner's wife and twice as rowdy. Don't get me wrong. Their zeal enhances the entire mystique around the winnowing, but . . . let's just say you should stick near your own color after dark."

"I appreciate the advice." Volencia grunted as something fell into her backside. Two young children engaged in a game of chase had collided with her chair and tumbled to the ground. The kids wore weathered yellow attire, threadbare at the knees.

A woman, their mother or an older sister, swept them up, one in each arm, and stammered an apology. She melted back into the crowd, taking her wriggling captives with her.

"Ahh, sorry about that," said Gauvin. "It's the festival. Gets even the younguns stirred up."

"No, it's . . . good. It's perfect," said the abrogator.

Chapter Twenty-Five: A Sympath on the Run

Ksenia loosened the string at the neck of her riding gear, allowing the mountain air to cool the heat of the midday sun. Snowmelt from the Great Crown spilled down the cliffs, forming ice-cold streams. She pulled off her boots, allowing her aching feet to soak in the shallows. Leaning back, she wriggled her fingers through the shoots of grasses and tender stems of wildflowers.

Her survey of the plot of land obtained by the Lacuna Trading Company left her with more questions than answers. The terrain had proved treacherous and challenged all the skills she had learned growing up in the lowlands. She shaded the light from her eyes and gazed back to the east, toward Stone's Grasp and the region she had navigated.

Sheer stretches of stone rose into the clouds. Splintered on occasion by rivers and streams similar to the one by which she lounged, the towering rock only seldom gave way to valleys of sage and scrub brush or meadows fed by the spring melt. Where the lowlands supported vast tracks of conifers, the ridges and rocky cliffs higher up in the mountain range allowed only small stands of timber to crowd together.

What could they want up here? It's nothing but mountain sage and craggy cliffs. I've barely managed to forage enough to eat.

A rodent resembling a weasel with perky rabbit ears popped its head aboveground and chattered at her with agitation. Ksenia considered using her gift to soothe the animal, but in her fatigue, she just waved a hand.

"Peace, friend. Even if I wanted to eat you, you're barely enough to make it worth the effort."

The creature chirped at her once more before diving back into its burrow. The entire interaction made her giggle, and she realized how the simple joy of laughter without the trappings of court made her feel like she could breathe.

Just finish this last day, then get back home. It's high time you settled things with Mother.

She rummaged through her travel pack, finding two small bottles of the perfume she'd made from the winter night's asylum. One bottle she planned to gift to her mother, and the other she used herself. She applied a drop behind each ear and under her chin, then replaced the bottle and inhaled the sensually sweet fragrance.

She had spent the last five days pushing hard into the Great Crown. The various switchbacks and lack of well-traveled roads made for slow progress. But Winter seemed equally eager for the journey, and together they pressed on. They had passed Midrock the day before, and that trip usually took two more days by caravan.

At first, she'd felt motivated by a combination of escapism and a curious desire to see what might interest the Lacuna in the strange parcel of land so close to the Balladuren ranch. As she gazed down the mountains now, she recognized the westernmost reaches of the ranch. Unbidden, memories of her family bubbled up in her mind: her mother preparing mountain basil bread, her father sitting on the porch by sunset playing his old five-stringed lute, her brothers racing on Aarindin. In the space of reliving those memories, she encountered a strong desire to abandon her survey and return home.

Soon enough. Soon enough, we'll be done with all of this, and then we can be free once again.

She recalled her conversation with the regent in which she described the sense of unfettered release that she felt when riding the foothills of the Great Crown. Part of her worried that the old lynx would be angry at her involvement with the Lacuna, and another part of her simply worried for the man. She had watched him manage endless conflict in the kingdom, all while worrying about the welfare of his children in the Outriders. *If only you could have the same opportunity to get away. If we all could once in a while, I think the world would be a far better place. Don't you think, Winter? . . . Winter?*

Ksenia wondered if she had forgotten to kindle her sympath rune, but she could feel the familiar tingly play of zenith across her hips. She pulled her boots on, shouldered her small pack, then stood to search the opposite bank where Winter had been grazing. The albino mare stood rigid, trembling, and stared unblinking directly at her.

"Winter, what? What's wrong? Answer me."

The Aarindin eventually blinked once, struggled to release a pained grunt, then staggered to the side on wobbly feet, finally collapsing among the grasses. Ksenia gasped and struggled to make sense of the scene unfolding before her. A man dressed in the tailored outfit of a refined merchant from the Delve stood in the place where Winter had been grazing. He appeared overdressed for hard travel, especially in the Great Crown, and seemed more interested in dusting off his pant legs than explaining his presence.

"Who are you? What did you do to Winter?" she asked.

The man cleared his throat, wiped his mouth with a pocket square, and answered her with a raspy voice. "Your horse is fine. I just borrowed her stamina. I've never felt so invigorated. The Aarindin are truly magnificent creatures. You see I . . . used up my mount following you here. She'll be fine after a rest, and I'll see her safely back to Stone's Grasp. My name is Alden Endule. I'm a member of the Lacuna as well. We've gone to great trouble to find you on Lord Kunzie's behalf. Now, why don't you save us the trouble and cross over to this side of the stream?"

"I don't understand. Why would Kunzie send you here for me? And who is us?"

The man replaced his kerchief and removed his pocket watch, assessing the time. He seemed to contemplate her question for a moment, then sighed. "Taker's grip, so that's what losing feels like."

Ksenia grew even more confused by the man's odd demeanor. Her gaze drifted over to Winter. The Aarindin lay on her side with labored breathing.

"Hold on, Winter. Rest easy, then get back home, get to the ranch. Tell Father what happened here."

Alden continued. "You've cost me a small bag of coin, young lady. I haven't lost a wager of that magnitude . . . well . . . ever. Who would have thought a simple scribe would be so adept at mountain travel?"

He looked up from his watch to consider her once again. "Grind it all then. Gevn, see to the young lady, will you?"

Five men walked forward from the grasses where Winter lay. While Alden appeared ready to discuss the finer points of gem smithing, these others approached like predators. Their steps were confident but measured. Each man wore light leather garb with boots fitted for rough travel. The one standing closest to Alden raised a bow, but the odd man touched his companion on the forearm. The hunter abruptly dropped the weapon as if the item suddenly weighed more than he could bear.

Alden tilted his head but kept his attention trained on Ksenia. "No blood, Gevn; means less chance of a tracker discovering anything about her travel through the area, remember? Weapons only as a last resort."

Ksenia lingered long enough to see Alden wink, then she turned and sprinted up the rocky bank. She scrambled down the far side, sliding on loose rock, using small trees to slow her descent, at last coming face to face with a sheer rock wall that prevented any farther retreat into the mountains.

Without much thought, she sprinted to the west just as the first two hunters cleared the ridge behind her. Panic fueled her steps for the next several minutes, and she surrendered to the simple urgency of the moment. She sprinted for everything she was worth.

After several minutes, her arms and legs began to burn, and her ankles ached from running across the uneven terrain. Facing the limitations of her physical stamina, she cursed inwardly.

Go to the capital . . . be the regent's scribe . . . grind it to the Drift! I knew the life of a scribe was a grind fest, but I never thought it would be the death of me. Come on Kess, think. You know this country better than anyone. Think!

She pushed on, struggling to maintain her footing and think of an exit strategy. A sharp turn left led down into a thick stand of timber and gave her a small sense of security. She continued to run downhill until she approached another stream, hopped across, then continued her flight to the west. As she ran along the banks, boulders at the stream's edge flickered in and out of her vision with a strange, staccato rhythm. Grey then green, grey then green, grey . . . then green.

She skidded to a stop and searched her surroundings until she found what she needed. Not twenty paces ahead, she spied a cave recessed in a rocky cliff overhanging the stream.

Let's hope you're home and in a mood to entertain guests.

She'd scrambled halfway up the rocks when the first of the hunters shouted behind her.

"Over here, she's down here!"

Ksenia could just make out their silhouettes through the trees when something scattered loose rock from the cave mouth directly above her. She looked up to spy the massive, ivory-chiseled underbite of a great cave lark. The muscled cat gripped the ground with its long claws and arched its back, stretching as it investigated her presence. She reached out with her gift.

"I'm a friend of your kind. I'm from the horse ranch in the valley."

There was an uncomfortable moment of silence, and Ksenia began to wonder if she had muddled the use of her gift. At last, a response yawned forth, the resonant voice sleepy and unconcerned. *"Yes. We know of you. Why are you here?"*

"I've come to warn you. Men are coming this way. Bad men who want to steal your cubs and take your food."

The cave lark flared its black nostrils and roared. Without waiting for further response, the beast leaped over her shoulder. Two more of the great cats bounded out of the cave in fast pursuit.

Ksenia dropped back to the ground and followed the bank of the stream deeper into the woods. *I'll have to face the Taker for that one someday. Giver, keep those cats safe.*

She ran farther to the west, leaving behind the screams of men and roars of cave larks.

Chapter Twenty-Six: Wrong Place, Wrong Time

LLUTHEAN STOOD AMONG the group, waiting for Dexxin to recover. He resisted the urge to withdraw three billow seeds for a toss. The sender's revelations and Savnah's assessment pulled a new tension through the air.

Lutney's dice . . . wrong place, wrong time. I should have gone with Bryn.

Kaellor knelt and considered Dexxin a long moment. Lluthean knew that look all too well and half expected his uncle to rebuke the Outrider.

Instead, Kaellor inhaled once and shared a look with Laryn, then placed a hand on the young man's shoulder.

"Dexxin, I know you did your best, son. We have a lot to accomplish and short time to see it through. You have the rest of your life to mend things with your brother and sister. But right now, we need everything the Outriders can give us. For the sake of the kingdom, I need you to be the man I believe you to be. Will you ride with us now?" asked Kaellor.

The sender stared up with reddened eyes and a look of astonishment. He nodded once, then climbed to his feet. "I . . . I can ride. You can count on me, Your Majesty."

Kaellor tipped his head once, then tugged at his bearded chin. "Alright, first things first. We have to assume that the Lacuna know we are here. Nolan, I need you to find the docent's trail. Karragin, you and Savnah have the lead once your brother gets a sense for things. Tovnik and Dexxin next; I'll be the rear guard. Any questions?"

They each seemed to understand the moment's urgency and made haste to retrieve their mounts. Nolan trotted out of the front gates, only to return a moment later. "I have it. Venlith's trail. It's thin, but it leads to the center of the city, toward the Sanitorium."

"Are you sure, Nolan?" asked Laryn. "She would have gone there every day, I expect."

"As sure as I can be," said Nolan. "Her signature was easy enough to find inside the home. There are faint echoes of her passing everywhere on the grounds, but in this trail, her resonance is the strongest."

"Good. Mount up. Nolan, you have the lead," said Kaellor.

Lluthean mounted his horse and fell in beside Laryn. Nolan led them out of the gate marking Venlith's home and turned onto a paved residential street that led straight to the city's center. He urged his Aarindin into a canter, and they all followed. Blocks of identical white stone, two-story homes with blue roofs passed by in a blur. Eventually, the street widened to a road with windowed shops.

Closer to the Sanitorium, the citizens of Callinora walked the streets. "Make way, make way! To the side, Outriders in service to the crown! Move to the side!" yelled Savnah.

For the first time since entering the strange city, Lluthean felt curious eyes linger on them all. Fortunately, people scattered to the side of the road, allowing them unhindered progress.

The paved road wound in a sweeping, artistic circle around the white tower. From a distance, two broad sets of stairs rose to arched double doors on the north and south sides of the Sanitorium. Crowds of people, scholars, healers, and the like gathered on the main steps. Nolan led them across an expansive green to a small door along the west side of the Sanitorium.

By the time Lluthean pulled alongside his aunt, Nolan had already dropped to the ground and jogged ahead a few paces. The scout approached the door set into the base of the tower and pulled on a curved handle.

He craned his neck over his shoulder. "It's locked. I can try to pick it, but I'm a little out of practice."

Karragin swiveled on her Aarindin and looked once at Lluthean, then directed her stony gaze to Laryn. "Your Radiance, can I assume we have your permission to break down the door?"

"By all means. Let haste be your guide," said Laryn.

They dismounted and waited behind the prime. Karragin took a moment to activate her gift, flexed her arms once, then shoved hard on the door. The hinges screeched in protest but held firm.

"Karra, use this," said Savnah, handing her a moonblade axe. "Wedge it in near the lock, then see if you can pry it open."

Karragin went to work on the door. She set the edge of the moonblade at the seal near the lock, hammered it into place with her fist, then pulled. The axe found purchase, and the screech of metal ended with a clanging pop. She threw the door open with a loud clang. Mutters of alarm erupted from the crowds on the main steps. The clamor caused Lluthean's horse to lift its head back in protest, but he held the reins firm.

Nolan withdrew a long hunting knife and disappeared inside, followed by the two primes, each brandishing weapons. Tovnik and Dexxin sprinted in after them. Lluthean placed a hand on his quiver and gripped his Logrend bow, finding reassurance in the weapon's familiarity.

He was stepping in to follow when his uncle gripped his shoulder, pulling him back. "Give them their due, Llu. This is what they trained for. We're not hunting vestek in there, and Neska isn't here to look after you. Besides, a bow isn't likely much good indoors in close quarters."

Kaellor reached up and retrieved the long knife he had secreted at the rear of his saddle. He flipped the weapon once, then slapped the hilt into Lluthean's hand. His thumb ran over the mottled stain of dried blood on the heel of the blade near the small guard.

"It's heavier than I expected," said Lluthean.

"It's more protection than your skinning knife. Let's hope there's no cause for you to use it in there," said Kaellor. His words were cut short by the sounds of splintered wood and the clamor of another door being wrenched open.

"I would rather have you armed against whatever the Taker might toss against us. If it comes to it, follow any commands issued by one of the primes. Go now. Your aunt and I will be right behind you," said Kaellor.

Lluthean reversed his grip on the blade, holding it hilt forward, edge down, and ran inside. Five steps in, he paused, allowing his eyes to adjust. Sconces similar to those from the outer walls bathed the interior in soft blue light.

The passage came to a four-way intersection. A door remained closed to the left, and the hall continued straight ahead, but stairs descended in a broad spiral to the right. The din of Karragin's demolition through yet another door echoed up the steps. He hugged the outer wall and bound down the stairs two at a time.

At the bottom, an iron-reinforced door lay mostly on the ground, splintered from its hinges. He stepped through to view another long hallway with doors on one side every twenty paces. Dexxin and Tovnik disappeared through the third door down.

Lluthean waited a moment, and Kaellor and Laryn arrived on his heels. "They entered the third door," he whispered. His uncle nodded once, then stepped forward, brandishing his guardian sword. Laryn followed, and he brought up the rear.

Lluthean stood in the doorway, looking in. The room beyond was more of a suite. A table and chairs sat to the side with upholstered furniture in the corners. Karragin and Nolan were studying a strange iridescent webbing that encased someone lying on a bed. Shimmering waves of blue light flickered through the enclosure.

Savnah held the edge of a moonblade axe to the throat of a woman standing off to the side.

"Is that a dozenth?" asked Lluthean.

"Perhaps," said Laryn. "Nolan, is Venlith in there?"

The woman held at arm's length by Savnah hissed an answer. "What is the meaning of this? If you disturb the docent while she recovers, you'll answer to the regent!"

The ginger-haired scout stared intently into the shimmering blue cocoon. "She is, Your Radiance."

Savnah's prisoner lifted a finger and pointed at Nolan. "Leave her alone, or face the wrath of the entire kingdom!" The woman looked around the room with a wild expression. Blistered sores festered on her face, hands, and wrists, making her appear feral.

"You have her, Savnah?" asked Kaellor.

"She's as slippery as a grot, but I'll manage," answered Savnah.

"Was anyone else in this hall or this room?" asked Kaellor.

"No, Your Majesty. I believe the doors offered a false sense of security," said Karragin.

Kaellor surveyed the room, walking a fast perimeter. "Good. Dexxin, Nolan, post up in the hall. Don't let anyone enter. Llu, stay at the door here but watch for anything coming from the opposite direction."

Lluthean moved to the side to make room for the Outriders. Dexxin nocked an arrow, and Lluthean thought to do the same, while Nolan took up a position near the ruined door at the entrance to the hallway.

The woman in the corner lifted her chin as Kaellor approached. They stared at one another for a long moment. "What is your name?" he asked.

"Inasia Kell. I'm a healer of the second order. You should release me so I can continue the docent's ministrations. I must reinforce the dozenth."

Kaellor reached forward and grabbed Inasia's hand, turning it over and inspecting the wounds. The woman sucked air through clenched teeth. "I'm no healer, but unless I miss my guess, you've recently tangled with ebon balm. What do you think, Laryn?"

Laryn had been inspecting the dozenth and now turned to consider the woman. Where before she wore a mask of curiosity, now his aunt considered the woman with intensity.

Laryn grabbed Inasia's wrist and placed a hand on her forehead. The murmur of her healer song vibrated through the room for several seconds. Laryn released the woman and stifled her gift. She shook her head from side to side in a mixture of disbelief and disgust.

"Why would a healer, pledged to eradicate sickness and suffering, be complicit in the abduction of the docent?" She reached forward and grabbed the woman's chin, drawing her full attention. "Before you think to lie to me, girl, I know that's no dozenth. It's a construct designed to facilitate sleep . . . but it can be used to subdue a foe as well."

The woman's eyes brimmed with tears. "It can't be. You're . . . not her. Her Radiance lost her gift years ago in a binding to . . ." Inasia turned to consider Kaellor. "Him . . . but you're not him . . . you can't be."

"Savnah, I think we have enough to bind her at least," said Kaellor. "Laryn, we must be fast. This was but one part of our mission here. Can you remove the construct?"

"Yes. It will take some time, but it's well within my skill now," she said.

Lluthean watched as his aunt pulled a footstool closer to the bed and sat down. Her healer song filled the chamber again. She inserted her hands into glowing fibers and, one by one, removed the delicate blue strands. The wispy filaments burned away in blue ash as they dropped to the ground.

He considered plopping down into one of the plush chairs, but a fell wind raised the hairs at the back of his neck. His ears popped as if he'd just dove too deep into the waters of the Shelwyn River. The feeling was accompanied by the roar of a straight-line wind.

Nobody in the room commented on the strange sensation; all had their attention on Laryn as she labored to remove the strands binding the docent. Lluthean stepped back into the hall.

"Dexxin, do you hear that?" he asked.

"Hear what?" asked the sender.

"That wind. I think it's coming from down there, from the other side of the hall." Without waiting for Dexxin's reply, Lluthean wandered down to the far side of the hall to stand by the last remaining door. Dust and debris streamed from under the crack at the bottom of the door, and when he grasped the handle, it vibrated. He looked back to Dexxin, who stared at him with a puzzled expression.

"Something is going on beyond this door," Lluthean explained, pushing the door open. The unmistakable odor of decomposing flesh wafted back into the hallway.

Similar to the room holding Venlith, the light of a dozenth revealed the lone simple bed. The strange wooshing sounds were emanating from the entrance to a dark tunnel in the corner of the chamber. Currents of air were being sucked into the strange portal. Despite the poor illumination, Llu could see the oily shadows streaming across the floor, sifting into the darkness.

Lluthean had just stepped inside when someone grabbed his elbow. "Llu, we should really get your uncle in here to see this," said Nolan.

"Can you hear it now? The roar of the wind sucking into the darkness there?" asked Lluthean.

"Just a whisper. How you heard that from the hallway is a riddle for another day," said the scout.

"Where do you suppose that even goes?" asked Lluthean.

He walked over to the tunnel entrance. Inside, the shadows appeared to twist and bend in a spiral pattern. He lifted a hand to investigate the oddity when something shifted from within the tunnel. Before he could step back, three creatures emerged from the dark portal, spilling into the room. One of them collided with him, and he fell back.

The frame of the bed rammed into the middle of his back, and his breath seized up. Lluthean struggled to both draw breath and organize his thoughts. The flat-headed beasts had no eyes and stood on gangly legs that bent at odd angles. One of them loomed over him and clutched a fistful of shadow. The creature raised its arm as if to strike a blow, then stopped and tilted its saucer-shaped head to the side.

"Umbral!" shouted Nolan. An arrow sprouted from the creature's chest. The umbral jerked with surprise and slashed its hand like a farmer tossing feed. The dark ball of nadir broke apart, but streaks of shadow still whipped forward. Nolan cried out in agony, then collapsed near the door, his bow clattering to the floor.

Before Lluthean could roll away, a gnarled hand reached forward and tore open his shirt, exposing his chest and shoulders. A single bone-white and withered finger touched the crab-shaped scar on his shoulder.

In the instant of their connection, the atmosphere of the entire room stilled. The wooshing air currents silenced and carried only sterile galvanic vapors absent of the scent of decay. Rivulets of shadow that had streamed into the dark portal now seemed to vibrate in place on the floor. The entire room fell into strange, wispy images of white and grey. Standing in place of the three creatures appeared the ghostly apparitions of two women and a man.

The figures wore grey, flowing robes, and thin rivulets of nadir trickled over the surface of their skin. Their dead eyes, as if cast from onyx, held no more expression than that of a snake. The female who had touched his scar kept her hand in place and rasped in a voice that seemed both to fill his awareness and yet originate from a distant shore. "You are touched by the shadow but stand in the light, brother. Come with us, and great will be your reward."

The woman helped Lluthean to his feet. He realized now that his breath came easy and free. "Who are you? Why are you here?"

The other two figures took swift action, stepping to the bed and raising thin black knives. With deft slashes, they removed the dozenth, the cocoon falling to the floor in leathery blue strips that held their luster for seconds before disintegrating. Faintly, Lluthean could just hear the echo of an alarm.

A disfigured and withered patient lay underneath. The person's face was so severely burn-scarred that Lluthean couldn't tell if the patient was male or female. The patient coughed and seemed to gasp, drawing in ragged breaths without the protection of the dozenth.

The ghostly man hoisted the patient over a shoulder, then turned to answer Lluthean with an equally raspy voice. The skin over his face seemed both wrinkled and yet stretched taut over his jaw. His answer came devoid of emphasis or inflection. "We come to recover the vessel. Ell'exoon is correct. You should return with us. One will remain, and you can take her place. Master would reward one able to stand both in shadow and light."

Lluthean looked back to the portal. Where before he saw only swirling shadows, now he made out silvery and black ribbons that fluttered about the entrance. Something within the portal beckoned him to step closer. A pleasurable vibration massaged across his scarred shoulder and tingled down his spine. He reached a hand forward and touched one of the ribbons. The sensation ran up his fingers and into his armpit. When he dropped his hand back, a residual ache of longing shivered across his chest.

He groaned as much from the sensation as its sudden absence. "Oh, Giver, that's—"

A wave of force shoved into his back, causing him to lurch forward a step. In his peripheral vision, the blue pulse of a wave of zenith passed through him but rocked into Ell'exoon.

"Get your hands off my boy!" yelled Kaellor. Dexxin and his uncle stood in the doorway, intense eyes incandescent with the cerulean blaze of zenith.

The woman lifted her hand from Lluthean's shoulder, and the room fell back into chaos. Her appearance shattered, and she resumed the monstrous flat-headed form standing on crooked insectoid legs. Standing so close to the portal, he recoiled from the torrential roaring winds that sucked into its vacuum. A wave of nausea threatened to overwhelm him from the intensely fetid reek of decay.

Dexxin managed to fire an arrow, striking one of the umbral in the abdomen. The creature appeared unaffected by the wound and hurtled globes of nadir toward the Outrider. A shimmering barrier of zenith flared across the doorway, absorbing the dark material. Without pause, all three umbral channeled continuous streams of nadir at the ward. Kaellor remained on the opposite side, hands held palms up, maintaining the barrier with a pained expression on his face.

Another arrow fired into the room, impaling one of the umbral in the shoulder, but it continued to stream nadir without pause.

The umbral holding the burned patient over a shoulder stopped channeling. With uncanny agility, it leaped onto the bed while the others continued to funnel streams of nadir at Kaellor's guardian ward. It stepped down from the bed and toward the portal, stopping directly before Lluthean.

The barrier and the roaring vacuum of the portal muffled Kaellor's shouts, but Lluthean sensed his uncle's cries were becoming more frenzied. A glance back to the door showed Nolan sprawled on his back by the entrance, unmoving. Dexxin stood wide-eyed near his uncle, who mouthed his name, "*Lluthean!*"

The umbral standing before him lifted a closed fist and unfurled blackened fingers that tapered to fine points, gesturing to the portal. The creature then placed its hand on Lluthean's scar, shifting his perception once again.

The room fell back into a peaceful silence, the smoky apparitions replacing the otherworld monstrosities. The man's voice rasped a haunting invitation. "Brother, come with us. Leave all the suffering of this world behind. Join Tarkannen."

Upon hearing the name of the abrogator spoken so plainly, Lluthean startled to full awareness and focused his intention. He gripped the blade his uncle had armed him with and savagely thrust up and into the umbral's chest. The weapon penetrated deep into the creature, who considered the gesture with seeming indifference as he buried it to the hilt.

They stood considering one another for a strange moment, and then for the first time, the onyx, dead eyes of the apparition showed an emotion: surprise. The blade quivered and shuddered before a painful, bitingly cold sensation leeched from the hilt into Lluthean's forearm. He tried to release the weapon, but his fingers spasmed, frozen in place.

He grabbed with both hands to pull back, but the pain intensified from numbing cold to a searing agony that held him fast.

Lluthean and the apparition screamed together until, at last, the umbral released his shoulder and backhanded him to the side. The blade released, and Lluthean flew into the wall near the portal. His head throttled into stone, and the floor seemed to tilt.

A trio of enraged screams echoed in the room as two of the umbral retreated into the tunnel, taking the patient from the dozenth. The last umbral continued to funnel a current of nadir at Kaellor's guardian ward until, a moment later, the dark portal winked out, and so did Lluthean's awareness.

Chapter Twenty-Seven: The Vessel

The rhythmic chanting of the Brognaus shamans echoed from the summoning chamber and throughout the caverns under the Torgrend Range. Volencia increased her pace, causing Eguma to lope along on all fours.

"You should have sent for me before they opened the portal, Eguma," she hissed.

The lithe grotvonen hung his head. "My told them to wait, but the Consort made the shamans to begin."

I see. What is it that drives them to action without my presence? The question heightened her sense of unease, and apprehension found purchase in her thoughts. "Run ahead, Eguma. I need you to light the way. I can follow. Get me there as fast as you can."

The grotvonen stretched out his stride and loped ahead on all fours. She followed on his heels, the staining of mushroom spores her only source of illumination. As they approached the chamber, she sensed currents of nadir flowing into the room. The shearing sound of the streams folding into the portal eclipsed the chanting of the shamans.

Rows of Brognaus shamans filled the expansive cavern. They sat on their haunches chanting; some clenched their eyes shut in concentration while others stared into the oily vacuum in the center of the chamber with intense focus. Several umbral sat among the chorus of grotvonen, weaving currents of nadir into the portal.

Volencia ran to the edge of the dark rift and peered inside. The black tunnel gently ebbed back and forth. The diameter seemed more expansive than the one she had used previously. Occasionally, the far side lined up, and she could make out the faint images of a room in what she assumed was Callinora. When he last umbral exited into the distant room, the tunnel undulated and bent enough that all she could see were streams of nadir running along the inside.

"Eguma! How many umbral passed through?"

A moment later, Eguma hopped to her side. "Three."

"Taker's bite!"

"Mistress?" asked Eguma.

"If I'm right, this can only hold four. If I try to enter, the entire construct will collapse upon or return. I can only join them if one remains behind."

Volencia paced about the front of the room, resisting the urge to dive through the rift. An unmistakable blast of zenith flared from within the rift, and the integrity of the tunnel began to unravel. The interior of the construct whipped about wildly like a length of rope caught in a violent storm.

The chorus of chanting shamans entered a frenzied state; the cadence and intensity of their guttural speech sent vibrations through her core. Inside the portal, the streams of nadir began to disintegrate.

It's not going to hold.

Volencia drafted two thick tentacles of nadir, folding the extensions of her will back on themselves, creating two rigid planks. She risked everything in the effort. If her control wavered even a moment, the feedback of the folded currents of nadir would travel back down the length and consume her utterly.

But it's the only way I can support the flawed structure.

Her planks of nadir slid inside the tunnel, where she reshaped them into rounded supports. She braced her feet and strained against the natural forces that threatened to pull the portal apart. After several long moments, the rift stabilized and returned to its gentle swaying motion.

A shadow obscured the far side of the tunnel, and she felt the umbral slide back through along her supports. It carried something over its shoulder, and another flat head spilled into the room. Volencia stifled her channeling, and the portal collapsed inward, causing her ears to pop from the abrupt vacuum. The last umbral shrieked in pain as the construct collapsed, sundering the creature in the Drift.

The lead umbral bent to place something on the ground with a tender gesture that defied its nature. Volencia knelt to inspect the wreckage of what might have passed for a human at one point. Thick ropes of burn scars covered the face and chest. Small strictured holes were all that remained where the eyes, nose, ears, and mouth should be.

In her fascination, she nearly missed the lifeless stillness of the body and the single wound that oozed dark blood from the chest. "Eguma! Something's wrong. It's not breathing. The vessel's been wounded. Get a shaman over here now!"

Eguma chattered a command, and two shamans scurried forth. One wore the unmistakable fetishes of an elder; bones rattled from the belt looped around its bloated belly. The other was most likely its apprentice. The younger one placed a clawed hand on the lifeless body and began to chant. The elder reached into a pouch and sifted a dark powder through thick fingers into the chest wound. Together, the two Brognaus growled long, haunting notes that overlapped. Faint flickers of zenith danced across the serrated wound. The edges curled in and sealed up, leaving a blackened scar. Several moments later, the vessel took a ragged gasp, coughed, then wheezed with shallow, labored breathing.

The apprentice shaman continued to growl the strange healing chant while the other fell into a trance, running its palms over the body, stopping over the abdomen. The elder pulled its hand back as if it had touched a hot cauldron.

"Grind it. I don't have to speak grot to know there's still a problem," said Volencia.

The elder repeated its strange assessment, then blinked its overlarge eyes. With agitated clicks and growls, it shared its findings with Eguma. Before the lithe grotvonen could translate, one of the umbral stepped forward.

Volencia sensed the flathead carry out another assessment of the vessel. The umbral pulled wispy filaments of nadir through the wounded body, causing it to shudder as if in pain. When the umbral stopped, it chattered angrily to the elder shaman, who growled back its response.

"Eguma, I need answers. What are they saying?"

"Mistress. The body arrived damaged, as you saw. The shamans restored what they can. This, it seems . . . was the vessel."

Volencia began to wonder if the grotvonen's command of the Kindred speech had lapsed into a sloppy mixture of tenses. "This *is* the vessel. Is that what you meant to say?"

Eguma held his hands out, showing empty palms. "No. This is the vessel no more."

A surging tide of emotion threatened to overwhelm Volencia's senses as she wrestled with the grotvonen's explanation. She didn't want to admit that all of her labor these last months, the entire trajectory of her life's choices, might be upended if Tarkannen lost his tether to the world of the living.

Without waiting for confirmation, she drafted a probing filament of nadir into the scarred body. Faintly, like an aftertaste on the back of the tongue, she sensed the resonance of the reductive force. But the shaman's assessment was right. There was nothing to indicate that Tarkannen remained tethered to the body lying on the floor. She fell to her knees, feeling defeated, empty, and numb.

One of the umbral sauntered over and dropped a globe of nadir onto the vessel. The tissue melted away, collapsing into a smoldering ruin. She barely registered the stench of the rotting flesh. The flathead spoke with clicks and tones that lacked the passion and urgency of the previous conversation.

Eguma lifted his face with a bright expression. "Some happy news for you, Mistress. Your master sends word through this umbral. He remains tethered to this world. Despite this." He gestured at the remnants of the vessel. "His anchor is more strong now than ever. We must prepare for the Rite of Sundering."

"How? How is master still tethered if the vessel is destroyed?" she asked the question more to herself than anyone in the cavern. Eguma chattered to the umbral, who responded with short bursts of angry clicks.

"This one says there was a traitor in the vessel's room, a young man with a shadow mark who refused the call. They fought, and somehow the tether . . . t-t-transferred to this other man," stammered Eguma.

Shadow mark? By all the dead in the Drift, nobody ever survived to inherit that. She considered pressing the umbral for more answers. "Tell me again, Eguma. Tarkannen's tether, it's intact? He remains strongly connected to us?"

The lithe grotvonen engaged the umbral in conversation, the cavern an echo chamber of their clicky, guttural speech. At last, Eguma turned luminous eyes to her. "This one says your master's tether is safe, safe and strong. It warns that you must turn your attention to the Rite of Sundering."

Volencia sensed the edge of a warning in Eguma's response and considered throttling the umbral with her power to coerce more answers. With an effort, she set the puzzle to the side and thought about the work ahead.

We should wait at least a few more nights for the crowds to swell. I can bring the grondle army into position, then it will still take two nights to march them all up here.

"Eguma, tell the umbral that in five, maybe six days, we will be ready to begin the Rite of Sundering."

Chapter Twenty-Eight: Company in the High Country

Bryndor finished grooming his mount and turned the horse loose to graze on the meager scrub and mountain sage near Reddevek's Aarindin. They had circled north around Callinora, climbing a good distance into the Great Crown to avoid the risk of encountering other travelers. A stream cut through the cliffs and gave rise to a flat meadow with a small copse of trees with roots that bulged up unnaturally in mounds clinging to the craggy ground. It seemed to Bryndor no small miracle that they found purchase among the rocks.

He lifted his eyes back to his horse. Habit, more than anything else, made him double-check that the mount remained close.

"He won't wander far," said Reddevek in answer to his thoughts. "They prefer to stick together, and Zippy will keep him close."

Bryndor dipped his chin and grunted with a soft smile. "I know. And still, I can't help but fall back on lessons learned from the past. Lluthean once allowed his mount to graze free when we took a cartography assignment for the margrave in Riverton. She was a strong-headed mare, and it took us three days to catch her. Kae was beyond angry for the delay and made Llu drive the wagon the rest of the trip."

"What's so bad about that?" asked Ranika. "I think I would love to ride in a wagon. It beats sliding off Zippy's backside like a loose pebble."

"Oh, I agree," said Bryndor. "But not Llu. He gets bored and likes to wander off-trail. It's just his way, I guess. He would ride a game trail for miles, circle back, and never get lost. Somehow, he always managed to find his way back to camp."

He joined Reddevek, who sat on a rounded rock, watching his boots dry near their campfire. The warden used a stick to remove a small tin from the edge of the flames. He popped the lid off to reveal a thin brown sauce.

"Looks like apple butter but smells a bit like bacon," said Bryndor.

"Boot grease. I got it from a Moonie a few days ago while scouting south of Callinora," said Reddevek. He used an old cloth to rub the oily mixture into his boots.

"What's a Moonie, Redd?" asked Ranika.

The warden looked up. "A Moonie? Nomads, merchant peddlers who roam the kingdom following the cycles of the moon. They can be a superstitious lot, but friendly enough once they get to know you. Their families travel in wagon caravans and always carry something you need. The last time we met, it was boot grease."

"So they never settle down in any one place? They don't have a home?" she pressed.

"I suppose that their home is anywhere under the moon. Wherever they stop, that's home," said Reddevek.

Ranika's brow creased in thought.

"That kind of freedom doesn't sound so bad," said Bryndor. He ran a thumb along the outside of his boot, finding the material coarse. "Mind if I use that when you're done?"

"There's more here than we need. Nika, stand in the stream and clean your boots, then set them by the fire here to warm, and I'll get to yours next."

Ranika shrugged and waded into the shallows, then bent over to remove trail dust and mud from her boots.

A sharp, deep bark announced Boru's return. The wolvryn appeared on a hilltop to the east.

"Is it just me, or is he back sooner than usual?" asked the warden.

Bryndor studied the wolvryn's posture and body language. *He's found something.*

He stood and made for the hillside. "Give me a moment. I'll link to him and have a look."

Bryndor signaled for Boru to meet him halfway, but the wolvryn sat on his haunches, demanding he make the climb. At the top, he paused to catch his breath. Not thirty paces away, Neska lapped at the edge of the stream as it meandered from the east. Stark cliffsides barred further travel to the north.

Bryndor collected his thoughts, then ran thick fingers over Boru's back, stopping at the muscled shoulders. He stilled his breathing to merge with Boru's senses and waited. A moment later, the world exploded with the wolvryn's perception. He became aware of the humid aroma of mosses and lichen growing along the bank and the tinge of a crisp mineral edge that flavored the water.

Boru huffed once, and Bryndor understood the wolvryn meant to draw his attention to something beyond their immediate surroundings. He expanded the survey, reaching out. A rich, musky, and floral fragrance pulled his awareness to something farther to the east. He strained with enhanced vision and discovered movement.

A woman ran along the stream at breakneck speed. She was the source of the entrancing fragrance, but she smelled of something else. Desperation flavored her sweat, and she panted with labor. Honey-colored hair matted to her forehead, and a sprinkle of freckles adorned a small upturned nose. The woman leaped from a boulder, landing with agile grace on loose rock only to continue her reckless dash.

What are you running from?

He drew his attention farther east and found his answer. A group of four pursued the woman. The front three held bows and deftly picked their way along her trail. The distinct metallic tinge of blood cut through their leathers and added to what Bryndor could only perceive as malevolent intent.

Behind these three, the fourth man followed. He kept pace with the group but appeared unlabored by the travel. Zenith flared from runes at his wrists and neckline. The man wore attire befitting a tailor or merchant from a high-end shop.

Bryndor released his connection to Boru. "Red? We've got company!"

Reddevek stood from the campfire and growled. "Up here? Taker's breath. What do you see?"

"There's a woman. She's alone and running this way. Four men chase her and have the stink of bad intentions about them. At least one of them is gifted, a strange fellow dressed in odd clothes."

Reddevek squinted. "What makes you say that?"

"Three of them wear leather gear made for rough travel. The gifted man looks like he belongs at a table counting coins."

Reddevek unfastened the leather straps over his axe and a long knife. He turned to consider their surroundings. "How much time until they arrive?"

"Four minutes, maybe five," said Bryndor.

The warden inhaled and nodded. "Alright, call in Neska."

With a curt hand signal, Bryndor led the wolvryn back to the campfire.

"Are you as good with that bow as your brother?" asked Reddevek.

Bryndor nibbled on his lower lip. "Nobody I know is as good as Llu, but I'm good enough, especially in daylight."

Reddevek grunted. "Honesty . . . refreshing. You and the wolvryn get back into the trees. When the woman gets here, I'll send her back to you. When they press forward, and they will, take out the ones who hang back. Those are usually the ones with bows. Then be ready to send in the wolvryn. If things grind sideways, get yourself back to Callinora. Under no circumstances do you place yourself in danger."

Bryndor collected his bow and quiver. "Where will you be?"

The warden sat back down by the campfire and pulled on his boots. "I'll be the bait."

The man spoke the words with strange acceptance; no bravado flavored his tone. Bryndor shook his head in disbelief. "What if we stand together and prepare to meet them? Don't you think we might—"

"No," Reddevek interrupted. "We didn't ride all the way from the Bend to risk the royal bloodline. Besides, your uncle would be a hard man to deal with if anything happened to you. Stay back in the trees, use your bow, deploy the wolvryn. Nika, you stay out of sight until I need you."

The two of them, Reddevek and his ward, shared stony gazes for a long moment. Something unspoken seemed to pass between them. Ranika eventually gave the warden a curt nod and offered no argument. Bryndor watched her walk over toward the Aarindin. Within three steps, streamers of oily shadow flowed across the ground and up her legs. Two steps later, her appearance wavered as if he was seeing her through a pool of water. Two more steps and she vanished.

Bryndor turned to see what the warden thought of Ranika's ability. The man rubbed a thumb over the edge of his long knife, grumbling. "Because I don't have enough to contend with today."

"Her secret is safe with me. Ranika can't hide from the wolvryn. I've known about her ability to vanish for some time now."

The warden pursed his lips, then nodded. "It's not something most folks will understand. Not yet, anyway. We'll speak more of it later. For now, find your spot in the trees and be ready."

Another hand signal brought the wolvryn along, and they retreated behind the cover of the timber. He picked his way up a rocky rise and squatted behind a dense cluster of thorny scrub brush. After commanding the wolvryn to sit and remain quiet, he peered through the briars.

Reddevek unholstered his axe, placed the weapon behind him, then sat back down, keeping the fire between himself and the hill to the east. He tossed a small branch and several handfuls of dried reeds onto the coals. Flames flared, and a thick column of smoke rose into the sky. Bryndor searched the area but couldn't find Ranika. He considered linking to the wolvryn sight to see where she hid, but at that moment, the woman crested the hill and skidded to a stop, surprise and relief evident on her face.

She trotted closer, making an assessment of their surroundings, stopping several paces away. Her hands clutched her knees, and she leaned forward, panting. Her speech came between gasping breaths. "If you're a man of Aarindorn, I could use your aid. My name is Ksenia Balladuren. I'm employed by the regent, and a group of men plan to kill me for my current mission."

Reddevek stared at the girl but made no remark. She looked over her shoulder, then struggled to stand at her full height. "You have two mounts, and . . . I'm a capable rider. If we leave now, we could escape, or I could borrow—"

"You're too young to have ever seen a wolvryn, but you've heard of them, right?" asked Reddevek.

The question caught the woman off guard, and she stammered, "What?"

"We saw you coming and those who pursue you. I have a man back in the trees, which is where you should be, but he keeps the company of two wolvryn, so don't cry out when you see them. They're . . . basically tame, and you'll be safe back there."

Ksenia looked past the warden into the tree line but stood frozen in confusion. Bryndor watched the exchange and stepped out from behind the briars to signal her with a friendly wave. The woman looked once at Reddevek, then jogged forward and into the timber. Her steps seemed uncertain or possibly clumsy with fatigue as she cautiously picked her way through the underbrush. She stopped several feet away, a glaze of bewilderment evident on her face when she saw the wolvryn.

"Ksenia, right? Come on, it's safe," he pitched his voice low. "I'm Bryn. This is Neska and Boru."

At his introduction, the wolvryn lifted their noses to the air but remained seated. Ksenia shook her head in disbelief but managed to step closer on wobbly legs. She held out a shaky hand, and Boru panted eagerly, then licked her palm when she stepped closer. Neska watched the interaction but remained aloof, shifting her attention back to Reddevek.

"Right, introductions later," said Bryndor. He nocked an arrow to his Logrend bow and drew his focus to the far hillside just as the first three hunters appeared.

Chapter Twenty-Nine: The Source of the Regent's Folly

A sharp wind gusted down the cliffs of the Great Crown and caused the flames of Reddevek's campfire to gutter. The rising smoke streamed off to the south, and he channeled into his arca prime, casting out a net of his awareness. Three men stalked down the hillside to the east, fanning out to encircle his camp. Each held an arrow nocked to a bow, casting nervous glances to Reddevek, and they stopped thirty paces out. Through his gift, he assessed their intentions. The two on the edges gave him little cause for alarm. One wore a ponytail, and the other was duck-footed. Their heartbeats thrummed like a pack of dogs who had cornered wounded prey.

The one in the middle, though, carried himself with professional detachment, making an assessment of the camp and the surroundings instead of approaching him directly in meaningless conversation. This man's temperament reminded Reddevek more of the cautious wolf. *Ponytail, Ducky, and Wolf. But where is the man that holds your leash?*

Wolf held his bow on his hip and squatted to the ground, studying a disturbance where a single flat stone had overturned, showing moisture on the top instead of the bottom.

You've got sharp eyes, Wolf; I'll give you that. Why did you have to be the one to walk directly over her trail? Gonna be a shame to send that kind of skill to the Drift.

Reddevek made a pretense of stirring the coals of the campfire, and the two predators, Wolf and warden, studied one another in silence.

"What do we do?" asked Ducky.

Wolf walked his fingers in the air, indicating they should walk around the camp and continue their pursuit.

"I wouldn't do that," said Reddevek.

The sound of taut sinew creaked as Ducky and Ponytail readied their arrows. Reddevek kept his eyes trained on Wolf, who surveyed the cliffs to the north and the trees to the west.

The warden cleared his throat, addressing the group. "And I definitely wouldn't do that. I'm not your enemy, and I'm not your prey. But take one more step, and I'll see you to the Drift. You and the fella that's yet to cross over the top of the hill."

Ponytail lowered his bow at the mention of their fourth companion. Ducky shifted his weight from foot to foot, and his aura smelled of uncertainty and fear. "Enough of this! I say we send this monk to the Drift and fetch what we came for."

A sharp voice broke through the tension. "Manners, Gevn. That's no way to greet a fellow Aarindorian, especially an Outrider."

Reddevek focused his gift on the man sauntering down the hillside. Something in his resonance conveyed barely restrained hunger. Bryndor was right. This last man wore refined clothing more suited to legal arguments in the court of the regent than ranging in the highlands of the Great Crown. He also held something in the palm of his hand. The small object glowed, and he spoke into his cupped hands in conspiratorial tones.

"We know each other?" asked Reddevek.

The man pocketed the strange object and turned his attention to Reddevek. "You don't know me, but it doesn't take much imagination to figure out who you are. Your Aarindin is nibbling the grass by the stream there. Lone Outrider, middle-aged, scarred face with a look that could wither most men. You're Warden Reddevek. I know you; at least, I know of you. Allow me to introduce myself. My friends call me Alden, but my associates refer to me as the Leech."

Alden waited for the name to register with Reddevek, but the warden just shrugged his shoulders and resumed prodding the coals in the fire.

"No? Nothing at all?" Alden pushed out his lower lip in a pout. "That's a shame since I knew your predecessors so well. Of all the agents the regent sent into the field in search of the lost Baellentrell heirs, you were the only one to escape my grip."

Reddevek turned over a small log, and sparks flurried into the sky, popping and hissing. "You're the source of the regent's folly? Why did they send Becks instead of you?" asked Reddevek.

"I've become more . . . discerning over the years. I only take jobs within the kingdom, and inside Stone's Grasp is even better." Alden walked in a slow circle, his hands in his pockets. He stopped beside Wolf. "What are you doing up here, Warden? What errand did the old lynx task you with that separates you from the main host?"

Reddevek leveled his gaze on the man, then shifted to Wolf, allowing his lazy eye to drift just enough to keep tabs on them both. Wolf hocked a glob of spit and cracked his knuckles, his stoic demeanor withering under the warden's glare. The man stepped close and whispered something to Alden, pointing at the ground and then the trees behind Reddevek.

Alden nodded, then cleared his throat. "You can come out now, girl! You've already cost a small wager and the lives of two men of the kingdom. It would be a shame to see harm come to the warden here."

Despite his threat, Alden made no advance, standing at ease. Wolf tapped the lower limb of his bow on the stony ground. *Stalling . . . what are you stalling for?*

Instinctively, Reddevek cast his awareness forward and up the hillside. None of the men before him, not even Ducky, seemed eager for a fight. Their auras remained alert, but something in the hostility of their collective energy had cooled.

Alden and his men continued to stall, so Reddevek channeled zenith through all of his runes, linking them in a rare task to sense not what passed before, but what approached. Tracking the alterations of zenith created when creatures passed by was one thing, but using his gift to sense those yet to approach was quite another. The effort would push him close to the draft, but he had a feeling he was missing something.

He pulled his gift back across the meadow and filtered the myriad of signals, ignoring everything smaller than a fox. Finding no hidden threats, he strained his senses to the west, past the place where Bryndor and the woman hid, past the wolvryn, back into the trees, and beyond. Just when he thought to suspend his survey, he felt the resonance of a party of six mounted men approaching from the west.

Reddevek allowed his perception to linger a moment, hoping that perhaps Kaellor and his Outriders were returning with the rest of their party. However, after only a brief inspection, he realized that nothing in the details of the group felt familiar: there were no gifted, no Aarindin, no Outriders.

He can't have had men circle around, not on this cliffside. Giver, we could use a hand. What's the smart play here?

He considered giving up the woman but understood that Alden had divulged too much of his identity to allow any of them to live—conflict was inevitable. With this realization, he committed to action.

Reddevek made a pretense of scratching his shoulder, then reached back to find the hilt of his axe. Just as his fingers found familiar purchase on the wood haft, the delicate vibration of a bowshot echoed from the tree line. Without waiting, he spun and hurled the axe at Ducky. The man crumpled forward with a grunt as the wedge buried into his abdomen.

From the corner of his vision, he saw Ponytail stagger back, the target of Bryndor's bowshot. Reddevek rolled to his feet and sprinted at Wolf. Alden retreated onto the hillside, but Wolf stood his ground. The man fumbled with his bow and nocked an arrow, so the warden threw his knife. The blade clanged off the bow, and the arrow discharged into the ground.

Reddevek surged forward, bellowing in rage. Wolf struggled to unsheathe a short sword. The glint of metal showed as the man lifted the blade from the sheath, but Reddevek tackled him to the ground. He allowed all his considerable weight to lever forth on an elbow, driving the bony edge into Wolf's lower ribcage. Ribs cracked, and the man gasped in pain.

The warden gathered himself and wrenched his knees forward, pinning the man's arms, then delivered a single elbow to the man's nose, followed by a punch into his neck. Wolf's head snapped back, then bobbed forward as he struggled to draw in air. He wriggled and writhed in desperation. His face, painted with blood, flushed a ruddy color, then blue. A whistling sound croaked from his throat as he struggled to draw breath.

Reddevek remained seated and retrieved his knife. He plunged the blade into each side of the man's chest, ending his suffering with the second stab. His fingers found purchase on Wolf's short sword, and he was lifting the weapon when something clamped onto the back of his neck.

Ice-cold, searing pain rippled down his back, causing all his muscles to seize up. The Leech's face leaned into view. "That's quite enough of that, Warden. I considered letting you live, but then I realized I probably said too much. Can't have you tracking me all over the kingdom for my accomplishments. So now I'll just drain you, kill the girl, and who knows? I might be able to fetch a fair price for your horse. Or maybe I'll drain him too. The amount of raw power I can siphon from one of those creatures is . . . utterly intoxicating."

Reddevek quivered on his knees but remained immobile, unable to turn or rise. He felt his innate stores of zenith flow in a countercurrent through the fibers of his runes. The sensation was abrasive as the energies sheared against the grain, and as it intensified, it reminded him of tearing away great patches of scabbed skin.

He struggled to relax his chest muscles and draw breath, the effort occupying all his attention. Delicate white stars streamed in the periphery of his vision. One of Bryndor's arrows stabbed into the ground only a foot away.

The Leech relaxed his grip but stepped around, placing Reddevek between himself and the tree line. Another arrow sprouted from the man's shoulder. The momentary break allowed Reddevek to draw in a fresh breath, but fast as a striking snake, the man snapped a hand forward, and the agony renewed.

"You've got a friend or two there, I see. I suppose I should have known that by the extra horse. Is that where the girl is hiding? All in the Taker's good time—"

The Leech arched his back and fell to the side. Ranika appeared behind him, slashing her blade through the back of one knee and then thrusting the blade up into the small of his back.

Reddevek toppled to the side, panting. He sucked in both air and zenith, pushing the current through the natural flows of his runes, the searing pain dissipating enough for his thoughts to collect. The girl stepped in as if to reclaim her dagger, but Alden flailed wildly, trying to grab her. Bright red blood sprayed on the ground from the man's fresh wounds.

"Nika, don't," he panted. "Step back. Don't let him touch you! He's done." Enough strength had returned to his arms and legs that Reddevek was able to roll to his belly, then pushed up to his hands and knees. He looked across the meadow to see Bryndor step from the cover of the briars.

The warden lifted a hand. "Stay there. More are coming . . . from the west!"

Heedless of his warning, the prince shouldered his bow and sprinted forward. Bryndor skidded to a stop, knelt down, and hoisted the warden to his feet. "Ranika, grab the warden's knife and that sword, then disappear into the woods. Mounted men are moments away. Meet us by the wolvryn."

The girl looked once to Zippy, then turned back to Reddevek, who nodded his agreement. She gave a curt nod and folded back into the shadows. Bryndor tried to pull Reddevek along, but they managed only a step before his legs buckled.

"Leave me here. Get back to cover. Use the wolvryn. You'll stand a better chance."

Without words, the burly prince pulled Reddevek to his feet, then up onto his shoulders. The ground passed by in a dizzying blur, making Reddevek's head spin as Bryndor began a labored but brisk walk back to the tree line.

"I'm not going to be any good to you in a fight. You should have left me there as more bait," grunted Reddevek.

"That was . . . one way to go . . . but the woman . . . Kess," Bryndor panted. "Ksenia . . . She's gifted. She's buying us time."

A few minutes later, and well camouflaged by the briars and timber, Bryndor set him down. Reddevek leaned back against a tree trunk. Echoing through the timber, men screamed and cried out in shouts of alarm.

Acting on instinct, he reached for zenith and, to his profound relief, found the flow easy and natural. He scanned back across the meadow. The auras of Ponytail, Ducky, and Wolf ran cold, showing the men well on their way to the Drift. The Leech lay unmoving but alive. *I'll deal with you later.*

He dragged his attention to their immediate surroundings, finding comfort in the intense burning auras cast by the wolvryn. Both stood attentive beside the prince, ears perked, tracking the sounds and scents of the approaching enemies.

Bryndor stood ready, bow at his hip, his heart thumping either from the exertion of the walk back or the anticipation of the coming battle. He kept a hand buried into Boru's fur, and the patterns of their zenith appeared to merge through Reddevek's gifted sight.

Kid's got stones.

Next to him, the young woman seemed lost in a trance. She remained poised in the position for several minutes.

Bryndor withdrew from his connection to the wolvryn, and an expression of surprise and respect played across his face. "That's it, I think. Kesnia sensed the other riders approaching. She's done more than even the odds. She's unhorsed and incapacitated every last one of them."

A horse galloped past them. Its unconscious rider was dragged by a lone foot in the stirrup. The horse whinnied and turned away from the wolvryn, eyes flaring to white. Its tethered cargo thwacked against a tree trunk with a wet crunch that carried the tone of a mortal injury to the warden's ears. The man was dislodged from the stirrup, and the horse ran across the meadow.

"Sometimes the Giver gives," said Reddevek.

Ksenia lifted her chin, sharp focus returning to her eyes. "Now, Bryn, send the wolvryn now, and they should have an easy time of it. Only . . . maybe tell them to leave the horses alone, for me?"

Bryndor nodded once, gestured a few hand signals, and the wolvryn sprang to action. Reddevek reconsidered the woman. "I think I missed something in our introduction."

"I'm also a sympath, but more than that, I'm Balladuren. There's not a common horse in the kingdom that I can't bend to my will," she said.

"Your brother's Kervin?" he asked.

"He is," she replied.

"He's a good man. Why aren't you in the Outriders?" asked Reddevek.

Ksenia wrung fingers around her left wrist and drew her lips to a thin line. "It's a long story."

Ranika walked around the edge of the briar patch and dropped a clutch of weapons beside him. He spied his bloodied axe, knife, and Wolf's short sword. Light glinted off the ruby set on the hilt of her dagger.

"You couldn't wait for me to help you retrieve that safely?" he asked.

Ranika shrugged in indifference. "I saw what he did to you, Redd. That's his blood on your axe. Two good whacks, and he stopped flailing around; didn't make a sound when I pulled it out. I think he's fading to the Drift now."

Reddevek grunted. "An easy passing is more than that fella deserves. I've half a mind to bandage him up, paint him in boot grease, and tie him to a tree."

Several minutes later, Neska and Boru loped back into camp. Gore splattered their muzzles and paws, but neither appeared injured. Bryndor made fast inspections of them both, then stood and shook his head. "None of the blood is theirs."

"Bryn, link up like you do and see if any of the others are left alive," said Reddevek.

While the prince surveyed the surrounding woods, Reddevek stood on wobbly legs and walked over to the dead man unhorsed by Ksenia's gift. His torso was wrapped around the trunk of a tree at a sharp angle.

Reddevek rolled him over and searched his clothing. Underneath a tan leather overcoat, he wore the uniform of a Callinoran guard.

Eventually, Bryndor turned back. "Other than us, did you find any people left alive?" asked Reddevek.

"No. We're safe for the moment," said Bryndor.

"This one was a member of the Callinoran guard, not that the place ever really needed guards. They keep their gates open to welcome any who seek assistance at the Sanitorium."

"How would they know we're up here? You think Kae and the others are in danger?" asked Bryndor.

"Danger? Not likely. That group is armed with more martial talent than the entire population of Callinora. I'm not sure these others were here for us. That whole time, I got the feeling the Leech was stalling, waiting for this other group to arrive. Somehow, he was communicating with them," said Reddevek.

"They were here for me. The Lacuna sent them. They can . . . talk to each other through zenith seeds," said Ksenia. She went on to explain how select members of the Lacuna carried seeds and how the gifted could use them to communicate with one another.

"That makes sense," said Ranika. "I heard that man who called himself the Leech speaking to someone. I thought he was whispering to a moonstone or something, like he was mad. He said, 'We'll hold here, and you drive her out into the meadow, then we can deal with them together.'"

"What do we do now?" asked Bryndor.

Reddevek resisted his first thought. The notion of setting a camp and taking time to rest seemed appealing on the surface. He inhaled a sharp breath to dismiss the idea. "Now we search the dead for answers and then regroup with the rest of your family. We need someplace private to sort all of this out. If the Lacuna have infiltrated Callinora, I'm not too sure any of the towns or villages along the way will be safe to rest up in," said Reddevek.

"We can go to the Balladuren ranch. I'm overdue a visit there, and I'm sure my parents would welcome us," said Ksenia.

"No offense, but can you be sure your folks aren't in league with the Lacuna?" asked Reddevek.

"I'm certain of it, especially after everything that's happened today. They would sooner dine with the Taker than befriend a circle breaker," said Ksenia.

After searching all of the bodies, they regrouped. Reddevek tossed two leather pouches to Bryndor. One held coins, and the other something that clattered like marbles. The prince opened both and inspected the contents. From the first, he inspected a myriad of Aarindorian coins.

"The gold ones are moons. If you hold them up under moonlight, you can see faint outlines of blue and red on each side," explained Reddevek. "You might as well get to know the local currency. The silver pieces are stars, and the copper are suns. A fifth of a copper is a ray, but the Leech didn't bother with any of those."

Ksenia leaned in and fingered the moons in his palm. "It takes fifty stars to make a moon. You're holding enough moons to buy a manor and staff it for a year in the high district of Stone's Grasp."

The prince handed a few coins to Ranika. "How many suns in a star, then?" he asked.

"Fifty again," she replied.

Bryndor replaced the coins and handed the coin pouch back to Reddevek, but the warden held up his hands. "I've no need for any of that. Do with it what you will."

The prince looked to Ranika, who dropped a moon, two stars, and a sun into her sock. "Thanks, but it's not safe to carry a lot of coin in a big city. I've got enough here."

He handed the coin purse to Ksenia. "You can likely find something meaningful to do with this, Kess. Put it to good use, maybe, since it came from the man sent to kill you?"

The woman's eyebrows lifted once in surprise, but she accepted the gift. "I think I have just the thing."

Bryndor upended the other pouch and studied the small clattering objects. After a moment, he paled. A pair of identical nuts and several opaque, marble-like objects filled his palm. "Red, are these what I think they are?"

Reddevek cleared his throat. "I've heard of an assassin who collected the eyes of his victims over the years, but I never thought it was true. The Moonies believe that if you harvest the eyes of a gifted while they are still alive, you can hold them up to the moonlight on a full moon and inside, see what they loved the most."

As he relayed the tale, Ksenia covered her open mouth with a hand. One side of Bryndor's upper lip snarled back in revulsion and disbelief. "That's awful," said the prince. He dumped the marbled orbs back into the pouch. "What should we do with them?"

"Give folks a measure of peace," said Reddevek. "When all of this is over, Nolan and I might use these to backtrack. We can probably find the families of all the people Alden murdered over the years."

"Giver's truth? You can do that?" asked Ksenia.

"It's a lot of work for a small kindness," said Reddevek. "But if it was my brother or sister, I would want to know. Folks can't move forward if they are stuck hanging on, waiting for the Giver to bless them with something when the Taker already had his due."

Bryndor placed the pouch into Reddevek's outstretched hand. "Ksenia, do you know if more of the Leech's men pursue you?" asked Reddevek.

"No. I've been on the run all day," said the woman. "There were two more, but I think cave larks killed them. I have no idea if he traveled with more than the five."

Cave larks? When all of this is finished, we need to get you into the Outriders. None of my sympaths have ever been so clever or so lucky.

"Good. Come then," said the warden. "Let's retrieve Zippy and some of the Callinoran mounts. We need to put some distance between us and all of this. It's the Giver's good fortune that we've escaped without serious injury. I'll not risk the Taker trying to even the scales."

Chapter Thirty: A Story for a Story

Ksenia dismounted the horse, a leggy strider she had commandeered from one of the Lacuna agents from Callinora. As she set her right foot on the ground, her left boot hung up in the stirrup, and she stumbled back a few steps, turning in a wild circle to come nose-to-nose with Bryndor.

"Sorry there, I'm not used to the saddle. In fact, I don't think I've used one since I was four or five," she muttered, more to herself than him.

Bryndor stepped back and glanced to the west, where Reddevek rode his Aarindin back to Callinora. "You ride like the warden, then? Gripped or . . . held fast?" he asked.

She nodded and stretched sore muscles in her hips and lower back. *Winter's grip has its advantages.*

Returning with the warden and the young man was a concession she found difficult to make. Her every instinct was to ride hard to where she had left Winter, or at least return to the Balladuren ranch to see if the Aarindin had found her way home. And none of that spoke to her concern for Rugen. If the Lacuna came after her, would they not also move to eliminate him? Was Kervin in danger as well?

Reddevek had listened to her concern but argued that the risks were simply too great for her to travel alone. His gruff words only grated on her nerves. "Far better that we play to our strength and meet any resistance with the benefit of a full Outrider quint and Kaellor's wards."

The resources the Lacuna had utilized to guarantee her removal were beyond anything she had ever conceived. The warden explained how they were behind other assassinations over the years, adding to the "regent's folly." The strain of it all froze her with indecision as her heart warred with the logic of remaining in their safe company. In the end, the young man, Bryndor, convinced her to ride along with them—he and his wolvryn.

She had never seen the creatures in real life. To ride alongside not one but two did mollify her unease a little. So, she accompanied them out of the Great Crown and down to the low country. For her part, the journey unfolded in silence, her thoughts bouncing from one concern to another. They set up camp on a hill where the blue lights off the walls of Callinora flickered in the distance, then Reddevek left to connect with the other half of their group.

After tending to her mount, she joined Bryndor and Ranika. She realized that she had spoken very little in the last few hours as she wrestled with her inner conflict. The two of them sat in the low grass, watching as the sun painted streaks of deep orange and pink on the far horizon. The young girl finger-combed through the tail of Neska while Bryndor ran a small chunk of beeswax down the length of the bowstring.

Taking a cue from their casual nature, she relaxed a little and sat down next to them. Several minutes passed in silence that she normally would have appreciated but now felt awkward as she tried to think of something to break the ice.

She watched the young man and recalled his prowess with the unusual bow in the mountains. He had waited for the exact moment the warden turned to reach for his axe and, without hesitation, loosed a killing shot into one of the breakers. "You sure you're not an Outrider?" she asked.

Bryndor shook his head and chewed on the inside of his cheek. "I've seen what passes for an Outrider, and I can't count myself among them. Savnah, Karragin, and the rest of their group are nothing to trifle with."

The name Savnah seemed only vaguely familiar, perhaps from one of Kervin's stories. But Karragin, she knew. "Karragin Lefledge? The regent's daughter? She's riding with the group in Callinora?"

"She and Nolan. They're in the same quint," he explained.

She frowned at the term. "You mean quad? As in four Outriders?"

Bryndor nodded. "Apparently, they're special, a mixture of two quads, so they combined what was left, and the five of them make a quint."

Giver's sweet breath. Who is this that rides with the warden, two wolvryn, and a . . . quint of Outriders in the company of the regent's children? With a conscious effort, she released the stranglehold of her right hand around her left wrist.

The larger wolvryn, Boru, loped forward from the shadows, tongue lolling, and greeted the other of his make. They touched noses, then pressed their cheeks together until Neska rumbled what sounded like a bothersome noise. Boru extricated himself and walked in a circle around Ksenia, sniffing at her shoulders and neckline, the long hairs of his tail batting her in the face enough to make her giggle. Next, he licked Ranika's cheek, then finally settled onto his haunches near Bryndor.

Without words, the young man gestured a hand signal, then settled into a trance with one hand placed between the great wolvryn's broad shoulders. They remained poised in silent communion for several minutes.

"What . . . what's he doing?" whispered Ksenia.

"Searching, I think," said Ranika. "They belong to one another. Somehow . . . Bryn can join or . . . I don't know . . . but he sees what Boru sees, and as I understand it, that's even better than a spyglass under the midday sun. His brother can do the same with Neska."

The more she learned about her new company, the more bewildering it all sounded. "What about you, Ranika? How did you get mixed up in all of this?"

"I met Redd in Callish. He needed directions and then someone to look after him while he got lost trying to find the Bend, Journey's Bend in the Southlands." The girl removed a poorly fitting hat, revealing tight, curly ribbons of fine, straw-like hair that sprouted at all angles. She scratched behind an ear, then deftly replaced the hat, pulling it on from front to back and somehow collecting the unmanageable locks under the brim.

"Once we made it to Journey's Bend, we met Bryn and the rest of his family. But not his Aunt Rona on account that she was killed by an assassin sent by the Lacuna. Redd nearly met Mogdure that day too. That's the nearest thing folks in the Southlands have to the Taker. Anyway, Bryn and his family made the trip north while Redd and I spent the winter in the Bend.

"I liked the Bend. Ms. Della was kind to me there. But this group, called themselves the Immaculine, were causing trouble for any gifted. So Redd and I lit out one night and came north into the Borderlands. That place was something; grondle roamed free on the plains near as much as other wild animals, but Redd was able to sneak us past them. We met up with Bryn, his family, and the other Outriders. Then we all snuck through these pillar things and ran into some bad people a few days south of here. Bryn's aunt and uncle needed to find someone in Callinora, but that's no place for wolvryn, so we volunteered to skirt the city and wait for the rest of them on this side. Then . . . we found you."

Ranika kept combing through the strands of Neska's tail as she recited the history. The girl seemed too natural and calm to make up such a story, and something in her carefree exposition allowed Ksenia to relax for the first time all day.

She thought back to the first part of the girl's story and felt the muscles around her eyes tighten as she considered some of the salient details. "Ranika. Are you saying you're from Callish in the Southlands?"

"Mm-hmm," the girl confirmed.

"Alright . . . and the Lacuna sent an assassin after Bryn's family in the Southlands? Why would they do that?" She asked the question more to herself than to the girl.

Ranika shrugged with indifference. "All I know is, until they showed up, it was a right peaceful place to be."

"It really was, wasn't it?" Bryndor commented.

"Welcome back," said Ksenia. "Are we safe here?"

"For the moment," said Bryndor. "Boru didn't find anything on his patrol, and we can't sense anything hostile."

The young man lifted the grey eyes of an ungifted. Ranika's eyes were hazel; possibly, that was a common trait in the Southlands. But he definitely had the look of an ungifted Aarindorian. And something else about him looked so familiar.

"Ranika tells me you can use the wolvryn's sight to survey our surroundings, but I can see by your eyes that you're ungifted. How . . . how does it work, exactly?" asked Ksenia.

"I think it has more to do with Boru than anything I bring to the table," said Bryndor. "The wolvryn allow it or enable it, maybe? It's how we found you up in the mountains."

"What do you mean?" she asked.

"We never expected to bump into anyone up there, so I turned them loose to hunt and explore. Your scent was easy to follow on the wind. But once I linked with Boru, I could sense the danger you were in."

His words left her with more questions, and he must have sensed as much by her puzzled expression. "You wear a perfume. It's nice, not like the heavy stuff the nobles of the Southlands might wear. But everything else about you at that moment indicated . . . desperation and exhaustion. Boru could see, smell, and even hear all of that. And he recognized the intention of the men who followed you. It gave us the time we needed to prepare for your arrival."

"Hmmm . . . can you do it with Neska, too?" she asked.

"I've only done that once, and I think she only allowed me in because of the danger of the situation. But both of them follow my hand signals," he explained.

"I'm a . . . sympath, like Karragin. Did she ever try to use her gift to communicate with them?"

Bryndor nodded. "Once, and to my understanding, Neska didn't take too kindly to it. Apparently, she considered it more of an intrusion. She's the clever one, though. So if you want to try it, I might suggest reaching out to Boru first."

Bryndor patted Boru on the hind flank, and the great creature rolled onto his back, enticing a scrub of his belly fur. When Bryndor didn't move fast enough, the wolvryn rolled to his side and flopped his enormous muzzle onto Ksenia's lap. The weight of his head surprised her. She shifted her leg underneath the soft part of his neck and knuckled the fur just outside his ears.

"I appreciate the advice. I can tell they are . . . beyond other animals. Maybe I'll wait until they know me better before attempting to reach out through my gift," she said.

"They're not like anything in the Southlands," said Ranika. "I saw them back in the Bend when they were just pups. I've never seen anything grow so fast."

The young man inhaled, and a look of understanding played across his face. "In our travels, we crossed over the Korjinth, and they sort of . . . absorbed zenith in ways that altered their growth. At least, that's what an expert in the Korjinth told us, and my aunt agrees."

"You crossed over the Korjinth? The mountains on the southern end of the Borderlands? I've read those are impassable," said Ksenia.

"They very nearly were, and it's a journey I should not like to make again. We almost met our end there," said Bryndor.

"That contradicts everything recorded in our histories. They all state that passage over the Korjinth is literally impossible," said Ksenia. She studied his face, looking for any sign of a ruse or possibly false bravado, but the young man seemed disinterested in her skepticism.

"Ranika, did you and the warden lead them across the mountains?" she pressed, searching for some explanation.

"No. We arrived by cargo ship from Callish. It cost a fair bit of coin to accommodate Mr. Zip, but Redd was never gonna leave him in the Bend," said Ranika.

"Mr. Zip is Zippy, his Aarindin?" she asked. "No, I suppose he would not lightly leave an Aarindin behind."

The entire tale, Bryndor and the company he kept, the wolvryn and his journey here, screamed of embellishment bordering on the absurd. *But sometimes, the Giver sets the most unlikely of gifts before us. Here I sit, one of the first in a generation stroking the chin of a tame wolvryn, and all I can do is question the veracity of his story.*

"It sounds crazy to me, and I lived it," said Bryndor, echoing her thoughts. "Two years ago, we were simple cartographers. When my Aunt Ro was killed . . . everything changed."

"I can't imagine," she said. "But you said you traveled here with your aunt and uncle. What's the story there exactly?"

For the first time that evening, the young man grinned. He dropped his head forward, and strands of his long black hair fell across his eyes, but they didn't mask his full smile. He pulled a leather cord off his wrist, swiped his hair back into a ponytail, and looked at her from the corner of his eye while knotting the leather strap. "You don't miss much."

Her face flushed. "I'm sorry. I meant no offense. If it's not something you care to talk about, I shouldn't presume to press. It's . . . I'm a scribe for the regent in Stone's Grasp. I . . . I suppose that I've developed a strange skill for catching the small details in the bigger narrative."

He held up his hand in the moonlight. "It would take more than a few questions from an agent of the crown to provoke offense."

Now she smiled, and a bit of warmth reached her cheeks. Agent of the crown sounded much more heroic than any image she possessed of herself.

"Tell you what. Nika told you parts of our story, but I can tell it's only enough to broker more questions. I'll fill in the blanks, all of it as strange as it might sound, if you tell us your story," said Bryndor.

"My story? My story doesn't really amount to much. Not compared to my brothers or everything else that's going on in the kingdom," she said.

He trapped his lower lip between his teeth and nibbled, then squinted. "You single-handedly unhorsed and incapacitated no fewer than six men in the mountains. I think there's a story there. So . . . a story for a story. I expect it's not every day the Lacuna pursue someone into the Great Crown plotting their murder. That already has the making of a pretty great tale. Start there."

And so she did. Other than Veeble Hebben in the archives, talking to another male peer had never felt so natural. Maybe it was because he was ungifted and played no games of power or influence with her. Maybe it was his wonder at watching her direct the mounts of the Lacuna in the mountains. Kervin once explained how a shared struggle against life-threatening circumstances instilled a certain kind of bond among the Outrider quads.

For all those reasons and more that she couldn't understand at that moment, her apprehension relaxed, and she found comfort in telling her story. At first, she began to describe her discovery in the archives and the reason she was surveying the Great Crown. She soon realized she would need to backtrack.

She reviewed a bit of her life on the ranch, her unique bond with Winter, everything that led to her post with the regent, and her introduction to the Lacuna through their efforts with the orphanages in the Sprawl. She lost herself in the narrative for a time, reliving her mounting unease, especially when speaking with Kunzie. Finally, she came back to her discovery in the archives and the reason she'd ventured into the Great Crown alone.

As she finished her tale, the night stars twinkled in the sky. Ranika had shimmied back against Neska and drifted off to sleep. They sat in silence for several minutes staring at the beauty of it all.

Eventually, Bryndor cleared his throat. "I'm sorry. I don't think any of us understood."

"Understood what?" she asked.

"Your bond with Winter. I get it now; why you wanted to go back. And I'm sorry that we didn't. If it was Boru, and I had left . . . nothing the warden might say or do could keep me from returning to him. We should have . . . listened better. If you want, in the morning we can ride back and check."

Those were the last words she ever expected this strange man to speak. His tender honesty made her nose sting, and she felt grateful for the cover of moonlight. She cleared the full feeling gathering at the back of her throat. "Well, she's a smart girl and knows her way back home. Besides, not once did I ever think I would have a chance to earn the favor of a wolvryn."

Bryndor chuckled. "Careful what you wish for. Once he knows he's in your good graces, he'll trick you into rubbing your fingers down to nubs of bone."

"Alright, Bryndor, mountain man of mystery. Tell me how your family attracts the attention of the Lacuna from an entire continent away only to arrive here in the most unusual company," she said.

He sighed. "I can do that, but only if you promise that it will change nothing."

Ksenia inspected him with hooded eyes. "Are you asking me to make a bet while holding less than all of the cards?"

He shook his head and stared up at the half-moon of Baellen. "You sound a bit like my brother there. It's been . . . difficult with all our travels to find friends, I guess. I would hate for any part of my story to change that."

Ksenia sat forward. "You're doing pretty good so far. Stop worrying. I pretty much completely spilled my guts to you, which, you should know, is something I never do. So, come on now. Story for story. Pay up, Bryn . . . Bryndor, whatever your name is. What is your surname anyway?"

The young man licked his lips. "My uncle Kae raised us, Llu and I, in the Southlands because we fled there after my parents died fighting Tarkannen in the Abrogator's War."

"Oh," she said, feeling sheepish. "Look, if it's a painful memory, skip past the parts you need to."

Bryndor took a deep breath and responded in an unusually slow cadence. "My full name is Bryndorllean, and my brother is Llutheandellen. Kaellor Baellentrell is my uncle, and Laryn Lellendule is my aunt."

She sensed that he was allowing the names to hang in the air, waiting for her to synthesize them into something meaningful. And all at once, she did.

Ksenia lurched to her feet, feeling momentarily lightheaded after sitting for so long. Her mind raced as she recalled the names from history. Then she remembered the preserved faces of the king and queen, frozen in the inner sanctum by a sacrificial spell of their own making. Her thoughts flashed to the moment she'd barged into the regent's chambers to divulge Karragin's secret message . . . and all the pieces snapped together.

"Giver's last breath. You . . . you're here . . . what . . . why would the warden leave you here with me? I can't possibly protect you from the Lacuna. No . . . this . . . this is bad, this is very bad. They know you're here, in Aarindorn!"

She paced back and forth, ruminating about the bits of inside knowledge she had learned and shared, all the while wondering if she had been complicit with the Lacuna's moves to subvert the return of the royals.

The Taker grind me for a fool; of course I have. I could have told the regent privately of the return of the royals, but I didn't, did I? Instead, I practically announced to everyone in earshot that they were returning! Before he even set foot inside the kingdom, I backstabbed the single nicest man I have ever met.

"Grind it all, grind it all, grind it straight to the grinding Drift!" she swore, then drew up short when he placed strong hands on her shoulders. She blinked away tears of anger and frustration and struggled to free herself, but he held firm. She looked into his eyes and saw a startled look of alarm. He held a single finger to his lips to garner her silence.

She sniffed back a sob once, then followed his hand gesture to sink back to the ground. One of the wolvryn rumbled a low, throaty growl.

Bryndor's voice whispered in her ear, and the Taker curse her; if the gentle heat of his breath didn't distract her from the self-loathing, his words did. "There's a group of armed riders from the west, from Callinora, I think. I count at least twenty, but their path should take them well south of us."

"If it's not Karragin and the others, what do you think they want?" she asked.

"I don't know. Merchants and common travelers don't ride under the light of a half-moon. If we stay down, stay quiet, they should pass. But if it comes down to it, can you do that trick with the horses again?"

His blind trust in her made the last vestige of her self-esteem wither with self-recrimination. She squeezed her eyes shut, forestalling the burning tingle of tears, thankful for the darkness, then nodded.

"Good. Follow me. Stay low. It's going to be alright," he said.

They belly crawled over to Ranika, who slept near Neska. Bryndor gestured a sharp command, and Boru huffed once in disappointment, then lowered his muzzle to the ground in silence. Ksenia lay there bookended by the large wolvryn on one side and the heir to the throne on the other. Eventually, the riders passed them by, making steady progress east. The entire time, a small part of her wished that the men on patrol would discover them all and that an errant arrow would put her out of her misery.

Bryndor drew himself to all fours but remained there, an ear turned up to the sky. "Do you feel that?" he asked.

And she did. A vibration like constant distant thunder trembled the ground. "If I didn't know any better, I would say it's a stampede. But no herd animal I know dares to charge like that at night."

He sucked on his teeth, considering her words. "One moment then." His expression lost focus while he attuned his senses to Boru. The wolvryn panted with excitement, and a soft growl rumbled in his throat.

Acting out of curiosity more than fear, Ksenia turned to the female. From her few observations, she knew that Neska was the alpha of the pair and held herself more aloof. A trickle of zenith caused the sympath rune to glow a silvery blue. Ksenia pulled her sleeve back and held her wrist to Neska's nose. The wolvryn sniffed once, then cocked its head to the side.

Ksenia offered a brief hope to the Giver, then began, *"Neska, I have the gift of your speech. I do not wish to intrude. May I ask you a few questions?"*

"You may ask." Neska's strong presence, calm and confident with the undertone of an almost maternal voice, resonated through Ksenia's gift. She also became immediately aware of the ambient sounds, the texture of grass and trembling ground, the west wind rippling fur, even the taste of the wind—all of that sensory information swirled through the link. The intermingled sensations exceeded anything she had ever experienced with Winter and belied a far superior intelligence.

An intimate feeling of awe settled over Ksenia, and she dwelled in the moment. *"Thank you. What is causing the vibration in the ground? It feels like a stampede."*

Without words, a deluge of commingled senses entered her awareness. The revelation caused her to gasp, and she barely managed to convey her appreciation before severing the link.

"I don't know how to explain it," said Bryndor.

"It is a stampede but . . . more. All manner of herd animals . . . horses, vestek, bartusk, and others. They're coming from the east. And more mounted men, another group of riders, is coming from the west. We need to find trees on high ground, and fast."

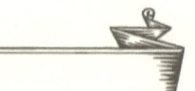

Chapter Thirty-One: Keeping Pace with the Old Man

The Aspect stood in his private suite watching the sun rise over Stone's Grasp, waiting for the sun to awaken the city to its full breadth of color and life. He lifted a cup of tea to his mouth but paused without sipping. The silence of the room sliced ever so delicately by the swish of a letter sliding under his door.

That a message arrived in such fashion was not particularly odd; the delivery, however, so early in the morning and not on the usual afternoon rounds, piqued his interest. A slow pace around the room ensured enough time for the servant to retreat from the door. He forced two deliberate sips of tea, though he was too preoccupied to enjoy the flavor. Eventually, he retrieved the letter.

Inside the envelope lay ordinary parchment. No fewer than twenty copies of the letter would circulate throughout Stone's Grasp, arriving to various merchants, guild leaders, members of the regent's staff, and select officials in offices of power. The tedious delivery system was Kunzie's attempt to conceal the true identity of the inner circle of the Lacuna.

The Aspect sighed, resigning himself to the continued need for secrecy. *The Giver rewards the cautious mind, and you're one of the few who can reveal the letter's true contents. All the other recipients will see a standard dinner invitation.*

He retrieved a vial of Eldrenol's solution. The medicinal oil, a rare commodity among the healers and alchemists of Callinora, prevented an abrogator from channeling nadir when ingested or inhaled. But in skilled hands, it offered a different purpose.

He held the colored bottle up to the light and grew concerned. Only a trace layer of fluid sat at the bottom of the vial, just at the tip of the dropper. If he had run out, the solution might be nigh impossible to obtain on short notice.

Kunzie and I will need to adopt something different. We could revert to using a secret code again, I suppose.

He drafted a swirl of air and held his breath while holding the dropper high. Thankfully, precisely three small beads of the solution dropped into the miniature cyclone. The liquid vaporized into a fine haze, and he hovered the cloud near the blank parchment, then allowed it to mist the page. Slowly, the words describing a dinner invitation vanished, and the previously invisible letters appeared. He suspended the cloud just long enough for the entire letter to develop.

Too much, and the entire page blackens; not enough, and it's all incomplete scribbles.

The leading edge of the parchment began to blacken as if burned by a flame, so he pulled the parchment away and dismissed the cloud of Eldrenol's solution, sending it into a corner of the room. Finally, he considered the message.

Aspect,

Inasia has been compromised. The details are fluid, but she overreached and moved to subdue Venlith. In the Taker's bad timing, the royals and a party of Outriders rescued the docent. Callinora is surely lost if the old crone remains aware despite our precautions. However, there is some good news. We know where they are and can meet them in force before they arrive in Stone's Grasp.

As a separate issue, the Leech has not returned to collect payment, nor have any of his associates.

Please use the inner council seed to contact us immediately. I've taken the liberty of moving agents in the field.

Your faithful servant,

Kunzie

He read the letter twice before rage overtook him. With barely constrained fury, he walked to the window, gently unlatched the lock, and leaned out into the cold morning air. In his fist, currents of air constricted under his will. The force squeezed with inexorable pressure as he refused to release it. The parchment condensed into a tiny pellet. Friction from the indurated knots of air began to swell, and a hot ember coalesced in his hand. When he could bear it no longer, he threw his fist forward, releasing the flow out into the sky, where it erupted in a plume of flame and ash.

The Aspect stumbled back, gasping. Small blisters welted up on the palm side of his hand and fingers. The pain, though significant, seemed inconsequential to his seething anger. It took him several more minutes to relax his breathing and collect his thoughts. Eventually, he retrieved the lockbox full of zenith seeds. A draft of air released the locking mechanism, and the box tipped forward on silent hinges. A gilded snuff box lay underneath the clutch of nuts. Under normal circumstances, he would avoid the intoxicant until late in the evening.

But these are not normal circumstances, and something tells me you're in for a long day, old boy.

He inhaled a pinch of snuff, his own cocktail of diluted vivith and a mild narcotic chaser, then waited for the aromatic powder to provoke the familiar pleasurable rush. In seconds, his shoulders relaxed, and he shivered in minor ecstasy as a tingly wave spread from his head, rippling down and settling in his genitals. Once the rush dissipated, he retrieved the unique flat nut from the bottom of the snuff box.

Before activating the zenith seed, he propped open the oval pendant with the picture of his family in his uninjured hand. *Give me strength, loves. We're close, so very close.*

He donned the hooded robe and cowled his face per his routine, then drafted a trickle of power into the zenith seed. With deliberate attention toward relaxing the muscles in his throat, his voice dropped, and he began. "Ill news at an early hour. Is Callinora truly lost?" he asked.

Kunzie's nasal voice responded, "I received a message by carrier pigeon, and the source is reliable. I told Inasia not to move on the docent until after spring assembly. Too much hangs in the balance."

"She must have had a good reason," said Burl.

"The docent has been aware of our meetings for a time; she announced as much to the regent a while back," said the Aspect. "If Inasia felt compelled to act, she must have made a move before Venlith took action to curtail our activities."

"She should have consulted with us first," grumbled Valdesta. "Her failure places everything at risk."

"It is an obstacle, but nothing more. Calm yourself," said the Aspect.

"I'll swallow the Taker's sauce if it doesn't!" the woman continued. "Our control of Callinora is the foundation for the manufacture of vivith. Without that connection, we can't refine the wild plant. Without vivith, we lose the Spicer gang. Without the Spicers, we risk losing control of the Sprawl. I can't peddle influence without it!"

The Aspect thrummed a surge of zenith into the seed, asserting his will before emotion derailed the conversation. "We all understand, Val. As I said, calm yourself. We knew that one day we would leave the vivith trade behind. It's why you and Kunzie have both worked to diversify our investments into legitimate endeavors. This only moves up our calendar."

"The truth is, I'm not sad to see us walk away from vivith," said Burl. "And the sooner we cut ties with the Spicers, the better. You can't store rotten meat in the locker with the finer cuts and not expect to spoil the lot."

"Indeed," said the Aspect. "Tell me, can we recover Inasia?"

"Not at this time," said Kunzie. "Kaellor Baellentrell identified himself and ordered her arrest. With the announcement and Venlith's support, more than half of our chapter members in Callinora have gone dark. I'm not even sure that Inasia still lives."

The zenith seed hovered in silence as they each considered the news.

The Aspect cleared his throat. "I understand. We will need to find and dispense a new line of zenith seeds to breakers. Time will tell if this line of communication is compromised. Was the prince accompanied by either of his nephews?"

"Just one, as I understand it," said Kunzie. "But we have learned from the senders that all three have returned to Aarindorn."

"Can we discredit his claim or their identity? Nobody has seen them for over thirteen years now," said Burl.

"No," answered Kunzie. "He is accompanied by his wife, Her Radiance Laryn Lellendule. Far too many people of influence are quite familiar with her story."

The Aspect felt the familiar tension rise between his shoulders and considered another pinch of snuff but knew he needed to remain clear-headed. *Taker's shit . . . just what we need, another prominent Lellendule on the board, and right at a time when we are poised to sway the regent.*

"How much time do you estimate before word reaches the capital?" asked the Aspect.

"We should have at least a week, possibly longer," said Kunzie. "I ordered an agent to burn the dovecote after I received the last message. We control the road from Callinora to Midrock and have active patrols from Midrock to Stone's Grasp."

"Are we certain that they will come this way? We've not been able to predict their actions in the kingdom even with the mumblings of the dream auger," said Valdesta. "My girls get more reliable information on their backs."

"I understand," said Burl. "There's been nothing useful, nothing that pertains to our current predicament. To your point, however, all of the nobles from the western duchies are on their way to the spring assembly. If Kaellor seeks counsel or to rally support among the noble houses, would he not first need to find a way into Stone's Grasp?"

"That's true enough," said Valdesta. "The girls have already seen a flourish of business, and two of the gaming houses in the Sprawl took in record purses last night."

"The hormones of young men and resco always seem to swell our coffers," said Kunzie.

"I only have a few minutes. Let's focus, please," said the Aspect. He continued, careful not to allow the tenor of his voice to betray his inner stress. "Zee, fill us in on the situation with the Leech, and then we need to address our next steps."

Kunzie understood and replied, "The situation with the Leech is just as I indicated. He left with a party of seasoned hunters and strict instructions not to spill Balladuren blood in the Great Crown. The mission was simple by his standards, and he should have returned two days ago. Yet, we have not heard anything from him or any member of his group."

"Has he ever chosen to delay his recompense? We all know of his strange predilections. Perhaps he's scratching an itch, taking his time. Could greed have caused one of his associates to try to replace him?" asked the Aspect.

"No and . . . no," said Kunzie. "The man was a consummate professional, and his hand-picked members were all veterans. They knew we would only complete the contract with him in person. It's why we've been able to secure his trust all these years."

"You speak of him in the past tense. Is it likely that a simple scribe defeated them all?" asked Burl.

"No, but the man's history is flawless. Not once has he missed a mark. He has filled over thirty contracts with efficiency. Always on time, always within the designated restrictions and circumstances, and he's always been at the meet for compensation. No . . . the girl's got a sharp mind, but her gifts are no match for his team. Maybe some natural disaster happened. I don't know. If you like, I can try to get agents in the field to learn more."

"No, it's of little consequence compared to the bigger picture," said the Aspect. "We have eyes on her brother, Rugen. Do we have any agents at the Balladuren ranch?"

"No, Aspect," said Kunzie. "Rugen came to join us here, and his younger brother, Kervin, is an Outrider on assignment at the forward base camp. There are two other brothers, but they hold allegiance to the old ways. If I send agents to investigate the Leech, I could have them survey the ranch and watch for her as well. At least if she returns there, we will get a sense for things."

Something inside the Aspect settled, a feeling of relief that perhaps the young woman would not need to be sacrificed. He gazed down at the pendant clutched in his palm.

"Whether we find her at the ranch or back in Stone's Grasp seems to make little difference. If she lives, she will expose our efforts in the Great Crown. The Giver's protective hand seems to have settled on her shoulders," said the Aspect. "Time is everything here. V, you've been quiet, so I know you are ruminating about profit and losses."

"Someone has to watch out for our bottom line! You two go through coin faster than a fat drunk reaches the bottom of a bottle of resco! First, we risk losing the vivith trade, and now we're giving up on everything invested in obtaining that tract of land in the Great Crown!" fumed Valdesta.

"Peace, sister, peace," said Burl. "Let's not lose our heads now. As I understand it, we hold enough vivith in storage to carry us well into fall."

"That's a fair point," said Kunzie. "Even if the manufacture of vivith grinds to a halt, I estimate that we have until Harvestmoon to address the Spicer issue."

"You all have valid points, keep your grip and listen," said the Aspect. "All your work was not in vain. That tract of land in the Great Crown was but a small step."

"A small step? You call all the palms I greased, all the clients I entertained, a small step? I spent years!"

"Enough!" The Aspect usurped control of the seed again with another pulse of zenith. "Stop griping, and let me finish. Together, we managed to abolish the outdated One Kingdom policy of land ownership such that any of us, noble or otherwise, can purchase land in Aarindorn. Nobody has the research or capital to make savvy investments except the Lacuna. You think too small, V.

"Can you imagine the taxes the LTCI could legally obtain if we owned all the land between the Pillars of Eldrek? Once we purchase the land rights to the agricultural fields used to grow crownberry, we control the resco trade. And on and on. So you see, my dear, your work was never in vain. I have been preparing our organization for greatness. I knew we would pivot to these endeavors. Events simply speed up our collective need to do so. The question for you three is, will you keep pace with one old man, or will I leave you behind?"

For the second time that morning, the seed hovered, a silent blue swirl of clouded zenith. At last, Kunzie broke the quiet. "The greatness of your vision was never in doubt, Aspect. I serve at your pleasure."

"I would rather hitch my wagon to a legitimate business than rely on vivith or the Spicers. No offense, Val," said Burl.

Valdesta sighed as her face appeared. She stared down at the floor for long moments and finally lifted her gaze with an expression so intense that the Aspect waved a hand through the zenith cloud as it appeared she was looking directly at him. "I understand. I'll follow orders and do what I must for the organization as long as I get mine. But when all the dust settles, I'm going to make sure that Balladuren girl gets hers too."

"Your passion is, as always, one of the reasons I invited you into this circle, V," said the Aspect. "My time draws short. We need another meeting in two days. Come prepared to discuss the management of Inasia's mistakes in Callinora and our next steps with the Spicers. In addition, we need to formalize our negotiations with the ungifted's Dedicant and the mobilization of the Church of the Giver."

Burl chimed in, "With everything else, are you still convinced involving the church is . . . necessary? Those are good people. It feels wrong somehow."

Valdesta chuckled, then said with insouciant sarcasm, "Brother, do not tell me that welcoming a group of believers galls you more than everything else we've had our hands into. Come visit me in the Sprawl again, then you can see how the righteous are already subverting themselves."

"I understand your misgivings, Burl," said the Aspect. "But we might need the motivation of true believers in the future, so we should at least continue to pursue their alignment. Now, Zee, tell me how we plan to stop Kaellor and his nephews from making a return to Stone's Grasp."

Chapter Thirty-Two: Scars from the Past

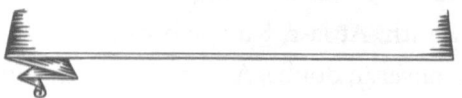

The intense, multi-tonal moan of the healer song vibrated through Laryn as she awakened her arca prime. The halls of the Sanitorium magnified her art such that she needed to expend but a fraction of her power. She reduced the flow of zenith, and the song settled to a soft murmur. Yet, even still, the vibration of her gift resonated through her knees.

Lluthean. It's just a knock on the head. You've suffered worse from your brother. Come back to me now.

Laryn intimated her thoughts through the myriad of delicate filaments, extensions of her gift that probed for any injury or lingering illness as a result of his contact with the umbral. Tovnik had reached him first while she finished restoring Venlith from the sedating effects of the sleeper's cocoon. The medic thought Lluthean was concussed but without other injuries.

When she completed her survey, she agreed with Tovnik's assessment. Yet, she sensed a subtle difference underneath Lluthean's innate resonance. She recalled the numerous other times that she had touched him with her art; her gift had always slid along the fibers of his inner zenith in harmony. But just now, something vibrated slightly counter to her probing. When she searched for the source of the aberration, it seemed to vanish, only to return as she migrated her surveillance to other parts of his body.

It must be a lingering effect of standing so close to the portal or the umbral. Perhaps Venlith will know.

Laryn redoubled her efforts to beckon him to consciousness, and at last, his lids fluttered open. Where Bryndor's eyes always reminded her of polished steel, Lluthean's smiled like the silver edging of the crescent moon of Baellen. Something always seemed to dance behind them. Just now though, he squeezed them shut and grabbed at his temples.

"Mogdure's . . . aching asshole," he said, then rolled to the side and emptied his stomach.

She patted him on the back a few times and waited for the episode to settle. "I've half a mind to leave you to heal without the ministrations of the gifted. Honestly, Llu, what were you thinking?"

He held up one hand in surrender but draped the other arm across his eyes. "I know, I know . . . dumb as a monk and twice as stubborn. Nolan, is Nolan alright?"

His immediate concern for the young Outrider soothed her frustration. She drafted a web of soothing zenith, then draped the invisible meshwork over his head. Within a few minutes, his breathing slowed, and the color returned to his cheeks.

"Thanks, Laryn. Sweet Giver, thank you," he said.

"Back to the Northland gods now, are we?" she asked. "Nolan is fine. He garnered more of the Giver's favor than you today. Apparently, the nadir strike fell apart before it struck him. I healed his broken ribs. All he needs now is a good tailor to replace his Outrider gear."

"I guess I sort of lost track of things for a moment there." Lluthean pushed himself to a sitting position and peered around the room.

"Nolan and the others are with Kaellor securing the Sanitorium. We're safe here, for the moment," she explained.

As he oriented himself, he staggered to his feet. "Laryn, the patient. There was a patient here, all covered in burn scars. These ghosty things came in . . . there was this huge hole in the wall, and the ghosty things tore into the dozenth. They took the patient and, and . . . oh Giver, I think I stabbed it, I don't know, I couldn't really tell. Is the patient going to be alright?"

"How is your young charge?" the voice of Venlith asked from the doorway.

Laryn rose to her feet. "He's coming around just fine. Ven, was there a patient in here, someone protected by a dozenth?"

The rapping sound of a cane punctuated Venlith's hobbled limp as she walked to sit on the edge of the empty bed. "Yes. He was an Aarin. One of those few left over from the Abrogator's War . . . so badly burn-scarred that we never could identify him."

"What's an Aarin?" asked Lluthean.

"It's how we address any nameless patient who arrives needing our services. Most of the time, it's just someone rendered temporarily unconscious. In Aarin's case, the healers suspended him, hoping to discover a means to heal both the body and the mind. We prefer to reference those in our care with a proper name instead of 'the patient with the horrible burns,'" said Laryn.

"So . . . Aarin then. Is Aarin going to be alright?" Lluthean pressed.

"Llu, what do you remember exactly?" asked Laryn.

Lluthean walked to the far wall and ran his fingers along the stone as if searching for a hidden door. He retrieved a brass candleholder from the bedside table and tapped it along the wall. He stepped back, rapping the brass edge against his thigh in a nervous rhythm.

"There was a hole right here, an empty blackness, like a cave into a starless night sky, and this dread wind howled from inside. When I stepped close to see inside the hole, these three creatures stepped into the room. Only they changed somehow and . . . took on the appearance of something else . . . ghosts maybe? Two of them used black daggers to cut through the dozenth and picked up Aarin. I tried to stop the one holding him, but when I stabbed it with Kae's long knife, it passed right through the ghost and . . . I'm pretty sure it sunk into Aarin's chest. Only, I . . . something . . . I don't remember what happened until waking up here."

"Lluthean, those weren't ghosts," said Laryn gravely. "You tangled with a trio of umbral. Umbral are from the Drift, semi-sentient things used by Tarkannen in the Abrogator's War." *And it's the Giver's embrace that kept you alive despite it all.*

"Young man," said Venlith. "What made you come in here in the first place? I wove Aarin's dozenth over ten years ago. It needed no maintenance, no upkeep. Other than a cursory check, nobody ever comes in here."

"I heard a noise, like the rushing of air through an open window in a violent storm," said Lluthean. "The sounds came from the hole, the . . . portal that was right here. And I think somehow . . . I was drawn to it."

"What else do you recall from the encounter? Did they threaten or harm you in any way?" asked the docent.

Lluthean's expression became abstract as he focused inward. His right hand errantly massaged his left shoulder. "I know that three flat-headed, eyeless things with legs that bent unnaturally spilled out of a hole in the wall here. But then, somehow they changed, and the whole room shifted. The rush of wind was like a loud waterfall until everything became silver and grey mist. And that's when they looked like ghosts of people. And they did speak to me . . . something about the shadows."

His lips drew to a thin line, and a wrinkle creased his forehead. "Grind it. I can't explain it, but it's like grabbing smoke. I can't . . . remember more."

Laryn caught the sidelong glance from her mentor and recognized the somber determination. The docent had employed the same persona over the years whenever she had to confront a patient with an awful truth, usually about a terminal illness they didn't want to address.

"Come here, Lluthean," said Venlith, the pensive expression worn plainly on her face.

Lluthean looked once to Laryn for affirmation. She forced a soft smile. "It's alright. Lluthean. Docent Venlith was my mentor, and I would struggle to count myself her equal in the healing arts. Let her have a look at you."

The room sang with the murmur of Venlith's healer song even before she laid hands on him. "Medic, close the door, but you may remain inside."

Tovnik tipped his head in deference, closed the door, and stood with his heels against the threshold.

A flurry of blue probing tendrils filtered through Lluthean. Laryn marveled at her skill as the docent simultaneously assessed multiple organ systems at the same time. For his part, Lluthean withstood the intimate probing without complaint. After a few minutes, Venlith stifled her gift, and the room fell into silence except for the strange clucking of the old woman's tongue as she considered her findings.

She reached into a pocket and withdrew a small leather clutch, popped open the clasp, and removed a palm-sized blue gem. Soft blue light, bright enough to facilitate reading, radiated from her palm.

"Is that the eye of a wolvryn?" asked Lluthean.

Venlith's head recoiled with surprise. "It is. Would you be so kind as to replace that candlestick?"

Lluthean complied, placing the candlestick on the bedside table. The docent set the glowing orb on the candlestand, then turned to consider him again. She stared with a quizzical expression. "You're Nebrine's son, alright. Now, strip off your shirt. Unless my gift has failed, you're hiding a miracle under there."

She tapped Lluthean above his breast with the end of her cane. He removed the thin leather jacket and unbuttoned his shirt, revealing the crab-shaped scar that spread across his upper chest and onto his left shoulder. Venlith grunted as she rose to a standing position and ran arthritic, bony fingers over the silvered edges.

At last, she sat back down on the edge of the bed and stared at her feet for a long moment, lost in contemplation. She lifted her head and motioned for Lluthean to cover himself, her gaze an expression of bemusement as she met Laryn's eyes.

"And so the student surpasses the master. That's a shadow mark, and it vibrates with your signature, Laryn." Venlith's statement hung in the air, the unspoken question demanding an answer.

"You are, as you always were, the clever diagnostician," said Laryn.

"Perhaps. But Laryn. I weave and repair, knit and mend, crafting . . . small works of art. What you've accomplished here is nothing short of a miraculous masterpiece," said Venlith.

Laryn felt the sting in her eyes but turned the sensation into a smile. "Sometimes . . . the Giver gives."

A smile that brought a rare twinkle into the docent's eyes accentuated deep-set, slashed dimples in her cheeks. "Well, I suppose she does at that, my child," said Venlith. She picked up the wolvryn eye, put it back into the leather pouch, and stood, the creaking of her prosthetic leg echoing in the room.

She took a few steps toward the door, then stopped. "Kaellor escaped the kingdom with two of Nebrine's sons. Can I ask what happened to your brother?"

"He is well and waits with Warden Reddevek outside of Callinora," said Lluthean.

"Well. Let's find that husband of yours, Laryn. I have questions that need answering, but they can wait until we secure the Sanitorium against the infestation that calls itself the Lacuna."

"What about the ghosts, the umbral?" asked Lluthean.

Laryn searched her mentor's face for long moments, and finally, the docent spoke. "Thieves only risk danger when there's treasure to be gained."

Laryn nodded in agreement. "Right ... Taker's breath," she mumbled to herself. "It's unlikely they will return if they got what they came for."

Chapter Thirty-Three: The Power of True Belief

Kaellor trailed behind the healer, Veldrek Lellendule, trusting his gift to alert him to unforeseen dangers. With the support of the Outriders, they had efficiently cleared the lower levels of the Sanitorium of anyone loyal to the circle breakers. Their members in Callinora had little taste and even less experience in combat. Savnah, Karragin, and Dexxin were keeping more than thirty Lacuna locked in a small amphitheater.

They ascended several flights of stairs to the upper tier of the Sanitorium to continue their search for anyone remaining loyal to the Lacuna. The middle-aged healer gripped his knees, panting when they reached the landing. After a moment, he stood and winked or possibly blinked with his unpatched eye, then pointed down the hall. Kaellor recognized the rune of the healer inlaid with silver and gold across the panels of a broad set of double doors.

Veldrek leaned closer. "Your Grace, there were five rounders in Callinora. Rounders are like captains; they run the meetings, organize the gatherings, and coordinate recruitment efforts. We've only found the one so far, Inasia, but it seems she was the main leader of the Lacuna here. If the others are in the Sanitorium, the odeum is the last possible place they might hole up."

Kaellor channeled zenith into the runes on his forearms, opening his awareness to the powers of balance and perception. Everything Veldrek said felt genuine, free from obfuscation. When Kaellor directed his attention to the double doors, a faint but unmistakable feeling of danger caused his senses to heighten.

"The odeum, is that another lecture hall?" asked Kaellor.

"Of sorts," said Veldrek. "It's smaller than the amphitheater and covered with a dome of zenith, much like the Founder's Memorial. It's mainly used for astrological studies, although on a clear night, one can see the lights from the top of Stone's Grasp."

"I've not set foot in the memorial in over a decade, but I remember the dome. It lets living things like birds pass but keeps out the elements, right?" asked Kaellor.

"Yes, Your Grace, although this one functions more like a glass dome, repelling everything. Since there are no other walls but the dome, it's a safety measure, I suppose," explained Veldrek.

"Anything else I should be aware of, any defenses or even a drop in the floor?" asked Kaellor.

The healer offered him a soft smile. 'No, Your Grace, nothing like that. The greatest danger the rounders might pose is the contagious nature of their lies."

"Fair enough. All the same, get behind me but stay close. I prefer to apprehend anyone in there peacefully."

"I'll be your shadow, Your Grace."

Kaellor kindled zenith into his arca prime and stepped forward, one hand firmly gripped on his guardian sword. He disengaged the latch and pushed the doors open. The thick panels creaked open to reveal seven people, men and women, standing around a ten-foot-high zeniscope; the silver central tube fitted with lenses was aimed into the heavens. The room appeared otherwise as Veldrek described: a large circular floor covered by a dome that appeared cast from light blue glass.

"Veldrek, you traitor," hissed one of the men. "I should have known you would be involved after the way your sister infiltrated the Sanitorium."

Kaellor tilted his head to Veldrek. "Something I should know about?"

"His words are not false, Your Grace. My sister, Volencia, threw in with the Usurper in the Abrogator's War. Several weeks ago, she opened a portal much like the one your nephew discovered, I'm afraid. We never determined her motivations. Regardless, my loyalties are to the Docent, Her Radiance, and Aarindorn." The man lifted his chin as he spoke.

"I believe you. Give me a moment," said Kaellor.

From the far side of the room, another man paced back and forth, taunting Veldrek and making disparaging statements about his family. Kaellor used the opportunity to read the room and funneled a trickle of his gift back into his rune of perception. None of the people inside appeared armed. The silent majority shuffled back several steps as the two men hurled insults at the healer.

Veldrek accepted the verbal abuse until one of them made a comment about his mother. The healer threw one of the doors wide open and moved to step forward. Unbidden, zenith ignited Kaellor's arca prime, and he erected a barrier across the threshold. Through the distortion of the field of zenith, he saw one of the men dive to the side, a thin trigger wire in his hand. A moment later, the reverberation of a tremendous munition detonated, and the room disappeared in a confusing flash of flame followed by roiling grey smoke.

Only muffled sound and light penetrated Kaellor's ward. With nothing combustible, the debris cloud settled relatively quickly, and the room appeared empty. The blue dome remained intact, encompassing a naked round platform.

Kaellor blinked away tears and waited for the ringing in his ears to lessen. "Let me guess, that was a priceless piece of observational equipment?"

Veldrek's attention lingered on the threshold, and he tapped a finger on Kaellor's guardian ward. Eventually, he regained his senses. "Apologies, Your Grace. The zeniscope, yes . . . quite valuable, although not irreplaceable."

"Taker's spit, what kind of scholar doesn't understand the basics of how munitions work? Even without the kickback from my barrier, they rigged enough explosives to effect the same outcome," said Kaellor.

"I don't think that the size of the explosion reflects ignorance," said Veldrek, a haunted expression evident on his face. "They never intended to survive this encounter. Their retreat here was a lure. I believe that they hoped to take us, more specifically you, with them."

Kaellor considered the man's words a moment, then shivered at the realization. "Conviction then? That's far worse, isn't it?"

"True belief, even if misplaced in a false ideology, is a powerful weapon, Your Grace."

Kaellor dismissed his ward but kept his gift primed. The acrid scent of sulfur and alchemics spilled back into the hallway. More out of curiosity than necessity, both men wandered into the room, each walking the perimeter in opposite directions.

They met on the far side, and Veldrek lifted a hand to shade his eye as he peered beyond the barrier. "Giver," he mumbled.

The healer rapped a knuckle on the translucent wall, testing its solidity. "Your Grace, I think they blasted themselves right through the dome. That long tube lying on the ground a few hundred paces away is part of the zeniscope."

"So much for peaceful dialogue. Were any of the people in here rounders?" asked Kaellor.

"Two of them. A woman that was in the back of the room and the first man, a healer of the second order. The others were regular breakers, though. I've seen them at the meetings Venlith charged me with infiltrating."

Several hours later, as they regrouped in the seclusion of Venlith's private offices, Kaellor still smelled a waft of sulfur lingering in his clothes. Collectively, they pieced together what they could make of the umbrals' intrusion into the Sanitorium. Coupled with the warnings from the Cloud Walkers, Volencia's initial break-in, and the reappearance of umbral, they came to a frustrating conclusion: the abrogators had laid claim to the Aarin because he was somehow an anchor for Tarkannen to the world of the living.

Kaellor lightly tapped a fist on the long rectangular table around which they all sat. "Grind it all to the Drift. We were but moments away from stopping Tarkannen and would have placed all of this behind us if not for the meddling of the Lacuna."

"The circle breakers have been busy in your absence," said Venlith. "Rooting them out of the Sanitorium hasn't been easy. Removing their stain from the kingdom will require even more concerted effort, and time. What are your plans moving forward, and how can we assist?"

Kaellor turned to Laryn and struggled to shift his focus to Venlith's question. A smoldering anger occupied his foremost thoughts. Offering him more grace than he felt he deserved, Laryn squeezed his hand. "Kae, eyes to the horizon?"

With an effort, he met her gaze, inhaled once, and released his frustration. "The truth is that we have not spent much time preparing for the next steps. Everything hinged on thwarting Tarkannen here. Once that was done, I thought we could turn our attention to seeking justice against the Lacuna. I made assumptions about the kingdom's stability, but I think that was an error. I suppose we must return to Stone's Grasp with all haste."

"Do the breakers know that you have returned to the kingdom?" asked the docent.

"I suspect so. We encountered a strong force south of here, and Dexxin, our sender, lost control of his gift just before we found you. His siblings are in the Lacuna, so we have reason to believe they are aware of our presence," Kaellor explained.

Dexxin sat at the end of the table, his chin resting on his forearms, staring blankly ahead. Veldrek sat beside him and placed a hand on the sender's shoulder. "Lift your chin, Outrider. The Lacuna knew of your arrival weeks ago. They control a dream auger who forecasted your journey along the west side of the kingdom."

Savnah leaned forward. "Do you know where they hold him? That dream auger is my brother."

"I am sorry, but I do not," said Veldrek. "While I was able to learn many things, the knowledge of your brother's location is a strictly guarded secret."

Savnah sat back in her chair, thumbs tucked into her belt, brooding.

They've wounded each of us in different ways, it seems. And while I've been focused on stopping Tarkannen, we've missed how deeply the Lacuna have embedded their claws.

Kaellor cleared his throat. "Before we discuss returning to Stone's Grasp, I think we need to take this moment and learn everything you can tell us about the Lacuna. Dexxin and Savnah have been helpful. We know about some of their financial leanings, such as the gaming houses and brothels, but I never expected to witness the strength of devotion I saw in the odeum."

Venlith tapped her cane on the floor twice. "Veldrek, I think it's time you made a full accounting of your observations."

The one-eyed healer nodded and described in detail everything he had learned from attending the local meetings. Occasionally, Savnah or Dexxin confirmed or expanded on certain elements of his report. The conversation drifted to recent introductions of new members from the Church of the Giver. Dexxin added his understanding of a possible alignment with the ungifted, who were now, apparently, an organized group in the kingdom.

Venlith spoke at length on her discoveries of the Lacuna's activities in Callinora. It started with the confession of a healer of the second order. The breakers had blackmailed him into procuring reagents required for the refinement of vivith. The docent was in the process of stopping the commercial enterprise when Inasia broke into her home and took her prisoner. When she finished, Veldrek placed a dormant zenith seed on the table.

"We recovered this from Inasia. It's called a zenith seed, though I've not seen its like at any of the meetings," said the healer.

He went on to describe how the zenith seeds worked, concluding with a demonstration. Kaellor watched in fascination as a vacant blue cloud hovered around the seed. The swirling zenith coalesced into the features of a man with narrow angular cheeks and a pointed nose. Shadows and a hood prevented a clear view of his face.

A nasal voice broadcast from the image. "Inasia? Is that you? We've had reports of . . . you're not Inasia. Who are you? How did you come by her zenith seed?"

Veldrek shifted his gaze slightly to Kaellor, who leaned close. The healer held up a hand, indicating he should remain silent. "No, Inasia was captured, my lord. She recruited me to the breakers and asked that I contact you when I could."

"What can you tell me of Callinora? Is it true that the royals are there? Who now controls the Sanitorium?" pressed the voice from the seed.

"Royals, my lord? I don't know what you mean. The Docent Venlith remains in power here. Other than that, I don't know. Armed men, possibly Outriders, stormed the Sanitorium, and utter chaos broke out. There are many of us loyal to the Lacuna who hide in the shadows."

The image of the strange man reappeared when Veldrek stopped talking but remained almost inanimate for a time. Eventually, the nasal voice echoed through the seed. "No . . . I don't think any of that is true. I know Callinora is lost to us, but that is only a minor setback. Are you in the room, Docent? Or perhaps my voice reaches the ears of a Baellentrell even now? I think that is far more likely."

With a furious effort of will, Kaellor resisted his initial impulse to reach into the cloud and strangle the man. Once he leashed his anger, he reached for the zenith seed. "Might I give it a try?"

Veldrek handed the seed to Kaellor, and the integrity of the cloud wavered. "Filter but a tiny fragment of zenith into the seed, but guard against letting much emotion into the channeling, or the draft will claim you," said the healer.

The zenith seed flared brightly, then dimmed as Kaellor labored to bring the image into focus. "This is Kaellor Baellentrell. I've returned with Her Radiance, Laryn Lellendule, to stop a resurgence of the abrogator, Tarkannen. Surely that is a struggle on which we can find common ground?"

The image in the cloud sneered, poorly obscured by the cowl and shadows. "So, the lost prince returns and spouts the same drivel that plunged the kingdom into the Abrogator's War. You had more than twelve years to think of something more original. A disappointment, really. Tell me, how did you manage to evade my friend, Vardell? A gifted guster with a talent for certain toxins."

The zenith cloud expanded with brilliant flows of cerulean blue, but Kaellor allowed the surge to continue unrestricted. "You should not taunt your betters, monk. I ended your assassin and sent him to the Drift, bereft of his gift, but not before he took an innocent life. If you had left us alone, I might never have had cause to return to Aarindorn. I've marked your voice, and my gift has marked your measure. I'm returning to Stone's Grasp, and there is not a force on Karsk that can stop me. You can step aside or be crushed by the full weight of my wrath. Tell your Aspect. I'm coming."

Kaellor stifled the flow of zenith just as a slight wave of dizziness passed. He relaxed back in his chair. "So much for diplomacy. Venlith, do you have the means to communicate with Therek Lefledge? Our return to Stone's Grasp should be coordinated with the regent."

"We are close. My brother is an infuser and loves to tinker. He's been working on a way to enable two-way communication. But as it is, we still rely on messenger pigeons, I'm afraid. The Lacuna never shared the zenith seed concept with us," said the docent.

"I understand. If you could, inform the regent to be watchful for our arrival and warn him against the Lacuna threat," said Kaellor. He turned to Dexxin. "Is your brother still able to relay a message to Therek?"

"Yes, but he remains loyal to the Lacuna, I'm afraid. My sister, Mullayne, might be more reliable, but she's posted with the overwarden at the forward base camp," said Dexxin.

"That's alright. We can only try to advance our truth, son," said Kaellor.

The door to the private office opened, and Reddevek stepped inside. He made a quick survey of the room. "Everything in order then?"

"It's getting there," said Kaellor. "We have yet to secure the rest of Callinora, but the Sanitorium is safe."

"I wouldn't bother looking too hard. On the way here, I passed two large mounted parties. I estimate no less than forty total riding hard to the east," said the warden.

"Are you sure they were with the Lacuna?" asked Kaellor.

"Pretty sure," said Reddevek. "They carried the stink of fear."

"Taker's breath. Well, whether they stop in Midrock or Stone's Grasp, we'll have a reckoning," said Kaellor.

Chapter Thirty-Four: Mingling with the Unsuspecting

Grasdok lumbered out of a cave mouth, the tarnished blade of his axe only dimly glinting in the late setting sun. Several Brognaus warriors wearing ill-fitted amalgamations of armor followed from the shadows, their luminous eyes squinting at the western horizon. The grotvonen interpreter, Eguma, trailed them all. Covered in mushroom spores, he continued to glow like a shambling beacon at the back of a dark train of Brognaus.

"Over here," said Volencia.

The grotvonen chieftain approached and lifted his chin in a savage attempt at a smile. His lower lip drew back enough to blanch, and yellowed, tusk-like teeth erupted from the unsightly, pallid grin. "Brognaus make tunnel. You smooth the path. We get . . . hoomans now?" Grasdok said.

"Yes. There are enough humans gathered in the tent city down the mountain," said Volencia. "I need you to take these sacks of mushroom spores and meet the grondle below Sifter's Valley. Once you gather there, coat the grondle with the dust. Make them glow like Eguma, especially on their heads. The people will think they are ghosts and run up the mountain in fear. Understand?"

The chieftain looked at the large sacks stuffed full of luminescent spores. His face creased up in a pained expression of confusion. "Eguma, explain to him everything I just said."

Her interpreter repeated the instructions, and still, Grasdok struggled to comprehend. "We no be hunting? No be . . . killing?" asked the chieftain.

Volencia turned to Eguma. "All in good time. I don't trust the grondle. The umbral will help lead the herd. But if they smell blood, they will rage and kill too many humans before we collect them into the ravine. They might even kill grotvonen. We can't toss the dead down the chute. All of them, every last one, must arrive in the shaman's chamber alive. We must have a thousand living people to complete the ritual."

She waited for Eguma to finish her explanation, a string of guttural noises, clicks, and occasional hoots flowing from the back of his throat. The lithe grotvonen paused and gestured for her to continue.

"I trust you, Grasdok. I need you to paint the grondle. The people will run away from them in fear. I will lead them up the mountain, they will follow me, and we can drive them into the ravine. Once we have them trapped, the shamans can begin the Rite of Sundering. I need your warriors to wear the glowing spores as well. They can prevent the tide of people from veering off course."

After Eguma finished the explanation, Grasdok looked disappointed. "Chief Grasdok, the Brognaus have excavated a mighty tunnel. All we need to do is see it properly put to use. Once the ritual is complete, you can do what you want with any remaining humans, and I'm quite sure there will be plenty left over. Get to the grondle. It will take you some time to move the herd closer to the tent city. If you find any human hunters or scouts, you have my permission to kill them, but only them. Wait until nightfall; three nights from now should give you enough time, then paint them in the glowing spores. Paint your warriors. Then, when the moon sits just above the mountain, raid the tent city. But save the killing for after the ritual."

When Eguma completed her translation, something resembling resolve played across the chieftain's toothy mug. He turned and gestured several warriors forward. They picked up the sacks and began to march down the mountain. She watched them disappear into the night, the glowing bags of mushroom spores visible for several minutes.

"Eguma, return to the shamans. Tell them that we should have the people situated in four nights. I will lead the humans to the ravine and wait for their signal."

"Yes, missstresss," said Eguma. He turned and loped on all fours into the cave.

Volencia picked her way out of the ravine and down the mountain. The crescent moon cast enough light to find familiar trails, but she made slow progress, only arriving above Sifter's Valley in the predawn hours. Torches flickered as she approached the tent city. The outermost ring had filled with an array of tents and carts shrouded in canvas and tarps of different shades of red.

From one end to the other, she walked in shadows and began to count. More than three hundred different campsites occupied the red tier alone. At least two hundred were set up in the yellow rows, and an equal number in the green. She assumed that most of the dwellings housed more than one person and, after performing a few calculations, released the breath she'd been holding once she felt certain that well over a thousand visitors were attending the festival this year.

A gruff-looking man climbed down from a wagon covered in a weathered canvas with a red patina. She peered over his shoulder to see a modest bed, but otherwise, he kept no company. He walked past her with a nod of his head, presumably to attend to the call of nature.

Your bed is likely as good as any other, and you don't reek like the grot.

The steps to his wagon creaked as she climbed inside. She settled herself on the edge of his small mattress and waited for him to return. The wagon shifted when the man stepped up, and his bearded face popped into view. Though his face remained shadowed, the way his silhouette paused at the threshold betrayed his surprise.

"I couldn't sleep either," she purred. "I thought maybe we could keep each other company?"

"We could at that, I suppose," he said and crawled into the wagon.

He turned to secure the flap of the tent, and Volencia stabbed out with a thin spike of nadir. The onyx barb bored into the back of the man's skull like an ice pick. Gasping in silent agony, the man arched his back in a spasm. The only sound came from the clatter of the knife blade that fell from his hand.

"Tsk tsk. The bard warned me not to mix company with the reds."

After a sharp twist of the spear of nadir, he collapsed backward beside the mattress. A gasping, ragged breath preceded a wordless death sigh, and he was gone.

She allowed the nadir to fester for several minutes, dissolving blood and fluids. Her abrogator's work complete, she dismissed the pick. Her fingers brushed lightly under the bony ridge at the back of his skull, and she could barely feel the defect left behind. She combed his hair back down, threw a blanket over his body, then pulled off her boots and made herself comfortable.

Several hours later, the chatter of people passing by roused her from sleep. Thin shafts of rose-colored light permeated the inside of the wagon. She rolled back the blanket to take one last look at the corpse of the man. There were no visible traces of blood, no bruising from her handiwork. To the average person, he appeared to have died in his sleep and rolled off the side of his mattress.

Just the first of many to come.

After pulling on her boots, she salvaged a pouchful of coins from his jacket. A peek through the front tent flap showed only sparse foot traffic at the outer edge of the red zone. When no one passed by for several minutes, she stepped out and slowly made her way to a thoroughfare that connected the different tiers.

The aromas of baked bread and grilled meat drew her onward. A middle-aged woman in drab burgundy clothing stood behind a makeshift bread stand. A man, most likely her husband, pulled dough into strips and then twisted them into rolls. Two teenage children basted the rolls with oil and herbs, then rotated them through a clever clay oven. The woman parted with three rolls for one of the coins.

A short walk into the yellow neighborhoods, she saw a grizzled man turning the flank of some kind of animal over smoking embers. "Are you selling this morning, good man?" she asked.

He nodded once.

"What are you roasting, and how much can I get for a coin?" she asked and flipped one of the shiny silver discs into the air.

The man deftly caught the coin and placed it in a shirt pocket. "It's not dog and more than enough to fill your belly, I wager." The edge of a cleaver carved a large slice onto a broad leaf. When he slapped the rolled-up parcel into her hand, it weighed more than she expected. A moan escaped her mouth after the first nibble of the burned end.

"It's good," said Volencia.

The abrogator wandered through the vendors, spending the dead man's coin on items she discarded minutes after making the purchase. She had no need of any of it: not the gloves, the extra scarf, the rain-proof cape, or the wool socks. What she enjoyed was the deception, and what she gathered was a sense of the crowd.

The mood of the people in the outer rows seemed aloof, suspicious even. They carried themselves with the kind of hypervigilance born of harsh mountain living. The closer she moved to the center, the more social and engaging people became. More than once, she entered a pleasant conversation with strangers wearing some shade of blue or green.

As the morning unfolded, Volencia became convinced that her earlier approximation of the population had grossly underestimated the family units. While it was impossible to take an accurate census with all the people milling about, the feel of the crowd seemed well over a thousand.

Closer to the King's Respite, a crowd had gathered around an outdoor stage to watch gleemen and jugglers perform. Immediately outside the tavern, the throng of people pressed close enough that she guarded her coin pouch on general principle.

The sound of stomping feet announced her arrival on the stone slab that served as the boardwalk before all of the permanent structures. Volencia kicked a bit of mud from her heels and migrated inside the tavern.

Patrons dressed in a scattered patina of colors packed into Cabe's front room. Gauvin, the bard, sat in his usual corner, piping away on the horned instrument he had played for her weeks before. Volencia found an open seat and ordered two tankards of honey mead. After lubricating the bard with a free drink, she spent a good portion of the day mingling in the company of the unsuspecting, all the while waiting for her unique version of the Winnowing of the Shades to begin.

Chapter Thirty-Five: Perfect Timing

Therek rubbed at his temples, warding off the beginning of a dull ache that seemed to be developing more from the bickering between the two petitioners than out of any legitimate malady.

Jaspen Holling, an affluent vineyard owner from Stellance, thundered on, pacing the hall. "Promises were made, verbal commitments, you see. I would never have invested so much capital without the near guarantee that I could divert but a portion of the upper Stellance River for irrigation."

Sensing a break in the man's bluster, his counterpart, the resource administrator in Stellance, spoke up. Skoon Fepl had proved himself a faithful steward of the office over the years. "As I stated before, there is precedent on this matter. There can be no proprietary ownership of water. I mean . . . it's water, a resource everyone in the kingdom requires and to which all should have reasonable access. And you understate the amount of water you intend on diverting. Your plans call for over ninety percent of the resource to be diverted to your vineyard! This would conveniently lead to the ruination of all your competitors in the region, not to mention the fact that your neighbors would wither from thirst. All while you build up enough resco stores to pickle the kingdom!"

"Administrator Fepl is correct in this matter, Lord Holling," said Therek. "As much as I appreciate the rare bottle of prewar resco, I have to side with the administrator in this case."

"Regent, you can't be serious," whined the aggrieved vineyard owner. He turned to face Therek directly, placed thumb to thumb and forefinger to forefinger, holding the circular gesture over a rather rotund belly, and momentarily sprung his fingers apart. "I was led to believe by mutual friends that the matter had been all but decided. Are you sure that there is nothing I can do to change your mind?"

Therek's fingers clawed around the arms of his chair. The open display of the Lacuna, so brazenly conducted, could be construed as treason against the crown. He considered taking the man to task, understanding all too well that he intended to bribe both him and the resource administrator right there. With deliberate effort, he released one hand and smoothed down his wispy brows. *Giver, grant me peace before I commit myself to ungentlemanly conduct.*

"Lord Holling," said Chancle. "The regent is charged with acting in the interest of the entire kingdom. Were he to ratify your proposal, all of your competitors and the good people of Stellance would surely pack the roster of petitioners for the next month, airing their grievances. As much as we all desire to have the Holling vineyard prosper, the answer at this time is no."

The rotund merchant clicked his tongue and pouted. He stared at Chancle, then Therek, and sensing that neither man intended to alter his position, turned to walk out of the room. He yelled over his shoulder as he left the audience chamber, "Giver's ripe blessings! I'm so glad I made the trip all the way here to partake in the regent's folly!"

Chancle waited for Administrator Fepl to exit, then turned and signaled the corner scribe to cease the recording. The scribe picked up his utensils and made a hasty exit. "Jaspen goes too far, Regent. Shall I have him brought up on charges of insurrection to the kingdom?"

Therek stood, his back stiff and knees aching, stretched, and sighed. "He does make my teeth ache. As I understand it, Lord Holling has overextended his debts. His creditors will no doubt take him to task. Besides, he was the last petitioner of the week. If we take action now, you and I will have to hold an emergency court as all the other offices are on break for the spring assembly at week's end. I don't particularly care to ruin the rest of my day, so let's leave the man to his misery."

Chancle bowed once. "Wise as ever. My agenda grows ever longer. I could use the afternoon to accomplish a few tasks. Have you reviewed the social calendar?"

"I have," said Therek. "I appreciate your diligence."

"There were an unusually large number of requests for private audiences this year," said Chancle. "Are you prepared for the obvious question that will no doubt grace the dinner conversation?"

"I know that some will argue to abandon the monarchy, and I am prepared to speak on the matter, yes."

"I see," said Chancle. "Care to share your thoughts with an old friend?"

Therek released a sigh of resignation. "I think I've waited long enough. I shall make a formal announcement in four nights. Could you have the staff prepare a zeniphone on the front of the outer balcony?"

Chancle tilted his head in agreement. "An address during the gala event? That would make for perfect timing, as most of the members of the assembly have made commitments to attend. Would you prefer to broadcast from the ground floor or up here?"

"The top tier makes sense given the momentous occasion, I think."

"As you wish. Might I suggest you wear a purple suit tailored to the latest fashion? The color would be seen to unify all of the gifted while paying respect to the Church of the Giver."

"I defer to your sense of style, my friend," said Therek.

"Will your children be available? I can have matching formal wear prepared," said Chancle.

"It's possible, but not likely. They are both on assignment with the Outriders."

"Well, best to be prepared. If I might beg your leave, I have a few details to attend to," said Chancle.

Therek waved a hand. "The sooner begun, the sooner done."

He followed the vice regent out of the audience chamber and walked to the Founder's Memorial. The gardener, Fagle Hoff, sat on the edge of the fountain, drying his feet. Clusters of Baellen's eclipse completely covered the surface of the water. The flowers had opened up in the shape of broad bowls with deep lobes. The midnight blue base of the blooms gradually blended to a royal blue color, and light blue accents silhouetted the edges of the petals. Their sweet fragrance permeated the entire garden.

"It looks and smells like your centerpieces are blooming with perfect timing," said Therek. "Your dedication is admirable."

His friend looked up and winked. "If only the Giver saw fit to bless everything in life with that kind of precision, aye?"

Therek walked over and sat on a bench opposite the fountain. "Sometimes it's difficult to see the Giver's hand in the moment, but much later, we often come to appreciate that events unfolded at the appropriate time."

Fagle pursed his lips. "There's a truth. You need to start writing those things down. Maybe get one of those scribes to follow you around and draft a tome called 'Therek's Truisms,' or maybe 'The Regent's Reality.'"

Therek smirked. "My children are the only legacy I care to nurture. I don't need my statements being abused by some future generation when they are removed from all context."

Fagle stomped into his boots. "There is always that concern, I suppose. Leave it to the youth to misquote the old lynx."

The jibe made Therek giggle. "Ahh, you have my thanks, Fagle. I needed that. Before I forget, I wanted to express my gratitude for all the work your people carried out. Our embertang stores remain secure, and the new munitions to fight the grondle threat have already been implemented at the forward staging area."

"Just doing our part," said Fagle. "Nolan and Karra, are they at the staging area?"

"I admit, I'm not certain," said Therek. "Elbiona tries her best to assign them missions of 'strategic safety.'"

"Nolan probably rolls with that just fine, but how does that sit with Karra?" asked the gardener.

"You know Karra. She's her mother's daughter. Sometimes, I think she's marked with an invisible rune of attraction."

"Meaning she attracts trouble?"

"I think 'shit' is the operative word," said Therek. Though he spoke with sarcasm, a warm sensation in his chest blossomed with pride. "Trouble, political intrigue, grotvonen hordes, and grondle attacks all pretty much combine . . ."

Fagle laughed. "Yup, that sounds like the right ingredients for shit pie."

They laughed together, then sat in companionable silence. Eventually, Fagle cleared his throat. "Is everything alright, Therek? Why aren't you in arbitrations?"

Therek flapped a hand. "I'm fine, old man. We canceled petitioners for the rest of the week in anticipation of the spring assembly. Soon enough, my time will be occupied by attending dignitaries with lofty opinions of their accomplishments. And yet, a lot hangs in the balance, so I'll entertain them all. Before it all begins, I thought to touch base with you once more and . . . if I'm honest, it's nice to clear my head."

"I can't imagine," said the gardener. He removed a kerchief and blew his nose. "I have enough trouble trying to get one group of people to march in the same direction. You've done a masterful job holding it all together."

"Thanks, my friend. You'll need to have your people on point during the gala. The fate of the kingdom might depend on their readiness."

"We are, as ever, loyal servants to the kingdom and the old ways," reassured the gardener.

"Do you have the Aspect's trust? Does he suspect where the group's loyalties lie?"

"Not as far as I can tell. I've attended a few closed-door meetings, allowing me to keep up appearances without exposing our members to their poison."

"And so the cards are dealt for the king's gambit," sighed Therek. "Thanks for the reassurances, my friend. I'm going to take a stroll. I'll see you soon enough, though. Your group is slated on the calendar of social commitments a few nights from now. Of all the activities Chancle planned for me, yours, I think, is about the only one I'm looking forward to."

"We'll see you then. I'll be the fella with a blue trumpet flower in my lapel," said Fagle.

"I won't miss it," said Therek.

Therek walked the memorial, allowing his mind to wander. He glanced at the words scrawled in High and Low Aarindorian along the bottom of the monument. He thought briefly of Ksenia and wondered if she had made much progress with the journal of Nivosh.

I'll have to ask her when she returns from the ranch. It will be good to see her parents too. I hope they can make it for the spring assembly.

He departed the memorial and walked outside to the royal plaza. From the cantilevered perch, he cast his gaze down across the castle, the city, and eventually, the kingdom. His hands gripped the smooth stone rail of the balustrade, grounding his thoughts.

Timing really is everything here. Giver, grant me the blessing of your perfect timing. You know the kingdom needs it. I need it.

He stood at the rail contemplating his decisions, both past and present, searching for something to offer him confirmation. A flash of light in the distance, far to the east over the Callinoran skyline, caught his attention. An eruption flared amber and then red. A thin trail of smoke lifted into the heavens. Several seconds later, a soft but resonant thump vibrated in his chest.

"Giver's tears, Venlith. What is it now?" He puzzled over the meaning of the apparent explosion for only a moment before walking briskly back inside. He hailed a page.

"Young lady, tell me you know your way around the castle?" Therek pressed.

"Yes, Your Grace," said the page.

"Good. Find Fagle Hoff, the master gardener. He left the Founder's Memorial only moments ago. Take this message and tell him I require his assistance immediately."

Therek scribbled the letter with uncommon intensity.

Fagle,

Events outpace us. I think I know where the son of Kaellex is. Come to me with all haste. I will meet you with Hestian Lellendule.

Therek.

He folded and sealed the letter with a zenith mark, then handed it to the young woman. "Go and be quick about it. Lives may hang in the balance."

Chapter Thirty-Six: Something Dark Stirs in the East

The rumble from the approaching stampede magnified, and the occasional grunts and squeals of herd animals added to the din. Bryndor shook Ranika awake while Ksenia worked to free the three Callinoran mounts.

She looked over the neck of one of the horses. The creature shuffled and stamped its feet, nostrils flared. "Are you sure you want me to turn them loose? How far is it to safety?" she asked.

"Yes. It will take too long to saddle all three of them, and I think you can each ride a wolvryn."

The woman frowned at him a moment but offered no argument. She slapped the horse on the hindquarter. It trotted off to the west, back toward Callinora. While she untied the other two, Bryndor pulled Ranika by the elbow.

He signaled Neska, and the wolvryn lowered her belly to the ground. "Nika, do exactly as I say, and you'll be fine. Throw a leg over Neska, then lean forward. You have to lie down on top of her. You can't sit her like a horse, or you'll fall off."

The girl brushed an errant sprig of hair from her face. "Like a stick of butter?"

Bryndor couldn't help but smile. "Yes, exactly. Don't be a stick of butter."

Ranika followed his instructions. "You can grab the fur by her neck, but don't touch her ears, or she'll leave you in the dirt. She will take you north. There is an outcropping of rock. We'll meet you there."

When he turned to offer the same instruction to Ksenia, he saw that she stood next to Boru but was holding the last Callinoran mount by the withers. "Can you ride bareback? Because I can."

Bryndor sucked at his teeth. "Not well enough to outrun what's coming. And I think I'm too heavy for Boru. There's no help for it. I'll be running regardless."

She frowned at him. "You sent Ranika on the other wolvryn. They're practically as big as a horse."

"He can ferry me through the clouds, no problem, but I'm not so sure about my weight on the run ahead," said Bryndor. He grabbed his bow and slung his pack over his shoulder.

"Through the clouds?" Ksenia considered him with hooded eyes.

"It's . . . another story. Look, I've got an easy eighty stones on Nika and near that much on you. Pick your mount, horse or wolvryn, and then we need to run."

Ksenia gripped the horse's mane in two fists, and the animal began to trot forward. She jogged alongside, hopped once, tossed a leg up, then began galloping off to the north.

"Moons," muttered Bryndor, more than a little impressed. "You and me, Boru, let's go!"

In the few moments that he'd debated with Ksenia, the sound of the approaching stampede intensified, and the ground trembled. Bryndor strained to see anything from the east. The leading edge of the far horizon rippled, but that was all he could make out in the moonlight.

He charged over the uneven ground. Fear carried him for the first few minutes, but then his arms began to ache. The fatigue started in his shoulders, spread across his chest, and eventually, his thigh muscles began to throb. More than once, he barely avoided stepping in a hole or rolling his ankle on the uneven terrain.

The swelling chorus of the stampede roared in his ears, louder than the thump of his heartbeat. His steps began to falter, and he stumbled but remained on his feet. Fueled only by a desire to reach safety, he pumped his legs, churning through patches of muddy ground interspersed with rocky terrain.

Finally, a dark shadow rose before him. He ran around to the back side of the boulder but found it empty. In the confusion and darkness, he had lost track of Boru as well.

"Neska? Kess?" he barely got the words out through heavy, panting breaths, but no answer came forth. He jumped up and realized there was no reasonable way to climb on top of the smooth rock.

Neska's deep bark echoed from the west, and he turned to see the shadowed figures of the wolvryn and the two women standing well above the grasses.

"Grind me for a grinding monk."

Shaking off a feeling of self-disgust, Bryndor started toward the other rocky outcropping with renewed urgency, but all his muscles were cramping. After thirty steps, he toppled, nose-diving into the mud before rolling once and landing on his ass. The abrupt tumble caused his lungs to seize up, and delicate white stars flared in the periphery of his vision. He struggled back to his feet, managed to gasp a painful breath, and staggered a few steps ahead.

A vestek side-swiped him, and he careened to the side, barely managing to keep his feet, but another ran right up his back, and he toppled forward. The hooves of at least two more struck him with the force of a hammer. He felt the weight of the blows more than any stinging pain.

Some component of the animals' unbridled fear swelled inside his core. Bryndor rose and focused on lifting his knees and continued to slog along. Several vestek sprinted by his side. One bounded over his shoulder, a hoof clipping him behind the ear. The shadow of a much more substantial beast, possibly a bartusk, galloped by, churning up clods of mud that peppered his face.

Grind it. It's already here.

Something massive pulled up alongside him, keeping pace. Bryndor lumbered a few steps to the side to give the large beast passage, but it bodied into him with a growl.

"Boru?" The simple word was all the wind he could accommodate.

The wolvryn sprinted ahead and lay down, belly to the ground. Bryndor stumbled on top of the wolvryn, leaned forward, and grabbed his coarse fur. Boru grunted but surged forward. Grasses slapped Bryndor's face as they sped over the ground. All at once, Boru heaved, and Bryndor felt his stomach lurch. Then they came to a stop on top of the safety of the rocks. Bryndor rolled off the wolvryn to his back, muscles spasming and an achy fatigue threatening to cause his chest to burst.

The raging sounds of the stampede rose to a crescendo as herd animals flowed around their perch in pandemonium. He lay there for several minutes, allowing his breath to recover. The air took on a musty quality of freshly churned soil and wild animal.

Boru licked him on the face and several times behind the ear. A stinging sensation blossomed from his scalp where the vestek had grazed him. Probing the area with his fingertips, he discovered a deep cut underneath his hair.

They lay there listening to the throng of creatures flowing around the stones that offered the only succor. Eventually, he sat up and wrapped his arms around his knees. The initial deafening wave of beasts had thundered past. The sounds of smaller groups of herd animals seemed to trot by with less intensity and more mewling.

"Lutney's dice, that was close, Bryn," exclaimed Ranika. "I haven't seen so many animals up close like that ever. Not even in the Borderlands."

"That was more than a half-mile, Brynd—Your Grace. Are you alright?" asked Ksenia.

Bryndor let his chin rest on his chest. "Yes. But first, please, a small kindness? Drop the grace talk. I don't . . . wear it well. And second, I don't suppose either of you has a spare cloth? I have a cut I need to hold pressure to."

"Roll over then, let me see," said Ksenia. He felt too tired to resist her suggestion and turned, realizing for the first time that perhaps he had suffered more injuries than he was initially aware. A warm hand probed under his shirt, causing stinging pains in several places.

"You're either covered in mud or blood or both. I can't see. Give me a moment. I have some things in my pack," said Ksenia.

A rasping sound scraped into the night air once, twice, and on the third strike, light flared across the rocks. "Ranika, I need you to hold this overhead. It's one of my brother's old Outrider torches. It sheds light but no heat. It should last about fifteen minutes."

Lying prone on the cold stone, Bryndor felt his strength leech away. The simple act of breathing started to trigger pain in the muscles of his back. His left cheek numbed against the stone, so he turned his head to the other side. The torchlight reflected off the eyes of hundreds of animals as they ran past.

An involuntary grunt of pain escaped his lips when Ksenia probed his shoulder blade. "Sorry. How does it look?" he asked.

"Not bad, but not so good," said Ksenia. "I'm no medic. I don't feel any broken bones, but the bruises you have here are—"

"Mogdure's bite, Bryn. What happened out there?" asked Ranika.

Bryndor sighed, trying to stave off a surging feeling of self-recrimination. "Just . . . alright, listen. Is anything bleeding? Are there any wounds that need to be cleaned?"

If there is a Giver, please let me avoid anything like the infection Llu suffered.

"No, nothing like that. Just the cut behind your ear," said Ksenia. "But your entire back looks like Ms. Della's mulberry cobbler."

"Good. That's good," he said. His mind drifted for a moment, awash with relief.

"Have you got anything to clean the cut with?" asked Ksenia.

"No, just a canteen of water," said Bryndor. "I didn't bother packing anything like that. Aunt Laryn is a gifted healer."

"I have a small amount of embertang. I can dilute it, but we won't be able to drink any of the water afterward, and it will likely ruin your canteen," said Ksenia.

"I suppose it's no less than I deserve for running to the wrong pile of rock," he mumbled.

He stared at the animals meandering nearby. Most still trotted by, but in the distance, others gazed back at the torchlight without blinking, their irises flaring yellow and red in the darkness.

"This might sting a bit. Are you ready?" asked Ksenia.

He inhaled a deep breath and tucked his chin once to expose the skin behind his ear. "Ready."

He felt too exhausted to clench up, but sweat beaded on his brow from the pain as Ksenia doused the wound, picked at debris, and rinsed it again. The embertang burned like a hot poker for several minutes. But the dilution must have made a difference because the pain ebbed and became tolerable. Eventually, it felt like she was tugging at his hair.

"It feels like you're tying my hair in knots," said Bryndor.

"That's because I am," said Ksenia. "I'm not a medic and have nothing to stitch you back together, but the cut is straight. I'm braiding the hair from both sides of the wound to hold it closed. I've seen my mother do this several times for my brothers."

He felt one last gentle pull before the warmth of her hand settled on the side of his neck. Her touch, at once sincere and intimate, distracted him from any pain, if only for the moment.

"Give me a moment to clean away the dried blood," she said. He barely registered the words as she rubbed the cloth over the side and back of his neck.

"That will have to do until we rejoin your aunt."

"I'm sure it will heal better than most I've had over the years," said Bryndor.

Pushing through the fatigue, he rose to all fours and crawled closer to Boru, placing his face against the wolvryn's cheek. They remained pressed together for a moment. "Thank you again, my friend."

The myriad of welts and bruises began to throb, and he found lying on the cold rock preferable to anything else. After situating his pack as a pillow, he tried to find something resembling a comfortable position.

"I'm going to have a look around," said Ranika.

Bryndor raised a hand in acknowledgment. "I don't fancy explaining to Reddevek how two of us got trampled. Stay up here where it's safe, if you would."

"I will," she said. As the girl walked the perimeter of the rock formation, the halo of light faded, and the entire panorama of the night sky appeared.

"Ksenia, what would make all of these animals flee in the night?" asked Bryndor.

"I was just asking myself the same question," said Ksenia. "There isn't a predator in these parts capable of driving that many different herd animals."

"That's some good news, at least," he said.

Dancing light accompanied the rapid skip of Ranika's footsteps as she sped back across the rock.

"Ksenia, did you say the horse you left behind was white?" asked Ranika.

"Yes, why do you ask?"

"Because there's a white mare standing off the far edge of these rocks."

Ksenia's face lost all expression, and she stared into the darkness. Her eyes glistened.

"Is it her?" asked Ranika.

Ksenia gently tipped her chin up and down but pressed her fingertips to her mouth in pensive silence. After several minutes, she blinked away tears and wiped a stuffy nose on her sleeve. Her posture stiffened, then she bent to retrieve her pack.

"There's help nearby. I'm going to ride Winter, but I'll be right back. I don't have any more torches, but I think I can find you."

Ranika tossed the remnant of the torch to the ground as it sputtered out, then removed something from inside her coat. A faint light shimmered in the palm of her hand, growing in intensity.

"What is that?" asked Ksenia.

"It's a moonstone. It won't glow as bright as the torch, but it will last all night. I'll keep it out so you can find us," said Ranika.

"Where are you going?" asked Bryndor.

"The entire herd of Aarindin are at the back of . . . whatever all of this is." She lifted a hand, gesturing at the roaming animals. "Something dark stirs in the east, back near the ranch. Something that set all of these animals running out of fear."

A graceful, muscular white horse trotted by. Ksenia squatted, then hopped onto Winter's back. She leaned forward and embraced the Aarindin around the neck.

"Did she tell you what they were running from?" asked Bryndor.

"I have a sense for something strange . . . I don't understand it, not yet anyway. But there is someone out there who might know," said Ksenia. The woman turned with an oddly severe expression. "My mother."

Chapter Thirty-Seven: Releasing the Reins

"**G**iver's last tear, Winter. I thought I lost you forever." Hot tears streamed across her cheeks as Ksenia leaned forward and embraced Winter's neck. She remained there, draped across the mare's withers, despite bumping into other animals and even other Aarindin.

"The bad man took my strength. I felt weak, like a newborn foal, but I made it home."

"The bad man can't hurt you anymore. He's dead. Winter, why are the Aarindin out here? Why are all these animals running in fear?"

"The night split open, and death spilled on the ground. All of us, every creature on the plains, could sense it." As Winter tried to express the phenomenon, broken images of a dark fissure jumbled together with other senses. For the first time in Ksenia's recollection, the Aarindin's communication was laced with the sensations of bitter cold and the unmistakable scent of decay.

As Winter struggled to convey the memory, Ksenia sensed they were wandering aimlessly in the tide of animals, carried west by the pressure of the group.

"Winter, focus on me. You said my mother is out here. Can you take me to her?" asked Ksenia.

Winter lifted her head and tightened her grip. *"Yes. It will be difficult. Keep your legs high."*

The Aarindin nudged her way to the side and broke loose from the pack. She circled wide and began to trot back to the east against the current of migrating animals. In just moments, they encountered another surge of frantic beasts migrating west, away from the direction of the

Balladuren ranch. The throng proved too much, and they turned for a time, navigating once again within the surging tide of animals.

Winter's familiar grip grounded Ksenia in the tussle and flow. The Aarindin staggered, hopped, trotted, and veered in different directions, all at the whim of the wild rush. Most of the animals they bumped into bounced off Winter's flank. Occasionally, a bartusk or another Aarindin ran alongside them, and Winter struggled to veer to the side.

Every time they abruptly altered pace or direction, Ksenia felt thankful for their intimate connection. Though she held her gift open to conversation, Winter remained preoccupied with moving them to safety. Slowly, they moved out of the main host and back to the perimeter with room enough to wheel about in an attempt to travel east.

In the commotion, Ksenia thought she had lost track of the perch on which Bryndor recovered. But within a few minutes of travel, Ranika's moonstone glimmered to the northeast. The young woman's silhouette was entrancing in the soft, shimmering light.

Winter's thoughts disrupted her fascination with the distant light. *"We have to skirt the trees. Lean forward and guard your head."*

Ksenia knew not to argue and bent forward with one arm over her head. Without direction, Winter regripped her, making the travel a surprisingly comfortable affair. Ksenia sensed the Aarindin gallop up and down several hills and bound over a stream. Then, Winter loosened the grip at last, and they fell into an easy canter.

"Your mother is there, at the top of this hill."

Ksenia stared ahead through the moonlight, waiting for the outline of her mother to appear. It wasn't until Winter slowed to a walk some ten paces away that she made out her mother's face. Before she knew it, all her months of anger sheared away, displaced by an intense feeling of safety she hadn't felt for days. "Mother!"

"Oh, breath of the Giver. You found her. Good girl, Winter, I knew you could do it," said Madola.

Without words, Ksenia and her mother hopped down and embraced. They stood long moments, and eventually, a few stray Aarindin wandered up the hillside.

"Did you cause that stampede?" asked Ksenia.

"No. I've never seen anything like it," said Madola. "And it wasn't just the Aarindin. There's vestek, Bartusk, wolves . . . you name it. If it can leap, run, or fly, it lit out of here like the Taker himself was giving chase."

"Did you send Winter after me? How did you find me in all of that?"

"Winter made it home and told your father and me about the men that chased you in the highlands. Your father and I were just getting ready to come look for you when I swear something from the Drift spilled out from a tear in the sky. It spooked the entire herd. I barely managed to maintain a connection to Winter. She challenged my arca prime to be sure. But then I realized she was running west in part out of fear and in part because she found your scent on the wind."

"In all of that and so far away? How is that possible?" asked Ksniea.

"Winter night's asylum. You're wearing the fragrance, and it's a good thing too. I'm not sure she would have found you otherwise."

Her mother pulled her in for another tight embrace and kissed her on the top of the head. "Come on, let's mount up and get home. Then you can tell your father and me all about this trip of yours into the highlands."

"Wait, I can't; we can't. I left someone important back there. You're never going to believe me when I tell you who it is."

"Unless it's the king of Aarindorn returning to claim his throne, I don't think we can chance it," said Madola.

"Well . . . I suppose it could actually be just that."

Madola scoffed and gestured for her Aarindin to kneel, allowing her to mount up.

"Mother . . . Mom . . . Madie Balladuren, stop," said Ksenia.

Madola walked her Aarindin around in a slow circle to face her daughter. "Child, there've been enough strange things going on tonight without you making a jape. Speak to me the Giver's truth and nothing more."

Ksenia swallowed. "I was rescued by none other than Bryndorllean Baellentrell and the warden, Reddevek. The warden rides to check on the rest of the royals in Callinora. I left the prince and his friend to come find you."

Madola's head cocked back as if struck by a fell wind. "The prince of Aarindorn, the heir to the throne, and you left him back there in all that?"

"They are safe, resting on top of a cluster of rocks. But he's injured . . . a little, and he's runeless, so we might need the wagon," said Ksenia.

Madola sat unblinking, staring out into the night. "How bad are his injuries, and what of his friend? Are they both injured?"

"Not bad. Bruises and cuts, and Ranika, his friend, she's fine."

Iridescent blue light danced across Madola's arca prime, and all the Aarindin, even Winter, perked their ears and stood at attention. "Winter thinks she can get us back there and that the girl is holding some kind of light. That will help, but it will be slow going."

Ksenia threw a leg over Winter's back and situated her hips before the grip took effect. Madola led the way back to the west, toward Bryndor and Ranika. As they traveled, her mother attracted more and more Aarindin, using them like a protective circle of calm tranquility among the wild herds. In just a few minutes, no fewer than twenty Aarindin walked around them, entranced by Madola's gift. As they traveled, more and more Aarindin wandered out of the shadows to walk with the group.

"So, tell me what you were doing in the highlands in the first place, and who were those men?" asked Madola.

"Rugen and I discovered that the Lacuna bought a tract of land in the Great Crown. It was a strange acquisition and too close to the ranch to be a coincidence, so he sent me out to scout around before I came home for a visit. Only, somehow, they learned about what I was doing and tried to stop me."

A few of the adjacent Aarindin grunted and nickered in annoyance. "There's a lot more to that story that needs a proper telling. How do a subcaptain in the city watch and a scribe in service to the regent get mixed up in all of that?" asked Madola.

Whether it was the comfort of sitting gripped on Winter or riding in the security of her mother and more than twenty entranced Aarindin, Ksenia told her mother everything. She began with Craxton's introduction to the Lacuna, the meetings she attended, and Karragin's use of Tacit to relay a secret message. She left nothing out, not even her betrayal of the regent's trust in divulging the return of the royals to Aarindorn, knowing full well that the information would be passed on to the Lacuna.

As they rode, she continued her explanation, describing her work for the regent and subsequent discovery of the properties held by the Lacuna, including the tract of land in the highlands. The words tumbled out, a welcome confessional to the last person she thought she would ever trust.

At last, she came to the end of the adventure, culminating with her introduction to the wolvryn and their escape to the rocks just before the stampede. They rode in companionable silence, the light from Ranika's moonstone shimmering in a slow wave in the distance.

"Mother, you haven't said much. If you need, I can help pacify some of the Aarindin," said Ksenia.

"I'm fine, Kess," said Madola, but she sounded exhausted.

"You don't sound fine. Why don't you let me help before you slip into the draft?" Ksenia nudged Winter a few paces ahead to keep pace and make eye contact with her mother. Tears brimmed Madola's eyes, and the woman blinked in frustration.

"I know, Mom . . . it's a lot," said Ksenia. "Had I known what I was getting into, I never would have joined them. I am so . . . sorry," said Ksenia.

"Oh, child. You don't owe anyone an apology. It was me. I knew that I pulled your reins, making you wander paths you would not choose for yourself. And I can see now how alone you were in the capital. It makes sense. The Lacuna made you feel welcome when others did not. Giver bless your father for putting up with me . . . I did the same thing to Rugen, but in different ways, and steered you both right into their web."

Ksenia felt weightless astride Winter, numb even, and for a time lost herself in the humble honesty of her mother's words. Eventually, with Ranika's moonstone casting a clear halo around the rocky perch, Ksenia found her voice again. "Thank you for sending Winter to find me."

Madola turned her face full into the moonlight, wet stains visible on her neckline and shoulders. She held out a hand, and Ksenia grabbed it. "No more small words. Not after everything you've been through. Moons, but it's hard to let go, Kess. Can you forgive me for not seeing that sooner?"

"I love you, Mom. I'll keep my eyes to the horizon if you promise to do the same."

Madola sat upright on her mount. "I can do that. Now, let's see to our young prince."

Madola guided the herd of Aarindin, now a group of over forty, to surround the rocky outcropping.

Ranika walked to the edge of their perch, holding her moonstone over her head. The intensity of the light it released seemed brighter than before. Bryndor rose with slow purpose and limped over to stand beside her, picking his steps carefully.

Madola stared at them both, and an awkward silence drew out. The prince, appearing more than exhausted, swallowed once and brushed hair back from his face where the wavering light from Ranika's moonstone cast cool shadows. "Ksenia, is this your mother?"

Madola leaned forward on her Aarindin and studied his face, then seemed to accept something about the young man's bearing before sitting back into a relaxed position.

"Is everything alright?" asked Bryndor.

"Yes, forgive me, Your Grace. You're not what I expected, but there's no doubt about you being Japheth's son, with a touch of your mother about the eyes," said Madola.

"You knew my parents, then?" asked Bryndor.

"I did, and I would be happy to tell you all about it, but why don't we see to you and your friend here first?" said Madola. "We don't keep horses or saddles. I'm afraid you'll have to ride one with each of us."

Without waiting for further instruction, Ranika knelt slightly, then hopped onto the back of Madola's Aarindin. "It's better this way, Bryn," said Ranika. "Otherwise, you'll slide off like butter."

Bryndor nodded his understanding. "It seems I'm in need of an escort. Would you mind if I . . . ?" He gestured to Winter.

"Not at all; one moment," said Ksenia. She directed Winter to stop beside the rocky perch, allowing Bryndor to drop down behind her.

She waited for him to place his hands around her waist, but the prince maintained a polite distance.

Ksenia spoke to him over her shoulder. "Bryndor, slide close to me. Winter's grip will hold us fast." She reached behind and slapped his thigh, encouraging him to slide closer. Then she grabbed each of his wrists and pulled his calloused hands forward. She made him interlock his fingers around her abdomen. Eventually, he shifted his weight forward, his contact warming her back, hips, and legs.

"Thanks," he stammered.

"Just hold on. I won't let her run, but I can't be known as the woman who dropped the heir to the throne. Giver knows I've got enough to deal with in Stone's Grasp as it is."

He offered no response, but the weight of his forehead rested on the top of her shoulder. After a few paces, he muttered, "I'm sorry. I feel like someone went at me with a hammer and tongs. I just need a moment to let the muscles in my back relax."

"It's no bother and the least I can do after everything you've done for me. Just hold on. We'll get you home," she said.

They rode in silence but for his occasional gasps of pain. Thinking to ease his burden, she channeled into her sympath rune. *"Winter, have you the means to grip Bryndor?"*

"Yes. I can do it, but something about him keeps me from making the grip."

"What do you mean?" asked Ksenia.

"I can sense where our bond should be, but it's slippery. Like trotting over ice. Should I keep trying to grip him?"

Ksenia puzzled over her words. *"No. Focus on your footing and a smooth walk. I'll mind the prince."*

They continued on amid the Aarindin herd, through the predawn shadows, and back to the Balladuren ranch.

Chapter Thirty-Eight: Searching for the Source

Karragin shifted her weight astride an Aarindin. Since her introduction to Trinney, the spirited filly, the relationship had proved more tedious than she cared for. In usual fashion, she had employed her sympath gift but now regretted their connection. The restless three-year-old craned her neck to make eye contact every few minutes. The last three hours had proved an exercise in tedium as the filly invited random conversation.

Ksenia pulled alongside her, riding Winter. "How are you two getting along?"

"She's a chatterbox," said Karragin. "Smarter than most, but more needy than Tacit."

"Give her a few days. I worked with her a fair bit last year. She's eager to please and more balanced in temperament than most. I'll bet she grips you by week's end. If it doesn't work out, Tacit is in the royal stables at Stone's Grasp."

Karragin watched as Ksenia's mother, a middle-aged sympath, paced back and forth across a pasture. Now and again, the woman turned to commune with the Aarindin that walked behind them. "Your mother seems driven to find answers this morning. How is it with you two?" asked Karragin.

Ksenia sat idle, but Winter pawed once at the ground. Since their collective reunion the previous day, Madola Balladuren, the matriarch of the entire family, seemed preoccupied. She had spent the last night managing angry tears upon learning how much danger three of her children had experienced at the hands of the Lacuna.

The previous night, the entire group, Kaellor and the royals, the mixed company of Outriders, and the Balladuren clan had gathered around Ksenia's family table. Ksenia led the conversation, answering questions about her recruitment and experiences with the Lacuna. The discussion naturally led to her work for the regent and the discovery of the unusual tract of land purchased in the Great Crown.

Bryndor and Reddevek contributed to those parts of the tale, and then the attention shifted. The group that had ventured into Callinora shared all that they encountered. By the time they retired for the evening, it was well past midnight.

When her daughter had revealed all of the details of the past months, Madola Balladuren sat in silent acceptance. This morning, with the return of the entire Aarindin herd, the woman appeared driven by purpose.

Most families clustered certain gifts, and with the Balladurens, the sympath trait ran strong, but in none more so than Madola. From what Karragin surmised, it was her arca prime, and the woman took it upon herself to interview more than half the herd to discover the source of the stampede several nights ago.

Ksenia reached for her wrist but rubbed warmth along her forearm in a comforting gesture. "It's better than I imagined with Mother. I never expected her to apologize. She worked to keep me from the Outriders out of fear for my safety, but now that she's learned about everything that happened this past week . . . well, I'll be surprised if she doesn't try to convince me to relinquish my post with your father."

"Parents, right?" said Karragin. "Still. Don't be too hard on her. I would give a lot to have my mother around to berate Nolan once in a while."

"Just Nolan?" asked Ksenia. Karragin offered her a half-smile.

A moment later, Madola's Aarindin knelt, allowing the woman to mount up. The breeze swept wispy grey hair across her face. "Whatever caused the disturbance, it's not here. Let's check the valley to the east."

They trailed behind her as Madola trotted up the next hill. From a tree line to the north, Nolan and Lluthean emerged, each riding Aarindin. The wolvryn, Neska, loped alongside them, keeping an easy pace. Nolan rode with the comfort of a gripped Outrider, and somehow Lluthean managed to ride bareback, appearing just as capable.

"Huh," grunted Karragin.

"What?" asked Ksenia.

"The prince . . . I thought I had him figured out, but he continues to surprise me, I guess."

"Which one and how so?" asked Ksenia.

"Lluthean, and it's lots of little things, I suppose. For starters, he rode a horse and saddle all the way here but now sits an Aarindin almost like he was born to it."

"Well, he sort of was, right? I mean, born to it?" asked Ksenia.

"Technically, that's correct. But he's basically like a runeless, cut off from his gift," said Karragin.

"Bryndor is the same. Winter could sense something about his gift when we rode here, but she couldn't grip him, though she tried."

Karragin sucked at her upper lip, tonguing the scar. "He and his brother, that whole family really, they have a different . . . skill set from any of the nobles I know. You can tell they're no strangers to hard living."

Ksenia nodded in agreement. "I got a sense of that too. When the Lacuna attacked us in the highlands, Bryn seemed composed, I guess? Like he was no stranger to surviving conflict."

"It probably didn't hurt to have two wolvryn at his side and the warden along for the ride."

"No . . . it was more than that," said Ksenia. "When the Leech's men approached, we hid in ambush, and the entire time, Bryndor whispered his observations about the hunters, weighing their strengths and weaknesses. When he finally shot one of them, it was the one most likely to give Reddevek a difficult time."

"That sounds like something your average prime would do," said Karragin.

"Right, except . . ."

Karragin conceded her point. "Except none of them has had Outrider training. It makes me wonder what life has been like for them all these years."

"Whatever shaped them, it's nice to meet a group unspoiled by the games in Stone's Grasp," said Ksenia.

Karragin considered her words, letting the silence draw out an explanation.

"I mean, it's like . . . everyone in Stone's Grasp identifies me either by my family ties or my gift. With Bryn, he just treated me like an equal. I didn't even know he was the prince until hours after our initial conversation, and by then, I had pretty much told him my life story."

Karragin noted her friend's use of the prince's common name and sighed. "Neither one of them cares for the titles or the honorifics. My brother loves that about all of them and can't wait to see how the Aarindorian nobles might react. But the political games in Stone's Grasp can become a grind fest if they arrive unprepared."

"That's the Giver's truth," said Ksenia.

Nolan pulled up beside Ksenia, and Lluthean managed to remain seated as his Aarindin fell in beside Karragin. The prince massaged his thigh muscles but made no complaint. "Any luck?" he asked.

"Not yet, but this last valley is the only part of the ranch we've yet to search," said Ksenia. "What brings you two out?"

"Why, mischief and mayhem, of course," said Lluthean.

Karragin felt her cheeks tighten but resisted the smile. It was good to see Nolan with a friend, but she hoped neither man would contribute to the delinquency of the other.

Nolan cleared his throat. "Kaellor returned with Reddevek and the others a while back. They found the dead Lacuna and backtracked until they found what was left of the men killed by the cave larks."

"Did they learn anything new?" asked Karragin.

"Sure," said Lluthean. "Don't mess with a sympath."

That comment did provoke a bark of laughter from all of them.

"How is Bryndor this morning?" asked Ksenia.

"I think Laryn's got him sorted out," said Lluthean. "When we rode by, he was teaching Ranika how to draw the bow."

They walked their mounts in slow pursuit of Madola. Something in the wind must have caught Neska's attention because the wolvryn loped ahead. They arrived to find the Balladuren matriarch walking around the perimeter of what appeared to be a sixty-foot-long section of scorched grass. The aberration silenced their casual conversation.

"Lluthean, would you mind sending Neska on a perimeter patrol? Just to be safe," said Karragin.

The prince shrugged and dismounted. He signaled the wolvryn to come, but she remained distant, and he sighed. "She's not too happy with me for leaving her behind when we entered Callinora. Give me a moment."

He took a knee, and Neska sauntered forward, licked him once on the forehead, then loped off over the hill.

The Aarindin tossed their heads and appeared reluctant to approach. They each dismounted and joined Madola. "This is it. Whatever made this caused the panic that started the stampede. But the images I saw looked different," mumbled the woman.

"Winter said something split open, and the smell of death fell on the ground," said Ksenia.

"Most of the Aarindin I interviewed gave me . . . frantic images," said Madola. "But all of them gave me the impression that something cracked open, like a fissure in the sky. None of them made reference to this."

Karragin noticed that the ground wasn't so much burned as wilted. Set in the shape of a giant wedge, the grasses and weeds folded over, leaning away from the narrow point of origin. "This has the look of a directional munition; only the ground would be scorched, and a blast this long would leave a crater at the point of origin. Nolan, can you make any sense of this?"

Her brother walked around the area, frowning in concentration. He stopped at the narrow end of the pattern. "There's no hint of alchemics or munitions. I don't sense a poison, either. You're right, though. The way everything bends away makes it look like something blasted out from here."

"The umbral in Callinora channeled currents of nadir. Could they do something like this?" asked Lluthean.

"I don't know," said Karragin. "The few times we've encountered an umbral, the nadir strike dissolved its target. Even stone seemed to melt away. This looks more like something . . . wilted everything."

Madola leaned down and pulled a few blackened samples, placing them into a leather satchel. "They have the same feel as plants after a hard frost. Do you know of anything capable of that?"

Karragin tongued the scar on her upper lip. "No. At least, nothing in my experience. Anyone else?"

She waited for a response, but everyone stared, fascinated, at the blackened ground.

"Taker's bite. This leaves us with more questions than answers," said Madola. "Even if this was an explosion, why would it cause such an extensive stampede? So many different animals . . . you would think they were running from a massive forest fire. It makes no sense."

Neska returned from her patrol, tail wagging. Lluthean signed, and she cocked her head as if considering him a moment but eventually walked forward. He stood beside her, hands buried in the fur at the back of her neck, and lost himself to the trance of her senses for a moment. He looked up. "The warden is riding this way, but there's nothing else that seems unusual."

Reddevek was tracking the Lacuna that escaped Callinora. Something must have happened for him to return so soon.

A few minutes later, Reddevek brought Zippy to a stop near the other Aarindin. His gaze fell across the blackened ground, but his expression remained unreadable. "Everyone mount up. Rugen Balladuren has returned from Stone's Grasp with more news of the Lacuna."

Madola set a brisk pace as they rode back. Rugen Balladuren stood on the expansive wraparound front porch, leaning against a stout post. His mother dismounted with the agility of an Outrider and pounded up the steps to stand before him. She slapped him twice across the same cheek, then gripped the front of his shirt and pulled him into an embrace.

"I know, Mother. I'm sorry. Believe me, I'm sorry. For all of it. For leaving, and for getting Kervin and Ksenia involved," said Rugen. He studied his feet until Madola placed a finger under his chin.

She wiped tears from her cheeks and stepped back, studying her oldest son. Her tone softened. "The man I raised might accidentally wade knee-deep into the mud, but he'll also find a way out before it gets any deeper. Tell me you've found a way out of the muck."

"I've got some ideas, but you won't like parts of it. Come inside. We've got a lot of things to discuss."

Chapter Thirty-Nine: Beyond Suspicion

"Nearly all of them were killed, run down by the stampede, near as I can tell," said Reddevek.

Kaellor struggled to imagine a wave of wild animals so vast as to overrun more than thirty mounted riders. Something about the timing of the umbrals' intervention at Callinora and now the strange stampede left him unsettled.

We're missing something. Giver grant me the wisdom to see it.

"All of the riders from Callinora? I can't say that's an injustice, but by the moons, have you ever heard of such a thing?" he asked.

When nobody answered, he cast his gaze around the table, studying the faces of his family and his fellow Aarindorians. Elbend and Madola Balladuren bookended their children, Rugen and Ksenia. All four wore sober expressions, but none of them avoided eye contact.

Laryn and his nephews sat mingled among the Outriders. None of them offered an explanation. At last, Ranika, of all people, spoke up. The girl sat in the corner, pulling her fingers through Boru's fur. As she spoke, she frowned, concentrating on removing a burr from the wolvryn's coat.

"I once saw thousands of rats fill a street in Callish. Smugglers had caused some kind of accident, an explosion in the sewers. The rats flowed through the street like a wild river. In turn, people, horses, and mules ran to escape the tide. When it was all done, more than six people were dead."

She plucked out the offending burr and set it on the table. "And that was just rats. The stampede was all sorts of big animals. It doesn't take much imagination to see how a whole ocean of them could trample a group of people."

"Thanks, Nika. Your point is well made. I just wish we knew how it all started or why. If we could question any of the Lacuna, we could learn something of what they saw that night," said Kaellor.

"It's possible a few escaped," said Reddevek. "But they're in Midrock or beyond by now."

"Might I make a suggestion?" asked Laryn.

"Please," said Kaellor.

"Whatever caused the stampede, be it the Giver's blessing or the Taker's grip, we won't have the answers today. We need to set that aside and focus on the two problems before us: Tarkannen and the Lacuna. We know that Tarkannen has a foothold in this world. It's why Elder Miljin sent us back. We can mount our best defense against his return from Stone's Grasp. For now, let's focus on how we will return home with the Lacuna embedded throughout the kingdom."

Kaellor sensed Madola shift in her seat with unease before she cleared her throat. "Laryn is right. We'll keep an eye out in the valley for any other disturbances, but maybe we aren't meant to know what caused it all—not today, anyway."

"Of course, I appreciate the counsel, and I agree," said Kaellor. "Dexxin, have your conversations with your siblings revealed anything that might help us understand the Lacuna's plans?"

The sender blushed but held his chin up. "No, Your Grace. It feels like Mullayne wants to tell me more, but I can tell that she and Craxton are holding back. I don't think they trust me right now."

"I understand, and I appreciate your honesty, son," said Kaellor. "Rugen, if I understand your theory correctly, the Lacuna purchased a strategic tract of land in the Great Crown in an attempt to control the water rights to all the rivers that supply this valley, the surrounding fields, and the ranch, right?"

"Yes. And in a similar fashion, they carry influence with many of the trade guilds and several other . . . disreputable revenue streams," said Rugen.

"Do they know you are here? Will they miss you?" asked Madola.

"Not likely. I was on my way to Dulesque, and this is only a small diversion. I'm charged with organizing an expedition to see if there is a direct route over the Great Crown to Faltusch. The Aspect plans to establish a trade alliance with the border kingdom and hopes to find a more efficient passage."

"It doesn't sound like the Lacuna are a martial force. While I fully understand that we will have to deal with them, are they in any position to prevent us from returning to Stone's Grasp?" asked Kaellor.

"Possibly," said Rugen. "They have the ear of a good number among the city watch. While many of their members reside outside of Stone's Grasp, who can say how many of the visitors for the spring assembly hold allegiance to the Lacuna?"

"Don't we have to assume that they will try to prevent us from returning?" asked Lluthean.

Kaellor turned to his nephew. "We do, but can you tell us why?"

"Well, from what Ksenia has said, the Lacuna know we are in Aarindorn. Between those zenith seed things, Savnah's brother, and Dexxin's siblings, there's no way that they didn't know we were in Callinora, and they must assume that we plan to make a return. The spring assembly seems like the logical time," said Lluthean.

Bryndor nodded in agreement. "But it's more than that. We arrested their agent in Callinora and restored Venlith's control there. Then, though it's no fault of ours, fifty or sixty of their members were killed during the stampede. They'll have to assume that was us and prepare a force of equal size, right? I mean . . . it's what I would be worried about if I were this Aspect fella."

Kaellor rubbed a knuckle against his bearded chin. Under the table, Laryn squeezed his hand, an echo of the pride he felt. "Your observations are spot on. We need to make the Lacuna think that we are approaching from the main gates facing south."

He stood and placed his palms on the table, then lifted his head, making eye contact with each of them. "I'll not ask any of you to do this lightly, and I'll understand if you decline. So consider my proposal carefully. There's no shame in refusing."

Zenith infused Kaellor's runes of judgment and perception. Something about the proposal felt right, and he stood up straight to address the room. "All we need is time to get inside Stone's Grasp. If we can make it into the inner sanctum, I'm pretty sure I can activate the castle defenses. They will only attune to a Baellentrell while the blue moon is dominant. To that end, we need a distraction."

He shifted his gaze to his friend, the warden. Reddevek listened intently, both eyes fixed on Kaellor's. "Reddevek, I would like to send you and Karragin in disguise, posing as Laryn and me. Tovnik and Nolan could potentially dress as Bryndor and Lluthean. The other Outriders could be your escort. If you arrive robed and hooded but surrounded by Aarindin, you'll either be mistaken for our party or allowed inside. If they mistake you for us, you will have a fight on your hands, and I won't be there to shield you. But even if you flee on the Aarindin, the diversion could be just the thing we need to slip inside unnoticed."

"Whether I'm to ride in disguise or as an Outrider escort, I will go," said Savnah. "The Lacuna have been pulling my strings for years. It's time I yank them back."

Dexxin nodded in agreement. "What I've seen in the last few weeks makes the politics of Stone's Grasp seem like fishing for minnows: all scales and no fillet. If getting you inside helps us prevent Tarkannen's return, count me in as well."

Kaellor's runes thrummed lightly, confirming the truth and conviction behind Dexxin's words. He looked to Laryn and saw an expression of understanding reflected in her eyes. *Moons, Laryn, you've done it.*

Laryn cleared her throat. "Dexxin, the plan would benefit from any communication you can give to the regent through your siblings, but it requires you to engage them beyond suspicion. They will have to believe you are passing honest information."

"I can do that," said the sender.

"Good, that's good," Kaellor agreed. "The Lacuna burned the dovecote in Callinora, so it's unlikely Therek knows how close we are. Whether your siblings believe you or not, the misdirection should only help."

Reddevek exhaled and folded his arms. "You have another way inside? Never mind, you must. Though I don't think a disguise will hold up under scrutiny, I'll do it."

Karragin, Tovnik, and Nolan echoed their agreement with the plan.

"What about us?" asked Ksenia.

"Rugen, I want you to continue on your mission to Dulesque but as a commissioned royal advocate. Send an expedition into the Great Crown and continue your plans to negotiate trade relations with Faltusch. Make no overt promises without checking with the regent. Do this, and I'll see what I can do to safely extricate your brother from the Lacuna."

Rugen bowed his head. "You honor me, Your Grace."

"Ksenia, I could use your eyes to identify known Lacuna leaders, any people in positions of authority. Also, it's been a moon since I've navigated the halls of Stone's Grasp, and we could use someone to guide us directly to the inner sanctum once inside. Would you be willing to accompany us back to Stone's Grasp?" asked Kaellor.

"Certainly. I'll take any chance to repair the damage I've caused," said the young woman.

Elbend Balladuren muttered something to his wife, then turned his attention to Kaellor. "Your Grace, as Kess indicated, my family owes you a great debt. How else can we be of assistance?"

Something in the man's earnest nature reminded Kaellor of the Tellends from Journey's Bend. "All of us . . . we've all made mistakes, Elbend, but I appreciate your words. If you and Madola were planning to return to Stone's Grasp for the spring assembly, then I would ask that you keep those plans. Giver knows we could use a friendly face or two when we address the high houses and nobles."

Madola patted the top of Elbend's hand. "We'll be there. We have a small manor house in the high district. It's not much by royal standards, but consider it a safe place to escape the politics if you ever have need."

"Good," said Kaellor. "Now, we need some means to approach the capital from the northwest without raising suspicion. Does anyone have ideas?"

"Could you approach one of the noble caravans arriving for spring assembly, maybe pose as guards?" asked Savnah.

"I thought of that, but we have no way of knowing for sure if they are loyalists or breakers," said Kaellor.

"I think I have an idea that can get you close to the capital, but I'll need a jar of honey, and we have to leave immediately if we are to catch them," said Reddevek.

"Alright, you have my attention. Who is them?" asked Kaellor.

"Have you ever heard of the Moonies?" asked the warden.

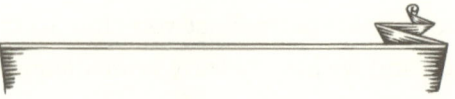

Chapter Forty: The Luna Rova

After provisioning fresh Aarindin, Madola and Elbend Balladuren utilized their skill with the new mounts, enticing them to grip each of their riders. Bryndor and Lluthean rode tandem, alternating with different gifted, and Ranika took her usual seat behind the warden.

Ranika shifted her dagger to the side of her hip and situated herself comfortably. Up close, the man's leathers exuded a heady fragrance beyond the normal stink of trail dust.

Shifting back a few inches, she grabbed onto the sides of his breeches. "Redd, you need a bath if you're to pass for anything resembling royalty."

"Zippy doesn't seem to mind, and I spend more time with him than anyone else. Besides, if anyone rides close enough to challenge my disguise, I expect I'll have time to do something about it."

"You'll make a good Kaellor, but I should probably find another to hitch a ride with. I doubt the prince would return with a passenger," she said.

"Fair point. How would you feel about riding with the Moonies? They travel in caravans of painted wagons. It might be slow going, but you'll reach Stone's Grasp all the same."

An uneasy sensation welled up in her throat at the thought of separating from the warden again. That part of her that set her to following the warden from Callish rose like an itch that just had to be scratched. She considered the suggestion in silence.

Reddevek spoke over his shoulder. "I'm not trying to get rid of ya, Nika. I worry about splitting up the group as it is. While Kaellor can likely keep them all safe, I would prefer to have you along with that group as an extra measure of security. I've trained you well, and you've proven your ability to handle yourself more than once. If I can't be there to watch over the royals, then at least you can."

"Have you told them about my . . . darkness?" she asked.

Reddevek's shoulders slumped a bit. "I wish you'd stop thinking about it like that. The only person who knows anything about your *gift* is Bryndor. Even then, he doesn't likely understand the specifics. Anyway, once we get things sorted out in the capital, you can wander the streets and see the sights. But if I understand things correctly, this might be the one chance to see a secret entrance to the castle. I, for one, would think—"

"You can stop trying to convince me, Redd. I'll go with them," said Ranika. She removed her hat, holding it in her teeth while she gathered her hair back with one hand, then pulled the hat back on with the other just in time to trap the offending strands and reclaim her tenuous grip on Reddevek before sliding off to the side.

"What's to happen to me after? Once things quiet down, and you're off doing whatever wardens do?"

"I expect that depends on you," said Reddevek. "Kaellor already promised me he would see to permanent housing for you in Stone's Grasp. You'll likely have your pick of a suite in the castle. Laryn's family owns a manor in the high district if you prefer. She made it clear that you are welcome there as well."

"Yes, but then what?" she pressed.

"What then what? What do you want me to say exactly?"

"What does a person like me do in Aarindorn? What will I become?" asked Ranika.

Several minutes passed in silence. "Hold on," said the warden, and he signaled Zippy to trot ahead and veer north, leading the company through a stand of timber and eventually along a well-worn wagon trail. "Sorry, I think we're getting close to the Moonies. Listen, Nika, every person your age asks the same questions. I did when I was your age. And I know you want the whole answer now. But life . . . life gives you bits and pieces over time. In Callish, your opportunities were limited. But in Aarindorn, you'll have the chance to see and do anything."

"Maybe I'll join the Outriders," she said.

"You should think about it. You would be an asset to them. But before you decide, you need to experience the kingdom and all it has to offer. You don't know what you don't know, if that makes sense."

It didn't, not really. But before she could needle him with more questions, they crested a hill to see a group of painted wagons camped by a narrow stream. It looked to Ranika like artisans had crafted tiny homes of wood, embellished the doors and elaborate trim with intricate wood carvings, then mounted them on oversized wheels. Ornate murals adorned the backs of the wagons, most depicting scenes of nature, all comprised of bright colors.

A thick-muscled horse pulled each of the strange boxy structures, and more than twenty fanned out along the stream. Men, women, and children meandered about in idle conversation. The adults wore white shirts with slashes of color along the sleeves and multi-pocketed leather vests that extended well below the waist. Men tied bright scarves around their necks, and women tamed great curly mounds of black hair underneath sashes of bright red or blue.

The Moonies reminded Ranika of some of the exotic traders and sailors from the port at Callish. But where the traders scuttled about with frenetic purpose, the Moonies carried themselves like an entire clan of people at a picnic.

Reddevek drew Zippy to a stop and waited for their party to gather. "The Moonies are welcoming and friendly, but I should go along to make introductions. Our group is more than a little intimidating. Have you got the jar of honey?"

Kaellor patted a bulging leather satchel on his hip. "It's right here."

The warden lifted a leg over Zippy's head and slid to the ground; Ranika followed. He turned to address the group. "Good. A few rules: don't call them Moonies. It's considered an insult."

"How do we address them?" asked Laryn.

"They refer to themselves as the Luna Rova The formal title for a man is do', sintra for women. This clan is part of the Rovinary family. Movshka is their speaker. He's like an oracle, gifted with the ability to look into a person's past, but he defers to a trio of elders, two women and a man."

Karragin's voice inserted into the conversation. "Warden Elbiona always directed us to engage the Luna Rova only when we needed equipment repairs when ranging. They prefer to barter. If we are not here for that purpose, they might insist on a mull."

"That's right," agreed the warden.

"Enlighten us, if you would," said Kaellor.

Reddevek cleared his throat. "Under normal circumstances, it's customary for us to carry out a hunt, provide food and drink, and deliver a great feast while the elders consider our request. The whole affair is called a mull."

"Is there a polite way to expedite the proceedings?" asked Laryn.

"There is a price to pay, but I can manage it. I'll take the honey down. It's a symbolic gesture of friendship and should indicate to Movshka my familiarity with their customs," said Reddevek.

Kaellor handed him the satchel with the jar. "You're sure about all of this, Redd? We can always take our chances together."

Reddevek shifted his weapons to hang from his back and threw the satchel over his shoulder. "I'm sure. Come down on foot when I whistle. Only those traveling with the caravan should approach. Shift any weapons over your back as I've done. It's an informal gesture of peace. For now, keep all of the Aarindin and especially the wolvryn up here. Nika, you're with me."

It felt good to stretch her legs as they walked down to the camp. Savory aromas belched out from small black stove stacks set on the sides of the wagons. Two boys raced across their path. One of them pulled a small fish on a string, and a lean cat with distinctive black and white tabby markings gave chase.

"Why did you have the rest of them stay behind, especially with the mounts?" asked Ranika.

"We're safe enough among these folk, but there's only one thing they prize more than their wagons, and that's a good horse. If we ride the Aarindin into camp, they'll assume we mean to barter the mounts for goods or services."

"So if we leave Zippy back there, they know he's not for sale?" asked Ranika.

"Exactly," said Reddevek. "And nobody haggles like a Moonie. Negotiations over something like the value of an Aarindin could take days. Never mind that they aren't for sale; we just don't have time for that kind of distraction."

"And the wolvryn?"

"It's the same as with the Aarindin, only the negotiations would take much longer and involve the entire extended family. Gathering them here could take weeks."

"What about me, Redd? Why did you bring me down?"

He shook his head with a smile. "First, the Moonies value children. But second, your company makes me appear less hostile or maybe . . . less dangerous. Does that make sense?"

"Mmm, only because the Moonies don't know us very well."

Reddevek chuckled. "Right you are, but careful; we're nearly in earshot."

"Sorry," said Ranika. "But, if it's an insult to call them Moonies, why do you?"

"Because when I say it, it's not an insult. I mean, it's only an insult if you're not a Moonie," said the warden.

"Oh," said Ranika. She realized she knew less than she should about Reddevek's past, and questions bubbled into her mind about his childhood, his parents, and where he grew up. *Does he have brothers and sisters? Lutney's dice, I never even thought to ask if he has kids.*

They approached the nearest wagon, a dark red boxy structure perched on unusually large wheels. Elaborate carvings of dragonflies covered every inch of the panels and framing. A weathered wood bench provided the backrest to a cushioned seat on which a woman reclined. She crossed knee-high black leather boots and puffed on a pipe with an unusually long stem as they came near.

"Sintra Rovinary, may the moons light your path," said the warden.

The woman blew out a thin stream of smoke and scratched under her chin with the pipe stem before taking another drag. She lifted her gaze back up the hill and studied the distant group before speaking. "The wheels take us where the moons lead us, Wolfespark. You've been away a long time, and you have a daughter now?"

Reddevek glanced at Ranika, and for the first time she could recall, the scar on the side of his face flushed. The warden cleared his throat. "Have we met before? I've only traveled with the Dev'advari clan."

The sintra stared at them both a long moment. Just when Ranika thought the question needed repeating, she closed her eyes in an odd slow blink that resembled a bored house cat. "I'm Dev'advari born. I married a Rovinary man and have followed the moons as a Rovinary. But I remember you and all the Luna Rova know of your story. You and your brother."

Reddevek placed a hand on Ranika's shoulder. "Ranika is my ward, my traveling companion, as are these others. I would have words with the speaker. If you please, can you direct me to Movshka's wagon?"

The woman pointed the stem of her pipe toward the stream. "His is the purple wagon with the gold trim."

"Moons light your path, sister." The warden dipped his head, then led Ranika around the camp.

"What did she mean by that name, Wolfespark?"

Reddevek grumbled something under his breath. "It's a long story, Nika."

"Redd, I've traveled across a good chunk of Karsk with you, yet it just now dawns on me how little I know of your past when you know so much of mine."

Reddevek sighed. "Alright, but for now, this is the last question today. And the only reason I'm telling you this is because I know you'll keep at me, little gnat."

He tipped the back of her hat forward, causing it to fall over her eyes. "I was born a Moonie, in the Dev'advari clan. They keep to the mountains rather than the lowlands and travel in tent caravans instead of wagons. They . . . used to keep wolvryn."

He seemed about to explain more, but as they approached a weathered wagon with cracked purple paint, a lean man with black eyebrows that framed milk-stained eyes stepped out of the front door and settled himself on the seat. The man called out, "Kevska! I need an ember for my pipe, child!"

"Yes, Pappa!" yelled a boy of not more than five years. He scurried under a neighboring red wagon and retrieved a small stick from within a campfire, the edge a smoldering ember. Holding the twig in his mouth, the boy deftly climbed up to his father's seat. Without words, Kevska held the ember to the pipe bowl. His father inhaled and puffed a few times, then blew out a long roll of smoke before easing back into his seat.

"Thank you, son." The man lifted his nose to the air, tilting his head. He addressed any in the surrounding vicinity, yet his opaque eyes seemed glazed over, unfocused. "I sense visitors among us in spite of my sweetleaf. Come then, who visits the Rovinary?"

"Speaker Movshka Do'Rovinary, may the moons light your path. I am Reddevek, son of the Dev'advari and warden in the Outriders. I'm here with my ward, Ranika. We represent one who would ask a boon of the Luna Rova. I offer a tribute of friendship."

Though Movshka's eyes remained unfocused, his lips tightened on the pipe stem as Reddevek introduced himself. The warden stepped forward and placed the jar of honey on the wagon near the man's feet. Movshka picked up the container, sniffing at the top, then tilted his head.

"As I understand it, you've been away from the Luna Rova a long time, but I see you've not forgotten our ways. Are you here for a mull?"

"Sadly, no. Our need is great, and we can't afford the delay."

Movshka stared ahead in silence, the end of his pipe bobbing as he bit down on the stem. "Come forward then and let me read you that I might know the true nature of your visit, Outrider," said Movshka.

Reddevek stepped forward and gripped the speaker's hand. Movshka turned the warden's hand palm up and traced the lines and creases. "Once we do this, you will be reconnected to the Luna Rova and forever part of the Rovinary song. The tie is unbreakable. Do you consent?"

"I do," said Reddevek.

Flickers of zenith swirled like smoky blue ribbons under the milky surface of Movshka's eyes, and he pressed his hand to Reddevek's, holding the warden in place. Reddevek stood still but began to pant, and a bead of sweat gathered on his forehead. Ranika took a step forward, her hand naturally falling on the hilt of her dagger, but Reddevek placed a hand on her shoulder.

"I'm alright. It's alright. Just . . . let him finish, Nika," said Reddevek.

What seemed like several minutes later, the Rovinary released his grip. His eyes faded to their murky stillness, and he puffed on his pipe, but no smoke came forth. "Forgive me. Your journey, Wolfespark, took longer to read than I imagined, and now . . . my pipe has faded."

The warden pushed his palms to his temples in obvious pain. "There's nothing to forgive, Speaker. I knew the price required if we hope to receive your aid. Allow me."

Reddevek retrieved another smoking twig from the fire and held it forward. Movshka puffed once again, sending the sweet fragrance of his pipe out in small rings.

"My thanks. Your request is simple. Anonymous transport to Stone's Grasp. You keep . . . unusual company," said Movshka.

"To be sure," said Reddevek.

Movshka turned and looked directly at Ranika, the strange vacant quality to his gaze making her shiver. "None more unique than you. Isn't that right, child?"

"I'm not sure what you mean," said Ranika.

The Rovinary reclined on his seat, using the top edge to massage the muscles in his back. "I think that you do. But relax . . . Ranika. Your secrets are yours. I would not divulge them without your consent. That is the Rovinary way."

He puffed a few more times on his pipe and, once he exhaled a long smoke trail, sat forward. "These are strange times. I'm glad to see that a son of the Luna Rova survived the stampede a few nights ago."

"Strange seems like a soft word to describe everything going on in these parts of late," said Reddevek.

"That's the Giver's truth. You've arrived behind dark tidings to our camp, Warden. But I understand that it's not a darkness of your making. Do you truly believe Tarkannen seeks to walk again under the moons?"

"You know that I do, that we all do. I don't have the means or the inclination to hide from your sight," said Reddevek.

"No, you don't," sighed Movshka. "And sadly . . . I must believe you. So, we will dispense with the usual ceremony and feasting. I can read that time is a commodity with which you have little to spare. Come then. I invite you into the camp with my blessing. Bring forward those who would travel with the Rovinary, but keep your soldiers at a distance."

"I understand. I'll be a moment. Wait here, Nika," said the warden, then he jogged back up the hill, leaving her alone in the Rovinary camp.

The speaker continued to puff idly at his pipe. "Do'Rovinary, why do your people call Redd, Wolfespark?"

"You have questions, and I have answers, but like all things, they come at a price," said the speaker.

"What's the price then?" said Ranika.

"A reading, information. You share with me your memories. They will add another stanza to the great story sung by the Luna Rova, and I will give you some of mine. The exchange will bind us together," said Movshka.

The notion of a relative stranger sifting through her memories unnerved her. But her curiosity outweighed her fear. "That doesn't sound . . . so bad."

Movshka smiled and nodded. "I will share this with you. Reddevek was given the honored name because he once returned a spark of the wolvryn to the Luna Rova. If you want to know more, you must wait another time. Your friends return, and it would take more than a few minutes to read an outsider with such a past as yours. But, the journey to Stone's Grasp will take two or three days. If you would like, young abrogator, seek me out."

Ranika chanced a glance over her shoulder, relieved to see that the others were well out of hearing range. The warden returned on foot with the royals, the wolvryn, and Ksenia. All the Aarindin and Reddevek's Outriders remained back on the hilltop.

"I will," said Ranika.

Movshka sat forward and pitched his voice for her alone. "But be careful. Some secrets are best left in the dark corners of the mind where they can't hurt anyone. Once I begin to sift through your memories, one never knows what I might find."

Chapter Forty-One: The Winnowing of the Shades

The rhythmic stomping of feet reached a fevered pitch as Gauvin the bard finished a rowdy song celebrating the passion of young love in spring. Laughter and spirit-fueled cheers rose when the song ended, and the crowd demanded more from the troubadour. The grizzled entertainer cleared his throat, strummed a cord, and began anew. Volencia excused herself, retreating to the back porch of the King's Respite.

Clouds obscured the half-moon of Baellen, and the southern slopes dropped into murky shadow. *Grasdok, you've got one task to accomplish. I'll use nadir hooks to skin you alive if you fail me in this.*

She strained, searching the darkness. As her eyes adjusted, she detected movement in the distance. A faint trail of glowing figures snaked from west to east, filling the southern reaches of the valley.

Gauvin's song ended, and a few patron's wandered onto the porch. A young couple wearing garments trimmed with green filigree walked out, arm in arm, whispering in quiet conversation. *Time to light the fuse.*

Volencia stepped close and placed a hand on the woman's arm. "Forgive me. Do you see something out there, or have I had too much of Cabe's honey mead?"

The man turned to consider her, saw the blue trim to her cloak, and dipped his head in deference. "Cabe's mead is strong, but I've never known it to cause—" His words trailed off as he stared into the darkness. "By the spirits, what is that?"

"Then you see it too? What could it be?" she asked.

"I don't know. It's nothing I've ever seen before," said the man.

"If I didn't know better, I would think the spirits have come out for the Winnowing of the Shades. Keep an eye out, will you? I'm going to get others," said Volencia.

She stepped back into the taproom and searched until she found a person with the right mix of self-importance and righteous condescension. The middle-aged man stood aloof from the crowd in dark purple clothing, nose held high, a glass of wine in hand.

"Excuse me, might I have a word? You look like a man of sound . . . composition. I wonder if I could get your opinion on something," said Volencia.

The man leered at her over the brim of his glass, lingering overlong at her neckline. "Lord Boffle. How can I help you, my lady?"

"A pleasure to make your acquaintance, my lord. I was just getting a bit of fresh air on the back porch when this younger couple and I noticed a . . . well I don't quite know how to describe it other than a strange disturbance below in the valley. I wonder if you could have a look and tell us what you make of it all?"

He drained the wine and held an arm out, inviting Volencia to step closer. She did so, tolerating his hand on the curve of her buttock, and escorted him to the back porch. Other patrons clustered together on the porch, staring into the darkness and pointing amidst a murmur of anxious conversation.

Volencia laced her speech with a shrill tone. "Giver's breath, there's more of them now, a lot more." The glowing herd of grondle meandered in rows at least five or six deep, spread out across the southern edge of Sifter's Valley.

Lord Boffle removed his wandering hand and stepped forward, intrigued by the phenomenon. Though the grondle remained perhaps a half-mile or more away, their ghostly silhouettes and vast number left no doubt that something bestial and otherworldly approached.

Volencia ran the length of the porch, then returned to Lord Boffle, panic flavoring her tone. "There's more of them to the east and look . . . to the west. They're coming this way!"

The mutters of the crowd became agitated chatter, and someone even yelled out. "It's the shades! The dead are angry!"

Volencia turned to Lord Boffle, but spoke in a voice loud enough for all to hear. "My family owns a tract of land high in the mountains north of here. It's consecrated holy ground. We could escape to the canyon there. If the shades follow, we could mount a defense, but here we're defenseless!"

"That seems rather hasty. No, no better to have a look ourselves. I'll send armed men down to investigate," said the purple lord.

Volencia stepped back to observe the gathering. More and more people joined them on the back porch, and soon others could be seen standing on the back porches of adjacent buildings watching the spectacle in the woods.

She returned to the taproom, where news of the strange occurrence was spreading like an ill wind. Gauvin made a pretense of tuning his lute but kept a wary eye on the strange behavior of the crowd.

"Why is everyone acting as if someone pooped in the punchbowl?" he asked.

"There's something, I can't explain it, but ghosts or spirits or something are climbing up the side of the mountain and . . . Gauvin, I'm getting out of here, and so should you. Lord Boffle is sending a few men to investigate, but something doesn't feel right. I'm headed for the highlands to the safety of my family's holdings. The canyon there is consecrated land."

"At this time of night?" asked the bard.

"It's got to be safer than waiting for whatever is coming this way. I swear it's like the Taker set all the restless spirits of the dead upon us. I pray, look for yourself, and when you see that I'm right, let anyone who wants know that there is safety a few hours north of here. It's a hike, to be sure, but I'll have a torch to light the way."

She walked out the front doors and began the slow climb through the tent city. Her intention was to stop and engage other families, spread the rumor of the specters approaching from the south, and offer a promise of safety to the north. However, within minutes, people were migrating to the south end of the King's Respite, eager to see for themselves.

Volencia used the confusion to commandeer a dun gelding. The horse stood tethered beside a familiar wagon. She peered inside and wrinkled her nose from the smell of shit. The corpse of the man she had murdered the night before lay prone, undisturbed, exactly where she had left him.

She grabbed the lead rope and whispered in the horse's ear. "Have you been unattended all this time? My apologies. Let's get you some water and see if we can't become friends."

After watering the horse at a nearby stream, she gave him a bucket of grain and found the saddle. The horse seemed eager to move and responded to her directions easily enough. They walked to the edge of the encampment and watched as a palpable fear kindled among the community, spreading faster than she expected, like a flame to dry tinder.

From her vantage point, she could make out the painted grotvonen closing in from the east and west. A crowd of revelers wearing all the colors of the rainbow gathered. One man, a father of two from the yellow tier, approached her. He led a lean horse by the reins. Two sleepy-eyed children sat on the mount. "Are you the lady who said there was safety to the north?"

"Yes. My family owns holy ground that should be protected from the shades. North of here, a good hike through the night, there is a canyon where we should be safe. I can lead you there, but we should wait for others to arrive."

A rough-looking woman wearing a faded orange skirt stepped forward. She held a walking stick in one hand but bounced it lightly on her shoulder like a baton. Her grip caused the scars over her knuckles to pale to silver when she spoke. "If you've got a safe place for us to go, we should begin before those things reach us. Mountain folk can manage safe travel at night, but most of these others will need a well-marked trail."

Screams of pain and shouts of alarm rose from farther down the valley. "That must be Lord Boffle's men. He sent them down to investigate; perhaps you are right," said Volencia.

Volencia lit a torch, held it high, and stood in the stirrups, then shouted across the growing group of people. More eyes than she could count reflected the amber torchlight. "Everyone, I can lead us to safety, but the hike will take most of the night. There is holy ground in a canyon to the north. Mounts and horses can make the journey, but the ground is too rocky for wagons; leave them behind. Pass the word back, and we'll begin."

"Why don't we scatter? Some of us could take to the east or west?" one man shouted.

"Take your chances if you dare, but there's safety in numbers," said Volencia. "Besides, you can see for yourselves that the only path clear of the spirits seems to be to the north."

Grotvonen clicks, wild hoots, and bestial growls echoed around them, emphasizing her point. A grumble of discontent and fear spread through the crowd. "Let's go then. Lead on before it's too late," shouted another man.

And with that, she circled the gelding to the north and began the long climb back to the valley, back to the grotvonen lair and her promise of deliverance.

Chapter Forty-Two: Mixed Blessing in the Wolf's Maw

Reddevek fed an apple to Zippy and watched as the Moonies welcomed the new arrivals. Most of the Rovinary focused their attention on the first wolvryn seen in a generation. That Neska and Boru rivaled the size of a draft horse made no difference. The entire clan turned out to bear witness to the creatures, and, in short order, the laughter of both children and adults dissipated any of his lingering reservations.

"Did you know they would get along so well?" asked Savnah.

"It's not less than I expected," he said.

"Other than Outriders, those are the first people I've seen around the wolvryn. I thought they would cower in their wagons, but they seem to treat them with, I don't know . . ."

"Reverence," said the warden. "In the highlands, the Luna Rova used to keep wolvryn before they were hunted to extinction. The clans there remain suspicious of any outsiders because of that loss alone." Memories he had long ago shelved flickered into his awareness, kindled by Speaker Movshka's touch.

He recalled the scent of the well-oiled skins used for both clothing and teepees, the gritty feeling of frost underfoot, and the way droplets of moisture gathered from condensation on the inside of their tents at night. And he remembered his wolvryn, Voozsh.

Unbidden, the voice of his mother scolding them both for wandering into the tent with muddy feet echoed in his thoughts.

Savnah hocked a glob of spit and cleared her throat. "You seem to know a lot about those people. I imagine you've had more than a few dealings with them over the years, then?"

Reddevek released the memory and drew his focus back to the present. He looked at the group of Outriders. Karragin and her brother Nolan stood beside their Aarindin. Tovnik and Dexxin sat their mounts, each waiting for his direction. He had a hand in training all of them, and a ripple of pride warmed his chest. They had come through a lot in the last several months, but still, the kingdom required more. It was quite possible he would be leading them into their last adventure.

"You could say that," said Reddevek. "Alright then, Karragin, send the mounts that Kaellor and Laryn used back to the Balladuren ranch. I assume they can make it back there without our escort?"

"Yes," said the prime. "Ksenia already set Winter on that path."

"We need to obtain clothes that appear a bit more refined than Outrider fatigues if we're to fool anyone into thinking that I'm the long-lost prince returning to the kingdom."

"Could we trade with the Moonies before they leave?" asked Nolan.

"I thought about that, but their style is a bit . . . garish for nobility," said Reddevek. "Anyone with a passing knowledge of Aarindorn would question the disguise from a distance."

"We're a day's hard ride from Midrock," said Savnah. "It's not much out of the way. I'm sure we could procure a high-quality mantle, cloaks for the rest of us, tailored clothing, and even dressing for the mounts. It might cost a bit more, but we could find what we need. My second cousin is a barber, and no offense, but he could tighten up your beard, sir."

He watched the two riderless Aarindin trot off to the west and signaled Zippy to lower belly to the ground, then climbed onto his back. "North to Midrock then. We'll spend the night, provision, and leave by the next day if possible. That should place us at the south gates to Stone's Grasp on the evening of the third day, which is perfect timing to give the others a chance to sneak inside before the Lacuna get a feel for things."

"What's our script then? I know too many people there, and I know for a fact that the Lacuna have a presence in Midrock. It's where I was recruited, after all. We need to get our story straight," said Savnah.

Reddevek thought a moment. Her point was well made, but any story to which they agreed needed to be laced with enough truth to make the script both easy to follow and credible. "Alright. We'll arrive as Outriders needing provisions and appropriate attire to accompany highborn dignitaries arriving at the south gates in three days. There are enough nobles making the trip for spring assembly that elements of that cover ring true. If anyone presses for specific details, claim secrecy as ordered by Overwarden Kaldera."

They ranged north, and he gave the lead to Karragin. Her intimacy with the Aarindin allowed them to push the mounts without causing injury. They arrived before the front gates of Midrock as the evening sun approached the horizon.

Midrock sat at the transition point between the foothills and highlands of the Great Crown. A paved central road climbed steeply, switching back every few minutes. At the edges of the settlement, smaller winding streets wound back and forth in a tangle of cramped neighborhoods. Squat two-story buildings, homes, and shops crafted from blocks of cut stone were crammed together at the edge of the winding streets. The districts rose in a steep wall that clung to the sides of the Great Crown. The dark peaks of the mountain range blotted out the stars above.

Lamp and torchlight cast flickering shadows as a throng of locals and visitors milled about, crowding the lower streets well beyond anything Reddevek recalled from prior visits. He realized the reason at once. Anyone who traveled from one of the western duchies or Callinora used the small city to rest up and provision before completing the journey to Stone's Grasp. This time of year, an excess of travelers for the spring assembly were using Midrock to good purpose. The sheer number of people made him scratchy.

"Savnah, we're not likely to find lodging here with so many traveling this time of year. This is your town. Any suggestions?" he asked.

The prime sat with her thumbs hooked into her belt, studying the press of people. "You're right. Most rooms will have been booked months in advance. How do you feel about staying at the Wolf's Maw? It's my dad's place, so I'm sure we can acquire food and lodging."

"Times like these, it's not what you know, but who. Lead on," said Reddevek.

"We'll have to make the climb all the way up, but the crowds will thin the farther we go."

She turned her Aarindin off the main winding road to a side street that climbed at a steep angle, bypassing the switchbacks. Zippy's head bobbed up and down with effort, and more than once, he had to duck down under the edge of a low-hanging building. Thankfully, fitted cobblestone pavers ensured sound footing. Reddevek wondered how the locals managed the climb in the winter months.

Savnah returned them to a paved switchback, and the Aarindin walked at a leisurely pace, unfettered by the crowds of people closer to the entrance. The smell of lanterns carried on the wind, their flickering lights keeping the shadows at bay. They rounded the last corner to stare up the street at a building carved directly into the mountain. The last blush of the setting sun cast a ruddy silhouette over the structure. From this distance, the crests of the building and the backdrop of the mountain took on the vague outline of a wolf's head, accentuated by lanterns set in depressions where the eyes would be.

An unmistakable aroma of smoked meats wafted down the street. Savnah encouraged her mount into a trot, and they followed. A crowd of hungry customers milled about the front door. She led them around the side to a stable adjacent to the inn and rang a small bell. A groom came out of the stables, took one look at Savnah and the others, then turned and opened a gate.

After seeing to the Aarindin, Savnah led them to a small side door with a combination lock. She scrolled through the letters, and the lock clicked open. The prime held open the door and welcomed them into a large taproom. The buzz of happy patrons accompanied the clank of mugs and table service on plates.

Sconces set against dark timber paneling shined down on round tables saturated with diners. An expansive bar ran the length of the far side of the room, above which rested a wood carving of a howling wolf. As they'd entered from the shadowed side of the room, nobody paid them much notice.

A woman holding an oversized serving platter on her shoulder spun around a patron and came to an abrupt stop when she saw them.

"Savnah? Giver's tits, it's been a moon! Wait right here." The woman delivered her tray of goods to a nearby table and quickstepped over. They shared a fierce embrace.

"Hello, Binta. I figured it was high time I show some of my Outrider friends how we eat up here in the Maw. Can we get a table?"

"Of course, follow me," said Binta. She led them up a flight of stairs to a balcony overlooking the taproom. A lone table sat empty. Binta lit a lamp on the table and pulled back a chair.

"Let me guess, Savnah's plate?" she asked.

"All around, if you please," said Savnah. "And let my father know I'm here, would you?"

"Of course," said Binta. The barmaid disappeared down the stairs only to return holding five foaming mugs of ale.

"Oh, actually, I don't know if we're . . . partaking . . . on the job in service to the crown and all," said Savnah.

Reddevek looked around the table, wondering if any of them understood the potential danger involved in the days ahead. Dexxin and Nolan stared with wonder about the establishment. Tovnik tipped back in his chair, clasping his hands overhead, while the two primes sat forward on elbows with all-too-serious expressions on their faces.

Grind it. They've each ridden through more trouble than me at the same age, and Giver knows I could use a drink.

"Binta, leave the mugs," said Reddevek. "We're due a little relaxation tonight, as long as it's in moderation."

They each reached for a pint, even Karragin. After knocking the base of her mug on the table, Savnah held her drink forward. "Fancy a toast?"

Reddevek had just lifted his mug to his lips. "Don't keep me waiting."

"Alright then," said the prime. "To Redd's Riders and second chances. I'm grateful to both."

They each knocked mugs on the tabletop, clanked them together, said "Moons!" in unison, and pulled a draw. Cold amber liquid splashed the back and sides of his tongue with a pleasing malty taste and nutty aroma. Reddevek took another swallow, considering the complex flavor. "Not bad."

Tovnik leaned forward over his mug. "Not bad? Am I the only one who expected more sauce from the toughest bitch this side of the Korjinth?"

"That was a bit tame, Savnah, especially for you," said Karragin.

"If you lot think you can do better, let's hear it!" challenged Savnah. When nobody spoke up, she elbowed Nolan in the ribs. "Let's have something from the regent's son."

The flushing of Nolan's cheeks flared to his ears, and he swallowed another mouthful to hide his discomfort. But instead of setting his pint down, he held it forward. "May your mount never stumble, and your will never break. May your stomach never rumble and your heart never ache."

The tap of mugs on wood followed by "Moons!" resonated again as they responded to Nolan's toast.

"How about you, sir?" asked Savnah. "Something from your early days as a rider, maybe?"

Reddevek remembered sitting around a much smaller table with his first quad years ago. The mead was sour and the tables sticky, but Karragin made the perfect stand-in for Elbiona. "Alright, I can't take credit for this one. It's from an old warden, back in the day. 'Here's to the Outriders under the moon, and the kingdom stone from which they're hewn. When their zenith fades, it will be too soon. All praise the Giver who lights the rune.'"

Thunk. "Moons!"

The next several minutes were spent draining the first mug, ordering a second round, and listening to Savnah find creative ways to toast with different parts of the Taker's anatomy. Binta brought shots of resco, which they all enjoyed. "One sip cures the rot, two makes you brave, three grants a dreamless sleep, and four grants the grave!"

Thunk. "Moons!"

Savnah set her shot glass down and blew out the volatile fumes. "Good ol' resco," she said. "Helping tenders like Dexx and Nolan to find a grinding partner since the Cataclysm!"

The table erupted in laughter as platters of smoked meat, bread, and thick, tangy soup arrived, causing the conversation to fade as they sampled the fare. The thump of heavy footsteps announced someone ascending the stairs. A balding middle-aged man with thick shoulders stopped at the top. He stood with his thumbs tucked into his belt, the unmistakable relative of Savnah. She pushed back from the table, rushed to him, and the two embraced.

They walked over, arm in arm. "Everyone, this is my father, Burl Derrigand, the best pitmaster in Aarindorn and the only man who could make the Taker blush with his wit. Dad, this is Warden Reddevek and . . . everyone."

Burl made the rounds, accepting compliments on the food and drink with polite conversation free from the typical Derrigand spice. After returning to Savnah, he leaned forward and presented her with a gift, placing the palm-sized package on the table before her.

"And what is this then?" she asked.

"Open it and see, you moon calf!" said Burl.

A single strand of blue ribbon tied in a bow wrapped around the thin wood box. Savnah untied the bow and removed a small foldable knife with a single blade. Silver runes ran along the outside of the handle. Savnah's lips drew to a thin line, and her face became unusually placid.

"He would have wanted you to have it, Savvy," said Burl.

"Thanks, Dad. I suppose he would," said Savnah.

She stood and hugged her father in another long embrace. When they separated, she rubbed her palms at her eyes and giggled. "Thanks for that, Dad. It's the first grinding time anyone in the riders has seen me shed a tear, I think."

"Well, that sounds like a moment we should commemorate," said Burl. He walked to the back of the room and returned with a serving tray. An ornate resco bottle of tinted glass sat in the center, surrounded by six glasses with bulbous bases and narrow rims.

"Is that from your stash of prewar resco?" asked Savnah.

"Only my best for Aarindorn's best," said Burl.

He poured a finger into each glass and raised a toast. "Some might say that if you travel with a Derrigand, that makes you the Taker's fools or the Giver's martyrs. But I say, thank you one and all. For everything you do for Aarindorn and for keeping my Savvy safe."

He tapped his glass on the table, and they all followed. "Moons!"

Burl replaced the stopper in the decanter and smacked his lips. "Excuse me for a while; I'll see to your rooms. Will you be staying long?"

"We've been recruited as an honorary escort for some nobles arriving for spring assembly, Dad. We're to acquire appropriate formal wear and then ride out to meet the new arrivals," said Savnah.

"I'm not surprised. I plan to attend this year as well . . . personal invitation from the regent. Something about an announcement affecting the kingdom, so I hope to see you all there." He turned to depart but stopped at the top of the stairs. "Binta will prepare rooms and will see to a breakfast at least before you depart."

The innkeeper bid them a good night, affording them a rare opportunity for fellowship without the struggles of the road. Reddevvek sipped at the amber liquid, savoring a smoky, rich quality that flowed over his tongue smooth and with little burn. He took stock of each of his Outriders. It marked the first time he could recall in which any of them had a chance to let their guard down. Karragin and Savnah exchanged friendly barbs, finding the young men at the table the butt of their jokes more often than not.

Savnah passed her brother's knife around the table so that each might inspect the gift her father had bestowed. When it fell into Nolan's hands, he opened the blade and studied its make. As he folded it back, a vacant expression played across his face, one that the warden recognized. Nolan stood and wandered to the balcony, staring down into the taproom.

The scout returned as the others became engrossed in one of Savnah's bawdy tales. He sat down and pushed the knife over to Reddevek. The warden leaned in close and tilted his head.

"There's a spot of dried blood in the locking hinge of the knife, but it's not Burl's," said Nolan. "If it's her brother's, the resonance is strong . . . fresh, and the trail is easy to follow."

Reddevek held his hand out, and Nolan turned over the pocketknife. The warden eased onto the chair's back legs and studied the blade under the table. He sifted his gift over the hinge and studied the pattern that sang through the dried blood. The resonance resembled Savnah's pattern, and he trusted Nolan's assessment.

337

Grind me, sometimes the Giver gives, and sometimes the Taker takes, but what am I supposed to do with this?

Chapter Forty-Three: Spun Glass and Dragonflies

The caravan of brightly colored wagons meandered along ruts cut into the rocky ground. Bouncing along in the covered wagon was more comfortable than Lluthean expected. He leaned over the side, inspecting the wheels. Some trick of their design or the strange braces under the carriage made the ride far less jarring than his experiences surveying the Southlands with Scout pulling their old cart.

A flash of silver darted in and out of the undergrowth to his side, Neska keeping pace. She shadowed the caravan at a distance despite his signal to approach.

Still angry at me for leaving you outside Callinora.

He stood on the seat and looked back. Bryndor sat beside Ksenia; the two of them rode in silence behind a Rovinary woman. The only sign of enthusiasm came from Boru, who loped alongside their rear wheel.

Lluthean sat back down beside Ranika. They shared a broad padded seat with Movshka. The Rovinary guided the wagon in silence, offering only occasional conversation, but Ranika made a fun traveling companion.

"What do you feed the wolvryn?" asked Movshka. "I remember seeing them when I was a boy. There was a moot, a gathering of the clans in the highlands, and the Dev'advari still ran with a few, but none so big as these."

"I think it has more to do with zenith than anything else. They absorb it, maybe, or it sustains them? Does that make sense?" he answered.

Movshka bobbed his head back and forth with indecision. "Maybe."

"Redd says that the Aarindin use zenith, so it's not such a stretch to think the same of the wolvryn," said Ranika.

Lluthean removed two billow seeds from a pocket and flicked them into the air with his thumb, considering the young woman at his side. He had realized in their short time together that her simple clothes disguised a clever mind, and that she had a way of seeing the world, then talking about it with unvarnished clarity.

"Llu, when we reach Stone's Grasp, how are we going to get inside without anyone like the Lacuna knowing about us?" she asked.

Lluthean continued flicking the seeds in the air, and Ranika plucked one out from an errant trajectory. She studied the round nut-like seed, nibbled at it, and frowned when the husk resisted her bite. When he sent his leftover one into the air, she tossed hers up, and he continued the rhythmic volley.

"I haven't given it much thought. Kae thinks he knows a way in other than the main gates, so I suppose we go where he tells us," said Lluthean.

"Yes, but don't you want to know about it before we get there?"

Lluthean shrugged. "What's it going to change? I'm as much a stranger here as you are. I suppose we'll figure out how to get into the city, wolvryn and all, once we get there. If we can sneak past the breakers in the process, good on us. If they find us and put up a resistance? Well, my money's on Kae and the wolvryn."

"Spoken like an acolyte of Lutney," she scoffed.

"Hmm, old habits, I suppose," said Lluthean. "I do try to remember that we're in the Northlands . . . it's the Giver this and the Taker that. Sometimes I slip, but you've got to admit, it's easier to remember two gods instead of seven."

"True, but I haven't found anything that sounds like 'Lutney's dice' or 'Foden's teeth.' Those just sort of . . . feel right in my mouth, you know?" she asked.

"Foden's teeth . . . I hadn't heard that one. But if you want some good curses, hang around with Savnah when we all meet back in Stone's Grasp."

They bounced along in silence for several minutes, and at last, Lluthean replaced the billow seeds in his pocket. He surrendered to a yawn, craned his head back, and stretched his arms overhead.

Ranika slapped him on the arm and stifled a yawn. "That's the fourth time today you've yawned. Don't you know those things are contagious?"

Lluthean shook his head and flared his eyes. "Sorry. I haven't slept well ever since we left Callinora."

"I can imagine. We've all seen plenty to give us bad dreams, and you more than most."

Unbidden, images of the umbral and the bitter wind that strafed through the portal rose to his awareness. A shiver spread across his shoulders as he recalled fragments from a dream the night before, where dark tentacles of nadir had lashed about him.

He refused to let the memory darken his mood and shook off the unsettling sensation. Ranika seemed to withdraw into herself, her gaze unfixed but staring ahead. "You worried about Redd?" he asked.

"No . . . sort of . . . yes," she said. "He sent me with your group as an 'added measure of security.'" She dropped her chin to her chest and tried her best to mimic the warden's growl when she spoke. "But I think he just wanted me out of harm's way."

"We've both seen him up close in combat. I wouldn't want to be a Lacuna tasked with barring him entry through the front gates."

"Sure, but they are walking right up to the hornet's nest, knocking three times, then standing around hoping not to get stung. All the while, nobody really knows how many Lacuna might come after them thinking he's your uncle."

"Don't forget he'll have Karragin and the rest of the Outriders with him. That is one group who can handle themselves," said Lluthean.

"If it's those five against ten, I agree. But what if it's thirty? What if it's fifty breakers?" she asked.

A flutter of uncertainty washed across his stomach as he imagined a horde of angry Lacuna bearing down on the small party.

The wagon bounced over a rut, and she shouldered into him. A sly smile stole across her face. "You like Karra, don't you?"

He turned to look directly at her and couldn't help but smile. "I like all the Outriders."

"Come on, that's not what I mean, and you know it."

The brim of her hat shaded her eyes, so he pushed it back with a finger, forcing her gaze. He hoped, on some level, to intimidate her away from the topic. They stared at each other a moment until she arched an eyebrow.

Grind it, but she's really direct.

"What gave me away?" he asked.

"You did, just now, you silly monk."

At that, he slapped a hand down on the edge of her hat, causing it to drop onto her face. Ranika giggled, removed her hat, and handed it to him. "Hold this for me."

Fine yellow hair poked through her fingers as she scrubbed her scalp, tossing the curls into a frenzied mess. She looked like a tufted billow seed after it sprouted, and he couldn't help but laugh. She lifted her forehead into the breeze, and the hair settled back in long, thin spirals.

"Alright, that's enough of that. My hat, if you please."

Lluthean handed it back. "Why do you cover it up?"

Ranika's eyebrows lifted as she thought about the question. "I suppose it made me stand out back in Callish, and that was one place you wanted to blend in."

"It's like . . . spirals of spun glass. You shouldn't cover it up. It's distinctive."

Ranika squinted her eyes. "I think . . . that you're trying to change the subject. I believe we were talking about Karra." She gathered her hair under the hat and replaced it on her head, then pushed the brim back enough to smile at him.

With a sigh, he conceded her point. "Do you think she knows?" he asked.

"There's knowing, and there's understanding. She's definitely smarter than most. But something tells me she pushes things like that to the back of her mind. She's all Outrider, all the time, from what I've seen."

Lluthean sighed. "That's the Giver's truth."

"What is it that you like about her instead of, say, Savnah or Ksenia, maybe?"

He thought about her question and wondered if he should answer at all, but something in the matter-of-fact way she engaged the conversation put him at ease. "Have you ever seen her smile? I mean a full, light-up-the-room, reach-the-corner-of-the-eyes smile?"

Ranika frowned. "Actually . . . no. Never."

"Well, after we first met, it seemed like a fun challenge to try to get her to smile like that at least once a day."

"How did you manage that?" she asked.

"That's just it. I didn't. I failed . . . miserably, in fact. But then, one day, a few weeks back, after that attack by the Lacuna, I saw her talking to Nolan. And for just that moment, something . . . the ice of her face melted, and this remarkable smile was there, just for a few seconds, and because you don't get to see it very often, it was . . . amazing. I can't stop thinking about that smile."

"It sounds to me like you should ask Nolan what he said," said Ranika.

"Oh, I asked him right away."

The wagon rocked and bounced ahead, and at last, Ranika shouldered into him again. "And? What did he say?"

"He said he told her their mom would have been proud."

"Woof. There's a kick in the berries," said Ranika.

Hearing the phrase, especially from a woman, made him laugh despite his best efforts not to. "How so?"

"As I see it, none of us motherless types like to talk about the loss of a parent. I mean, how do you begin to work that into a conversation?" asked Ranika.

"Hmm. I see your point," said Lluthean. He straightened his back, set his shoulders, and cleared his throat with theatrical purpose. "So, Nika, what happened to your mother?"

"Seriously? Llu, don't be a monk."

"Sorry. I was just practicing. You're right, though; that's a weird conversation starter," said Lluthean. "I'll have to find something else."

Movshka gave a gentle flick of the reins, turning the wagon to the north. "My wife loves dragonflies. In the summer, she paints a single finger with yellowbud resin. Then, she sits back and watches as the males take turns trying to mate with her pinky. She could spend all day watching them."

Lluthean signed to Ranika. *"Did I miss something?"*

"Dragonflies, silly. You need to find Karragin's dragonflies."

Chapter Forty-Four: The Giver's Rare Touch

Bryndor sat in silence beside Ksenia on a wood bench behind a Rovinary woman. Theirs was the fourth wagon in the caravan traveling toward Stone's Grasp. Cliffs of the Great Crown rose on their left, and in the far distance, where the peaks of the range curved to form the eastern boundary on the horizon, lay Stone's Grasp.

He ran his fingers along one of the intricate dragonfly carvings set into the side of the bench beside his thigh. He had tried to engage the Rovinary woman in conversation, inquiring about their customs. She deflected his inquiries with vague answers about "tracking the moons" and "in the Giver's time." Sensing that she was in no mood to offer further conversation, he settled back on the bench and chewed on the inside of his lower lip, trying to enjoy the ride.

Lluthean rode in Movshka's cart directly ahead of them. His brother's head popped up for a few seconds, then disappeared. Thinking of his brother made him painfully aware of their differences.

He would have contrived seven different things to talk about. One for each of the Southland gods, then two more again for those of the north.

Ksenia rode on the bench next to him, staring off into the distance. Boru ran by the rear wheel of the cart and occasionally jumped ahead, seeking attention and affirmation. Something in the wolvryn's exuberance and constant desire for play lightened his mood, and realization washed over him.

"It's Winter, isn't it?" he said.

Ksenia turned to him for the first time all day, rolling her left wrist inside the clutches of her right hand.

"I'm sorry. I don't always make for very good company, I'm afraid," said Ksenia.

"Are you worried about her?"

"Not really, no. But I was listening . . . with my gift. She's happy enough to be returning to the ranch. But my gift only stretches so far, and I lost her voice a few hours ago. I've just never been away from her for more than a few days since . . . well, since I found her on the ice."

"On the ice? What's that all about?" he asked.

"She was foaled early, in the worst part of winter, and the mare abandoned her to the elements. I found her before she perished."

With deliberate thought, he picked out a Northland expression. "Giver's mercy, how did she survive long enough?"

"There's a wild vine that blooms in the coldest months of winter. It's called winter night's asylum. If you are lucky enough to collect the petals, they can be distilled into a fragrance that merchants sell for a small fortune."

"Is that the perfume you wear? The one you had when we first met in the mountains?"

She frowned and smiled, appearing confused that he would notice such a detail. He tilted his head toward Boru, who bounded over a short bush. "In the mountains? When we first met? I linked to Boru. That fragrance was the first thing the both of us noticed about you."

She nodded understanding. "Well, I found the clutch of vines. When the flowers drop, they radiate enough heat to melt the ice and snow. Winter was lying in a lush bed of the petals."

Bryndor shook his head in wonder.

"Don't believe me?" she challenged.

"Oh, but I do; that's just it . . . I do," he said. "I shouldn't be surprised, I guess, but somehow I always am."

"What do you mean?"

"Well, I've seen so many strange things in the last few years. Umm," he chuckled. "When I think of them, they're like a log jam in my mind. So . . ." He paused, trying to sort out all the different examples of the strange wonders he had encountered. "Until a little over a year ago, I had no idea what wolvryn were, or zenith, abrogators, or grondle. My own uncle can summon a barrier that reflects explosions, and my newfound aunt can bring a person back from the edge of the Drift."

Bryndor withdrew from his memories and looked past the freckles draped across her nose and cheeks to search her eyes. He cleared his throat. "So . . . what's one more miracle but another reason to . . . I don't know, find a bit more wonder in the world, I guess."

He lost himself in the sincerity of her gaze and realized she seemed to be studying his face as much as he was considering hers. At the realization, his ears burned red. He dropped his head forward, allowing his hair to cover his face.

Grind it; how does Lluthean do it?

He took one breath and pulled his hair out of his eyes to find her still staring at him. "What?" he asked.

She shook her head as if to say "nothing," but only smiled in silence.

Bryndor arched his back and set his palms on the bench to shift his weight off his butt cheeks, which had numbed ten minutes ago. The side of his hand bumped Ksenia's, and as she was doing the same thing, the realization caused them both to laugh.

"Sintra Rovinary, how long can your horses pull these wagons before we stop and camp?" asked Bryndor.

"Another four hours today," said the woman.

"So . . . as I recall, I owe you a story, right?" he asked.

Ksenia nodded. "Yes, you do, in fact. Story for a story, I believe you said."

"Alright, what do you want to hear?" he asked.

"Tell me about the Southlands."

He wrinkled his nose. "Really? But the Southlands are . . . well, there's just normal folks down there."

"Isn't that where you and your brother found the wolvryn?" she challenged.

Bryndor smiled and nodded once. "Indeed. The Southlands then."

He spent the next several hours talking about growing up in Journey's Bend, Rona's influence in their lives, and the difficulty making friends under the influence of the mantle that erased most people's memory of their identity. As he allowed himself to relive parts of his past that he had previously buried, a small piece of his awareness sat beyond it all, watching. This marked the first time he had shared stories about Rona without the smothering, oppressive sense of empty loss.

Instead, he remembered Rona's smile through the window of their home by the Shelwyn River. The scent memory of the kitchen after she brewed tea gave rise to other recollections, and he slipped into stories about how the slight woman managed to corral them all, even Kaellor, to her bidding.

Eventually, he described Journey's Bend and the hunt that led Lluthean and him to the wolvryn lair in the Moorlok. When he finished that part of the story, Sintra Rovinary grunted her appreciation.

The woman held the reins lightly in one hand and puffed on a fragrant long-stemmed pipe with the other. She glanced over her shoulder. "It doesn't take the speaker to know you've been touched by the hand of the Giver. Nobody survives a feral wolvryn."

"I can't argue the point," he said.

Ksenia stretched her arms overhead and then rubbed at the small of her back. "I've got to stretch my legs a bit."

"Sintra, I'm going to join her. I'm no stranger to driving a wagon. If you need a break, let me know."

"Only Luna Rova drive Rovinary wagons," said the woman with a wink. "But I appreciate the offer. Mind the back wheels when you drop."

He hopped down and crossed behind the wagon to fall in beside Ksenia. The muscles in the middle of his back still ached from the injuries he'd incurred during the stampede, but walking relieved the stiffness. Within moments, Boru inserted himself between them. He stroked his fingers against the grain of the fur over the wolvryn's spine and stopped when his hand ran into hers. He withdrew with a laugh and craned his neck to see over Boru's shoulder. Neska loped forward to walk on Ksenia's other side.

"It didn't take you long to get comfortable with them."

"I thought they were hunted to extinction. After your family, I'm the first Aarindorian to walk beside a wolvryn in a generation. Sintra is right; it's truly the Giver's rare touch."

"Have you tried to use your sympath gift with them yet?" he asked."

"I spoke briefly to Neska, just before the stampede, but that was under duress, so I haven't tried with either of them again."

"After Karragin's experience, I can understand. Though . . . I was curious to see what you might learn about Boru. I can communicate with him through the Cloud Walker hand language, and we can merge our senses, but it's not the same as an actual conversation."

"I'm willing to try it," said Ksenia.

"Can you manage as we walk, or do you need to be sitting?"

"Walking is fine. Give me a few minutes."

If Ksenia used her gift, it made no sound like the healer song, no brilliant flashes of zenith like one of Kaellor's wards. But something in Boru's demeanor changed. His breathing slowed from a casual pant, and he turned his head to the woman. Boru's next several steps seemed hesitant. His reluctance lasted only a moment, and then the wolvryn leaned his head against her shoulder, causing her to stumble. She giggled, and they resumed a casual stride.

They walked in silence for several minutes. At last, Ksenia released a wistful sigh. She stopped in place to watch as Neska bounded up a hill and Boru gave chase. When she turned to look back at him, she wore a thoughtful expression.

"What?" he asked.

"It's not what I expected, to be sure. The way they communicate, all the senses bleeding into each other . . . truly brilliant."

"It's not like that when you communicate with Winter?"

"Sometimes, I guess, but mostly, she's been conditioned to form her thoughts more like ours, so it's seldom such a rich experience. And don't get me wrong, Winter has a sharp mind, but nothing like those two, especially Neska."

"You spoke to them both? Kess, that's . . . incredible. I would love to be able to do that. I wish I had your gifts."

Ksenia stopped and blinked at him a few times, appearing genuinely bewildered.

"Everything . . . alright?" he asked.

She smiled and nodded, then caught up. "Yes, good, thanks. I'm just not used to anyone from Stone's Grasp thinking much about my abilities."

"Sounds like the place is packed with silly monks," said Bryndor.

"More than you might think," she agreed.

"So . . . what did Boru sound like when you spoke to him? What did they say?" asked Bryndor.

"At first, it took me a few minutes to understand how they express themselves. He has a voice that's deep and gentle but kind of . . . goofy, I guess? And he was preoccupied with some game of chase. I think he's bored, of all things."

"He is," said Bryndor. "He and Neska will need to hunt, and then she'll lead him on a game of chase. We'll not see them for a few hours."

"That's . . . remarkably perceptive and exactly what Neska said."

"You hang around them long enough, you recognize the signs," said Bryndor. "Sometimes they are easier to read than people."

"Are you sure you're not a sympath?" she asked.

Bryndor shrugged. "I don't know. If I'm gifted at all, my ability to channel zenith was restricted by the mantle my parents wove around Lluthean and me. But I've had training and enough time with the wolvryn to understand them."

The freckles on her cheek wrinkled as she considered his words. "Remind me why they did that, the mantle thing?"

Bryndor puffed his cheeks out. "Sintra Rovinary, how much longer till we reach camp for the night?"

The woman shaded the sun from her eyes and considered the horizon. "Two hours."

"Are you sure you want to hear this? It's a long story, to be sure," said Bryndor.

"You haven't bored me yet, and I'm not so good as Boru at games of chase."

"Alright, what do you know about the Abrogator's War?" he asked.

Chapter Forty-Five: Dangerous Missions

Nolan lay in his room, staring out a small window at twinkling stars hanging just above the ridgeline of the Great Crown. After another round of ale, he had collapsed on the bed, seeking to abandon his sense of guilt in sleep. Discovering the blood on Savnah's knife had sobered him beyond reprieve. Reddevek's order to conceal the matter left him utterly restless. He absolutely hated keeping secrets and had spent the last two hours imagining the different ways the truth would be revealed, and he'd be blamed for withholding the information.

A rap on his door accompanied the first blush of color as the sun kindled the far horizon. Nolan hopped up, the cold floorboards drawing him to full attention. While he would have typically lingered in bed, the disturbance was a welcome sensation. *Rescued from myself, at least.*

He opened the door to find Reddevek dressed in his Outrider fatigues, axe on one hip, a knife just shy of a short sword on the other. The warden glanced at him with one eye. "Meet downstairs in five minutes."

Nolan arrived in three minutes. He sat down at the same seat from the night before and traced the watermark left by his mug of ale. After circumscribing the edge, he looked across the table at the other watermarks. All but one formed a complete circle, but he couldn't now recall if that was where Savnah or Dexxin had sat.

Karragin's chiding tone entered his mind. *Reading futures in watermarks now? When did you develop that rune, brother?*

Elbows propped on the table, he dropped his face into his palms and waited for the others to arrive. Karragin descended the stairs first, navigating with catlike silence, her arrival only announced when she tousled his hair.

"Morning, brother," she said. "You don't look like you slept very well. Is the ale still sloshing around in your head?"

"Something like that," said Nolan.

A rumble of heavy, thumping footsteps pounded down the stairs as Savnah arrived, followed closely by Tovnik and Dexxin. They took their seats, and Reddevek ascended from the taproom, his fingers dipped into three wood mugs, a pitcher of water in the other hand.

The warden poured water into the three mugs and took one for himself. "Sorry, these three were the only ones I could find." He drained the mug and poured himself another before taking a seat.

He glared at the table surface as if waiting for an argument to break out. After a pregnant pause that drew out into awkward silence, he looked up to Savnah and Dexxin, who sat side by side. "Tell me that you two are out. Good and truly done with the breakers. If you're not out completely, I'll release you from the Outriders, and we'll part company right now, no consequence for past transgressions. But before we move forward, I have to know."

Savnah's eyebrows arched up, but she nodded in understanding. "Karra's vision gave me a second chance. I've been out since that first muddle with the grondle on the Borderlands."

Dexxin swallowed. "It took me longer, maybe as long as Callinora, but I'm out, and for what it's worth, I think Mullayne is too, but Craxton might take more time to come around."

"Good enough. He's your brother, and we all make special considerations when it comes to family, which is why I'm changing your mission this morning. Savnah, the knife your dad gave you last night, can I see it?"

She withdrew the knife from a pocket and slid the folded blade across the table. Reddevek caught it as it dropped into his hand, flicked it open with his thumb, then stabbed it into the center of the table.

"There's a trace amount of blood staining the hinge of the blade. You can see it if you look close," said the warden.

His words caused Savnah to sit back in her chair as if struck by a fell wind. "You . . . have my attention."

"Good," said Reddevek. "Because the blood is recent, not more than two or three days. The resonance is strong, and while it's similar to your father's, it's not his."

He let the words hang in the air, and they etched a war of confusing realizations across Savnah's face. She blinked, paled, twitched a lip, and eventually shook her head in disbelief. "No; that would mean that Dad had contact with Kovesk."

She stood up so abruptly that her chair tumbled back. Her nostrils flared, and she paced back and forth, opening and closing the leather straps that locked her moonblade axes at her belt.

Reddevek cleared his throat. "I'm going to ride alone to the south gates of Stone's Grasp while you four—"

Savnah stepped forward and pounded a fist on the table. "Where is he then?"

The room fell silent once again, and even the warden gave Savnah the space she needed. Slowly, she regained her composure, collected her chair, and sat back down. "Sorry, sir."

Reddevek grunted once. "It's less than I expected."

He waited a bit longer to be sure she had mastered her anger. "As I was saying, I'll ride to the south gates alone. You four are going after Savnah's brother."

Savnah stared at the knife slack-jawed, as if considering something, but the look of indecision only lasted a moment, and something darker than resolution passed over her face. She pinched her lips together and responded with a curt nod.

The warden grabbed the knife and folded the blade, then handed it to Nolan. "Pass your gift across the bloodstain, Nolan. You should get a strong read."

Nolan studied the warden's face. With uncharacteristic empathy, Reddevek winked once, then turned to address the others. Nolan puffed out his cheeks and made a pretense of activating his gift to imprint the blood resonance.

"Got it," he said and slid the blade back to Savnah.

Karragin turned to speak, but Savnah spoke over her, glaring at Karragin with a ruddy face. "Don't you say it, Lefledge. I'm not staying behind. I know the risks, but if anyone is going to set my brother free, it's me."

"Good," said Reddevek. "Because here are my orders. For this mission, you're still a quint. Savnah has the lead as prime for this one. She knows the territory. Nolan can get you close. Find her brother, sneak in under the moon, get in, and get out. Retrieve any intelligence on the breakers that you can find. After all that, Dexxin, if you're able, check with your brother to learn if it's safe to return to Stone's Grasp. By the time you arrive, we should have the capital secured. If not, then regroup at Callinora; that would be the safest place from the breakers that we know of. Any questions?"

The two primes stared at one another. Savnah, a broiling thunderhead of constrained rage, Karragin still as winter. Savnah's intensity caused Nolan to push back into his chair. At last, Karragin blinked once and turned back to the warden. "How are you going to pose as Kaellor if you are alone?" asked Karragin.

"Let me worry about that," said the warden.

"If you knew about this last night, why didn't you say anything?" asked Savnah.

"Because you all deserved last night, and I needed to be sure that the blood trail didn't belong to your father."

"And you're absolutely sure?" asked Savnah.

"I'm sure. I followed your father last night; he had late-night business in the center of town. The signature of the blood led away from him. I followed the blood trail to the northeast gate. There's a footpath that climbs into the Great Crown. I'm guessing it's used by goat herders, so you should be able to ride the Aarindin most of the way. You follow that path, and Nolan will lead you to your brother."

"Have you seen my father this morning?" asked Savnah.

"No, and I order you to steer clear. Your Derrigand temper has a reputation, and I can't have you jeopardize this rare opportunity. As soon as we are done, you ride out. I'll provide any cover story if your father asks. There will be time enough to settle things in the Derrigand household once Kovesk is free. Am I clear?"

"Yes, sir," they responded in unison.

Reddevek stopped to glare at each one of them in turn. "We've each got our part to play. Don't think that just because I'm diverting you from decoy duty that your mission isn't dangerous. Kovesk has been an invaluable albeit unwitting asset to the Lacuna. He will most likely be surrounded by a significant force."

The warden paused one last time. "When the Giver sets a gift before you, you don't set it aside. You use it. So use this, Savnah. Get your brother back."

Reddevek waited for them to indicate a final acceptance of the new mission, then spoke with more reverence than Nolan could ever recall. "Friends, keep your eyes to the horizon."

"Eyes to the horizon," they echoed back. The skid of wooden chairs on floorboards announced the end of the meeting as the Outrider quint stood and accepted another mission.

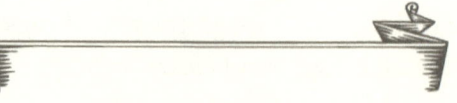

Chapter Forty-Six: The Giver's Last Breath

Trinney nibbled at a patch of grass under a bruised and clouded skyline. Karragin stood beside the Aarindin, stroking the mount's shoulder. The subtle magnetism of the Aarindin's grip passed under Karragin's palm. *Ksenia was right about you, after all. Eager to please and ready to grip.*

Savnah sat on the ground, whetstone rasping away at the edge of an already over-polished moonblade axe. With Reddevek's description of their current mission, the woman had shackled her characteristic cheeky nature. *I suppose if I read a prophecy forecasting my death and then rode forward to challenge the veracity of the prediction, I might keep my own counsel as well. All in all, she's managing better than I would have thought.*

The more Karragin thought about it, Savnah ran the quint much as Karragin would. She delegated Nolan the task of following her brother's blood trail but then diverted the rest of them off course, keeping to valleys and following streams and thin patches of timber when possible.

She had charged Karragin with linking to the Aarindin, using their superior sense of smell to track Nolan's mount from afar. Of all the Aarindin in the group, Trinney proved the most attentive and valuable in the task. Savnah's caution allowed them to reach Nolan without any contact from the farmers and folk who called the mountains outside Midrock home. The filly had led them to Nolan's secret observation post on a wooded bluff.

Now the group waited in silent surveillance of an abandoned church. The building, crafted of mountain rock and thick timber beams, rose three stories. A short wall ringed a garden with a Giver's Stone; the stone pillar topped with a depression would hold the ashes of the dead until the Giver saw fit to receive them in the wind.

A regular patrol of guards walked the grounds. Some wore partial uniforms of the city watch from Stone's Grasp. Others dressed in dark leathers, and all of them wore an assortment of weapons, including swords, axes, and crossbows. Nolan sat in rapt attention, using his gift to track their movements and numbers. He stood slowly and walked over to join them.

Savnah set her whetstone aside. "Get a sense for things, Nolan?"

"Yes," he said.

"Alright, gather around. Let's hear what we're up against," said the prime.

Nolan waited for Dexxin and Tovnik to approach, then began his report. "There are twenty-three people in addition to Kovesk. He's housed on the third floor, but they did let him out to walk the garden earlier." Nolan stopped and looked at Savnah. "He looked good, healthy, no injuries."

Savnah rolled her fingers in a circle and arched her scarred eyebrow, motioning for Nolan to continue.

"Right," he said. "At least half of the others are gifted. Two of them are just kitchen staff and the like, probably the bare minimum to feed and provision the lot. The others are well armed with crossbows and weapons made for close combat."

A distant, low rumble of thunder echoed across the mountains. The wind in the canyon had stilled, and the swollen clouds hovered low overhead.

Nolan continued. "They've got a lone Outrider, a munitions guy. I can't recall his name. He washed out a few years ago, I think. Anyway, he's not part of the routine patrols but—"

"It means the place will be rigged to blow if we're not careful. Good job, Nolan. Give us the possible entry points," said Savnah.

"I can sense incendiaries at the front doors and scattered about the grounds. But there's a potential breach point into the main building near the garden. The door appears solid, but it's not. When Kovesk returned from a walk, one of the guards had to wedge it back in place," said Nolan.

"Whether or not the Giver sees fit to give us the cover of rain, we'll make the run tonight. Nolan will lead us past the munitions and to Kovesk. Karra and I will make entry. We'll leave the Aarindin here at our extraction point. Tov and Dexx, you see that ledge halfway down the ravine there? That's your position. It will put you in bow range to cover our retreat. Shoot anything that tries to follow us. We'll go in ghost protocol, of course; paint your blades for shadow work. As much as I would love to end every single one of those guards down there, it will be safer for us to try to slip in and skin out under cover of the storm. Any suggestions?"

Karragin watched her friend carry out the mission briefing with professional detachment and felt more than just a sense of kinship or pride. Everything they had been through together, the shared misery of slogging through the grotvonen caverns covered in filth, fighting grondle, fighting bartusk, fighting to find a path free from the Lacuna . . . all of it made her grateful for the gift of second chances. She rubbed a hand across her forearm, across her rune of premonition, and sent a silent prayer of thanks to the Giver.

"It's a good plan," said Dexxin.

"Karra? What say you?" asked Savnah.

"It's good. Rain or not, when night falls, let's go free your brother," said Karragin.

Her words drew the shine of dew across Savnah's eyes, but to her credit, she pursed her lips together and gave a curt nod. "Right then. Nolan, don't burn yourself into the draft, but keep an eye on the place. Let me know if you discover anything else. Tovnik and Dexx, you should see about picking your way down to that ledge while there's still a bit of light. Any questions?"

She waited for anyone to reply, then broke the silence. "Eyes to the horizon, friends."

"Eyes to the horizon," they echoed.

Karragin channeled zenith into her sympath rune and made the rounds, giving each of the Aarindin instructions to remain in the wooded bluff. Nolan stepped close and pitched his voice low.

"There's one other thing. I found an old resonance belonging to Savnah's father. He's not there now, but he's definitely been here before," said Nolan. Karragin studied his face with her flat expression, so Nolan continued, "She's . . . not the same today. She's been a good prime, like you. I didn't know if telling her in front of everyone would undermine all that."

Karragin pursed her lips and nodded. "I get it. I'll let her know if it feels right. You should get back to your post."

Nolan picked his way back to the edge of the bluff and hunkered down in surveillance of the church. Karragin turned, intending to approach her friend, but Savnah found her first.

The prime hooked her thumbs over her belt and waited to ensure the others were not within earshot. "Karra, would you mind speaking to the Aarindin? No sense, you know . . . climbing back up here if the mounts wander away in the middle of the night."

Karragin studied Savnah's face. The woman made a pretense of examining the angry storm front. Under normal circumstances, the behavior would be expected. But this was Savnah, and she never bothered with such concerns. Karragin made an effort to soften her tone.

"It's already done. But you knew that, sister. So . . . why don't you tell me what you really came up here for?"

Savnah stared ahead and blinked, spilling tears down her cheek. She placed a finger to the left side of her nose and blew snot out the right, then took a deep breath. "Taker's grip. I was holding it together until you used that sister line."

"Sorry. It's long overdue, don't you think?"

Now Savnah smiled and huffed out a breath of air. She turned gleaming eyes to Karragin, an expression of pained regret poorly masked by her feeble smile. "Giver's truth right there. Alright . . . sister. Would you mind lighting up your rune of premonition? I think I could use some of that Lefledge good fortune today."

A furrow creased Karragin's brow. "Seems you're not the only one feeling out of sorts today. I should have done that already. I might already have a little bit of good news, though. Your father . . . he's not inside the church. Nolan searched for his resonance. There's a cold signal but nothing to indicate that he's here."

Savnah scratched at the back of her neck. "That only simplifies the mission. Dad and I will have our reckoning one day. Still . . . for now, it's a kindness."

Karragin lifted the edges of her mouth in a soft smile. "Give me a few minutes."

She sat on the ground and withdrew into herself. Ephemeral thoughts drifted in her mind, each receiving acknowledgment but then sliding away like raindrops on oilskin. She slowed her breathing and siphoned zenith, steeping and suffusing herself in the currents. Holding the power inside for a time, she allowed the force to linger at the edge of her sympath rune and then her arca prime. Her focus drew to their mission, and when it felt natural, she allowed the flow to suffuse her rune of premonition.

Shadowed images shifted in a dizzying array. She bore witness as Nolan led them under cover of rain. Lightning flashed, and thunder cracked, disorienting her all the more. She, Savnah, and Nolan crept over the low wall. Nolan guided them past munitions traps and through the back door of the church. Moments later, they left with a young man bearing all the facial features of a Derrigand, but just as escape appeared imminent, an explosion ripped across her vision, and Nolan and Kovesk lay dismembered on the ground.

Another set of images hovered at the edge of her vision, and she concentrated there. The shifting scene flooded her awareness. Now the assaulting company included Tovnik, while Nolan stayed in the cemetery, but this time, the assault took longer, and guards discovered their escape, cutting all of them down under a flock of bolts.

She forced her gift to unravel yet a different situation. She and Savnah crept in alone, taking their time. They managed to avoid several munitions traps and even reached the third floor where Kovesk was being held. But the images ended with Savnah dead on her back. Dark blood oozed from five crossbow bolts in her torso. Red lifeblood fountained from a bolt in her neck while another embedded itself in her cheek, causing her eye to bulge out at a ghastly angle.

Karragin pulled back a moment and floated in her gift, waiting for alternatives to present themselves. Eventually, she contrived several different scenarios, each ending with the death or apparent mortal injury of multiple members of the quint. Each new circumstance left the iron tinge of blood in the back of her mouth and lingering screams of pain haunting her awareness. At the last, she saw herself following Savnah through the front doors of the old church. Something about the approach felt right, but she needed to push her gift to see how that possible future might unfold.

"Karra! Karra, come back!" Nolan's wounded voice echoed in her mind.

Something stung her cheek, and Karragin opened her eyes, finding she had flopped to the ground and was lying on her back, panting. Cold raindrops spilled from a starless, dark sky and speckled her forehead. She sat up, and a wave of dizziness caused the sky to tilt to the side.

"Grind it. How long was I under?" she asked.

"More than an hour, I wager," said Savnah. "I tried to shake you out of it, but you seemed to drop in deeper than I've ever seen before. I wasn't sure if that was good or bad. So, I called up Tovnik and Nolan."

Karragin rubbed at her cheek, the remnants of a slap tingling on her jaw. Savnah handed her a waterskin. "Sorry, sis. I didn't know what else to do and didn't want you catching the draft," said Savnah.

She nodded her understanding, took a long drink of water, then allowed them to help her to her feet. Standing between them, her prime sister, her brother, and the medic, memories of watching each of them die in agony flickered in her awareness.

Tovnik unstoppered a vial and handed it to her. "Drink this. It's concentrated lammen berry juice. The taste is awful, but it should restore you from the edge of the draft."

She tipped the small bottle back and swallowed the contents. The bitter liquid drew her lips back in an involuntary grimace and left her throat as dry as ash. Another gulp of water made no difference in the persistent sensation. She tried to speak a complaint, but her voice only croaked as her tongue and cheeks withered to dry husks.

"I know. What's worse, the medicine or the malady, right? Take this," said Tovnik, fumbling with a kerchief from which he produced a wad of purple leaves. "Chew them up, then keep the plug on the side of your mouth for a time. It helps with the aftertaste."

Without hesitation, Karragin tossed back the entire bundle and began to chew. Tangy, sour juice replaced the desiccated sensation in her throat, and her tongue relaxed in her mouth. She breathed a sigh of relief and noticed the sense of malaise and dizziness leaving her. *Still, I don't know what's worse, a bit of the draft or a mouthful of muck?*

"Alright then, Karra. Let's have it. You saw something, so tell me," said Savnah.

"Our plan is a good one, but it's going to fail. There isn't any way I can see that we escape as a quint," said Karragin.

Savnah hocked a glob of spit into the darkness. "I know that. Don't you think I know that already? I know there's more than a good chance that I will die. Kovesk predicted as much. I'll not let the fear of that possibility keep me from freeing him."

"It's not just you, Savnah. If we approach the church from the back stairs, more than one of us dies. Depending on who goes in, Kovesk doesn't even make it out."

Savnah searched Karragin's eyes, shifting her focus from one eye to the other. Karragin nibbled at the scar of her upper lip as the prime began to pant and gripped her axe heads, tears welling up fresh in her eyes. "Karra, I can't leave him. Even if it means the Giver's absolute last breath in my life . . . I'll do anything. Just please . . . tell me what to do."

The mission is over. We must return to Stone's Grasp and regroup. Consult Father or the warden, find another way. The words looped over and over in Karragin's mind and found purchase on her tongue. But as she watched her friend wrestle with the awful, inevitable truth, something rare happened. A stinging sensation gathered in the back of her nose, rose up, and forced her to swallow to dissipate a swollen ache in her throat. Karragin blew air through her nose, sharp and brisk, and squashed her initial response.

She looked from Savnah to Nolan, then Tovnik. "Every time we try a breach through the back doors, more than one of us dies. So . . . we go in the front."

Chapter Forty-Seven: Following Their Nature

The dun gelding lathered at the mouth, and Volencia used a thin tendril of nadir to leech away some of its fatigue. The trick allowed the animal to continue at the pace she required, but it would likely drop dead very soon.

She had made the trip up to the canyon proclaimed as the hallowed ground five times now, encouraging and ushering the refugees from Sifter's Valley to the promise of safety in the highlands. There were now well over thirteen hundred in the canyon; many had come on horseback, and others on foot. Most carried no belongings, retreating up the mountain with the surging crowds.

Now they huddled together in groups scattered across the canyon floor. Some gathered with their extended family or with those wearing similar colors; others seemed united by simple shared misery.

At the far end, close to the chute that led to the summoning chamber below, the mountains pressed in like a ravine. Anyone attempting the ascent would find it a difficult affair. The grotvonen had little difficulty scaling the steep sides and were waiting in ambush for any who attempted the climb. She'd posted them a hundred feet up, hidden behind rocks and the meager timber, with instructions to kill anyone trying to climb out. If anyone navigated the steep paths, they would have little energy left to mount much of a defense.

The chieftain, Grasdok, had managed the grondle effectively. At first, she worried that the herd would rage, killing grotvonen and humans alike. But their brutality only made a more than effective motivation for the weary to migrate to right where she needed them to be.

She had forgotten how ravenous the grondle could be. Earlier, she rode past the crowds, checking their progress, until she reached the outskirts of Sifter's Valley. She had discovered three grondle attacking a family of four who were trying to escape in a wagon. She remembered warning people that wagons would never make the journey, but the purple clothing told her all she needed to know. *Minor nobles; likely thought they knew best and wanted to travel in comfort. Can't blame them, I suppose. Just acting according to their nature.*

The grondle had charged headlong at the wagon and slaughtered the horses first, falling on them with axes and spears. The largest wielded a great hammer. She had never seen the weapon wielded with enough force to brain a horse. The sight was an impressive feat of strength, quite literally stopping the animal dead in its tracks.

Next, they rounded up the family, killing the parents and one older boy with brutal efficiency. That left the girl, a screaming adolescent. The grondle couldn't decide how to divide the spoils, and an argument broke out, leading to a strange three-way tug of war. Before they tore the child apart, the alpha wrestled her free. Once he had the trophy in hand, he grabbed the girl by the feet, swung her overhead like a rag doll, and dashed her head against the ground. That put an end to her wriggling, and he used an axe to divide her into three reasonably portioned chunks.

They devoured the child right there, bones and all. Blood stained the front of all three, painting them in shades of red and black. The eerie glow from the mushroom spores might fade under so much gore, but the sight of their ruthless violence would make anyone flee up the mountain. And it did. Even the bravest of the mountain folk fled up the steep passes to escape the worst imagining of their nightmares come to life. While none had laid eyes on grondle before, all of them could imagine the embodiment of tortured spirits made flesh through the Winnowing of the Shades.

They migrated with purpose through the night and into the next day. Now, late in the afternoon, as the last refugees climbed up the canyon, Volencia rode back out one last time. Not more than a quarter mile away from the canyon, the ring of grondle trekked up the mountain. The dun gelding flared its nostrils and flattened its ears, threatening to bolt back up to the canyon. The horse bucked and reared until she lashed it in place with a constricting web of nadir.

Grasdok rode a grondle toward her and dismounted, then lumbered forward to greet her. Black dried blood stained the bristles of his chin. He gnawed casually on something, a shiny nub of rounded bone with shreds of muscle still attached. It took her a moment to realize it was a human foot. He worked over the delicacy with no more concern than a chicken leg. The chieftain swept a beefy hand back across the herd. "We are here. Hoomans . . . enough?"

"Yes. You did well. We have more than enough to complete the ritual. Wait for the sun to set, then bring the herd close to the entrance to the canyon, but don't enter. The humans need to see you and believe they are on safe ground. Once you hear the drums, start pushing forward. Don't kill any of them; just force them forward at a slow pace. We need as many alive as possible until the Rite of Sundering is complete."

The chieftain scratched the bottom of a tusk and picked at a piece of meat, sucked it off his clawed finger, then lifted his chin to the canyon. "How we know when rite is done?"

"The rite is done when the drums stop," she explained. "Wait until then, and anyone remaining in the canyon, human, horse, or otherwise, are all yours."

Grasdok pulled his mouth back in a feral grin that paled his lips. "Is good . . . good plan."

"Alright. When the drums start, move the people slowly forward; then the drums stop when it's over." She lifted the bonds of nadir holding her horse, and the gelding reared back then bolted, nearly tossing her from the saddle. With an effort, she regained her balance and leaned forward, giving the horse free rein. It sprinted back to the canyon, past several pockets of people, then staggered, listing to the side. Volencia dismounted just before the animal collapsed to the ground, panting.

The refugees huddled together, too exhausted to give her dying mount much notice. Volencia walked along the outskirts of the refugees and made her way to the ravine. High above, a man screamed, the wail followed by the sounds of something tumbling through the trees, snapping branches as it fell. The corpse of a young man crunched into the rocky ground with the deathly clack of bones breaking against stone.

She climbed onto an adjacent boulder to better address the crowd. "People of Sifter's Valley, hear me. Do not lose hope, for this is hallowed ground. The spirits and shades that harry us will not enter here, but you must remain in the canyon."

The abrogator studied the crowd. *I can't believe this actually worked. I knew fear clouded the mind, but not so much as to make them believe that grondle represent their tortured spirits. Still, a few might need more convincing.*

She pointed at the corpse of the man, the handiwork of her grotvonen perimeter patrol. "Even if we try to scale the cliffs, it seems the spirits will find us."

A man yelled out, "How long can we stay here? There's no food or water, no shelter!"

"I know. Bear with me. There is a way out. I need to prepare the way. My ancestors made a slide at the far end of this ravine; it will deliver us to safety on the other side of the mountains, but there is a price."

"The Taker always has a price," shouted another man. "So what is it?"

"There is a gate at the bottom. I can unseal the way when the moon rises. To use the slide before then will drop you to your death. But if we hold out until then, I can give us safe passage."

Voices in the crowd muttered, some angry, others laced with fear. Most of the people, though, were too shocked to listen, and others were simply too far away to hear her. Volencia searched the crowd and found Cabe sitting on the ground next to Gauvin, the gleeman. Both men looked as bone-tired as the rest of the refugees. *Perfect.*

She hopped down and walked over to them. "I'm glad you made it when so many others did not. Cabe, where is your daughter? Surely, she . . ."

The innkeeper lifted his head in the direction of a group gathered fifty paces away. "She's well enough, checking on some friends over there."

"Good," said Volencia.

Gauvin peered up at her, a haunted expression in his eyes. "I've heard tales of beasts like the ones we saw, but never imagined anything so . . . evil."

Cabe wiped a sleeve across his brow. "It doesn't seem real. If I had not seen them myself, I would have thought revelers had too much mead. But I saw them, the . . . shades, or spirits, whatever . . . trapped inside those beasts. It's unholy."

"I mean no offense," said the bard. "But you seem awfully calm about this whole mess. The things I've seen today made even the toughest mountain folk run in fear."

Volencia forced a misty-eyed expression. "I'm . . . struggling to figure out how to move us forward, and I'm more scared than you can imagine. What if things don't work out? What if I've led you all the way up here for nothing?"

She stared at the ground, waiting. Eventually, Cabe stood and patted her shoulder. "You've given us a chance," he said. "And that's more than anyone else offered us today. How can we help? You mentioned a slide, a way out of here?"

She sucked in a breath, thinking about how to frame the lie. "My ancestors consecrated this canyon against evil spirits for a reason. I can't say that I understand it all, but there's an exit, a slide carved into the backside of this ravine with a blood gate. My mother used to tell me stories of the blood gate waking the drums under the mountain to open the way to safety."

Both men scrutinized her words. At last, Cabe broke the silence. "Your ancestors must be Dernegian, and everyone knows of their skill mining gemstones that harness zenith. But the gate you're describing sounds like dark magic."

Gauvin rubbed at an ear. "Not dark magic exactly . . . blood magic, like the Beskens. I've played the courts of that coastal city, and the people there rely on all manner of magical devices that require a blood offering to work. Some can only be triggered by those of a certain bloodline."

Cabe sighed with acceptance, as if the entire situation made a strange kind of logic. "Do you have to go down there alone? It sounds dangerous; maybe one of us should accompany you," said Cabe.

"As I understand the lore," said Gauvin, "if there's blood magic involved, we should wait. All the stories I've ever heard where heroic adventurers attempt to subvert such a device end badly. Better to let the one with the proper bloodline make the journey."

She nodded in agreement. "I think that's right, Gauvin."

She took a moment to survey the refugees before continuing. "The people . . . we've all been through so much, I didn't think I should mention anything having to do with more blood. But, as I understand it, my blood, smeared on the lock when the moon is in the night sky, will open the gate and allow safe passage. I think that when that happens, there will be a drumming . . . a sound to let us know that the way is clear. Everyone should be able to slide down, and if they come one at a time, they should come out on the other side of this mess."

Cabe pursed his lips. "So . . . no . . . you can't tell them all that. More than half would take their chances with the shades on the mountain. After what those beasts did to the few armed guards in attendance, I don't have to tell you what a bad idea that would be. Better to keep it simple."

"Alright. How do you think we should proceed?" she asked.

The innkeeper searched the crowds. "If we can't use the slide until tonight, we've got time. Gauvin and I will gather the heads of families and explain to them *some* of what you told us." He looked to the bard for confirmation.

Gauvin sighed and offered a weak smile. "In stressful times, people need a plan. They need to see a way out. Otherwise, they tend to follow their nature, and for some folks, that's not pretty."

"Agreed," said Cabe. "When night approaches, I'll post up at the entrance to the slide with a few men and make sure that people don't come down too early."

Volencia sighed, then offered them a half-smile. "If you two can manage that, I'll do my part down below. If it works—when it works—send the first people down when you hear the drums, I guess."

The two men wandered over to a group of refugees and engaged them in conversation. These two became four, and they, in turn, approached another group of stragglers. Volencia had been holding her breath. She exhaled and turned to walk to the back of the ravine. For now, at least, it appeared that Cabe would be able to sway the masses to enter the slide at the appropriate time.

What happens if this falls apart, if they don't drop in at the right time? What happens if I can't free Tarkannen from the Drift? What if it's all been for nothing?

She sat at the edge of the slide, appearing to stare into darkness while searching the recesses of her mind. The number of sacrifices she had made over the years, all in the quest for more control, more power . . . all of it hinged on freeing Tarkannen, on the secrets he could share and the mastery only he could impart.

The sun dipped low enough that a shaft of light skipped over the mountains and into the glassy, smooth interior of the slide. She ran a hand over the surface, polished free of imperfections by countless globes of nadir.

Stop caving to your lesser nature and make it happen.

With that thought, she used her hands to push herself forward, alarmed at how fast she plummeted into darkness. She wedged her feet down and placed her hands flat to slow her descent, expecting to feel some heat or friction, but the slide dropped her unerringly down to the grotvonen summoning chamber.

Cold air blasted her face and penetrated her clothing as she flew down. The disorientation of falling through darkness caused her stomach to lurch into her throat. In the periphery of her awareness, she registered the familiar stale and humid air of the grotvonen warrens and realized that the end of her journey drew near. Volencia gave in to the drop and siphoned nadir, holding it ready and clutching her hands over her abdomen.

She became totally weightless as the chute spilled her through the ceiling of the great summoning chamber. The rancid stink of grotvonen assailed her senses. She lashed out with tentacles of nadir, flailing about, but couldn't find purchase. In a panic, she flared the extensions, and one of them struck something solid.

She hoped it wasn't the floor of the cavern and put all her focus into the lashing. Her fall was arrested as she swung like a pendulum through the air, then crashed into solid stone. She hung dazed and spinning for several minutes, shoulder and back throbbing in pain.

Eventually, she lowered herself to the floor. She dispatched the nadir coils and sent probing tendrils into her back and shoulder, numbing the pain and reducing the swelling of the bruised tissues.

That's about the best I can hope for.

Volencia swept her gaze across the chamber, where a dim light caught her attention. Eguma stood like a faint beacon beside the Consort. Several umbral were perched on bent legs around a pool of refined liquid nadir. Occasionally, one of the umbral reached into the dark mercurial substance and removed an impurity, like pulling a thread from the outer layer of a cocoon. They flicked the offending filament into the air, where it dissipated.

"Eguma," she hissed. "They were supposed to wait for me before starting. What if they had attracted the attention of something other than Tarkannen?"

Eguma pulled on the frayed edge of his shirt. "I can not control the umbral, mistress. Waiting is not . . . their nature, but they keep watch in your absence. Besides, we still need the shamans, and they come soon."

The surface of the nadir pool rippled; something from the depths was threatening to push through. The umbral seemed unconcerned, but Volencia channeled a thick blade of nadir in preparation to repel any unwanted guests. She watched as a bubble formed, thinning into a raised mound. Something seemed to press up from the underside of the pool, and for an instant, the nadir thinned enough that she thought she could see two sigil-riddled hands press up and out. For the time being, the pool resisted anything exiting the Drift, and the bubble melted back.

But very soon, we'll set you free.

Chapter Forty-Eight: The Killing Field

REDDEVEK WALKED OUT of the Wolf's Maw feeling unsettled. A shave and haircut had done little to alter his mood. The task set before him placed him well outside his comfort zone, and the fact that he had dismissed his Outriders left him with no supporting cast to carry out the planned deception.

Why did I ever agree to this in the first place? The Taker's luck will find me dead at the end of a Lacuna blade, trussed up in frilly robes. At least I got the whelps out of danger.

And that thought, at least, did mollify his mood a little. He slung a heavy pack over his shoulder, surprised by the weight of the kingly silks, robe, and costume crown purchased from the minstrels who had performed the night before. Then he recalled the small cluster of munitions he'd secreted into the bottom of the pack.

He found Zippy, tipped the groomsman, and made his way down the switchbacks that wound through town. Looking farther down to the front gates of Midrock, he could see that the roads already were congested with more people than he cared for. The sooner he left the town and got onto the open road, the better.

Zippy picked his way around the caravans and wagons of people making the trip to Stone's Grasp. After eating trail dust for a few hours, Reddevek directed the Aarindin into sparse timber, choosing game trails over the open road. He tried not to overthink how he might create a diversion at the front gates of Stone's Grasp and instead wondered how the Lacuna might react.

By all accounts, they seemed poised to respond with violence. *The trick will be to remain out of bowshot yet still close enough that they think I'm Kaellor.*

He shifted the pack on his back, considering how to deploy some of the munitions. The vendor he had procured the fireworks from had stated that they had no martial benefit. Still, Reddevek felt pretty sure he could do more than grab everyone's attention if he directed the firework like a missile instead of an overhead display. He'd chosen three "moon sparks" that were supposed to shoot white and blue cascades of light in a sphere-shaped burst.

It's not exactly Kaellor's guardian ward, but it will have to do.

Despite separating from the crowds, a pervasive unsettled feeling continued to seep into his awareness. If he were honest, any novice in the Outriders could accomplish the task of impersonating Kaellor before the Lacuna. The subterfuge involved seemed minimal, given that they would view him from a distance. But once the breakers thought he was the prince, then what? His plan was to engage as many as possible in combat, then lead them on a chase across the kingdom.

It'll either be the Taker's foolish gamble or the Giver's bright blessing. Either way, I'm not the only one risking my life for the future of Aarindorn.

His thoughts wandered back to the quint he'd assigned to rescue Savnah's brother. Sitting in the tavern, watching them bond over ale, shared misery, and near-death experiences, he felt justified in altering the mission plan outlined with Kaellor.

The Lefledge siblings had developed into a formidable duo. Any doubts about Nolan's scouting prowess lifted when he considered how the young man had led them into the Great Crown and through the grotvonen warrens. Karragin managed the responsibility of leadership better than most. He had imagined that her stiff nature would make it difficult for those around her to find camaraderie, but something in seeing her rare smile around the table last night had sealed his decision to send them on a different mission.

Now he wondered if he should have accompanied them, yet . . . he also knew they could likely more than manage any resistance the Lacuna offered.

Tovnik had turned out to be an effective healer and a capable archer. He could have left the Outriders the prior year with his obligation fulfilled. *It's got to be the Lefledge woman. I suppose, were I of an age, I might follow her to the darkest corners of Karsk as well. It will be interesting to see where that goes.*

Savnah and Dexxin, however—those two had surprised him the most. Their betrayal and alignment with the Lacuna had enraged him enough to consider a field court-martial and summary execution. He never imagined either of them capable of so much change.

They've all fought against Tarkannen's forces. Seeing an umbral up close . . . that's enough to convert most heretics, I'll wager. But how will we convince the rest of Aarindorn?

His thoughts drifted to Ranika, not for the first time that morning. He smiled at the memory of her calculating glare when he proposed that she join Kaellor's group for the final push to Stone's Grasp. They both knew that he only wanted her out of harm's way. Kaellor and the wolvryn were more than enough to ensure the princes' safe arrival. Sneaking into Stone's Grasp instead of riding headlong at the front gates to the city while wearing a royal disguise seemed like a pretty good way to ensure she had a chance.

Giver knows when this is all over, she deserves that more than most. He grunted. *She'll need it more than most. Her street smarts will get her only so far in a kingdom of zeniphiles. I wonder how long it's been since an abrogator with a conscience walked Karsk? Probably longer than the last time one stormed the gates.*

He ruminated over all the young people under his leadership. His time with Ranika had changed him, and he was only just now realizing the full extent of it. In times past, he preferred to give orders, expecting others to obey. He chose not to care if his way was rough or even brutal, if his words were callous or harsh. Life was more manageable that way. If you never invested in the tender during their first year of training to join the Outriders, you found it a minor consequence when you had to cut them loose.

Somehow, the street urchin from Callish had opened his eyes to the power of simply showing up, and in the end, he had learned that investing in another person was its own reward.

He sighed, twisting a knuckle into an ache in the small of his back. *Giver, if you listen to any of this, see a broken-down warden through one last mission, and I promise to try and be the man I am when I'm with her . . . for everyone else . . . with all the others . . . grind me, you know what I mean.*

Zippy's head lifted ever so slightly, and his ears perked forward. Reddevek studied the ground ahead while removing the safety straps from his weapons. He had become complacent, lost in his thoughts, and wandered more than thirty paces into a glen without surveying it first.

Zenith thrummed through his arca prime, and he cast his awareness all around. The signals of four humans sang back through his gift, their trails fresh. Two waited in ambush, hidden by the grasses only twenty paces ahead. The other two had already circled behind him.

He thought about the bargain he had just made with the Giver and briefly considered announcing his identity in the hopes of a peaceful resolution, but the twang of a bow shifted his focus from one of peace to one of vengeance. Burning pain flared across the side of his neck as the arrow passed.

"So be it." Reddevek surrendered to his training. Instinct and battle rage overtook him. Zippy surged ahead, signaled by the motions of his hips and feet. The Aarindin veered to the right, and Reddevek swept his single-bladed axe in a fluid overhead arc, slid his hand down to the end of the haft, and gripped at the perfect balance point, catching one of the assailants with a satisfying crack as the axe blade split breastbone when he passed.

Zippy looped around in a circle to the bowman. The man was rushing to nock another arrow. The warden threw his axe; he missed, but the throw still caused the archer to fumble his weapon. As Zippy thundered past, he kicked a hoof out, catching the man in the ribs.

Reddevek shouted a command, and the Aarindin released his grip, hooves churning up clods of soil as he charged the front assailant on the left. The warden dropped into the grasses, setting down his pack, being mindful of the cargo. He tracked the other figure, who had circled behind. The man took three steps and stopped, appearing to take a stance, one foot before the other in a side profile, while aiming at the Aarindin with his bow.

Only the swishing reeds announced the warden's attack as Reddevek surged through the grasses just in time to prevent another bowshot, his dagger plunging up under the man's ribs, ripping until he heard the expected pop as the blade penetrated the inviolate tissues. The bowman panted, mouth agape, unable even to scream. The warden snarled, twisted the steel, then wrenched it free.

He turned before the bowman collapsed, focusing on the last of the four attackers. Zippy bellowed and snorted in rage, then reared back and crashed his front hooves down once, then twice, before trotting off in a circle, neighing and tossing his head.

Grasses strafed across his cheeks as Reddevek dropped belly to the ground for cover. He cast his gift in a wide net in search of more enemies. Only the four signals appeared, and of those, only one seemed alive, the archer who'd caught a hoof as the Aarindin charged by. Reddevek waited to be sure that the life force of the other three had faded. With their deaths a certainty, he crawled through the field to find the last bowman.

A middle-aged man wearing well-camouflaged hunting leathers lay on his side, his breathing ragged. A broken bow lay nearby, the string tangled in Reddevek's axe. The cold steel of his short sword resting on the man's neck announced the warden's arrival. Sweat trickled down the man's face and jaw, running over the edge of the blade, and he moaned softly with pained breaths.

The archer struggled to hold thumb to thumb and finger to finger, forming a quivering circle, then he sprang the fingers apart. Bright eyes stared at him above a sharp nose and angular chin. "Mercy. Lord Kunzie will pay . . . pay for my safe return."

"Why did you attack me? Are the Lacuna hunting Outriders now?"

"Lord K-Kunzie just said . . . look for anyone . . . traveling on Aarindin and . . . heading to the east, to-toward Stone's Grasp. Please, my boys . . . are they dead?"

Reddevek pressed a palm to his eye, refusing to answer the question. "Why Aarindin? Why not any of the other travelers on the road?"

"Gifted . . . only gifted can m-manage the Aarindin . . . and besides . . . everyone knows that the Outriders . . . they're loyal to the d-dead crown."

"Taker's blind eye, man, is that really what you monks believe? Outriders are loyal to Aarindorn . . . all of it." Reddevek pulled his blade away and pinched the bridge of his nose, disgusted by the revelations of the conversation.

He lifted his head across the field and swallowed his bile at the lie. "I think two of them got away. Probably went to get reinforcements. How many other patrols are out here then?" pressed the warden.

The man nodded, appearing eased by the news. "Yes . . . likely so . . . umm . . . m-maybe a dozen. Most of us were recruited from the Sprawl. I d-don't know . . . please. The pain, you've got to help me. I'm a m-man of Aarindorn. Same as you," he gasped.

Reddevek sighed, defeated by the futility of it all and exhausted by the receding tide of battle rage. His shoulders dropped. Why did it always come to something like this? Choices were supposed to develop your character, not blacken your soul. He gripped the hilt of the short sword. "Not anymore."

Before the man realized the finality of Reddevek's response, he'd chopped the sword blade down twice in rapid succession. The first chop parted neck muscle and vessels, splattering blood on the grass. The second clunked through bone and cartilage. Bootheels rattled in the dirt for a moment; then, the archer lay still.

Reddevek retrieved his weapons, cleaning the blood on the clothes of the dead and inspecting their faces. Up close, he could see that all three had handsome eyes set above narrow bridged noses and angular chins . . . brothers. All of them were his sons. The discovery that he had butchered an entire family, a father and three sons, leeched any motivation to move from the spot.

He lingered there, surrounded by the dead family, considering the senselessness of it all. What did it matter if they stopped Tarkannen from returning when Aarindorn was already rotting from the inside?

Zippy nickered softly once, but the sound was muted as he gripped the pack in his teeth. The Aarindin set down the pack, then sauntered in a slow circle, turning to face him. Reddevek pulled his gaze from his feet to find the compassionate acceptance of his Aarindin staring back at him. He lost himself in the unflinching expression of his friend's dark eyes.

Eventually, he shouldered the pack and walked around Zippy, inspecting him for any injuries. A shallow cut ran along his chest and another on his flank, blood already dried to black. The warden stopped and placed his head alongside the Aarindin's.

"Giver's mercy, you're no worse for any of it. And believe me, that's one blessing I'm thankful for tonight. If we go on, Zip, this is it. After this, it's you, me, and Nika into the Great Crown. We'll join a Moonie clan and leave all of this behind. They're gonna absolutely love you. What do you say?"

A soft, huffed nicker escaped Zippy's mouth. Reddevek craned his head back. Somewhere, in the depths of the gentle onyx orbs, zenith flickered, a cerulean blue acceptance of the warden's proposal.

"Eyes to the horizon it is, my friend."

Zippy knelt, allowing Reddevek to throw a leg over, then the great mount rose and left the killing field behind. Reddevek shoved the day's trauma into a corner in the back of his mind. He would unpack that, like so many other horrors, someday. But not today.

They rode well into the evening, Reddevek flaring his arca prime and directing them away from other riders and groups of people. The tactic led them in a serpentine pattern, but they made steady progress east. Fatigue crept into the muscles of his back, achy and pervasive.

At one point, when he rekindled his arca prime, a cluster of more than eight signals approaching from the north chimed into his awareness. Reddevek urged Zippy into a canter and released his gift, mindful of the draft and hoping to lose any pursuers in the dark.

After ten minutes, he surveyed the path to the north. The way appeared free of any humans, but when he directed his attention behind them, the signals reappeared bright in the field of his gift.

"Taker's bite, they've got horses, Zip. Time to show them what an Aarindin can do."

The mount responded to his urging, and they raced down a gentle slope, around instead of through stands of timber, over rolling hills, and down into sprawling valleys until finally emerging onto the vast plains that spread for miles before Stone's Grasp. They sped under the light of Baellen.

Reddevek felt the dampness of the Aarindin's sweat under his legs and drew Zippy to a walk. He cast his gift about, searching for any pursuers. The unmistakable flares of hunters both behind and now in front of them flared in the sight of his gift. Reddevek wilted forward over the Aarindin's neck. "I'm sorry, Zip, it's like . . . like they knew we would be out here."

The Aarindin murmured a lively whinney that sounded oddly eager. It reinvigorated Reddevek's spirit. He scanned the field and the beacons of riders too numerous to count and started to laugh. A maniacal acceptance of being forced down a pathway of endless violence overtook him.

It would be an end that the Moonies would record in song and story to recount forever, if only anyone would bear witness to it. "I am Reddevek Taim! And if you're a circle breaker, then run to the Giver and beg for her favor, because tonight I'm bringing the Taker's wrath!"

The warden hefted his axe in one hand, sword in the other, rasped them together, and urged his Aarindin forward. Zippy surged to a gallop, smooth and easy, closing the distance in seconds. Reddevek scanned the enemies, thinking to identify a resonance of fear. But the entire line stood resolute, their auras unflinching. Even their mounts seemed eager for conflict.

The Aarindin realized their good fortune before he did, and Zippy slowed to a trot and stood a hundred strides before the steadfast line of riders. A zeniphile in their ranks cast a bright nimbus of light, silhouetting more than twenty Outriders. As one, they charged, dividing to ride around the warden, attacking his pursuers.

A lone rider, separate from the main host, rode forward at a walk. A familiar grizzled face came into view under the moonlight. "Bringing the Taker's wrath? I haven't seen that kind of fire in you for an age, little brother," said the overwarden.

Reddevek signaled Zippy to walk ahead and drew up beside Kaldera. They interlocked forearms in a formal gesture that belied the intimacy of their friendship. Reddevek huffed a laugh. "Giver bless you, Kal. I thought you were the Lacuna. They've been dogging me all the way here."

Kaldera nodded understanding, then lifted his chin back to the sounds of fighting. "We've had to dispatch five or six groups of them already. I'm glad I found you before they did."

"How did you know to come find me out here?" asked Reddevek.

"Do you know what a speaker's true gift is, Redd? Once they've read you, touched your mind, they can reach out and touch it when they have need."

"Movshka?" asked Reddevek. "He's read you before?"

"Years ago, when I was a tender on my first mission and forgot to approach their camp on foot. I nearly lost my Aarindin in the exchange. Letting the speaker read me was a small consequence at the time. Anyway, his communications are nothing more than broken images and dream fragments. It took a few nights for me to understand what was happening," explained Kaldera.

"I'm glad you came when you did. I was ready to make a messy end of things." Reddevek turned Zippy in a slow circle toward the fading sounds of battle. "What do we do now?" asked the warden.

"Now, little brother, I ride back to the forward base camp to secure the fortifications. Our patrols have encountered packs of grotvonen and grondle roaming too close to the Pillars. You, I believe, are to impersonate the return of a prince. You should have enough time to rest up and make the gates by sunset. I thought you might appear a little more imposing if you were accompanied by a flank of Outriders. What do you say?"

Chapter Forty-Nine: All About the Details

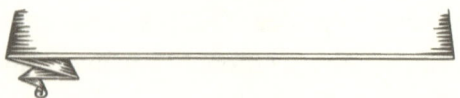

Travelers from all corners of Aarindorn crowded into Stone's Grasp. They crammed the streets of the lower districts, filling the taverns and gaming houses. Occupancy was at an all-time high, not just in the brothels but the inns as well. Nobles took up residency in their estates in the high district, each arriving with an entourage of servants.

Vice Regent Chancle Lellendule had organized a diverse array of food and beverage vendors for the arrival of so many guests. The aromas from a veritable menagerie of grilled meats rose up to his observation point on the royal plaza. The expansive cantilevered balcony offered a complete view of the capital. Nobles and their families arriving for the spring assembly milled about the lower baileys of the castle grounds like so many ants over a discarded morsel of crownberry muffin.

He stood at the stone railing and wondered, not for the first time, how these people might shape the future of the kingdom. He had a good sense for the political sentiments of the merchants and few nobles who resided locally, but the rest, all those arriving from Stellance and the western duchies, were tricky to pin down. *So much hangs in the balance this year. I've done my best to move the kingdom along the right path. Let's hope your words can unify them, Therek.*

Movement drew his eye to the broad set of stairs to the side, and he waved at a familiar face. His older brother, Hestian Lellendule, walked up the last few steps. The wind whipped through the man's wispy, ginger-colored hair, faded white at the temples. Hestian stopped at the top of the climb, palms on knees, panting.

"Hes, I could have saved you the climb, brother. Duty will draw me down the steps eventually," said Chancle.

Hestian stood up straight, arching his back in a gesture that accentuated his prominent midsection. He blew one long breath through pursed lips and scratched at the smartly trimmed beard along his jawline. "I'm overdue for the exercise. The old lynx keeps me sitting at the desk managing duty rosters, signing requisitions, and creating supply inventories . . . it's enough to make my teeth ache."

They embraced for a moment, Chancle finding comfort in the familiar feel of his brother's muscled shoulders. "Yes, well . . . these are strange times we live in," he said. "While I hope there is little need for a national army, nobody can dispute the disturbances at the border. And as merchants expand trade into the border kingdoms, our security as a nation becomes even more—"

A twisted swirl of wind gusted around the both of them in a torrent so loud that neither man could hear beyond its roar. Hestian held up a hand, dismissing the whirlwind and forestalling further explanation. "Save your speeches for the nobles, Chance. Did you not hear me the first time? I've had my fill of it for the week. So why don't you come down, and we can find our way to the bottom of a vintage bottle of resco?"

Chancle had to admit that the opportunity to lose himself in an evening of drinking with his brother sounded like a lot more fun than entertaining the nobles, but he also knew how much was at stake this assembly. "As much as I hate to disappoint you, I'm far more afraid of what your lovely wife might think were she to discover us taking up residence in a seedy corner tavern. Where is Evonda?"

Hestian leaned out over the rail, pointing to a tent with a maroon banner flapping in the breeze. Several wine barrels rested in the shade of the awning. "We're partial to that particular wine vendor from Stellance. She and Larik are putting in an order for the manor house."

"You got your son out of the Outriders for the assembly?" Chancle asked.

Hestian puffed out his barrel chest. "What good is the burden of office if I can't exercise a little executive privilege now and again?"

Chancle shook his head in disbelief. "I've never known a man more duty-bound than you, brother. You're the great loyal guster, but I think at the moment that your hot air is blowing in the wrong direction. No . . . I'll bet Larik happened to be on assignment and was granted leave by the overwarden."

Hestian chuckled once. "You have the right of it. His quad and a few others are on security detail. They escorted some of the nobles from Beclure and Dulesque. He's only got a few hours and is back at it, so Evonda pressed him into her service."

"Using a gifted outrider, an empath no less, to obtain favorable terms with a poor wine merchant from Stellance . . . that's rather crafty. I like it," said Chancle.

Hestian grunted. "He's not a poor wine vendor. Holling knows his way around a distillery and turns out an exceptional product, but let's not pretend he doesn't turn his fortune with his negotiation skills—skills supported by his own empathic gift. Evonda enjoys the game, the haggling. She'll rely on her own gifts, but if things don't turn her way, she's not averse to letting her son offer counsel."

"They do make a formidable duo at the bargaining table," said Chancle.

"Indeed. If things go well, we'll have the manor house stocked with a rare vintage in a few days. Will you have time to stop over?"

Chancle barely registered the invitation. Coordinating all of the small and large tasks he had set in motion was occupying more of his attention than he cared to admit.

"Chance? Brother?" Hestian's hand on his shoulder drew Chancle's awareness back to the present. "It's a lot this year, isn't it?"

"A lot hangs in the balance, Hes. I've done all I can to help steer Aarindorn to prosperity, to safety . . . and yet—"

"No matter how hard you lean on the rudder, sometimes the boat simply goes where the current takes it," said Hestian.

"Yes, sometimes it does feel that way."

Hestian left his hand on Chancle's shoulder and jostled him back and forth, a compassionate expression on his face. "After this week, there will still be grondle at the border, grot in the Great Crown, Lacuna and loyalists, gifted and runeless . . . you can't change any of that. So stop trying."

Chancle suppressed a surge of heat building at his neckline. He leaned back to consider his brother as he mastered the swell of emotion. "I've lost too much and given too much to stop. It's all I am these days, it seems."

"I know," said Hestian, a sly twinkle in his eye. "That's why I'm suggesting that you and I sneak away and enjoy ourselves while we can."

Taker's teeth, it's tempting . . . forget it all and drift away under a haze of resco and snuff.

A raspy voice cut into the conversation as Therek Lefledge covered the distance from the doors with but a few sweeping strides. "It's either the Giver's divine blessing or the Taker's mischievous shadow when I find two Lellendule brothers standing in whispered conversation, surveying the masses."

Hestian turned, his beard highlighting a full smile. "Can't it be a little of both, my friend? I remember a night long ago when we convinced you to accompany us to an illegal gaming hall in the Sprawl."

Therek answered the man with a knowing look, part mirth and part regret. "First, that was actually quite a long time ago. And second, don't remind a man of his flaws before he steps in front of the assembly."

Chancle came to the regent's rescue. "As I recall, with your help, we managed a purse so large that the gaming house had to close, and you met your wife for the very first time. All in all, a pretty good night."

They shared a laugh, and Therek bowed his head. "Point well conceded then; that was a rather good night."

They stood together at the stone rail, surveying the activity below. A warm breeze scalloped the waters of Lake Ullend in the distance, the ripples glinting in the late afternoon sun. "Storm clouds gather to the south and east. Do we have you to thank for the fair skies over the city today?" asked Therek.

"It's a blessing of the Giver," said Chancle. "I've not had to tax my gift beyond monitoring the winds today. That storm front should skirt over the lake and allow for the alchemics and fireworks show to be enjoyed by all. All the same, I'll do my best to keep the streets dry."

"Once again, you have my thanks," said Therek. The regent shaded his eyes against the setting sun and grunted. "Even a caravan of Moonies seeks to join the revelry this year. That's rather unusual."

"If you like, I can have a quad or a contingent of the city guard inquire about their affairs," said Hestian.

"I wouldn't worry overmuch," said Therek. "Moonies rarely venture inside the city walls. From my understanding, they don't trust the confinement. They were likely attracted by the crowds."

"I agree," said Chancle. "All the travelers arriving for the spring assembly have congested the roads for weeks now. Peddlers and sideshows always use the opportunity to attract more business."

Therek walked a short distance to a podium set in the center of the balustrade. A polished stone globe with swirls of silver and gold rested on a pillar beside the makeshift stage. The regent placed his palm on the sphere and tilted his head, listening. A soft whirring sound echoed throughout the entirety of Stone's Grasp, resonating throughout the city and muting the clamor of the crowds for a moment. He cocked his head back in mild surprise and removed his hand, stilling the zenith-powered device.

The regent returned to their position at the rail. "Chancle, did you place receiver globes throughout the entire city?" he asked.

"You indicated that you had a momentous announcement to make tonight. I thought it appropriate for everyone in the kingdom to have an opportunity to listen to your address this year," said Chancle.

Therek stared back across the city. "How did you . . . Giver's breath, man, that must have taken weeks to prepare." A genuine expression of appreciation settled in the depth of his eyes.

"It required a bit more planning than past assemblies, but sometimes big announcements need big gestures . . . and sometimes it's all about the details. "

Therek shook his head in disbelief. "I don't say it enough, but well done. The kingdom owes you a debt greater than it knows."

"Therek, any chance you would care to enlighten some of your closest friends as to the content of your address this evening?" asked Hestian.

The regent opened his mouth as if to speak, then closed it and smiled. He looked over Hestian's shoulder to a servant carrying a tray of muffins. "Young man, are those crownberry muffins?"

The servant stopped and bowed, holding the tray forward. Therek stepped forward and retrieved three of the pastries, handing one to Hestian and Chancle. With little concern for public decorum, the regent sunk his teeth through the top crust and chewed nearly half of the muffin in one bite. Long fingers shredded the wrapper, and he finished the treat with ravenous fervor, then lightly brushed the crumbs from the front of his shirt.

Hestian shrugged and took a bite of his muffin, then moaned with approval. "You two are hopeless," said Chancle.

"What value is there in life if one can't take but a moment to enjoy something as simple as a crownberry muffin?" asked Therek. "Besides, you've earned the right to enjoy the fruits of your labor on this night more than any other."

Chancle lifted his muffin up as if to toast the words and nibbled at the treat. With uncharacteristic levity, Therek quickstepped, if lurching stork-like strides could ever be considered to move in such a fashion, and returned with three small flasks filled with amber liquor. He handed out the spirit.

"Two sips for bravery before we begin a week of politicking?" asked Therek.

"I would rather sip three and have a dreamless sleep," said Hestian.

"And miss all that your brother set in motion this week? I should think not. The Giver's blessing to us all," said Therek, and he lifted his glass.

They clinked the flasks together and sipped at the resco. Chancle blew off the fumes of the volatile liquid, savoring the subtle undertone of smoky wood and vanilla. Therek pursed his lips out and frowned, considering the liquor. He tossed back the second sip and threw the glass over his shoulder.

"Duty calls. I need to mingle with the crowds before the address. See you on the green," said Therek.

Chancle watched his friend descend the steps, a light bounce in his gait.

"Have you ever seen that man more happy? It's like he's had a vision of things to come," said Hestian, eyes squinted in mock suspicion.

"Not for a long time. I think it looks good on him. The regency has been more burden than he cares to admit."

He allowed the second sip of resco to linger in his mouth for an unusually long time before swallowing. The liquid burned in his chest as it flowed to his stomach, causing him to errantly rub at the area. His fingers brushed lightly over an oval pendant under his shirt.

Hestian watched the gesture and pointed with his chin. "They would be proud of the man you've become, what you've worked for all these years, Chance."

Chancle absorbed the words for the kindness that they were and was about to offer a brotherly reply when he noticed dust clouds gathering on the horizon far outside the gates to the city. He stepped closer to the rail and shaded his eyes. "Have you got your pocket zeniscope? There's something on the horizon. Can you see what it is?"

Hestian reached into a pocket and withdrew the cylindrical zeniscope, extending the device to its full length and holding it to one eye. He held his breath, searching, then handed the tool to Chancle. "It's a whole flank of Outriders led by a rider dressed in white. Is it the overwarden? I didn't think Kaldera cared for theatrics."

Chancle scrutinized the rider for several minutes. Even with the enhanced clarity of the zeniscope, the man's face was impossible to make out. The rider was gifted, to be sure, as he was managing an Aarindin with ease. He wore a white cowled robe that flowed behind the mount, and a gold circlet rested on his head. The road dipped behind a hill, and Chancle lost sight of him, but a gnawing sense of unease bubbled in the pit of his stomach.

Chancle collapsed the spyglass and handed it back to his brother, then made for the steps. "Where are you off to?" asked Hestian.

"Attending to a few last details, brother. I have to see a merchant from Bekson's Fine Restoratives. I'll see you on the green or find you after the regent's address. You should bring your family up here to enjoy the view of the fireworks. It's sure to be an impressive display this year."

Chancle took the steps two at a time, his thoughts racing faster than his feet. *Taker's ill timing. He's riding right up to the front gates. This could still work out, but I've got to find Kunzie.*

Chapter Fifty: Joy and Pain

A cold rivulet of rainwater flowed along Karragin's jaw, dripping from her chin and spattering onto her chest. She sat on a two-foot-high boulder beside Savanh, who crouched outside the front doors to the church. Thunder boomed and echoed in rolling consecutive volleys across the valley. A striation of lightning flickered across the horizon, highlighting an intensity in Savnah's gaze.

Their eyes met, and Karragin dipped her chin, more water spilling from her forehead and nose. Despite the miserable conditions, the rest of her remained reasonably warm and dry, protected by her oiled Outrider gear. *Thank the Giver for small miracles.*

The front doors of the church creaked open, spilling amber light onto the steps for a moment. A guard dressed in the overcoat of the city watch from Stone's Grasp slammed the door shut, muttered an oath to the Taker against the elements, and clutched at his collar. The man kept his eyes down, descended the steps, and began a brisk perimeter patrol.

He returned minutes later, climbed the steps, and disappeared inside the church. Savnah stood, preparing to ascend the steps, when a longer fork of lightning flooded the valley with a few seconds of light. Something metallic glinted in the shadows only a hundred paces away. Karragin grabbed at Savnah's belt and tugged her back.

Without protest, the prime retreated behind a column of stone. Karragin held a finger to her lips, then signaled to watch. A minute later, a horse-drawn covered wagon approached, stopping in front of the church. The wagon had all the look of a reinforced cage used by the city watch to transport criminals: a squat wooden box with a single iron-barred window on a flatbed with wheels.

Two men wearing hooded cloaks hopped down, their faces obscured. One tied the horse to a hitching post, then both disappeared inside the church. Savnah signaled for Karragin to circle around, and they made a fast search of the wagon, meeting at the back door to the crude cell. On signal, Karragin pulled open the door, but the cage stood empty.

"Not a day too late. It looks like they're here to move someone," said Karragin. "This must be for Kovesk. We could wait and grab him when fewer breakers stand guard."

Savnah grunted once. "My brother has waited long enough already, and besides, there's no way to know if you could call off Nolan's diversion." She gripped one of the bars to the cell. "This changes nothing. It just means we get to exact some justice on a few more breakers. Get ready to breech once Nolan signals."

Karragin considered pressing her friend for more time but could tell Savnah had set her mind. They returned to the side of the front steps. From within the church, the shouts of men carried through the rain and thunder.

Savnah stood and twirled both moonblade axes once, rolled her shoulders, and hocked spit to the ground. Karragin recognized her resolve immediately.

"Savnah, wait for the signal," hissed Karragin.

"We can't. I recognize those shouts. We go in, now. Assault the door, Karra."

She studied the prime's face and knew at once the woman had crossed a line in her mind. *Right. No going back now.*

Against her better judgment, Karragin flared zenith into her arca prime. She squatted down and hoisted the boulder onto her shoulder. It reminded her of one of the atlas stones she had trained with back in Stone's Grasp. She was preparing to heave the boulder at the front doors when an explosion erupted from the backside of the church.

"That's the signal, Karra. Do it!" said Savnah.

The boulder flew through the air, blasting through the front doors and detonating several munitions. Flashes of white and yellow light flared across the threshold, and the scattered shrapnel of several shatterbites sprayed into the mud. The horse pulling the wagon reared back and whinnied in pain or fear. Savnah ran up the steps, charging into the foyer.

Karragin slashed her cutlass through the horse's tracings and sprinted behind her friend. Savnah veered left, and Karragin stepped right, but they encountered no resistance. They fanned out into a large room, assuming defensive positions. Karragin swept her gaze to the sides and up high, finding the bodies of five men strewn about. Their blood painted the walls and floor, the result of the munitions. The scent of fresh iron mixed with the acrid sulfur fumes. A dismembered thigh inside a shredded pantleg lay oddly propped up in one corner. A pair of boots sat in the center of the entryway, each holding the bloodied stalk of a leg bone.

Savnah lifted her eyebrows once. "The grinders don't mess around. Watch for tripwires on the stairs, then."

A vibration rattled through the floor as more munitions detonated from the backside of the church. More shots followed with pounding footsteps overhead, running in the direction of Nolan's diversion.

They crept up a flight of steps at the side of the room, and Savnah pushed the door open, stepping again to the left while Karragin lunged in to the right, knife in one hand and cutlass in the other. They wove a serpentine pattern down the hall, searching for tripwires and taking turns stopping at each doorway.

A set of stairs disappeared up into the darkness. Savnah was turning to step up when a door on the opposite side slammed open, and three men filled the hall. The prime spun back, swiping one axe blade clean through the belly of the first, then blocking a wild sword swing from the next man.

Karragin stepped into the space she created and stabbed the second man clean through the chest, her knife plunging in with little resistance. She slashed the cutlass against the trunk of the third man, but it rattled off a vest of chain mail under his shirt. The man grunted once, surprise causing his eyes to widen and flare white as Savnah's other axe thunked up under his chin. She wrenched her wrist once, splitting his jawbone, then withdrew the axe blade, allowing him to slump to the ground.

Karragin looked into the room the three men came from in time to see a fourth man winding up to throw some kind of munition.

"Get back!" she shouted. She closed the door and hefted a fresh corpse in each fist, bracing them against the slab of wood. A concussive force blew the door open, and she flew across the hall, landing several steps up into the stairwell with the bodies draped on top of her.

After that, everything was a chaotic muddle of muted sounds, flashing lights, and vibrations. She shoved off the dead men in time to see Savnah brandish her axes and charge to the left, down the hall. Dizziness slowed Karragin's reactions, and she struggled to overcome the sensation.

With an effort, she staggered to her feet, stumbling down the few steps in time to reach the landing just as men filled the hall to her right. A wild axe swing flew over her head. She ducked, and the blade wedged into the wood paneling. The error gave her a chance to slam the hilt of her cutlass onto the man's foot. This was followed by a zenith-fueled punch directly up into his face. His nose caved in, the blow lifting him off the ground and into the man behind him.

Her leg snapped forward, kicking out with all her strength, and where a line of four men stood one moment, they became a tangled mess of limbs the next. In the short reprieve, Karragin allowed a shoulder to rest against the wall, the disorientation from the detonation lingering and the sounds of conflict remaining strangely muted.

Something thudded, vibrating the floorboards, so she chanced a glance back. Savnah filled the hallway, retreating with axe blades flashing high and low. Men ran forward only to fall at her feet. At least four corpses lay dismembered; blood painted everything from the floors to the ceiling.

Karragin turned back to her pile of men and methodically stepped in and around, plunging her cutlass with rapid succession through the wriggling mass until she was convinced that all were dead.

She turned back to Savnah, who ran toward her, yelling something. The prime staggered with a limp, the fletching of two crossbow bolts lodged into her thigh. Savnah jumped into the stairwell. Karragin looked back down the hall. Two rows of guards were aiming crossbows out of the doorway from a room at the far end. The first row knelt to reload while the second row fired.

Karragin pressed her back against the wall in time for two bolts to fly past her, but a concussive force hit her in the left upper arm, spinning her around and flaring searing pain down to her hand. She dropped her knife, fingers strangely numb. More light flared from the far room as a woman stepped into the doorway, igniting not one but two munitions.

Grind it!

With her good arm, Karragin reached down and grabbed the ankle of one of the dead men in the hall. She launched the body, flinging the corpse like a rag doll directly at the woman. The floppy missile collided with the top of the doorframe, spinning into the room as a jumbled mass of noodled arms and legs. The demolitionist tried to step aside but was too slow and toppled back into the rows of archers.

Karragin dove into the stairwell beside Savnah and growled from the stabbing pain in her arm as much as anything else. "Cover your ears!"

She felt more than heard at least five sequential blasts. Thick smoke rolled into the hallway, stinging her eyes and nose. A lone man coughed, staggering forward from the smoke. He doubled over at the landing to the stairs, leaning on a sword and overcome with retching. Savnah's axe cleaved through the backside of his neck, sending his head rolling down the hallway.

More smoke billowed out from the room at the end of the hall, but no more guards spilled forth. Karragin pushed to her feet, sucking in a breath from the sharp pain in her wounded arm. She spoke, and even her own words seemed muffled, like someone was speaking from the other side of a door.

She pointed at the bolts protruding from Savnah's thigh. "Are you channeling? If so, let's get those out, make a fast tourniquet, and get to your brother."

Savnah lifted her chin once, and Karragin read her lips as much as heard her speak. "I'm ready."

Karragin grabbed the end of the bolts, and neither wiggled; both seemed wedged into bone. *At least the vital parts are on the inside, and the bolts are on the out. Here goes.*

With a quick jerk, Karragin popped the bolts free. Fresh blood streamed from the wounds, but nothing pulsed out under pressure.

"I've only got the one good hand. Set your axes down and tie off your leg before you make a bloody mess."

Savnah holstered her axes, tore off the bottom of her undershirt, then wrapped it tight around her thigh. Karragin's eyes stung from the growing wall of smoke rolling down the hall. Through tears, she understood Savnah's question. "What about you?"

Karragin tapped the end of the bolt protruding from her arm and felt intense burning radiate down to her hand. Fresh beads of sweat broke out on her forehead. "There's no help for it just yet, and I don't have your gift. I can go with one hand if I have to. Let's find Kovesk before the flames reach the rafters."

They climbed the stairs to another hallway obscured by smoke. Savnah crawled on hands and knees, and Karragin duckwalked, avoiding the worst of the smoke. They discovered corpses with fresh wounds, dark blood congealed on the floor. Savnah turned over the first one to find a single neck wound. She reached the second one, who must have been one of the guards that arrived just before the breach. The man's cloak was as rain-soaked as his shirt was bloodstained, and a gaping wound had been cleaved under one collar bone.

Savnah turned back and mouthed, "Was this you?"

Karragin shook her head once in the negative and sliced a hand forward. Savnah nodded in agreement and crawled on. Two more corpses leaned against the only door at the end of the hallway. Discarded crossbows lay beside them, a man and woman. The woman was dead, but only just so, as dark blood still oozed from an axe blade wedged under her rib cage. The man twitched on the ground, lying face down.

Savnah started to turn the man over when something caused her to do a double-take. She stared at the axe handle a moment, then wrenched the axe blade free from the woman's corpse. As she studied the weapon, she wore an expression that seemed a strange mixture of fear and rage. "This is Dad's axe." Savnah stood and shouldered the door open.

"Savnah, wait!" Karragin took a breath, gritted her teeth, and ran in behind her friend. She felt the vibration of Savnah's weapons clanging to the floor, followed by the prime dropping to her knees. Karragin slammed the door closed and turned to engage the enemy.

A desk sat on one side of the room, accompanied by a dresser and bookshelf. A four-poster bed stood in the far corner under a window. Next to the bed rested a plush chair. A lone man stood over a body sprawled in the chair, its legs extended with one foot pointing north and the other south.

The man turned, and Karragin recognized Kovesk from her visions. Tears streamed down his face, and he wiped bright red blood from his hands, though he appeared to have no physical injuries. He shook his head and spoke in barely audible tones. "He said he knew you would come, Savvy, but there were too many ears in the tavern, and the breakers had lost their way. He said he couldn't let you be the one."

Karragin drew her focus to the person in the chair. Burl Derrigand reclined in death, his head turned to the side, lifeless eyes as murky as the smoke rolling under the door. Five crossbow bolts impaled the man: two in the gut and three in the chest.

The floorboards shuddered and popped under Karragin's feet. Her head felt dizzy, ears muffled, and Taker's stones did her left arm ache, but the press of flames below spurred her to action. She heaved the bed away from the window, breaking off a post in the process. She used the splintered wood to bash out the window, then shouted into the night, "Now, Dexxin!"

Karragin stepped back, ensuring that Kovesk and Savnah remained out of harm's way. The siblings huddled together in an embrace on the floor. An Outrider arrow darted through the window, landing in the mattress of the bed. A thin line was attached to the fletching of the arrow.

Karragin retrieved the line, snapping it with a sharp jerk of the wrist, then began to wrap it around one of the posts of the bed. With only one arm, she made clumsy progress.

"Savnah Derrigand, move your moon-kissed ass and give me some help here!"

Savnah stood and took the line from Karragin, pulling hand over hand until the thin line became a rope. This, in turn, she pulled tight around the bedpost. Once secured, Karragin shoved the bed back farther, causing the rope to draw tight.

Savnah tapped her on the shoulder and spoke her words with exaggerated expression. "Karra, how do you fancy getting down there with one bad wing?"

"Because all I need is one good wing." Without wasting more words, Karragin sheathed her sword and stripped the top sheet from the bedding. "Help me roll this into a rope and toss it over the line. Use the rest of the bedding if this works."

Savnah made quick work of the loose fabric, twisting the sheet into a crude rope that she tossed over the zipline. Karragin nodded her thanks, gripped the sheet with her good arm, and leaned out the window. Cold rain splashed on her face once again, but with less intensity. Her torso twisted slightly, and the motion caused the bolt in her arm to shift. She gasped and swallowed back a wave of bile. Allowing zenith to infuse her with strength, she pushed out into the open air. The sheet clung to the rope, and she stopped only five feet out. "Grind it! Come on!"

She whipped her arm back and forth until the sheet began to slide on the line. In herky-jerky fashion, she made the descent in less time than she might have imagined, and Tovnik assisted her to her feet. She turned to watch as Kovesk and then Savnah came down the rope, sliding in a similar fashion.

Moments after Savnah's feet landed on rain-soaked ground, the line fell slack, and a loud crack erupted as the roof timbers collapsed. Angry flames rose despite the heavy spring rain, casting amber light on several bodies scattered about the grounds. Outrider arrows pincushioned the corpses.

Looks like we weren't the only ones keeping busy.

She felt a tap on her shoulder and turned to see her brother. He mopped back rain-soaked ginger curls and beamed a smile at her. His mouth moved, but all Karragin could sense was the vibration as another crack of thunder rolled across the valley.

The severity of her hearing deficit finally pressed in on her. She had assumed it would dissipate, but a faint low-pitched ringing was all she could hear. Nolan coughed into his hands, and she heard nothing. She must have betrayed something in the confusion of the moment because his expression turned from one of happy relief to concern. She sighed once and tried to speak without a tremble in her voice. "The worst part is over. I'm not going to worry, so neither should you."

Nolan nodded once and waved Tovnik over. The medic assessed her injuries, then focused all his attention on her wounded shoulder. She glanced over to Savnah. The prime stood with her back to Karragin, one arm around her brother, shoulders shuddering in spasms of what Karragin could only assume were tears mixed with both joy and pain.

Chapter Fifty-One: A Passage in Stone

Kaellor stretched on the wagon seat, casting a curious eye across a pasture and to the tree line. Two shadows shifted; the wolvryn, he presumed. Beyond the timber, a vast wall of white mountain stone rose up, thin veins of silver flowing over the surface. He had observed the walls surrounding Stone's Grasp for miles now; they all had. But up this close, the sight of them caused a fullness to rise up in his throat.

We made it home, brother. I only wish you were here to welcome us back.

"Come on, old man," said Laryn. "The walk will do us both some good."

Her words pulled him from his thoughts, and he handed the sheathed guardian sword down to her. The Rovinary wagon train had pulled off onto the grassy field west of the outer walls of Stone's Grasp. Several hours back, when they had merged onto a well-traveled road, the boys directed the wolvryn to keep well out of sight in the woods to the north, allowing them to blend in with the countless other travelers from across the kingdom.

Kaellor turned to the young man driving the wagon and offered his thanks. "Tell your speaker you'll always have friends in Stone's Grasp. And let him know that we are in your debt."

The young man tipped his head in silent acknowledgment. Kaellor retrieved a small shoulder pack and hopped down from the wagon. The broad muscles in the small of his back ached more than he'd expected, and he groaned. "I can't believe the boys and I used to ride something like that all over the Southlands."

Laryn waved him over. "Come here."

He stepped close, and Laryn strapped the sword to his waist. They embraced, hugging one another to massage sore muscles as much as to share affection. The murmur of the healer song hummed in his ears as she used the intimacy of their connection to trigger her gift. In moments, his pain and fatigue dissipated.

"You've got the Giver's touch, love," he whispered. "You've learned some new tricks. I didn't think you could take away things, though. Zenith is a lot, but it's not reductive."

"When we were with the Cloud Walkers, I found I could insert a small plane of zenith as a temporary block. I used it often to control the pain of broken bones or childbirth. Your sore muscles are little by comparison, and afterward, it's fast work to coax the soft tissues to renew themselves."

He pulled back and brushed a lock of silvery-white hair from her face, tucking it behind her ear. His focus shifted from the pigments in her solid blue eye to the one mixed with flecks of red. "When this is all over, the four of us should travel back there. I don't think I've ever been more at peace than we were among the Damadibo."

"I would love nothing more, but how about we see to getting inside Stone's Grasp first?"

"Agreed," he said and kissed her on the forehead.

The sound of boots shuffling through the grasses caused them to turn. Lluthen and Ranika walked in tandem, with Bryndor and Ksenia not far behind. The Balladuren woman stepped close, playfully bumping her hip against Bryndor and causing him to stumble. *It doesn't take an empath to see how those two are getting along.*

The thought of it, one of the boys finding happiness, friendship unmarred by the mantle, gave him renewed cause to smile. Bryndor recovered his balance, then stopped, staring up at the walls in the distance.

Lluthean bounced a green apple off his bicep, causing it to arc through the air, where Ranika caught it, only to toss it back as he repeated the gesture. They stopped in front of Kaellor, and he plucked the apple from the air, took a bite, then handed it back to Lluthean.

"You know those are for eating, right?" Kaellor teased.

Lluthean shrugged once, swung his pack around, and found several more apples, handing one to each of them. "A parting gift from Movshka."

Kaellor lifted his gaze back to the Moonies. They busied themselves setting their wagons for the evening, tending to the horses, and preparing cookfires. The speaker led four horses to a nearby stream. He must have sensed Kaellor's eyes upon him, for he stopped and waved. "Giver's good fortune to good people!"

"Until we meet again, I'm in your debt. Eyes to the horizon, my friend!" Kaellor yelled back.

Movshka tilted his head in respect and led the horses off.

"Well," said Kaellor, "we should get moving. I can't recall how long the hike is through the timber before we reach the walls, and then finding our way in is another matter entirely."

"We've seen nearly every kingdom in the Southlands, Kae, but none with walls so massive as these. What exactly are we looking for?" asked Bryndor.

Kaellor nodded. He had been waiting for the question. "We need to skirt around to the north end of the city. The castle was constructed with wards that respond to the touch of the king and queen. During the Abrogator's War, your parents unlocked a passageway. It's how I was able to escape with you two in secrecy all those years ago. I'm hoping we can find it and gain entrance. From there, it's a lot of tunnels and stairs, and we should come up somewhere inside the castle."

Bryndor frowned but held his tongue. Lluthean finally asked the question they were all thinking. "We don't really have a king or queen. Will these wards respond to your touch, Kae?"

He scratched at his beard, realizing that in the days of hard travel, the whiskers had grown enough to swirl. "That's the question, I suppose. I have to admit that when I was younger, I never concerned myself with the wards other than how to activate them. From what I recall, we have to stand in the inner sanctum to accomplish that. Anyway, let's concern ourselves with finding the passageway, then see if the wards respond to at least one of us."

They set out, reaching the timber within fifteen minutes and leaving the Rovinary wagons behind. Not more than ten steps into the tree line, the wolvryn loped forward. Boru sought affection from each of them, but Neska remained aloof, nose lifted to the air.

Lluthean nickered and signaled her over, but she just cocked her head to look at him curiously. Only when he knelt and offered her a piece of jerky did she approach. He ruffled the fur about her neck, but as soon as she devoured the treat, she hopped back a few paces.

Lluthean stood with a sigh of regret. "She still hasn't forgiven me for leaving her behind in Callinora."

"That should teach you never to spurn the affections of a woman, Llu," teased Ranika.

"Should we set them out on a patrol?" asked Bryndor.

"No. Nobody has seen a wolvryn in these parts for years. Let's keep them close to avoid any unnecessary encounters," said Kaellor. He led them farther into the timber, keeping the walls in sight.

They picked their way along game trails, through forest thick with brambles and underbrush. The path took them up and down foothills, but always north, which meant climbing higher toward the Great Crown. Before long, Kaellor's legs ached, his breath became labored, and sweat made his clothes cling to his skin.

After nearly two hours, they reached the northwest corner of the city, where the walls turned, breaking away to the east. There was enough space between the edge of the wall and the mountain cliffs to allow them to walk two abreast.

"Are there guards on the walls? Ramparts and such?" asked Bryndor.

"I suppose there could be," said Kaellor. "When your father sat the throne, his presence maintained the castle wards. Think of them like zenith-powered barriers keeping out enemies. It's possible that in our absence, guards might have been placed."

Kaellor stepped closer to the sheer mountain rock and stared up along the north wall but saw no sign of sentries. He looked back, checking the position of the sun. Amber light filtered through the timber at a low angle. "If there are guards, I think they would be hard-pressed to see us up close here. We've got maybe an hour of full sun, then another hour before we'll need torches. Let's see if we can find the passageway before then."

He took the lead walking beside Laryn, the path now easier to navigate as it followed the base of the walls without climbing farther into the mountains. After more than an hour, and with the sun setting low, Kaellor stopped. Ten paces ahead, the castle walls melded directly into the sheer side of the mountain, halting farther progress.

This is too far. The passageway out was on the northwest corner of the castle. We must have missed the entrance. Either that, or it's been sealed up. I didn't even imagine that. Grind me for a monk.

He closed his eyes, trying desperately to recall that night years ago when he eloped with the boys packed away, one in a front sling, the other over his shoulders. Images flashed in his memory: the massive stones crushing Laryn, the awful screams of the dying, the howls of Tarkannen's hordes, and the smell of so much blood.

"It was too much," he grumbled with self-recrimination and lifted his gaze to Laryn. "That night, years ago. I think I was in shock. My brother was facing death. I thought at the time that you died . . . all seemed lost. I didn't imagine I would be coming back, and so I didn't mark the way in my mind. But I know it's somewhere on the northwest corner. We must have passed it."

"It's alright, Kae," said Laryn. "We just have to backtrack. Do you recall, was there an alcove or a doorway, anything that might indicate the passage?"

"I don't really know. I never thought to look back." He took a deep breath and allowed himself a small measure of grace. *You're not the scared prince anymore. Lift your eyes to the horizon and find the solution.*

"We have to be close," said Kaellor. "Let's each of us walk with a hand on the wall. Feel for any irregularities. Boys, can you set the wolvryn to using their senses? Maybe they will be able to sniff something out before we do."

"Kess, that's a bit more complicated than a patrol command," said Bryndor. "Could you explain to them what we are looking for?"

"Yes, give me a moment," said the woman.

Boru and Neska approached and sat before the sympath in what appeared to be postures of attention. Ksenia sighed a few times and shook her head. The conversation seemed to linger for a few minutes, and at last, Neska turned and loped back toward the northwest corner of the castle. Boru trailed her, the two of them blotting out the fading sun. After a hundred paces, they trained their noses to the ground.

"Not as easy as I hoped?" asked Bryndor.

"Well, I couldn't really mix the sight, sound, and smell of a secret doorway that I've never seen before into a form of communication they would understand. In the end, I asked them to search for a passage through the wall, like a cave, and to notify us of anything unusual." She shrugged, clearly hoping that the request was enough.

"It's better than we could have done," quipped Lluthean. "And it looks like it might have worked."

The wolvryn paced back and forth, sniffing at the base of the castle wall. Kaellor jogged the distance to catch up to them, patting the wolvryn on the shoulders. He stepped forward and ran his fingers along what appeared and felt to be a nondescript, seamless stretch of stone. After several minutes of searching, Kaellor pounded a fist on the wall.

He rested a hand on the pommel of the guardian sword and considered pulling it out to bash his way inside, but knew that was an instinct born of frustration.

"Kae. Move to your right," said Bryndor with a strange, haunted tone.

Kaellor looked over his shoulder to see his nephew standing with his arm wrapped over Boru's shoulder, a distant expression glazing his eyes. "With Boru's senses . . . I see it now. There's a faint outline of zenith in the veining of the stone. It's in the shape of an arch."

Kaellor sidestepped until Bryndor nodded, then ran his fingers along the stone. He followed several tiny silver striations in the stone, waiting to feel the expected thrill and buzz of zenith coursing through the wards, but discovered nothing unusual.

"It's right here," Bryndor said, his voice resuming its normal intonation. He grabbed Kaellor's hand and ran his palm in an arch, following a silver vein that only now revealed itself. The familiar thrum of zenith rippled under Kaellor's touch, and a soft rumble of stone caused the ground to vibrate underfoot.

Kaellor stepped back and marveled as the stones appeared to sift and melt, retreating into the wall to reveal a perfect archway five feet wide that peaked more than four feet overhead. Neska leaned her nose into the passage, then pulled back but panted and wagged her tail.

The familiar sight of the archway blossomed as a wave of utter relief inside Kaellor. He felt himself smiling. "Giver's sweet breath, that's done it. This is it."

Chapter Fifty-Two: Confronting the Past

Bryndor watched his uncle step quickly through the archway that appeared in the outer wall. Laryn followed, and then Lluthean, Neska, and Ranika walked inside. He set his palm on the archway, studying the cold rock. It felt smooth as supple leather, and he rapped a knuckle on it, reassured by the dull thump of bone on stone.

Ksenia stepped forward, giving him a quizzical look. "It's just . . . I think I feel a little like the Moonies. I've been free to wander the world my whole life, and now I'm left to wonder, once I set foot inside, will I ever enjoy that kind of freedom again? How will anyone respond to me, to us? I'm not even gifted," Bryndor said.

"I'm going to tell you something, and then we're going to follow your family before we get left behind," she said.

"Alright."

"You're not at all what I expected, and nothing like any of the nobles I've ever interacted with, and that's . . . something quite rare and beautiful. You're gifted with more life experience than most people three times your age. I think you have the chance to reshape what it means to be noble, to be Aarindorian. But that only happens if you come inside." Ksenia took two steps in and turned, holding out her hand. "So, what do you say?"

Bryndor gestured to Boru to follow, gripped her hand once in reassurance, and walked under the arch. Cool, damp air chilled him, and he paused, waiting for his eyes to adjust. A musty smell that reminded him of freshly turned-over soil displaced the fresh air from outside.

After forty paces, the tunnel branched left and right. They'd already left the fading light of the archway behind and could barely make out a flicker of motion as Ranika disappeared around the next corner.

They hurried to catch up, and the hallway opened into a round room with branching archway exits. Kaellor ran his palm along the wall of the room, holding a wolvryn eye up for illumination. Ranika also held her moonstone high, adding its pale glow to the room.

His uncle turned, but his vision was focused on something distant. "This is close to the room where your parents cast your mantle, binding all signs of the gifts that you might inherit. And the castle knows a Baellentrell has returned. I can feel the veining begin to pulse with zenith."

Kaellor reached into a pocket, retrieved the other globe, and tossed it to Bryndor. "Hold it aloft. I'll take the lead, Nika in the middle, and you bring up the rear. We should all have plenty of light to get along."

Bryndor ran a thumb over the smooth orb. It filled his palm and looked like polished crystal with indigo fragments that emitted blue light. He turned to see what Boru thought of him holding the petrified eye of his mother, but the wolvryn only seemed to smile and gave his tail a lazy wag.

Kaellor took the middle tunnel, walked a few steps, then returned and chose the one leading to the right. He walked cautiously at first, then began to pick up the pace. From the back of the line, Bryndor could sense his uncle's excitement as he muttered to himself. "Uh huh . . . this looks right. And there should be steps beyond this turn . . . yes, here we are."

Kaellor gathered them at the bottom of a set of spiral steps wide enough to walk two abroad. They formed a cylindrical tower that stretched up beyond the nimbus of light cast by the crystalline wolvryn eyes. Kaellor stepped up on the first stair, then turned, a puff of dust lifting from his boots.

"Mind your step. These stairs haven't been used since the Abrogator's War. Before we go on, I need you all to swear to keep these passages a secret. No one else can learn of our entrance here. This knowledge has been handed down from monarch to monarch. I only learned of these passages under dire circumstances."

Lluthean poked a thumb over his shoulder. "We sort of left a door wide open on the backside of the castle."

"I know," said Kaellor. "I'll return and find a way to seal it up once we have established our presence. Until then, we don't need to jeopardize the security of the castle. Tarkannen is bad enough. If the Lacuna are as thick as we fear, we don't need them becoming aware of any of this. Am I understood? Nobody can know."

Kaellor fixed his gaze on each of them, waiting to establish eye contact. "Not your parents, not Reddevek, not our friends . . . nobody. Understand?"

After he seemed assured of everyone's understanding, Kaellor nodded once and ascended the stairs. They climbed what felt like the equivalent of three or four flights, coming at last to a landing. Kaellor pulled at cobwebs and dusted off the outline of a door, exposing a stone placard set at shoulder height into the frame. A dense lattice of silver veins spidered across the surface.

"Llu, place your hand here. See if the wards respond to your touch," said Kaellor.

Lluthean stepped sideways and reached out a hand, laying it flush to the stone. When nothing happened, he lifted his eyebrows in anticipation. Kaellor grunted once. "Now you, Bryn."

Bryndor shifted position with the others, repeating Lluthean's actions and returning the same result.

"Taker's tiny bits, what did they craft that mantle out of anyway?" said Kaellor.

Everyone looked at him, waiting for an explanation, and he dropped his head once, then looked up with chagrin. "Even an ungifted Baellentrell should be able to use the placards. They do this."

He placed his hand on the placard, and a sound like static skittering between two sheets echoed into the stairwell. Zenith flickered through the veining of the stones, outlining the doorframe with blue light. A stone door drifted open on silent hinges as if supported by air.

"Follow me. Bryn, close the door when you come through."

Bryndor waited for everyone to walk through and shouldered the door closed, finding that it swiveled noiselessly until slamming into place with a colossal thud. "Sorry, I assumed it was heavy."

He turned to look back at the door, surprised to see only a bare stone wall.

"No help for it now. Besides, these halls are empty," said Kaellor. He led them across rooms with long, empty tables and stacks of chairs pushed to the side, indicating that they had not been used in a long time. They made several turns, crossed another room, climbed a short set of spiral stairs, and finally walked down a hallway with sconces that flared to life when they approached. Brilliant white and blue light chased away the shadows.

Kaellor stopped at a door at the end of the hall for a moment, catching his breath. He pocketed his wolvryn globe and withdrew his guardian sword, holding it in a defensive position with the blade down.

"Beyond this door is a hall that leads to the inner sanctum. Inside is where your parents banished Tarkannen," said Kaellor.

"It's most likely to be empty. Nobody comes down here except the regent or anyone sitting for their Rite of Revealing," said Ksenia.

Kaellor tilted his head. "Still, stay behind me until we know it's safe."

He activated another placard, waited for the door to unlock, and shouldered it open. They spilled into a broad hallway with a flight of steps rising into the shadows at the far end. A plush black carpet with a brilliant blue moon set in its center ran the length of the room. The crescent of a waning red moon listed to the side, almost as if an afterthought. A massive set of floor-to-ceiling double doors sat in the middle of the corridor, ornate runes and carvings set into the face and doorframe.

"All these years, and I had no knowledge of this exit," said Laryn.

"Me either, and I've been down here more than most," said Ksenia.

Kaellor walked to the far end of the room, peering up the steps. He returned and pulled open the double doors, ushering everyone inside. Bryndor walked into the sanctum, a domed room with a vaulted ceiling. A large oval pool filled flush to the floor occupied the far side of the room. To the right of the pool stood the statue of a giant man carved from the same white stone, covered in silver runes from head to ankle. The figure held his arms forward, palms up, and stared ahead.

To the left, two life-sized figures, a man and woman, stood with their arms forward, palms also up, frozen in time. They seemed to be staring up at the statue on the opposite side of the room. A shimmering, gauzy barrier encased them. Kaellor stepped forward and stared first at the woman, then brought his full attention to the man.

His eyes brimmed with tears, and he spoke with a throaty voice. "We made it back, brother."

Kaellor cupped the cheek of the statue and lingered a moment, then stepped back. "Boys, this is your mother, Nebrine, and your father, Japheth."

Bryndor felt his feet shuffle forward of their own accord, a strange numbness of surreal realization at seeing something long imagined from far away arrive suddenly, unexpectedly, before him. He stood next to Lluthean and studied the figures.

His mother was, beyond all his imaginings, simply lovely. High cheekbones, a delicate nose, and striking blue eyes full of purpose stared ahead. Through the weave of the magical preservation, he could see light-brown rivulets of hair fall on lean shoulders. Delicate freckles graced her nose and cheeks.

"Giver, Llu, you've got her face, her jaw, same nose . . . that's really weird," said Bryndor.

"You're one to talk. It's like someone cropped your hair, trimmed a beard, and plopped your head right onto our father's shoulders here," said Lluthean.

Bryndor stepped back, allowing Lluthean to step in front of their mother, and he considered their father. A manicured beard accentuated a strong jawline. The first indication of crow's feet silhouetted eyes that held the same intensity as his mother. Bryndor held a hand up, turning it over and comparing it to Japheth's, finding them identical but for his own calluses. Other than that and the trimmed hair, it was oddly like looking in a mirror.

He lost track of the number of times he walked a slow circle around the pair, committing every detail to memory, even the spatter of gore on their boots. Boru sauntered up and offered a soft whine, nuzzling against Bryndor's shoulder and pulling him from the immersion of that moment.

Bryndor blinked hard, eyes stinging from unshed tears, and threw an arm over the wolvryn. "Boru, meet . . . Mom and Dad. Mom, Dad . . . this is Boru."

The oddity of the moment gave them all room to laugh. Bryndor found his other arm snaking around his brother and felt jostled as Laryn, Kaellor, even Ksenia and Ranika, joined them in a warm huddled circle.

When the moment felt right, they separated. Bryndor turned to Lluthean, but words escaped him. They shared a look, as brothers often do, one that conveyed all the meaning and understanding required to express appreciation for arriving at the end of a shared journey.

He turned to Ksenia, who stood silently beside him. She shook her head. "I can't imagine . . . how are you?"

Bryndor swallowed. "I'm not sure how to answer that yet."

THRONNNNG! THRONNNNG! THRONNNNG!

A deep, resonant vibration, as if a massive bell were ringing out, erupted in the room, sending tremors throughout the walls. The consecutive shocks caused a tickling sensation to travel through his feet into his core. He squinted as zenith flared from blue to an intense white, streaming out from the giant statue.

After the better part of a minute, the onslaught of light and sound stilled. Kaellor stood under the statue, still holding one finger overhead, touching the underside of the giant hand. Currents of zenith smoldered in slow tendrils across the silver runes of the statue, streaming into the veining on the floor, merging into the walls.

Kaellor lowered his hand and sighed. "I'm a monk twice over. I didn't think it would be that easy to ignite the castle wards. If the Lacuna didn't already know we were here, they certainly do now."

Chapter Fifty-Three: The Rite of Sundering

AN ELDER SHAMAN STOOD off-center in the summoning chamber. Fetishes of feather, bone, and gemstones dangled on thin chains looping from ear to snout. He held a thigh bone in each clawed hand, the shafts riddled in intricate sigils, the rounded ends dyed in a ruby-black lacquer. Volencia assumed that the mystical paint came from human blood. As to the thigh bone, she couldn't be sure. The length seemed too long for a human, and the ends bowed back at an odd angle. And then she realized what it was. *It's the leg bone of an umbral.*

She wondered, not for the first time, at the complexity of Tarkannen's planning. Using powers beyond her knowledge, her master had enslaved a Consort of umbral. At least one of them had two leg bones inscribed with sigils of dark power before being sent from the Drift. Now those bones were part of a dark ritual to release him from captivity. Looking back, she could see other pieces set up on the board: the grondle herd, the Brognaus tribe with their rare caste of shamans, and the attempt to rescue the vessel.

She thought of the other abrogator, Verrador. *How many other soldiers have you placed in the field?* She grew frustrated by the lack of clarity and found herself thinking of the man gifted in nadir shielding more and more. What mission did he carry out for Tarkannen now? Why wasn't Volencia informed of that part of the plan? Hadn't she given enough to be trusted?

Maybe it's because I've failed to release him before now? Or because we never infiltrated Stone's Grasp?

The umbral that was Mallic stood as proof of the consequences awaiting those who failed to live up to their potential. What must that be like, to have your soul stripped away and used to animate one of those strange creatures? Was there an awareness of what you were before? Was there some fragment of Mallic scratching to get out, or was there simply . . . no more Mallic?

She scanned the chamber for the remnant of Mallic but recalled that it remained on the surface with the grotvonen chieftain. Grasdok was charged with pressuring the people down into the chute and preventing their escape. Should the grondle herd become unruly and begin to indulge their true nature, the chieftain and lone umbral would be pressed to control their bloodlust.

You're acting like a nadir-sick teen. Focus. Get through this day, and then you can leave this filthy chamber behind.

She exchanged a nod with the elder shaman. Hairs about the creature's muzzle and across its shoulders had long ago turned a silvery white. She didn't recall seeing any others in the Brognaus marked by the distinction of age and wondered what their lifespan was. The thing stared back at her with eyes that appeared less vacant and more pensive than she expected.

Beside the elder shaman, the rest of the umbral, the Consort, huddled over the black pool of refined liquid nadir. The scent of moldering flesh and decay wafted up from the surface. Shallow waves rippled as each of the underworld creatures wove thin black filaments into the construct. Acting with coordinated motions, they looked more like a group of spiders weaving a complex web than the architects of Tarkannen's Rite of Sundering.

Over the next few hours, members of the Brognaus clan filtered into the cavern, packing themselves into tidy circular rows. With so many of them marked by the luminous mushroom spores, they cast the chamber in a sickly yellow light. The air grew thick and oily with their collective reek. Despite spending months among the grotvonen horde, the stench overwhelmed Volencia's senses. She fashioned a filter of nadir across the veil on her face, insulating herself from the oppressive heat and humid stench generated by so many of them crammed into one space.

She had never seen them act with such coordinated restraint. Typically, the grotvonen warrens echoed with random clicks, hoots, and growls. The workers scurried past her chamber at all hours of the day. As they entered now, however, the entire tribe carried themselves with the quiet formality of a funeral procession.

The young and old, the warrior and worker castes, all assumed their positions in silence. Once they squatted in place, only the occasional twitch of an ear betrayed their still forms. Finally, the rest of the shamans arrived, setting up in two circular rows, their drums of bone and hide positioned between muscled, hairy legs.

Blue moonlight filtered in from the shaft directly overhead. The polished lining of the chute from the surface reflected the moon of Baellen down through the chamber as a muted green miasma. Volencia realized that the time was drawing near. A strange sense of anticipation rushed through her mind, and for a moment, she worried she had slipped into the frenze.

Her thoughts raced again, and she wondered if she had done enough, if the people she left on the surface would begin to drop through. Would

Grasdok maintain an orderly procession and keep the grondle from raging into the humans? She fleetingly thought about climbing back up. Lashings of nadir would probably allow her to make the ascent, but could she make it in time?

The elder shaman barked once, drawing her attention back to the crowded chamber. She watched with rapt anticipation as he lifted one of the thigh bones overhead and struck the master drum.

A thunderous, coordinated thump resonated throughout the chamber as the drummers matched the elder shaman's beat. When the echoes faded, he struck again, and the deafening beat vibrated through her body, tickling her core. The slow strikes continued, reminding Volencia of the footsteps of some giant creature plodding in a slow circle overhead.

A red, glowing fissure formed on the surface of the nadir pool, appearing to rise from a depth far greater than the shallow, viscous slick should be able to accommodate. She stared, transfixed, at the portal. Something from the other side probed at the rift, pushing and testing the limits of the barrier. The outline of two hands caused the black pool to bulge up for several seconds. When the pool's integrity resisted passage, the hands receded, and the surface became a flat slick with a central glowing fissure again.

Something caused the moonlight overhead to flicker in intensity. Twenty heartbeats later, a person spilled out of the chute. A woman wearing a drab yellow skirt plummeted through the cavern, the hem catching air and covering her face as she toppled.

Just before she landed, her head appeared, face a rictus expression of utter terror, mouth agape in a scream drowned out by the Brognaus drums. The woman struck the center of the nadir pool, the vibration of her bones and organs crashing against the barrier thrumming into Volencia's heels.

The woman's entire body, clothing and all, vanished into the nadir pool. The central fissure flickered a bright red color for an instant, then faded to a dull ember.

One down, nine hundred ninety-nine to go.

A man wearing purple robes fell through the ceiling next, his ruddy face a mixed expression of surprise, terror, and confusion. He collided with the pool and was consumed by the ritual. Next, another woman dropped, then two children, a man, another woman . . . and so it continued, with a person spilling through about once every ten to fifteen seconds.

Volencia held nadir at the ready, prepared to lash out with a tentacle to guide the people into the pool. After monitoring the ritual for over thirty minutes, she released the nadir and relaxed. All of the sacrifices, whether male or female, big or small, spilled out of the chute to plummet directly into the fissure. It mattered not whether they wore the refined purple silks of the minor nobles or rough-spun threadbare clothing with faded red embellishments; all of them collided with the rift, strengthening the breech and magnifying the power of the Rite of Sundering.

After an hour, the glowing fissure intensified into more than a simple ember, bathing the floor in a red light. The elder shaman kept a steady cadence but added an extra drumbeat, making a syncopated rhythm. The others matched him perfectly, and the umbral bent to their task, maintaining the integrity of the ritual. The Brognaus tribe recognized the progression of the ritual and began adding soft hoots, creating a primal chorus.

Volencia allowed herself to lean back against the stone wall and laughed in disbelief. *It's working. This is really happening. After all these years, I get to be the one to set him free.*

She studied the sigils on her forearm and wondered what more power would feel like. She had become a formidable master with her control of nadir. What else could she accomplish once Tarkannen scribed more of the sigils to her flesh?

Chapter Fifty-Four: The Taker's Run

The burning crescent of the sun dropped below the horizon, and the first stars twinkled overhead. Chancle suppressed a swelling tide of frustration. He had not managed to navigate the crowds of nobles without getting snared into meaningless pleasantries and introductions. At last, he gave up and sent a runner to check on his contact in Bekson's Fine Restoratives.

The young woman returned to him on the top tier of the castle. She arrived breathless as he extricated himself from a conversation in which a Beclurian Endule was complaining about the weather on the long ride to the capital.

"Did you find him?" pressed Chancle.

"No, Your Grace. Every shop in the Delve is closed for business in anticipation of the opening night's festivities. I'm sorry."

"I feared as much. You have my thanks. Tell anyone who asks that I personally relieved you of duty for the night. Go enjoy yourself."

At that, the young woman's weary expression brightened. "I will. My thanks, Your Grace."

She melted into the crowd, and Chancle walked with stiff purpose to the balustrade beside the podium erected for the regent's address. He scanned the crowd one last time with Hestian's spyglass, searching in vain through the throng of revelers mingling among the lower tiers of the castle grounds.

His brother emerged from the wine vendor's tent, cheeks already flushed after sampling the fare. Hestian looked right up at him and raised a glass of red wine. "Have one for me, brother. Giver knows I could use another drink."

He didn't need the spyglass to find Therek. The old lynx stood head and shoulders above anyone else. The man truly seemed happy this night, even taking turns holding babies while mingling with the different families.

Where are you the one time I need you?

Chancle brought the zeniscope back to the south gates to inspect the progress of the white-robed rider. An entire flank of Outriders accompanied the man. Within the hour, they would reach the entrance to Stone's Grasp.

From his elevation on the highest level of the castle, Chancle expected to see a flurry of activity as guards migrated across the ramparts to meet the unannounced arrival. But the ramparts remained empty.

Where is the city watch?

Closer inspection revealed several men posted on the walls, but their attention was centered on the festivities below: the various nobles, musicians, and dancers. *Something is off. Captain Oren maintains tight discipline. He would never condone a breach of duty, especially with so many visitors to the capital.*

Chancle walked to the edge of the balcony and waved at one of the soldiers. The man cradled a crossbow in his arms and walked across the rampart with little enthusiasm. "Can I help you, Your Grace?"

"Yes, I need to speak with Captain Oren about a few final details. Do you know where I can find him?"

"There's a purple tent sponsored by Bekson's Fine Restoratives just inside the curtain wall on the entry level. I believe he's there. But you should hurry. The sun has set, and the fireworks are set to go off after the regent's address. The best place to see the show is from the green on the upper tier. Most of the nobles are gathered there already, Your Grace."

Chancle's eye twitched in annoyance. *How is it I've managed to see to the most minute of details yet had no knowledge of his tent?*

"My thanks," said Chancle.

The guard waved a hand and strolled back to his position overlooking the crowd. *If I didn't know better, I would think the man had marinated himself in resco.*

Chancle had nearly crossed the second-tier green before being accosted by Jaspen Holling, the vineyard owner from Stellance. An attractive woman young enough to be his daughter waited at his elbow. Jaspen leaned in as Chancle tried to pass by.

"Your Grace, I hope you'll partake of a rare vintage, the Holling Select, a prewar red. I brought it over myself as an . . . aspect of good faith."

"Good faith? I'm afraid that I don't understand," said Chancle.

Holling leaned in. "I knew the regent would never grant me the water rights I requested. That only drove up the price on my reserve. As it stands, the Holling Select has nearly doubled in price, and besides, I'm reopening the old family mine at the back of the estate. I couldn't have more water running across that area. Drowned miners make for poor business."

"Yes, I suppose they do," said Chancle.

Holling pointed back up the steps. "Your Grace, you're going to miss the show, and I'm told the best view is—"

Chancle nodded. "Yes, yes, the best view is from up top. If you'll excuse me, Lord Holling, I have to attend to a few details. Do enjoy the festivities."

Chancle evaded further small talk, wandering past and around groups of familiar faces, many vying for his attention. Eventually, he reached the bottom-tier green, breathless, and marched along the inside of the curtain wall to a lavish purple tent. At least six posts supported the expansive structure.

Taker's breath. I never approved of such an expansive display inside the walls.

Savory aromas welcomed him inside, and his eyes adjusted. A replica of the bar from Bekson's Fine Restoratives ran the length of the sprawling tent. Dishes of savory meats, grilled vegetables, platters of sausages, and cheese covered the bar top. A barkeep walked over, welcoming him inside.

"Your Grace, it's a pleasure. I'm afraid my selection is limited to a fifth-year resco, a seasonal Stellancian white, and a Beclurian red. What can I pour you?"

Chancle searched the tent. Several patrons sat at tables in idle conversation. None of them wore the refined clothing of the nobles. In fact, several appeared to be members of the city watch. "I was told Captain Oren might be here. I need to have a few words with him."

"Certainly he is. Step right this way."

The barkeep led him to the far corner, then turned down what could only be described as a narrow canvas hallway illuminated by a string of crystals emitting a soft yellow hue. They passed two small rooms set up for games of chance but empty of patrons, then turned into a generous back room.

Several people sat around a circular gaming table, engrossed in a game of cards. A lady dressed in fine silks sat with her back to him, Captain Oren to one side and the merchant Kunzie to the other. The merchant threw three cards down and drew three more, a pointy nose lifted up in consideration of his fortunes.

The barkeep cleared his throat. "My lady and gentlemen, I present the Vice Regent Chancle Lellendule."

All three turned to regard him as the barkeep departed. A painted folding fan covered the woman's face as she turned to inspect him with eyes that seemed familiar. Captain Oren stood to attention, appearing startled, and Kunzie laid his cards on the table with a look of bemusement.

"Your Grace," stammered the captain. "How can I help you?"

"You've been here the whole time?" asked Chancle.

"Not the whole time, Your Grace," said Oren.

Chancle kept his eyes locked on the merchant. "Not you, Oren. Him."

Kunzie reached for a glass of wine, swirled the red liquid, took a sip, then sighed. "I've been right here the whole time . . . Your Grace."

"We've all been here," said the woman. Recognition caused his mouth to run dry, and Chancle placed fingers lightly on the top of her fan, directing her to lower the veil. "Valdesta. So . . . what are you three doing here exactly?"

"Umm, cards, I guess, Your Grace," said Oren.

Calculations of the events of the last few weeks jumbled in Chancle's mind. *How will this all play out? Are we to show all our cards or continue the game? Best to play your hand, old man.*

"There's an empty seat at the table. May I join you?" he asked.

"By all means," said Kunzie. He gathered the cards and shuffled the deck. "Oren, stop standing at attention when there's nobody to impress. Take a seat, man, all friends here."

Chancle gestured an open palm of invitation to Oren's chair and took the empty seat for himself. "The game is always more fun when chance is involved. More people means more chance."

"Just so, Your Grace," grunted the captain.

"Care to shuffle and deal?" asked Kunzie.

Chancle set a handful of coins on the table, took the cards, and began to shuffle. Nimble fingers split, expertly flicked the cards in an arc, then mixed the deck in a blurred flurry of action. At last, he set the deck before Oren. "Care to cut the deck, Captain?"

Oren's nobby finger tapped the top card, indicating that the shuffle seemed thorough.

"What's the game then?" asked Chancle.

"King's gambit, nothing wild," said Kunzie. "First round dealt, second one runs the river, third hand tops the castles, and fourth pulls from the rubbish pile."

Chancle nodded and began to deal the cards, placing the last card, the gambit, face down for the reveal at the end of the hand.

"While I'm here, Oren, I wanted to speak to you about the lapses in security. Surely, you know about the arrival of a rider accompanied by what appears to be a flank of Outriders. Why aren't you taking steps to stop him or at least determine his identity?" asked Chancle.

"Why would we want him to do that? We should welcome the man right up there with all the other nobles to enjoy the show," said Valdesta. "One last royal hurrah!"

Chancle considered his cards and began organizing the beginning of the Taker's run, a powerful but rare combination that weighed heavily on either a lucky draw or the king's gambit. Valdesta's last words tickled a nerve.

"Surely your employees will offer the visiting nobles other diversions after the . . . grand display," said Chancle. He turned to Kunzie, holding the deck forward.

The merchant pushed a silver coin to the center of the table. "I'll take two."

Chancle exchanged the two cards with Kunzie, then tilted his head to Valdesta. She matched the bet.

"You're either bad luck or a crafty dealer. The lady will take four." Valdesta inspected her cards, organized her hand, and finally lifted her eyes to meet his. "My establishments are more than prepared to delight the masses, though I doubt many nobles will have the chance to sample the goods."

"I see," said Chancle. "And how about you, Oren?"

Oren pushed a coin to the center and held up three stubby fingers. Chancle exchanged the cards, then placed his wager. "Dealer takes one."

Chancle discarded a crescent of moons, hoping to pull the Taker's blade, the one card that would complete his hand. Instead, he drew the gibbous moon. *Rubbish. Let's hope that's not an ill omen.*

Kunzie shifted in his seat and cleared his throat. He placed three fingers on coins, sliding them into the pile. Valdesta folded, and Oren matched the bid. Chancle studied his hand. Somewhere in the periphery of his awareness, he knew he should fold, leave the game while he still could, but he had already come this far, so he pushed three more coins into the pile and prepared to turn over the king's gambit, the wild card that anyone could add to their hand.

His hand hesitated on the card. "What's to become of us after tonight, I wonder?"

Valdesta squinted her eyes but remained quiet. Oren scraped the top edge of his cards on his beard stubble. "Brighter days for all, I expect," said the captain.

"That's not the question he's really asking. Is it?" asked Kunzie.

Chancle conceded the point. "I suppose I should be more . . . transparent, since it's just us here. I should ask, why is it so important that all the nobles gather to watch the fireworks on the upper green? That's the one guarded by all the sentries with crossbows, so its security can't be questioned, I suppose, but surely everyone in Stone's Grasp will be able to see the show this year."

Oren set his cards down, his expression sobering. Kunzie played at grooming his thin mustache, and Valdesta leaned forward on folded arms.

Chancle flipped the wild card over but didn't bother to look. "Were you even going to tell me to avoid the green? After everything we've been through?"

Oren's sword rasped as it slid from the sheath, the blade resting on his lap, the point mere inches from Chancle's belly. "I think you can see that the show was meant for . . . all of the nobles, Your Grace," said the captain.

Chancle just nodded. "May I ask why? Did you lose faith in the vision, or was it never there?"

"Oh, there's plenty of people that have faith in your vision," said Valdesta. "But in the end, you can't stiff the queen of grifters."

"Profits, Val? Have I not enabled you to thrive beyond your wildest imaginings?" asked Chancle.

"You did, in years past. But of late?" she sighed. "Nobody takes from the house and gets away with it."

"So we're to part company over what . . . a donation of embertang and a small strip of property in the Great Crown? Kunzie, surely you're not so shortsighted?"

The merchant appeared chagrined. "I'm a true believer, Aspect. But the man I follow can't be a member of the noble class. That defies everything we've held central for years."

A grunt escaped Chancle's lips. "How long have you known it was me? What finally gave me away?"

"We grew suspicious after Ksenia Balladuren barged into the regent's chambers to announce the return of the royals," said Valdesta.

Chancle thought back to the day, realization washing over him as a cold wave of regret.

Kunzie sighed. "The scribe was our man on the inside that day. The docent made him leave the chamber. That left just three of you to learn of her news. You, the regent, and the docent."

Chancle lifted his fingers from the table, gesturing a soft rebuttal. "What about her brother, Rugen? He was there as well."

Kunzie nodded. "Aye, he was, but the Aspect contacted me straightaway after the girl broke the news, long before Rugen had the chance to divulge his information."

"Well, there you have it," said Chancle.

Oren shifted his gaze to Kunzie, and they shared a look. The merchant nodded, tipping his pointy nose down. Oren inhaled once.

A concussive sound vibrated through the ground, followed by three painfully loud detonations.

Thronnnng! Thronnnng! Thronnnng!

Chancle seized the moment of confusion, flaring zenith into the wind rune on his arm. He pulsed a column of condensed air under the table, causing it to surge up to the tent ceiling. Canvas sheared, and one of the support timbers cracked. He pulled hard on zenith and released another current of air in a tight arc. Oren, Valdesta, and Kunzie toppled back. The force propelled Chancle through the tent to collide with the stone wall of the castle.

His breath came pained and ragged, but he staggered to his feet and stepped over the deflated tent. Bodies moaned and shifted several paces away. A lone card fluttered down to land beside him. The Taker's blade lay face up.

The Taker's run it is. And he slipped into the shadows.

Chapter Fifty-Five: Trading One Evil for Another

As dusk settled, Reddevek and his flank of Outriders reached the paved causeway before the south gate to Stone's Grasp. A lone guard stood at his post outside the gate. The upper ramparts, usually patrolled by at least a few supporting members of the city watch, appeared empty. He drew Zippy to a halt, infused his arca prime, and cast a wide net across the entrance.

Only the resonance of the guard, curious and somewhat apprehensive at their approach, manifested in his awareness. One of the other Outriders named Bacall, a prime gifted with unnatural sight, approached. "Everything alright, sir?" asked the woman.

"I'm not sure. If this ruse was to work, we should have been met by either a grand welcoming party or a sizable force of resistance," said Reddevek.

He released his hold of zenith and turned to consider the flank. The overwarden had reorganized the quads into more formidable groups of eight. Four such groups clustered around and behind him. Bright faces stared back, most familiar, though others looked to have no more experience than a tender.

Reddevek turned Zippy in a half circle to face them all and cleared his throat. "Listen up. This night is going down one of two ways: peaceful and quiet or rowdy as a tavern brawl. From this point on, nobody gets in or out of Stone's Grasp. The Lacuna are traitors to the kingdom, but lots of good people follow their lies. Tonight, our job is to put a leash on the range of their destruction. We do that by bottling up as many rats as possible. We'll let the regent and his staff sort out the details later. Once I assign you to your posts, station yourselves outside the gates and bring them down. Better to let the iron bars ward off the curious. Rely on your reputation to repel any interested in crossing the gates. Recruit the cooperation of the city watch by order of Overwarden Kaldera. Any questions?"

One of the Outriders from the back spoke up. "What if they still try to pass the gates?"

"Your reputation will work, I suppose, until it doesn't. Then you have my permission to use nonlethal force. Lethal force is reserved only in defense of your life. Anything else?" asked the warden.

"Who holds authority? The Outriders or the city watch?" asked another.

Reddevek nodded understanding. "The watch has say on the inside of the gates. You rule anyone stepping outside. As far as we are concerned, nobody steps outside or crosses your path to enter until you are relieved by myself, Kaldera, or an agent of the regent's offices."

He waited for any further questions. Sensing none, he singled out the group on his right. "You eight will guard the western approach. It's a smaller gate that leads into the protected timber, so you're not likely to see much action but stay alert. You on my left, your group will take the east gate. The group in the back has the bigger task of holding this gate. Bacall, your eight ride with me."

A toe stroked over the Aarindin's flank signaled Zippy to turn and approach the south gate. Reddevek stopped beside the lone guard. "Do you recognize me, sir?"

The man nodded once. "Name's Griggs, and I never forget a face, Warden Reddevek."

"Griggs . . . no offense to your skill, but why are you posted here alone? Where are the sentries from the ramparts?"

The guard scratched at a sun-leathered neck. "Oren's orders. He's pulled most of the watch up to the main castle to oversee security for the opening night of the spring assembly. Supposed to be quite a show, as I hear it, with music, dancers, painted ladies, and the like. After the regent's address, there's even supposed to be a fireworks display. Your riders will likely see it from the gates."

"Did you hear my orders to the Outriders just now?"

"Aye, I did, sir."

"How does that sit with you, Griggs?"

"The way I see it, man pulls an oar in one direction while his brother pulls in the other, they just turn circles. You can count on me, sir. Soon as you pass, I'll drop the bars just like you said."

"Good man," said the warden, and he directed Zippy into a trot.

Once inside the walls, the portcullis screeched, followed by a loud clang as the iron bars dropped into place. The grounds remained barren of foot traffic, and Reddevek encouraged Zippy to a trot. The clatter of six Aarindin echoed across the empty market district.

Reddevek seldom ventured into the city at night, usually choosing to find lodgings outside the confinement of the walls. While he preferred to keep his own company, the desolation gave him a sense of foreboding. "Light up your gifts. Bacall, you see anything unusual?"

The prime swiveled her head like an owl, surveying the immediate vicinity. "Not much to speak of down here. No movement. Ramparts are empty, like you said. A few civvies bedding down for the night, merchants, I would guess. Lots of heat in the Sprawl. No surprise there."

Reddevek grunted. "You can see that far? With accuracy?"

"Yes, sir," said Baccal. "I can't get an accurate headcount, too much action in the Sprawl, but the crowds move as expected, no sign of any organized force coming this way."

"Alright, what about the castle grounds?"

Baccal lifted her gaze into the night, the blaze of zenith flickering in her eyes. "The ramparts there are . . . covered in city watch. All three greens are crowded, but none as much as the top tier."

"We need to make the curtain wall. We can skirt around or ride through the lower city. Either of those look better than the other?"

Before the prime could answer, a deep, rumbling series of three thunderous booms detonated from deep in the castle, reverberating out through the city.

Thronnnng!

Thronnnng!

Thronnnng!

Cascading sheets of zenith blazed, starting from a central focus in the castle, racing along the walls of Stone's Grasp, and eventually flaring through the silver veining of the stones through the outer walls surrounding the city. Reddevek reassured Zippy, then dismounted. He walked over to one of the walls and placed his thumb over one of the silver veins.

A fluttering tremor vibrated into his skin in the rhythm of a heartbeat. "He's done it." Reddevek walked fifty paces, tracing the vein, expecting the resonance of the castle wards to dissipate but finding reassurance everywhere he searched. He walked back to Zippy, a lighter feeling in his step, and chuckled.

"He's actually done it."

"Sir?" Baccal asked, a slight quaver in her voice.

"You might not be old enough to remember, but when a Baellentrell resides in Stone's Grasp, he or she can engage the castle wards. It would seem that he's accomplished that task without us," explained Reddevek.

"Not that, sir," said the prime. "Running this way is a man . . . I believe it's the vice regent. He's either leading a group of armed men or being pursued."

Reddevek sighed and hefted his axe and sword. "The Taker always has a price. How many?"

"More than a dozen, and farther back, more are spilling out of the castle."

"Can we make the buildings three blocks up? There's a natural bottleneck. We can recover the vice regent. I doubt he's in league with the breakers."

"We'll get there first easy enough," said Baccal.

"Split up, five over there, three with me. We'll use the shadows. Protect the vice regent, repel the Lacuna!"

Zippy cantered over the paved streets, and they pulled to a stop where the buildings narrowed. A covered boardwalk brought the bottleneck to a defensible width. They all dismounted, sending the Aarindin out of the narrow lane. Reddevek ignited his arca prime and assessed Chancle's aura as the man ran toward them. Fear and trepidation flavored his signature, but those behind him carried the unmistakable intent of violence.

As they waited and watched, the muffled voice of the regent echoed through the empty streets, somehow oddly amplified. He spoke in calm, reassuring tones. The regent made a few introductory remarks, then promised to begin his formal address soon. They held position, and within a few minutes, the panted gasps and footsteps of Chancle broke the silence. Reddevek reached out and grabbed the vice regent by the robes, hauling him to the side of the building.

Chancle swore an oath, but the warden cupped a hand over his mouth. "It's Warden Reddevek. You're safe, Your Grace. What's going on?"

The vice regent studied Reddevek's clothing, appearing confused. Eventually, recognition spread across his face, and he laid a hand on Reddevek's shoulder. "Giver's sweet breath . . . Warden. The Lacuna, it's a coup; they've gone absolutely mad. They've set a trap for the nobles, gathering most of them on the upper green. It's . . . a killing zone. They've infiltrated the city watch and plan to use them to assassinate as many as possible. I only just found out, and some of them are after me."

"Any sign of the regent or a Baellentrell?" pressed the warden.

Chancle nodded his head. "Therek should be relatively safe. He's about to deliver an address, but I've not seen a member of the royal family."

Clopping footsteps approached, and a man shouted, "He went down this way, toward the market!"

"Get yourself somewhere safe," said Reddevek.

"I can fight. I've not worked all these years to see Aarindorn fall into the hands of traitors and thugs," said Chancle.

"These Outriders are trained to work together. Let them do their job, but if any need support, have at it."

Reddevek stepped out from the corner of the building in time to take the first Lacuna with a sword chop across the upper chest. The man slammed to the ground, and the warden quickstepped, catching the next man mid-step with an axe across the knee. That one crumpled to the ground, allowing Reddevek to spin and cleave the back of his head.

All around him, his Outriders sprang from the shadows, engaging in a furious surprise attack. Breakers grunted and fell with hardly a sound before being put to the sword.

"Move up in the shadows. Hold and repeat," growled the warden.

They crept up the boardwalk, waiting in ambush.

A second group ran forward, unable to slow down but sensing something amiss by the bodies covering the road. Reddevek sprang into the fray, ducking the swing of a sword before plunging his own short sword into a breaker's midsection. The tip caught on chainmail, so he reversed the grip on his axe and hammered the end of his sword, feeling the resistance give. The man grunted in surprise.

The warden slashed the blade out in time to block the swing of another. His axe swept up into the man's chin, splitting him to the nose. He turned to see three others dressed in the uniform of the city watch. Two wielded weapon and shield; the third hung back, cocking a crossbow.

One of the men pointed a sword down the road. "Stand aside for breaker's justice, Warden. Our fight's not with you but the vice regent. He's been pulling our chain for years. He's one of ours, and we're sending him to the Drift."

Instead of a response, Reddevek lunged to the side, the searing burn of a sword thrust arcing along his flank. He hamstrung the man with his axe and took him in the chest with the sword as he fell, stepping back to avoid an overhead swing of a mace. He hooked his axe over the lip of the mace-wielder's shield and heaved backward, then caught the man in the belly with his sword as he stumbled forward.

The twang of the crossbow sang out, and a poker of hot pain seared into the front of his hip, staggering him back. The edge of a bolt quivered, protruding from his leathers. Reddevek glared at the breaker holding the crossbow only six feet away.

"You little grinder!" The man struggled to cock the crossbow, and Reddevek hurled his axe. The effort caused his hips to twist, sending hot wires of pain into his thigh. He staggered back as his blade sank into the breaker's chest, the familiar clack of split breastbone giving him a momentary reprieve.

After that, the warden gave in to his rage. Reddevek lurched ahead, blocking thrusts, stabbing, and slashing. Three more breakers fell around him, gutted or incapacitated. He gripped the top of another shield, and something smashed the fingers of his hand, but the distraction allowed him to slide his sword blade over the top, catching the breaker under the eye. They fell together, Reddevek's wounded leg giving out.

All around him, the sound of melee and combat continued as more and more Lacuna filed into the block. A coordinated thrum of crossbows was followed by a peppering of bolts. Five of his Outriders and at least four breakers staggered, impaled by the bolts.

Bacall squatted next to Reddevek, looked once at the dark pool saturating his leathers, then reached under his arms, pulling him back to the shadows and a relatively safer recess on the boardwalk.

She shouted over her shoulder, "Kap, toss the shatterbites! Faille, man down here!"

One of the Outriders stepped from the shadows, appearing younger than a tender and just as dazed by the violence around them. He held a cluster of munitions. A flicker of zenith flared from the runes on his forearm, and the munitions sparked. Kap stepped onto the street and heaved one munition after the other, releasing them moments before a crossbow bolt caught him in the shoulder, spinning him to the ground.

A moment later, shatterbites erupted in concussive, blinding flashes. Men from the next block screamed in pain, and a cloud of dust billowed up. All was silent for the next minute save for the cries of the wounded.

"Faille," hissed Bacall, "the warden needs aid!"

From the other side of the road, Faille darted forward. Reddevek propped his back against the edge of the building, aware of the healer song as the medic went to work. Bacall crawled forward to drag Kap, her wounded munitions man, back to safety.

Reddevek was about to order Kap to sit tight when a shock of pain erupted from his wounded hip, taking his breath away. Another thrum of crossbows split the silence, and the bolts showered all around them. Somehow, the prime managed to avoid injury as she dragged Kap back to the shadows.

Reddevek sensed by the way Bacall sagged her head that the young munitions man was lost. Chancle stepped from a shadowed doorway, crouching beside them. The warden gripped the medic's wrist, bringing a stop to her ministrations.

He sighed. "You two need to go now. Take the vice regent, ride out of here. Regroup with those at the South Gate, then ride to Kaldera and tell him what happened here."

Bacall searched his face, then drew her lips to a tight line. She held up Kap's pack. "One last play. There's enough demolition packed in here to bring down the block."

"We don't want to harm innocent civvies," growled Reddevek. "Leave the pack with me, and go."

Bacall smiled. "Nonsense. The buildings are empty. I already checked. It will buy us some time. Then we're all riding out, sir."

She hoisted the pack and crept up the street into the cloud of dust. Chancle stepped forward, quietly retrieving two crossbows and a handful of bolts. He squatted next to Reddevek, arming the weapons in the safety of the shadows before training his sight into the darkness up the road. "Might as well be prepared," he said.

The murmur of the healer song lifted again as Faille resumed her work, sealing up the wound on Reddevek's hip where the bolt struck. The medic knew her craft; he could already feel the pain ebbing. His entire pant leg was soaked; he must have lost more blood than he realized. As the battle rage faded, he felt a little giddy, and his thoughts jumbled.

Without thinking, he spoke out. "Outriders gave their life for this. What did that breaker mean, Chancle?"

The vice regent stared back up the road a moment longer, then something in his regal bearing softened, and his shoulders dropped. Chancle turned a sad expression to him. "I never meant for any of this. I just wanted to see a free Aarindorn rise from the ashes of the Abrogator's War and never again face ruin at the hands of an elite caste. But it seems I've only managed to trade one evil for another."

His words did not completely make sense, but they still cut through the foggy feeling, unsettling his concentration. "Chancle, what . . . what did you do?"

Chancle blinked just before the first of his crossbows fired. The murmur of Faille's song ceased, and the woman arched her back, the barb of a single bolt punching through her chest with a blossom of blood.

"You're the Taker's piss. I'll be waiting for you in the Drift," said Reddevek.

The second crossbow discharged, and Reddevek felt the bolt crunch just right of center, scraping off his breastbone. Fiery hot pain followed the strange staggering concussive force of the bolt, starting, oddly enough, in his back. His breaths came short, labored with pain. The lightheaded sensation intensified. A salty taste welled up in the back of his throat, and he resisted the urge to cough but couldn't help it. Frothy blood spattered onto his chest, staining his white robe and congesting his nose.

Bacall's footsteps echoed from the dust cloud. Reddevek tried to cry out a warning, but only a garbled growl escaped. The prime drew her blade and crouched, recognizing the betrayal at once. Chancle lifted his hand forward, made a twisting motion, and gusted a funnel of wind that lifted the woman, launching her back up the street. She cried out in alarm, and then a blast wave erupted, the payload of the munition pack detonating.

A tunnel of darkness began to funnel Reddevek's vision to a narrow point. Chancle's legs strode out of his sight, back down the street. The regent's voice, oddly muffled, played at the periphery of his awareness. Orange firelight flickered, the sulfurous scent of munitions wafted across the ground, and he thought about how nice it would be to sit around a campfire with Ranika one more time.

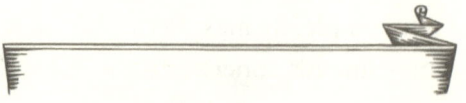

Chapter Fifty-Six: The Ascent

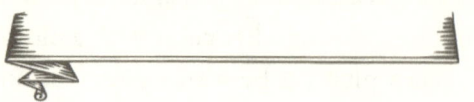

Luthean pulled his attention away from the statues of his parents. His mind continued to sift and record every detail of their preserved state: the delicate way her nose upturned, the varying pigments of grey in their irises, a serrated scar on his palm, and another on the underside of her chin. Maroon and black blood splatters stained the lower edges of their robes and painted the toes of their boots. From the knees up, he exuded a sense of strength. She conveyed all of that and more; she was absolutely lovely, flawless even.

As the deafening activation of the castle wards subsided, everyone had turned to look in Kaellor's direction, but something in his mother's intense expression held him fast. He willed her to motion, thinking if he pressed his desire with enough . . . intensity, she might speak or embrace him . . . even smile. He stood in place, enthralled, hoping beyond hope that something of a miracle might happen in this world of the strangest miracles. But both she and Japheth remained perfectly still behind the shimmering, gauzy patina of zenith that preserved them.

Eventually, the persistence of a faint sound in the cadence of a voice piqued his curiosity. It echoed as muffled speech, like someone speaking from the other side of a wall.

"Is that . . . is the castle . . . talking to us?" he asked.

Kaellor turned a puzzled expression to Laryn, and they all strained to listen. Eventually, Ksenia offered some clarity. "I believe that's the regent, but he sounds far away."

She walked out through the double doors and turned left down the receiving hall. They followed her to another door that opened to a broad circular stairwell where the echoes of the voice sounded much more clear.

"Yes, it's Therek. Unless I miss my guess, he's projecting his voice somehow," said Ksenia.

Indeed, as they strained to make out the regent's words, Lluthean understood him to say, "Keep calm. Everything is as it should be. I will commence the formal address in short order." After that, the phrases bled into one another.

"Ksenia," said Laryn. "This tower rises all the way to the highest reaches of Stone's Grasp, does it not?"

"Yes. From the top, it's a few turns and a short walk to the royal plaza," she answered. A curious expression played across her face. "I think we've arrived in time for the opening night of the spring assembly."

"All in the Giver's good timing, I suppose. It's so strange being back here," said Kaellor. He looked inside the room with the stairs. "I thought we might be at the end of the journey for today, but it seems we've one last climb to make. What do you all say?"

"Is it safe?" asked Bryndor. "I mean, we're here, but like you said, nobody is going to miss our arrival now. What about the Lacuna and all that?"

Kaellor nodded and took Laryn's hand. "We might have to ferret out a few rats, but with the wolvryn and in full command of my gift, I don't think anyone will be able to offer us much trouble. Let's see what our old friend Therek has to say."

Kaellor began the climb beside Laryn. Bryndor and Ksenia walked through next, followed by Boru. Lluthean started the climb with Ranika at his side. He turned to see Neska sitting on her haunches at the bottom of the steps.

He signaled to her in the hand sign of the Cloud Walkers. *It's strange, I know. But trust me, Neska. Please come, I need you.*

The wolvryn considered him a long moment, but only when he turned and climbed another ten steps did she follow. *Maedra, Giver . . . whoever you are, you have my thanks. Give Neska your peace if you . . . care to do that sort of thing.*

"What are you thinking, Llu?" asked Ranika as she panted beside him, following his pace on the steps.

"Hmm? I was thinking about Neska. Wishing there was some way to help her feel . . . comfortable, I guess?"

"What do you mean?" asked Ranika.

"She's been distant ever since Callinora. I don't know if it's this place, or all the people, or something else."

Ranika removed her hat, holding it in her hands and running her fingers through the spirals of her hair. "From the moment we met on the Borderlands, I always thought she was the vigilant one. Sometimes I would wake up and check on things in camp, and Neska was always the first one I would bump into. Maybe she's just less trusting than Boru."

"Maybe," he said.

They continued to climb for several minutes in silence, and he cast a glance over his shoulder. Neska made steady progress but remained twenty steps below. Bryndor and Ksenia muttered to themselves, something that made them both laugh between panted breaths. His uncle and Laryn set a steady pace, climbing the steps in silence.

"Are you excited, at least?" she asked.

"I don't know what I am, really. Kae said it best. This whole thing is strange." He paused to catch his breath and continued, "It's odd to have come so far, to a place we've been thinking about for nearly a year now. And yet . . . I have no idea where we're going, where these Taker-cursed stairs lead."

He leaned to look down the center of the cylindrical room. The bottom steps were lost in the shadows far below. "I've seen some grand kingdoms in the Southlands, but grind me, none of them had a castle that required this many steps to reach the top."

They continued the ascent. "How about you? What do you think of Stone's Grasp?"

Ranika bobbed her head from side to side. "I haven't given it much thought. I keep wondering what Redd is up to. Riding Zippy can be challenging, but it beats these stairs any day of the month."

Lluthean couldn't argue the point, and their conversation was stifled as they labored to keep pace with the others. Finally, they reached the top. After a brief rest, Ksenia pushed a door open and led them through several turns, eventually exiting into a wide hallway.

The regent's voice resonated full and clear, an amplified baritone rumbling through the walls. "And so we come to this place as a divided people needing unity. It's in this spirit that I've given my next announcement considerable thought, for I should like to announce—"

A distant lone detonation interrupted the regent, and a faint quake vibrated through the castle stones. Zenith flared through the silver veining of the walls.

"Something's not right," said Kaellor. "Boys, prepare your bows; keep the wolvryn in check but ready. The rest of you, stay behind my shielding."

Lluthean signaled Neska to accompany him on point. She dipped her head, then shook as if trying to free something from an ear, and walked to stand beside him. He lifted his arm to scratch under her chin and felt reassured when she rubbed the cheek of her broad head against his shoulder.

Zenith flared over the runes visible at Kaellor's jawline and wrists. Lluthean nocked an arrow before his uncle withdrew the guardian sword and shouldered open a set of double doors.

Lights from countless shimmering overhead spheres blossomed all around them. And so much sound . . . the clamor of more people than he had ever seen at one time greeted them as they walked cautiously onto the royal plaza. To the left and right, the expansive stone floor spread nearly fifty yards in each direction. Several servants stood spellbound, gazing out to the city, and gave them no notice. Far ahead, a lean man with gangly arms towered over a podium, speaking to the crowd.

Kaellor led them forward, and as they approached, the distant city came into clear view. Thousands of lights twinkled well beyond where he imagined the natural horizon should be. Armies of people milled about three separate tiers or plateaus below.

Lluthean shared a look with his brother and wondered if the same astonished expression appeared on his face. Neither of them had ever seen such a large population gathered in one place, and the city dwarfed anything they had visited in the Southlands. In the distance far below, a fire spread among the buildings of a city block, trails of smoke visible against the flames.

Most of the people in the crowd had turned their attention toward the explosion, giving the regent and the approaching royals little thought.

Kaellor sheathed his sword but kept a hand gripped on the hilt. "Therek Lefledge, it's been a long time, old friend."

The regent stiffened, remaining with his back to them a moment, then turned a slow circle. When he smiled, the wispy ends of long eyebrows flared. The old man clasped his hands together, then held them wide in a welcoming gesture.

He stepped from the podium to embrace Kaellor, turned to Laryn, and took in the rest of them. "You found them? All of them?"

Laryn stepped forward and giggled, embracing her friend. "Thanks to your guidance, I did. Allow me to introduce my nephews, Bryndor and Lluthean, and their wolvryn Boru and Neska. You know Ksenia, our guide, and this is Ranika, our dearest friend."

Therek shook his head in disbelief. "And you're all finally here. The Giver lights the path, but the Taker shadows the destination. I . . . began to doubt my gift." His eyes misted over.

Kaellor cocked his head. "You foresaw our arrival, yet still made me climb all those steps?"

"Not exactly. There's time for all of that later. The fire . . . in the merchant district, was that your diversion?" asked the regent.

"No," said Kaellor. "But the castle wards, that was us. You seem troubled. Is everything alright?"

Therek frowned. "Not yet, but it will be very soon." He focused on something internal for a moment, considering Kaellor's words. "Let me see to that before it burns out of control. Then we'll make proper introductions."

He stepped to the podium and placed his hand on a polished stone sphere. When he spoke, his voice amplified throughout the city. "Citizens of Aarindorn. I need everyone to remain calm. It seems we have ourselves a small fire in the upper merchant district. There is no danger inside the curtain wall, and I encourage everyone in attendance of the spring assembly to remain here for the time being. I further call on all aquamancers to employ their gift to subdue the flames. Once that is settled, I will conclude the address, and we can begin the night's festivities. Until then, enjoy the food and drink and dance to the music. The night is young, and we'll yet see the fireworks to welcome a time of renewal for Aarindorn."

The crowd muttered, but in tones that seemed eased by his words. Therek waved to a servant. "My friends and I are going to retire to the Founder's Memorial. Please see that refreshments, food, and drink are delivered for a party of seven, and until the fire is controlled, see that we are not disturbed."

The man bowed once, and Therek lifted a hand toward the doors they had used to enter the plaza. "Ms. Balladuren, if you could be so kind as to lead the way."

Ksenia led the group back through the double doors, around the broad hallway, and to the Founder's Memorial. Neska and Boru pushed their way into the garden and disappeared into the undergrowth.

"There's a dome here like the one in Callinora," said Lluthean as they settled onto benches.

"Just so, Your Highness," said Therek. His gaze lingered on Lluthean long moments before shifting to Bryndor. "Apologies. You have to understand, your parents were dear friends of mine, and your resemblance is nothing short of a miracle of the Giver."

A line of servants arrived with trays of food and drink. After they set up the refreshments, Therek escorted them out with a warning not to be disturbed until the fire in the merchant district was extinguished. The regent strode back on quick feet.

"Friends, please . . . eat and drink, but keep your heads clear. A lot hangs in the balance, and we'll need to work together to see the kingdom through this long, dark night."

Chapter Fifty-Seven: Rise of the Abrogator

THE ENDLESS TRICKLE of victims fueling the Rite of Sundering continued for well over two hours before any complications arose. With increasing frequency, they started falling in groups of two and three, then sometimes four or more, and many appeared bloodied by the traumatic passage. Each time a cluster of people plummeted from the cavern ceiling, the elder shaman altered the pacing and tempo of the drums to accommodate the increased number.

As far as she could tell, none of the sacrifices were wasted. Every time one of them struck the rift in the pool, the collision magnified the size and intensity of the fissure, now a wide crack of molten material so bright that she had to avert her eyes after a few seconds. Still, Volencia grew concerned that Grasdok and the umbral had lost control of the grondle herd and berated herself that she had not kept a close tally on the number.

Several seconds passed in which none fell from the chute. She searched the entrance at the ceiling to discover a clot of limbs bottlenecked. Fear fueled her to action, and she lashed out a spear of dense nadir. The onyx shaft plunged into the writhing mass with a hiss, dissolving and reducing the obstruction. Dismembered limbs and parts of three torsos toppled out of the chute. She whipped a tendril of nadir, deflecting the dead tissue to the perimeter of the cavern and preventing contamination of the ritual.

Shamans slowed the beat of their drums, and the tribe chanted with a more restrained cadence. Volencia stared at the empty orifice, waiting for the next sacrifice to drop through. *There must be another obstruction farther up. Either that, or the grondle have raged and ruined everything.*

Four leggy nadir tentacles sprouted from her, two on each forearm, and she used them to scale the interior wall of the cavern. She reached the place where the walls arched up to the ceiling and cast a glance back to the glowing fissure on the floor. Either the rift had lost something of its hot intensity, or from this distance, the light seemed less offensive to her eyes.

She plunged one of the tentacles into the rocky ceiling, finding a secure purchase before using the other to repeat the anchor. She surprised herself with how swiftly she closed the distance, pressured by absolute necessity. Just as she reached the opening, the scream of a man echoed down the tube, and seconds later, he plunged through, dropping down to feed the ritual. The fissure blossomed with renewed vibrance, and Volencia sighed inwardly.

She chose to remain perched like a spider for the remainder of the ceremony. A higher-pitched voice—a child—squealed as she slid through the opening. Volencia recognized the terror-stricken face. *Cabe's daughter, Retta. That must mean the numbers up top are thinning. We had better be close.*

She watched the girl drop, arms flailing, hair whipping about her face. The elder shaman trilled an unusual drumroll, then slapped both of the sigil-riddled thigh bones across the hide once. The entire ensemble matched him, and the cavern fell to silence save for the screams of the child and a groaning, wrenching sound rising out of the rift.

Retta hovered just above the surface of the fissure. Either the intensity of the light had altered Volencia's vision, or waves of power were rippling over the child, making her seem to pass beneath a flowing current. The umbral backed away from the pool, ending their mindful maintenance of the ritual.

Retta inhaled a breath and began to scream, but her body was torn apart, then plunged into the rift. The deep rumbling, groaning sound rose in frequency, becoming a harsh shearing noise, terrible and invasive. The grotvonen wailed, even the shamans, and all clutched their ears; all save the umbral, who stood with fascinated attention.

Tears streamed down Volencia's cheeks, and she pressed palms to her ears. An utterly putrid, rancid reek rose from the glowing fissure, so strong that Volencia gagged on the awful taste of it. She considered retreating up into the chute to escape the misery of it all, but two hands appeared on the edges of the fissure.

Another scream echoed from above, and Volencia filled the channel with a plug of nadir. She folded the weave back and forth, filling the chute just in time to prevent another person from falling into the cavern. She would have to maintain the construct, but what did it matter if her master could finally emerge?

Like a spider tethered by a long strand of webbing, she dismissed all but one of the nadir tentacles and lowered herself to the floor. Through the descent, she could make out one muscled forearm, then another. Black sigils wriggled on every surface. A bald head emerged, slicked in an oily black fluid.

Tarkannen grimaced and opened his mouth in a silent scream of agony. He shifted the back of his shoulders to one edge and pushed against the other. The sound of searing flesh hissed to her awareness, and the smell of burned flesh cut the tainted underworld reek. The rift resisted his efforts and seemed to constrict, as if to claim him once again.

He lowered his head, appearing to accept his fate, then curtains of nadir flooded through the fissure so intensely that the cavern fell momentarily into darkness. More of the otherworldly creaking and groaning echoed in the chamber, and the rock under her feet vibrated.

Tarkannen's swell of nadir receded into the glowing fissure, and she watched as he lifted one naked, sigil-laden leg out of the Drift, and then the other. He squatted beside the rift as it began to retract inexorably, becoming a thin glowing crack in the nadir pool in but seconds.

The cavern fell into silent darkness, and her eyes adjusted to the faint illumination of grotvonen painted with mushroom spores. She sauntered a few steps forward and fell to her knees. "Master, you made it."

Tarkannen stood to his full height, oblivious of his nakedness. Sigils covered every surface of his skin, shifting and wriggling but only rarely revealing the pale skin underneath. He lifted his nose to the air and searched the cavern, resting his eyes on her. "You." His first attempt at speech was garbled, and he coughed, clearing his throat. "You have done everything that I asked. Well done, Volencia. Rise and let me see you."

Volencia stood and retrieved the purple robe she had confiscated from one of the nobles of Sifter's Valley. She held up the garment, and he stared with confusion for a moment. "Mmm, yes . . . I've forgotten some things, but learned so much more in my time in the Drift. Still, I sense that I've lost some of that knowledge in crossing back through." His lips drew to a thin line, and sigils flared back from his mouth, making his lips appear all the more pallid.

His eyes shifted back and forth, attentive to a puzzle only he could see. "That's an unfortunate development. Nonetheless, I've retained enough."

Tarkannen surveyed the shamans, the umbral, and the host of grotvonen. He held a hand out and produced the guttural, clicky speech of the Brognaus. The elder shaman loped forward, head bowed, and her master stroked the creature behind the ear with affection.

"Why do you maintain a focus of nadir up there?" he asked.

"It's plugging a chute. We crafted a tunnel that drops from the surface and used it to deliver the sacrifices required for the Rite of Sundering. I didn't know if allowing others to drop would disrupt your emergence," she explained.

"Release it for now and save your strength. We have work to do."

"At once," Volencia dismissed her connection to the webbing of nadir plugging the chute. She expected to see people begin to drop through, but another clot of lifeless limbs was wedged at the opening.

"There should be enough refined nadir left to craft a conduit directly to Stone's Grasp. We should arrive easily at the inner sanctum and the deepening well. Come, Volencia, bear witness to all that we have labored for."

Tarkannen waved his hands over the pool of nadir, swirling the surface into a vortex. The oily black substance converted into a mercurial slick, emitting faint light and eddied by random ribbons of color. A portal formed, like the one she had used before, and at the far end, the foot of a large statue appeared. She recognized the statue of Eldrek.

"Follow me, child. I can maintain the conduit for both of us," said Tarkannen, and he hopped inside.

Chapter Fifty-Eight: The Sons of Japheth and Nebrine

Flakey crust broke apart, and a tangy berry filling grabbed at the sides of Bryndor's tongue. In three bites, he'd devoured the pastry and reached for another crownberry tart. He sat on a bench in the Founder's Memorial, listening to the discussion between Laryn, Kaellor, and the regent, Therek Lefledge. Ksenia sat beside him, nibbling on a pastry. Lluthean returned from a stroll through the garden, his curious hands fingering the waxy leaves.

The gardens seemed like a peaceful sanctuary, a welcome chance to regroup. But the sheer size of the population outside still weighed heavily on Bryndor's mind. He chewed errantly, thinking back to all of their journeys in the Southlands. Standing on the royal plaza scanning across the masses . . . he had never felt so insignificant.

Ksenia handed him a plate of cheese. "You're supposed to nibble a bite of this in between bites of the tart. I'm told the flavors compliment one another, though I've always been partial to the pastry myself."

He took a small piece of cheese, nibbled at the edge, and considered the creamy flavor.

"You haven't said much since we climbed the steps," she said.

"It's . . . a lot more than I expected. Those crowds . . . how is any one person supposed to lead that many people?"

She glanced at Therek and the others, then turned back to him. "With the help of wise counselors . . . and good friends, I expect."

That gave him a small measure of peace, and he returned her smile.

The regent stood beside Boru, scratching long fingers under the wolvryn's jaw. Therek's wispy eyebrows rose up in amusement when the wolvryn licked at the man's neck, then flopped his broad head over the man's shoulders. Though the regent stood a head taller, Boru's sheer mass nearly toppled Therek backward. He had no choice but to reach out and embrace Boru in an awkward hug. The entire interaction caused the man to burst out laughing.

"Apologies," said Bryndor. "He's become a bit of an attention monger."

Therek ruffled the fur behind Boru's ears and came to sit beside them on a bench. Boru followed him and plopped down on the ground, hoping to entice more affection. "There's no need. Seeing them after so many years, it's another blessing of the Giver to offset the Taker's meddling. I had a brief vision of your return a few nights ago. You approached me at the podium. I had no clear idea of the exact day or the timing, and so I stalled until I began to question the blessing. And I never saw these wonderful creatures in the images."

"Sometimes the Giver gives," said Laryn.

"And sometimes the Taker takes," finished Therek.

"You mean the Lacuna. Is it all that bad?" asked Kaellor.

"It's become far worse than I imagined a year ago," said Therek. "They've managed to infiltrate every level of government, every town and duchy. Even my own offices hold spies that favor the breakers."

"What about the noble families? The Endules? Llentrels?" asked Laryn.

"The families ruling Dulesque and Beclure and those here in Stone's Grasp have been resistant but not immune to the overtures of the Aspect and his followers. We have a few groups we can call upon if outright civil war erupts. Your arrival here might be the very thing that sets the course of the kingdom for generations," said Therek.

Kaellor scratched at his beard, looked at Laryn, then back to Therek. "None of us are dressed in appropriate attire to entertain the people of Stone's Grasp. But it sounds like we should address the crowds as soon as possible. Would it help if one of us spoke a few words? Maybe set the tone for the spring assembly? How do you think we should proceed?"

"The Giver bids the wise man to step cautiously around the feral wolvryn," Therek recited. "And yet, there must be a definitive declaration of your return. The kingdom needs the stability of your leadership."

The low rumble of a wolvryn growl interrupted the conversation. Neska prowled forward from behind a tangle of broad-leafed plants, her mass filling the paved walkway. Ranika stood at the wolvryn's flank, crouched with a knife in hand. Moments later, eight uniformed guards crept into the gardens, crossbows loaded and aimed. Bryndor reached a hand toward his bow.

One of the men in the front held his cheek flush to the weapon; a tremor caused the tip of the bolt to tremble. "Enough of that. Call off your dogs and keep your hands off the bow. Regent Lefledge, Your Grace, I need you to come with us back to safety. Then we'll deal with these . . . interlopers."

Therek's shoulders sagged. "You wear the uniform of the city watch but act with all the honor of a circle breaker. Do you have any idea what you are doing? Treason is punishable by death."

"Just my part to ensure a peaceful transition. Captain Oren ordered me to bring you to safety, and there's the matter of a reward for such . . . heroic duties," said the man.

Therek seemed to ponder the man's words a moment, then said softly to Kaellor, "I assume you've managed your arca prime since your return?"

Kaellor flared a sphere of translucent blue zenith; the barrier separated them from the guards. The front line of Lacuna discharged their crossbows, the bolts skittering harmlessly off into the garden. Kaellor's fingers twitched, and Bryndor recognized the signing. *Send in the wolvryn, ready your bows, keep at least one alive.*

Lluthean must have understood the message because before Bryndor could act, Neska charged the group from the side, scattering those in the back row with loaded crossbows. Boru leaped a moment later, charging into the fray. Bryndor stood, bow raised, and saw an arrow streak forward from the corner of his eye. Lluthean had already incapacitated the leader, and fletching sprouted from the man's chest.

Bryndor waited for a clear shot, but the wolvryn savaged into the group, a maelstrom of teeth and claws. In seconds they had crushed, maimed, and killed the entire party of eight.

Kaellor sighed. "Dammit to the Drift, boys, I said keep one alive."

"Sorry, Kae," said Lluthean. He whistled and shouted a command. Neska backed away with fangs bared. Boru shook his head, thrashing the corpse of one of the guards against a wall before returning to Bryndor's side.

They observed the maimed bodies for a moment to be sure that all of them were dead. One man spasmed on the ground, grunting in pain. Kaellor gripped his hands in the air in a crushing gesture. A soft thump vibrated through the pavers, and the ward seemed to lock in place. "Keep your bows ready but stay here."

He withdrew the guardian sword and stepped through the ward. *"Did you know he could do that?"* Bryndor signed to Lluthean. His brother shook his head, eyebrows raised in surprise.

"What are the Lacuna planning tonight? Speak truthfully, and I might be merciful," said Kaellor.

The man spluttered and tried to laugh. "You can't stop what's comin'. Any moment now . . . with the first flare." He convulsed in a spasm of pain, and a mixture of blood and foul-smelling fluid drained from a rent in his belly. "Like . . . shooting fancy fish . . . in a barrel."

Kaellor kept his eyes on the man, speaking loud enough for all to hear. "Therek, does that mean anything to you?"

As the wounded man gasped his last breath, Therek stood to his full height. "Giver's mercy. He's talking about the nobles. Many of them are gathered on the top green to watch a fireworks show. There are whole families down there, children, grandchildren. If the breakers control the city watch . . . I should have seen this coming."

"There were more guards than I could count walking the ramparts over that top outdoor garden area," said Lluthean.

"We could handle them in pieces, but not before they killed scores of people. How much time do you think we have?" asked Kaellor. He dismissed the guardian ward and sheathed his sword.

"The show isn't supposed to start until after my address, but I don't think we can assume that they intend to wait," said Therek.

Kaellor pulled a hand over his eyes and across his beard in frustration, looked at each of them, met eyes with Laryn, and finally smiled.

"Eyes to the horizon, love?" she asked.

"Eyes to the horizon," he spoke, sounding more exhausted than Bryndor expected.

"There might be a chance to avoid further bloodshed if we take the podium," said Laryn. "Address the people and welcome them to the spring assembly as if this was all part of our plan."

Kaellor nodded approval. "I can create and maintain a ward around us for hours before being taxed. All of you stay close to me."

"Should we leave Neska and Boru in here?" Bryndor asked.

"No. Bring them along. Many people my age and older will recognize them and respect their power and majesty. Others will think twice before rushing the podium," said Kaellor.

"Perhaps at least one of the princes should remain behind, as a matter of strategic security," said Therek.

Kaellor considered the idea and searched first Lluthean's face, then settled his gaze on Bryndor. Zenith flecked his eyes with cerulean intensity, but something in his expression softened. "I appreciate the counsel, but we've come a long way, and if the journey has taught me anything, it's that we're stronger together than apart. I'll lead us out. Bryn, you and Boru bring up the rear."

They filed out of the memorial and made their way to the royal plaza. Kaellor stopped at the door to ensure everyone stood prepared. "Not more than ten steps behind me."

He pushed through the doors, and Bryndor gripped his bow, expecting the rush of another group of Lacuna. Instead, a guard was propped up against the wall, bleeding from two crossbow bolts. What appeared to be two other members of the city watch lay dead at his feet, the grisly sword wounds oozing dark blood.

Kaellor stepped forward, assessing the plaza, but nobody else seemed aware of their presence. Countless globes and sconces bathed the plaza in a nimbus of light that obscured the night sky. In the distance, guards stood just inside the shadows on the ramparts, staring down into the green. Ksenia pushed forward to crouch by the guard. "Bextle, what happened?"

The man looked at Kaellor and Laryn, then back to Ksenia. "Craxton's been in contact with Dexxin . . . told me everything. How we've all been . . . fooled." He shook his head, self-loathing evident by his expression. "I tried to stop the men from coming to get you, but only managed to take out two before the grinders shot me."

Ksenia looked up to Laryn. "Can you help him? He's a good man."

Laryn had already squatted next to the guard and activated her gift, the healer song a soft murmur against the crowd noise.

"Laryn, we might not have time for this," said Kaellor.

She looked up, a fierce intensity in her eyes. "This is exactly what we have time for. This man, leaving the Lacuna, seeing them for the disease they are . . . this is what we've been working for. Leave Ranika or one of the boys and a wolvryn with me for protection. I'll see to this, and you go with Therek."

Kaellor sucked at his teeth, shaking his head, mumbling something about stubborn Lellendules. "Alright, Nika, Llu, and Ksenia, you're on guard duty here with Neska until Laryn can finish. Bryndor, bring Boru and come with me."

Kaellor stepped back and held a fist forward, bringing another guardian ward into place. He gestured as if pulling on a rope, securing the barrier around Laryn and the wounded man, then turned to the podium.

Therek wasted no time marching to the podium and placing a hand on the strange stone sphere. His voice carried across not just the crowd but seemed to echo across the entire city. "My friends, I apologize for the delay and offer you the thanks of the office of the regent. Ever since the Abrogator's War, we have gathered in the spirit of unity. Welcome to the 14th Annual Spring Assembly of Aarindorn at Stone's Grasp. May the Giver bless you and keep you."

Therek continued his preamble, welcoming the crowds and even sending greetings throughout the rest of the city. As he spoke, Bryndor's attention surveyed the panorama before them. The royal plaza defied gravity, jutting out from the mountain cliffs. Looking down, he had a clear view of the castle grounds as they spread out in three massive tiers that stepped down toward the rest of the city.

Stone ramparts, broad enough to allow four people to walk abreast, surrounded each green space. Very few guards milled about the lower two levels, but Bryndor counted well over fifty men and women, Lacuna he guessed, standing at attention on the west side over the uppermost green. Even by the dim light, he could make out that all carried crossbows, and several seemed fidgety to his eye.

He reached a hand back to his quiver, bouncing the base. The familiar weight and rattle of arrows told him it was full, but even if his aim was perfect, he could only manage to eliminate ten to twelve hostiles. *How exactly are we supposed to subdue them if they decide to attack with crossbows? There's no way we can keep them from showering the people below.*

As Therek continued his address, Lluthean came to stand beside them, Neska padding at his side. Kaellor looked back to Laryn, then to Lluthean. Ranika and Ksenia knelt beside the healer, protected inside the blue dome.

Lluthean shrugged. "What? I'm only following orders, and today I'm more afraid of your wife than I am of you," he said in answer to Kaellor's unspoken question.

A commotion of movement broke out as the Lacuna gathered at the far end of the rampart. They huddled up around a central figure.

"And so," said Therek, "it brings me tremendous pleasure to announce that I can finally step down as your regent and introduce Kaellor Baellentrell, prince of Aarindorn, who has returned to us with his nephews, the sons of Japheth and Nebrine, Prince Bryndorllean and Prince Llutheandellen Baellentrell."

A silence settled over the crowds, a sea of astonished faces turning to regard the group of men. Therek was welcoming Kaellor to the podium when a voice from the ramparts broke out, speaking through a handheld device that magnified his shouts. "Don't listen to the regent! He has been fooled by these imposters! Men and women of the city watch, breakers one and all, I am Captain Oren, and I order you to attack the imposters now!"

With military precision, the Lacuna already stationed on the ramparts raced forward, the first row dropping to a knee, the second aiming, and as one, from both sides of the ramparts, they unleashed a volley of crossbow bolts. Kaellor erected another protective dome of zenith, and the missiles clattered against the shielding, dropping to the ground.

Therek placed his hand on the sphere, attempting to regain control. "Captain Oren, you are both a fool and a traitor! Could anyone but a Baellentrell summon a guardian shield?"

A second and then a third volley of crossbow bolts showered the guardian ward in answer to Therek's challenge.

"All of you, I beg you to stop. It's not too late for peace, but this is your last chance!" Therek bellowed.

The ranks of Lacuna continued to alternate and fire crossbow bolts against Kaellor's shield. Two guards ran forward, holding what appeared to be bags of flour. Boru lurched as if to attack, but Bryndor signaled him to wait. They poured the contents on the ground, making a pile of sandy grit, then stepped back several feet. Each man appeared to generate a cyclone of wind, swirling the gritty substance around Kaellor's shield.

The blue dome flickered with static for several seconds, then nearly winked out. Kaellor withdrew his guardian sword and attempted to reinforce the ward. It flared a brilliant blue and seemed to hold, more crossbow bolts clattering to the ground. And then it didn't. A crossbow bolt wedged into the podium by the regent, and Kaellor turned a shoulder as another bolt flew by.

Kaellor took a knee and grunted, planting the guardian sword into the stone and clearly straining to recreate and maintain the shield. "I can't keep up both wards. Empty your quivers now! Concentrate everything on the east side! Send the wolvryn after those gusters!"

Bryndor wasted no time. He signaled Boru to attack, drew, and fired. He didn't even wait to see if one arrow landed before drawing and releasing the next. As he and Lluthean fired, men and women in the eastern ranks began to fall back. People on the greens shouted cries of alarm. Therek's voice broke over the din. "Salveen, Fagle, now is the time! Fulfill your vows for Aarindorn and come to our aid! People of Aarindorn, rise up against the Lacuna menace now!"

"Bryn, Llu, I'm sorry; that grit eroded my ability to channel. I can't hold it much longer. Be ready. We'll charge the group on the east. Arm yourselves from the dead as we go!" Kaellor shouted.

Kaellor waited for another volley, then dropped the ward and sprinted forward. Bryndor and Lluthean ran behind him, waiting for an opportunity. Kaellor pulsed consecutive arcs of power before them as they ran, knocking bolts from the air as they closed the distance, then tumbling the Lacuna back.

Kae sprang forward, taking advantage of the confusion, sword slicing left then right, piercing then recoiling. His fluid motions paused a moment, and he jabbed down into the chest of one of the Lacuna. He kicked back once, spun and lunged, then kicked back again. A longsword and two short swords slid back to Bryndor and Lluthean. Kaellor pulsed another crescent of zenith, and more breakers stumbled backward.

"Press forward in hand to hand. Don't give them room to fire!" Kaellor yelled.

Bryndor gripped two hands around the longsword. Lluthean crouched low, retrieving the other two weapons, then rolled into a lunge and slash, a Lacuna falling to his strike. A crossbow bolt arced past Lluthean's ear, and Bryndor felt his body move without thinking. He lifted the blade, lurched ahead five steps, and cleaved into the man who had fired at his brother.

The blade caught the man in the flank, a vicious side swipe. The guard folded over the wound, and Bryndor twisted his wrist and sliced back, opening a rent across his abdomen. He stepped back into the space Kaellor had created, blocking, then cutting, retreating two more steps, then turning and tripping a woman who stumbled into Lluthean's thrust.

A sword slice burned across his shoulder blade, and he cried out in a rage. Dropping low, he spun and swung out, catching a breaker below the knee, then used the pommel to crush in the back of the man's skull as he stumbled.

The next several moments tumbled out as a surreal melee as Kaellor flared arcs of his guardian power, and the three of them weaved in and out of one another. There was no formal battlefront. With Kaellor dispersing the guards in various directions, they continued to rush from different sides.

Bryndor sliced through torsos, cleaved into arms, and turned in time to avoid the most vicious slashes, but caught glancing blows from others. He took more than one breaker in the collarbone and even hacked into the skull of a man setting his feet to swing at Lluthean.

He dipped his face into his elbow to wipe away gore, thankful the sword allowed a two-handed grip, as his hands were slick with blood. Kaellor blocked and killed two for every one that he and Lluthean managed. A fragment of Bryndor's awareness realized that all the training, footwork, and drills were allowing his body to react when he could not otherwise think fast enough to do so.

Both wolvryn charged into the ranks of the breakers. Boru's jaw clamped onto the thigh of a man trying to reload a crossbow. With a savage toss of the head, the wolvryn threw the breaker over the ramparts. His screams were quickly lost in the din.

With the reinforcement of the wolvryn, the eastern flank of the city watch disintegrated into utter panic. Bryndor cut down one man running from Neska. He saw others become incapacitated by fear or confused about whether to reload a crossbow or abandon the weapon in favor of standing their ground with a sword. He took advantage of every moment of indecision, stabbing and slashing through their ranks.

In just minutes, they reduced the eastern ranks to eight Lacuna. Most were incapacitated, some from arrows, others from the brutal melee. Kaellor lifted his hand to send another pulse of zenith at the group, but they tossed down their weapons and retreated down the stairs.

Bryndor stood tall, panting, eyes searching for the next opponent. Bruises and small cuts rose to his awareness on his forearms, hands, and right thigh. *Grind me, when did all that happen?*

He glanced to Lluthean, who shook a hand in pain and pulled a dislocated finger back into place. His brother bled from the nose, and a dark bruise flourished on his temple. Kaellor panted, hands on hips, and limped a step. The broken shaft of a crossbow bolt protruded from his thigh. A shallow cut crossed his chest, and numerous nicks wept blood on his arms.

Both wolvryn prowled in a protective circle around the three of them. A glance back to the podium showed the mangled bodies of the gusters.

"Anybody seriously injured?" asked Kaellor.

"I'm good," said Bryndor.

Lluthean finished pulling his finger into place, then looked up with a shrug. "I've been better." Then he twirled his swords and smiled. "But this will do."

"Good. I've lost the ability to summon new wards. It's all I can do to protect Laryn. Something in that grit those gusters used, I don't know, something related to Veramanth's decoction maybe. We'll have to be much more careful from here forward. Let's get back inside. We can regroup within the safety of the walls."

They were turning to walk back to the podium when screams broke out from the green below. The other fifty Lacuna from the western rampart had begun unleashing volley after volley of crossbow fire into the crowd below. Waves of people, the young and the old, fell to the ground, defenseless against the attack. Some few gifted in the crowd managed to mount defenses, but in less than a minute, over a hundred civilians lay on the ground, their lifeblood blooming onto the green.

Even if he and Lluthean had more arrows, they could only hope to mitigate the onslaught as more Lacuna climbed from the second-tier green armed with sword and shield to prevent any nobles from escaping the killing zone.

A voice broke through the clamor. "That's enough. Breakers . . . hold!"

In the commotion, Captain Oren had taken control of the podium and set his hand on the stone sphere that magnified Therek's voice. The regent knelt before him, Oren's blade at his throat. Six heavily armed breakers stood in a circle, forming a wall of swords and shields around the regent and the captain.

"You imposters will surrender now, or I will continue to unleash the full might of the Lacuna below," commanded Oren.

Bryndor looked past the podium to Laryn. She, Ksenia, and Ranika stood behind Kaellor's ward by the door where Bextle lay propped up against the wall. Kaellor signed to her, and she stared back, unyielding.

"Grind it woman, get out of here," cursed Kaellor in a low voice.

"What's our play, Kae?" asked Bryndor.

Before he could answer, Oren continued, "If you don't think I'm serious, look below. Then look out at the city. The Lacuna control the Sprawl, the Delve, the commons, and everything in between. Warden Reddevek lost his life trying to get to you. It's a shame . . . a good man. How many other good people must die to preserve a dead crown?"

Bryndor felt an inner pang at the loss of his friend. Reddevek had been central to their progress through Aarindorn and treated Ranika like a daughter. When all of this was over, he would be sorely missed. The dancing light of flames rose from different parts of the city, and smoke carried on the wind, evidence of conflict in other parts of Stone's Grasp.

Kaellor's guardian sword tapped into the stone, both his hands over the pommel. The gemstones of smoke and purple hues flared indigo light through his fingers. He shouted in defiance. "I call you a coward and a murderer of innocents! You belong with the abrogator Tarkannen, who seeks to reclaim Stone's Grasp. You can't hope to defeat him without us."

Oren sneered, and his voice rumbled throughout the city. "That old line? I expected something more creative. Your brother killed the Usurper in the Abrogator's War. A war that this nation suffered because of nobles vying for power. Well, never again!"

Lacuna, armed with crossbows, jogged over to take up positions on the eastern rampart. Bryndor watched it all with a calm detachment. Some part of him hoped Tarkannen would return and lay waste to everything these miserable people held dear. He looked over the rows of crossbows and saw Ksenia and Laryn, then regretted his anger. Maybe the abrogator didn't have to destroy everything.

The front row of Lacuna took a knee and cocked their crossbows; the second row stepped behind them. Bryndor looked across to the western rampart and saw more Lacuna wielding longbows capable of bridging the distance taking aim. They all held, waiting for Oren's command.

Oren lifted his hand from the stone sphere, made a startled gesture, and grabbed at his throat. He croaked a strangled noise and dropped to his knees beside the regent. A scarlet fountain erupted from a gash across the front of his neck. Ranika appeared behind him, only just now visible. She wiped the bloodied blade of her ruby-hilted dagger on the man's shoulder.

Bryndor's initial elation at seeing the man fall vanished when he saw Ranika's face. Shadows swirled over the surface of her skin, and the placid stillness with which she considered the dying man gave him pause.

One of Oren's guards turned with surprise and swung wildly at her, but she ducked and vanished in the commotion. The twang of a crossbow diverted his attention, and Bryndor sensed Boru shudder as a bolt wedged itself in the wolvryn's shoulder. Boru roared and crouched to surge forward as two more crossbows discharged.

Bryndor felt himself fall outside the normal tempo of time. The air in front of them rippled with currents of zenith suddenly made visible. Ribbons of force coalesced in his vision, streaming across the ground and flowing through the air. The currents shifted from light blue to indigo, their undulating edges reflecting a cerulean sheen. The force began to leech in, penetrating his skin, muscles, and bones, suffusing his tissues with a pleasurable vitality.

But something in his core opposed the influx of power. A fullness gathered as a hot ache in his belly, giving him the sensation that something was distending his guts from the inside. The wedge of resistance rose into his chest, flaring throughout his blood, accelerating, intensifying, and blossoming into a searing flare of agony as the mantle forced out the flow of zenith.

He struggled to cry out, but his muscles seized up. His neck corkscrewed, and back arched near to the point of breaking as muscles cramped beyond his control. From the corner of his vision, he saw that Lluthean also struggled, enthralled by the spasms of torture. He gasped, expecting his chest to split open as the two forces warred inside him.

The intense infusion of agony seemed to last several minutes, time in which nobody moved except for Lluthean, who shuddered with the same misery. When he thought he could bear it no longer, the wedge inside him fractured apart. In an instant, the force of resistance dissolved, and the pain receded. He collapsed to his knees, afraid to move for fear of awakening the painful spasms.

The palpable currents of zenith flowed around his body, coaxing him from his state of shock with caresses akin to a pleasurable current of warm water, but he felt wary of letting the power back inside.

Bryndor splayed his fingers and waved a hand through the air, struggling to understand the strange occurrence. An expression of utter curiosity played across Lluthean's face, magnified by the scintillating sparkle of zenith that flickered in his now-blue eyes. And he noticed something else—delicate gold runes had risen from his brother's chest and neckline, adorning his jaw in a complex pattern of interconnected runes.

So this is it . . . no more mantle.

As he stood, motion swayed in the corner of Bryndor's vision, and the pace of the world crashed all around him. Kaellor fell back, struck by another crossbow bolt; more of the missiles flew past them. Boru turned to bite at another bolt in his back hip, and Neska darted back and forth, somehow avoiding the missiles but unable to charge ahead.

Bryndor stepped over to help his uncle, but Kaellor held up a hand and grunted in pain. "You have your gift, son. Unleash it. Whatever it is, use it now!"

He searched for the currents of zenith and relaxed his guard. Unrestricted, the force flooded his core. The flow crashed into him like a massive wave against the shore. He shuddered and inhaled, this time with pure ecstasy. The surge of zenith gathered across his shoulders, where it beckoned for release. He amassed the power, savoring the feeling and allowing himself a moment to understand how he could shape it to his purpose.

The torrential flood of power flowed from his shoulders, down his arms, and erupted from his hands as a continuous arc of blue flame accompanied by a thunderclap. His hair flew up and clothes fluttered back as if buffeted by a spectral wind. The air before him warped from the heat, and the stones beneath the blue fire glowed like embers in a forge.

Crossbow bolts scattered like leaves on the wind. When he suspended the flow, the entire group of Lacuna, more than twenty guards, lay as unrecognizable mounds of smoking ash. Another clap of thunder boomed overhead, and a flash of rune fire erupted on the far rampart as Lluthean discharged his own blast.

Innately, Bryndor sensed that the force inside him required further release and in a different manifestation. He gathered zenith into his hand and felt it coalesce above the armed Lacuna by the podium. With a furious effort, he labored to make the rune fire constrain to his will, dividing the mass into separate pillars of flame. Six identical cerulean blue columns of fire slammed down from overhead, consuming the armed breakers standing around the regent.

Bryndor heard a scream of rage and realized that the cry had come from his own ragged throat. When he released the surge, Therek crouched alone by the podium. Six blackened mounds of melted steel smoked around him.

Feelings of uncertainty and horror gave way to awe as he considered all that he had devastated in but moments. A last echo of thunder carried across the city. In the distance, the remnants of Lluthean's wrath lay as a blackened mass of bodies on the western rampart, smoke trails rising into the night sky. Down below, where armored breakers had arrived on the green, more mounds of bent metal smoldered. Gradually, he became aware of the wounded moaning and crying from the green below.

Bryndor looked to Kaellor. He remained on his knees, panting in pain. Dark blood oozed from his uncle's wounds, but Kaellor's expression held only admiration and respect.

"Bryn, get to the podium. Tell the people who you are, get them to stop . . . fighting. We didn't return to rule a kingdom of ash," Kaellor gasped.

The thought of speaking to the entire city gave him more pause than fighting an armed militia with crossbows. Bryndor shared a look with his uncle, and understanding was communicated in that desperate moment.

He swallowed any apprehensions and turned to approach the podium. Laryn ran past him to attend to Kaellor's wounds. Bryndor walked over to Therek and stared at the stone globe. "How does it work?"

"You place your hand on the globe. It will attune to you and broadcast your voice throughout the city," said the regent.

"What . . . what should I say?" he asked.

Therek smiled, a twinkle in his eye. "I've seen this moment, Bryndor. All you need do is tell the people who you are. Let them know your family has arrived."

Bryndor placed a hand on the stone globe. It felt more like a ball of supple leather, warm to the touch. He sensed a whirring murmur as the other globes placed about the city synchronized to his voice. "My name . . . is Bryndor . . . Bryndorllean Baellentrell. I'm here with my brother Llutheandellen. We are the sons of Japheth and Nebrine. If you are loyal to the Lacuna, you have this one night to flee Stone's Grasp while we tend to the wounded. Tomorrow, we lift our eyes to the horizon. Those who renounce the breakers are welcome to stay and continue the fight against Tarkannen and his minions, because that is the true fight, and the abrogator is coming once again. The Lacuna have murdered innocents, people dear to me. If you call yourself a circle breaker and remain in this kingdom, this is your final notice for a peaceful departure. Stay behind, and we'll bring the Giver's rune fire down on every last one of you."

To emphasize his point, Bryndor channeled another swell of zenith and cast a massive orb of blue fire over the city. The detonation erupted in a flare of blue streamers followed by a gust of hot wind and the reverberant peal of thunder. The vibrations from the demonstration of his power rippled throughout all of Stone's Grasp.

He lifted his hand and stared out at the ocean of people. The entire city seemed to quiet, considering his words and ultimatum. He turned to find Laryn. She was focusing her art on Kaellor's wounds, and already, color had returned to his face. Boru lay belly to the ground beside them, panting, but with a reassuring smile on his face as Ranika stroked his head with affection.

Therek placed a reassuring hand on his shoulder. "Well done, Prince Bryndorllean."

Ksenia's voice caused him to turn. "I didn't know you had that in you."

Bryndor sucked at his teeth, his cheeks flushed. Eventually, he smiled. "Neither did I. I think it was the zenith? Maybe?"

He shifted his attention to the regent. "Llu and I eliminated all of the Lacuna that were up here. Let's see if Laryn needs our help, then look to tending to all of the wounded."

Before he could respond, cascades of blue static raced along the stone walls of the castle, building in strength and emitting a shearing sound. The streams of zenith gathered overhead as brilliant, iridescent blue webbing. An enormous dome flared with light and surrounded the entire castle. Just outside the barrier, a giant writhing tube of blackness, like some massive, wriggling eel, materialized in the night sky and slammed against the barrier. The collision of the two forces caused sparks of blue light to erupt from the dome in a shower.

The black tunnel snaked around the barrier and thrashed against the castle wards for several seconds, each time causing a colossal boom as if the barrier were an otherworldly drum. Finally, the nadir construct undulated into the night sky and disappeared. The castle wards persisted for several more seconds, then dissipated, once more revealing the moon of Baellen shining high in the night sky.

Chapter Fifty-Nine: Abrogator Interrupted

Volencia studied how Tarkannen folded sheets of nadir around them as they slid through the portal. Encased within the insulation, she experienced none of the biting, shearing force from the inside of the passage. He even managed to diminish the dizzying effect of twisting through space as the construct conveyed them across the entire continent of Karsk.

Her awe persisted right up to the moment when the conduit collided with a barrier. A shower of zenith sparks flashed into the end of the portal, and Tarkannen grunted, laboring to shift the portal. He stepped away from the edge and molded the inside of the tube, reshaping it to his will.

The portal thrashed against the barrier in several consecutive impacts. Each time, Volencia struggled to protect herself, but the shock waves eroded Tarkannen's protections. Her shoulder flared with burning pain, and she pushed back just before the tube of nadir melted her flesh away.

Scrapes and burns blossomed on her face, her hands, and any part of her body that touched the lining of the conduit.

"I didn't free you so you could kill us! This isn't working!" she shouted.

Tarkannen raised his hands to steer the portal one more time against the barrier surrounding Stone's Grasp. She could see through the portal, through the zenith-fueled wards, and recognized the familiar outline of the city and even the cistern where she had met Tarkannen all those years ago.

She laid a hand on his forearm. "I know . . . it's so close. But we'll find another way. Please, cousin. If you keep this up, I won't survive."

The myriad of black sigils flared and shifted with unnatural frenzy under his bare scalp and the back of his neck. Eventually, the markings of power settled, and Tarkannen sighed. Without words, the abrogator threw his hands forward, streamers of nadir lasing the portal away from the wards covering the capital city. She felt the transport return to a smooth flow.

Through the wall of the conduit, the moons and stars glimmered brighter than she had ever seen before. Then, rather abruptly, the familiar constellations faded, and they passed through several seconds of pure blackness. The sensation was more than disorienting, and she grabbed the back of Tarkannen's shoulder to steady herself.

Eventually, distant, twinkling lights appeared all around. Some pulsed with various hues of light from white to indigo, others muted by smoky shadow. As Tarkannen directed them along, she lost all sense of time and space. An exceptionally bright light caught her eye. Initially, it seemed very distant and, yet, in moments, appeared as an enormous sphere, larger and more brilliant than the moon of Baellen.

"Are we . . . are we still on Karsk?" she asked.

Tarkannen kept his attention forward but spoke over his shoulder. "Not anymore, but we will be back in moments. We are passing through currents of the Drift. What you are seeing, those lights? Those are other worlds, places where the struggle between zenith and nadir have already settled."

Volencia puzzled over his words and studied the various objects as they swelled and faded from view. Ribbons of zenith flowed all around and undulated alongside vast inky flows of nadir. The currents intermingled around the different worlds, some beaming with bright streamers of zenith and others roiling with dense clouds of nadir.

"Have you ever been to any of those other words? Worlds where the currents of nadir seem to dominate zenith?" she asked.

"I've only studied them while I was trapped in the Drift. We could never survive there. Each world is different. Some worlds are just clouds and vapor; others are molten rock or endless torrential storms. Creatures of mist occupy that one we just passed. I've seen another one, landless and completely covered with water. It's populated by all sorts of life accustomed to those surroundings. Many of the worlds are empty, and others are infested with enormous floating creatures that glide without rest."

"Did you find the grondle from one of those worlds?" she asked.

His head tilted in appreciation of her observation. "Yes. They come from a world obscured in the shadow of nadir. Their world is overpopulated, and resources are scarce. Attracting a herd seeking new food sources was an easy task."

Several more worlds rushed by, some near and others far, each possessing unique combinations of swirling shadow and light.

"You said that in each of these worlds, there is a struggle between zenith and nadir, but that they are settled. What about our world?"

Tarkannen grunted. "As far as I could tell, Karsk is one of the last worlds left in play, and it's. . . a struggle that could break our world, which is why we need to return to the Deepening Well in Stone's Grasp. It's the only way I can become the Eidolon and maintain the barrier between our world and the Drift. And believe me, I've seen the forces of the Drift decimate worlds that failed to maintain that precious separation."

He shook his head, a rare gesture of disbelief. "Utter annihilation."

Volencia pondered his words as Tarkannen continued to manipulate the conduit. It was the first time in years she had a significant conversation with her master and the first time he revealed a glimpse of his true motivations. Some part of her felt small at the realization that all her efforts were driven by a base desire to obtain more power. She wondered where she fit into this new struggle.

The conduit shimmied and lurched. Immediately before them, another world appeared, surrounded by chaotic zenith and nadir striations. The currents clashed in violent opposition streaming around the world, and she knew by his description that this was Karsk.

"We're coming back, brace yourself. We left along a dense stream of nadir, but we'll have to punch through the currents of zenith," said Tarkannen.

A loud rasping sound, like colossal sheets of rock and metal wrenching against one another, vibrated along the sides of the conduit. Volencia's feet burned from the intense vibrations, and her joints began to ache.

She yelled above the din. "Why didn't we just go back the way we came?"

Tarkennen's neck bent to the side, and he thrust his hands into the walls of the conduit, straining to stabilize the portal. He channeled more nadir than she thought possible, the power flowing through him in a torrential surge. She considered attempting to reinforce the structure when, at last, the portal returned to a smooth flow.

Blue moonlight illuminated the surroundings, and once again, she recognized familiar constellations.

Tarkannen panted with exhaustion. "How long do you think that journey back took us?"

"I don't know, it felt like. . . I can't really say. Weeks, maybe?"

"Seconds," he said. "By passing through the Drift, we lost only seconds. And if we return to our point of origin in time, there should still be enough refined nadir to salvage something from tonight's . . . miscalculation."

Only moments later, they stepped out of the portal and back into the summoning chamber. Tarkannen spoke a mixture of guttural commands and clicks, and the grotvonen and umbral proceeded to empty the cavern.

He wasted no time and approached the fading pool of nadir. His hand, covered in shifting black sigils, hovered over the surface as if testing hot coals on an old fire. "Stand back."

A saber of nadir coalesced in his grip, and he struck at the edge of the pool once, twice, and a third time. Instead of the clang of metal, the familiar shearing sound of a nadir blade echoed through the cavern. The pool continued to recede, consumed by the Rite of Sundering and his subsequent portal, but three jagged rods of crystallized nadir remained.

"How do you intend to put those to use?" she asked.

Tarkannen cradled the black shafts in his arms and paced the chamber with a restless nature. "Every survivor has to improvise when their plans are interrupted. You . . . made me realize that. Sometimes, the master learns from the pupil, yes? I can use these to craft weapons or even shift weather patterns across the Northlands. But first, we need to follow the clan to the surface. I plan to test their might against Dernegia. From there, we take Kreeg. Verrador is already at work in the warrior kingdom. After that . . . Aarindorn. Once we have Stone's Grasp, everything will be made whole; my plans, so long ago interrupted, can finally be completed."

She studied his face, the way the onyx sigils swam under the surface of his skin. Sometimes, they moved away from his eyes, revealing pale skin and a fleeting expression of regret. Then the flows of nadir shifted, and his malevolent countenance returned.

This was the man she followed, the man she had given her life for. He alone could lead her to greatness. And she was the one who brought him back to Karsk.

Chapter Sixty: More with Less

Nolan rode point, leading the party out of the woods. After rescuing Kovesk, Savnah had relegated herself to caretaker for her brother. The two of them rode behind the rest of the group, the joy of their reunion tempered by the death of their father.

For the first half-day of the journey, Savnah stared at the back of her Aarindin's neck, wide-eyed, muttering to herself, "Why didn't he ever say anything? All this time, Dad could have told me. But we never talked, not about the important stuff. I mean, we could have fought the Lacuna together. I thought the deadener meant me, Kov. I never thought about Dad. It was always going to be me."

For his part, Kovesk tolerated but refused to engage in any wallowing. The tears he had shed in the old church seemed the only ones he cared to allow. While Savnah had been kept in the dark regarding her father's involvement with Kovesk's incarceration, Kovesk, it seems, had been all too aware of Burl's role in keeping him locked away. Father and son had a reckoning at the end when Burl spent his last breaths apologizing.

As Savnah struggled to reconcile her father's betrayal with the man she thought she knew, Karragin was left to reassume the role of prime of the group. But she remained even more stoic than usual, even withdrawn. His sister directed him to find a way back to Stone's Grasp, stating that she trusted his ability to get them home. However, when he sought out specifics about the route, she snapped, "Just get it done, Nolan. See us to Stone's Grasp. Avoid contact with anyone who might be Lacuna, so that means pretty much everyone. Got it?"

That was two days ago. He had been burned by Karragin's hot reprimands before, but usually, she came around sometime later and cleared the smoke. This time, though, she rode in silence and kept her own council. So, he assumed the default leadership of the group and chose to take them on a serpentine route through the highlands of the Great Crown. The journey took and certainly felt longer by their collective silence and the somber mood that had settled over the group.

Adding to the general melancholy, Dexxin learned from his siblings that Stone's Grasp had fallen into chaos. His brother, Bextle, had been grievously wounded but saved by Laryn. The royals managed to make it to Stone's Grasp, but the Lacuna had attempted a brutal coup that led to the deaths of countless innocents.

Martial law had been invoked after the discovery of Reddevek's death, and that news, above all, had been the wedge that isolated them each within their own thoughts and leeched away any motivation he had to move forward quickly. His hips felt achy and heavy on the Aarindin's back.

A sea of memories invaded his thoughts, causing him to flounder: the first time he met Reddevek, when he was rescued by the warden on the Borderlands while training as a tender, following the man's example as a scout, watching him fight Lacuna on the plains south of Callinora. Unbidden, the memories resurfaced over and over.

Somehow, Nolan managed to guide them out of the Great Crown in relative secrecy. His Aarindin jogged around a bend that led out of the woods and onto a field. In the distance, just outside the timber of Stone's Grasp, a caravan of Moonies camped by a stream. Nolan awakened his arca prime. A meshwork of tracks and trails, some recent, others old, presented through the filter of his gift. He studied and sorted the tracks for a time, and was relieved that there were no fresh signs of wolvryn or Aarindin or his friends. With Savnah's distraction and his sister in an unusually foul mood, he didn't relish the thought of acting as the primary liaison to the Rovinary clan.

He gave the camp a wide berth and swung south, finding the west gate. To his surprise, two quads of Outriders were posted, and the gate was closed. A flicker of zenith streaked across the silver veining of the white stone walls. Nolan studied the anomaly, waiting to see if it would recur, then wondered if it was just some trick of the sunlight.

He drew to a stop and looked over his shoulder, waiting for his sister to give an indication of how to proceed. Karragin rode with her chin dipped into her leathers. She looked up once, squinted at the group of Outriders, then waved Nolan ahead as if to say, "You handle it."

Tovnik's mount drew even to Nolan. The medic had become a valuable part of the quint and an even better friend these last months. He poked Nolan in the ribs. "What did you do this time?"

Nolan sighed. "That's just it, Tov. I haven't a clue. Are you absolutely sure she didn't crack her head in that fight with the Lacuna?"

Tovnik schooled his face from one of concern to comfort. "You know as well as I do that Karra only begrudgingly tolerates the intimate nature of a healing. And I have to admit, Savnah's leg injury and that shoulder wound pressed my skill. I used the last of my reserve to heal some minor barotrauma to her ears, and my gift mended that as far as I could tell."

They rode in companionable silence, and the medic seemed lost in his thoughts. Eventually, Tovnik sighed. "I did approach her once I recovered my stamina. She wouldn't let me attend to the bruises too numerous to count. Anyway, I'm fairly certain her disposition only reflects minor discomfort and nothing serious. I'll keep watching and let you know if I sense that her condition deteriorates."

Nolan's head tilted forward, and ginger curls bounced in front of his eyes. "I'll likely learn all about it when we're standing in front of Father."

The medic lifted his chin to the other Outriders ahead. "What do you suppose that's all about?"

"Might be that the Lacuna had more influence in the city watch than we assumed? Let's find out together," said Nolan.

"The sooner we get past the gates, the sooner we get a hot meal."

That thought did lighten his mood a little. Nolan nudged his Aarindin ahead. A somber cloud seemed to hover over the group of Outriders meandering around the gate. They offered no salute or greeting.

Nolan walked his Aarindin forward. He raised a friendly hand and waved. "Umm, good morning."

Larik Lellendule, a prime of his quad, stepped forward. "Long time no see, tracker. Your father's going to be happy to learn of your safe return. I assume you're not our relief rotation?"

"No . . . I'm trying to get through and . . . Larik, are you guarding this gate here?" he asked.

"Orders are, nobody gets through, not in or out, on account of the Lacuna and Warden Reddevek," said Larik. He looked over Nolan's shoulder. "I thought your sister was prime. Is she alright?"

"She's fine, we're all just tired, and she sent me forward to see us through," said Nolan. "We've never held guard duty outside Stone's Grasp. Is the city watch that busy?"

"Turns out the watch was infested with Lacuna sympathizers. They've been temporarily disbanded. Your father deputized a militia of runeless to patrol the streets in the daytime, and the Spicers keep the peace at night."

Tovnik leaned forward. "How bad is it in there?"

A troubled glower darkened Larik's brow. He stared at Nolan's group a moment, then his expression softened. "Nolan, exactly how long have you been in the field?"

"In the field? Months now, it seems. But away on this last objective . . . four, maybe five days now. Reddevek charged us with our last mission near Midrock. We were supposed to meet him here, present our findings and such."

Larik scuffed the toe of his boot in the ground, then turned and barked an order. "Make way and lift the gates. Outrider coming through!" Larik shook his head. "I hate to be the one to tell you all this, but Reddevek . . ."

Nolan held up a hand. "Dexxin's a sender. We know about the warden."

Larik searched the party with renewed appreciation. "Aye, it's . . . hit all of us hard. He was the best of us. You should probably avoid the Sprawl and the market districts. The Lacuna—there might still be pockets of resistance there. Make straightaway for the castle. Find your father. He'll be wanting to see you, I expect."

A screech rang out as the guards winched up the iron bars of the gate. Nolan sat on his Aarindin, wondering what they might find inside.

"Nolan," said Tovnik. "It sounds like we need to make straightaway for your father. Can you manage it, or do you want me to take the lead?"

Nolan shook his head. "That's alright. I can manage." He led them through the Crown's Timber and eventually to the Timber Gate by the stables, where they dismounted. He gave brief instructions to the groomsman, hoisted his pack, and set out at a brisk walk.

At the gates to the curtain wall, more Outriders and a separate contingency of guards took their names. Fortunately, the Outriders recognized them and waved them through. Inside the grounds, tidy rows of bodies lay covered in white sheets. Debris was scattered about the green: shreds of tents, discarded plates and utensils, and broken crockery.

A few families stood over the deceased in mourning. Nolan led them up the broad set of stairs to the second green, where more bodies lay shrouded in sheets. Workers had started erecting a massive pyre on the green, the acrid scent of pitch thick in his awareness. In the center of the green, workers had already erected a ten-foot-wide Giver's Stone in anticipation of holding the ashes of the dead.

They walked up to the third tier to find it vacant save for peculiar black patches on the once-pristine green lawn. A brief inspection with his gift revealed the stains as the remnants of human blood. The gardens here lay in similar disarray with broken statues, more rubbish, and more than a few discharged crossbow bolts.

When they reached the last step and walked out onto the royal plaza, each of them stood at the balustrade, taking in the obvious signs of conflict. Even Savnah stood in silence, unable to make a snarky remark. Nolan wondered what had happened. *What caused those patches of scorched stone and earth, not just on the green, but on the ramparts as well?*

Eventually, the familiar voice of his father caused him to pull his gaze away from the scene. Therek called his name, and he jogged over. For a moment, he wondered if he should salute or offer a formal report. Therek seemed to understand, tilted his head, and held his arms wide. Nolan fell into the smothering embrace and, for the first time in weeks, felt his shoulders relax.

"Karra! Come give an old man a hug," Therek called. But Karragin continued to stare at the desecrated grounds, her shoulders set, head swiveling to the left and right.

"Karra, come say hi to Father!" Nolan yelled. But his sister lingered at the balustrade, even leaning forward to look directly down onto the green. And that's when it hit him. "Oh, Giver."

"What is it?" asked Therek.

"All this time, on the way home, I thought she was angry, but I think it's something else. I don't think she can hear us, Dad. Give me a moment."

Nolan walked the short distance to his sister, the sun causing his shadow to fall over the railing. She turned, and her placid expression brightened a little when she saw Therek. But Nolan stared at her, waiting. She averted her gaze and made to step around him, but he stepped into her path.

Karragin stopped and searched his eyes. Without words, he tapped the front of his ear with one finger and waited. The muscles under her eyes tightened, and tears brimmed then streaked down her cheeks. Nolan sagged his shoulders as if to say, "Why didn't you tell me?"

But he knew his sister well enough to know why. So he put on a brave face, smiled, and nodded. Something in his acceptance of her privacy made her smile back, and they embraced. There would be plenty of time in the days ahead to learn about everything that happened in Stone's Grasp. For today, he would content himself with listening instead of speaking, and with the knowledge that sometimes, one could actually say more with less.

Epilogue: From Under a Dark Hood

Valdesta closed her establishments for two weeks after the funeral proceedings in Stone's Grasp. The entire city had entered a mourning period for the loss of life. The procession for Warden Reddevek and his Outriders took nearly a full day. The scent of burned timbers from all the funeral pyres still lingered on the wind.

Never one to squander an opportunity, Valdesta used the time to recover from her injuries in relative secrecy. When Chancle brought the tent down, she'd suffered a broken wrist and a knock to the head that rendered her unconscious for two days.

She'd awoken in one of her private suites on the top floor of a tavern and gaming hall in the Sprawl. Her first order of business involved summoning a back alley mender to tend to her injuries. Though the man lacked the skill of a true healer from the House of Moons, the care was rendered with the added guarantee of anonymity. And with everything that had happened, Valdesta didn't care to venture out of the Sprawl.

As her second order of business, she deployed runners to check on her other businesses and business partners. The regent had moved faster than she thought possible, arresting Kunzie and confiscating his holdings. She mentally ticked through the multiple business ventures they'd partnered in, from textiles to timber to land ownership and legal gaming houses. Only one thing likely saved her: in all of their dealings, she never used her actual name, instead claiming the identity of Tixon B'gin.

She looked out the window and down to the market, where the top of an empty timber gallows stood as a stark reminder of the kingdom's justice. Kunzie and anyone definitively tied to his dealings with the Lacuna had met the Taker at the end of ropes that now swayed errantly in the wind.

She sighed with regret that she never got to know the man better, and felt thankful that he took her secrets to the grave. He must have, or she would have seen her neck stretched on the same gallows.

Her business dealings suffered further from estrangement with Salveen and the Spicer gang. Apparently, the old lynx managed to court Salveen, offering the woman a legal stake in the gaming and hospitality trade and an import license free from tariffs for five years. Valdesta wondered how favorable the terms must have been to make the Spicers give up their lucrative control of the Sprawl and vivith. Then she realized they never really gave up control at all. Three gang members walked proudly down the boardwalk wearing armbands of red and blue silk coiled into a rope.

They're still running things, just not in the shadows anymore.

Two street urchins skipped across the street and walked into the last building on the row, an orphanage. She had never set foot inside that particular poor house before, crammed as it was with the runeless and other less fortunate members of the kingdom. Somehow the ungifted had climbed up from the lowest ranks of society amidst the turmoil of the last few weeks. Valdesta rolled her eyes. *And how did I not see that one coming? Why didn't Kunzie? Taker's teeth, his son was runeless.*

That night when the world turned upside down and the Drift spewed itself on her doorstep, everything changed. Everyone had taken to calling it "the Reckoning." A Baellentrell returned to the capital, activating wards left dormant since the Abrogator's War. The Lacuna's planned takeover of the city met resistance at every turn.

In the Sprawl, the Spicers subdued and apprehended any breakers trying to create mayhem. In the Delve and other districts, the ungifted arrived en mass to keep the regent's peace. Under order of the Dedicant, the runeless worked with the few Outriders to apprehend members of the city watch loyal to the breakers.

All that work culminated in three days of hangings. Everyone knew that the gifted at Callinora possessed more delicate means to lay a person to rest, but the regent had erected the gallows to make a point.

Reckoning indeed. Point well taken.

One of her most trusted runners, Kyvan, her sister's second son, crossed the street and entered the tavern. Moments later, his footsteps pounded up the stairs, and he knocked on the door. She turned from the window, situated herself in a plush armchair, and bid him enter. "Come in, Ky."

The young man looked once down the hall, searching the shadows with twitchy eyes. He stepped in and closed the door. Once assured of their security, he reached into a pocket, withdrew a snuff pouch, and inhaled a pinch.

"Kyvan Murk, if your mother could see you now, she would switch your ass till it shined like the moon of Lellen," said Valdesta.

Kyvan plopped down onto a chair beside her and tossed a leg over one arm. He gave her a grin marred by the absence of several front teeth.

"Don't matter much, Aunt Val. Red moon, blue moon, it was all the same with Mom . . . switch or paddle . . . I still never learned much."

Valdesta shook her head. "You best be weaning yourself from that poison. The supply of vivith will run dry in a month, and then where will you be?"

"I know, I know. I've got it handled."

She stared at the wreckage of her nephew. He was lean before he fell under the influence of vivith, but the drug had left him emaciated. His sleeves hid a myriad of self-inflicted scabs on his torso and arms. It was no small miracle that he hadn't lost all of his teeth, but he still smacked his lips back and forth with a restless nature.

At least the drugs make you overcautious, I suppose, and that's one thing I could use these days.

"What did you learn from your visit to the Delve?" she asked.

"The vice regent was seen hopping over the walls the night of the Reckoning. A few witnesses on the ramparts say he floated down on a current of air." Kyvan held his hand out like a paddle and soared it through the air.

"And after that?" she asked.

"Nothing. Nobody has seen or heard from him. Apparently, his brother, Hestian, has been in a rage. The man commissioned a group of mercenaries to hunt down and kill him—his own brother! But then, who can blame him, right? I sent word to our contacts in Stellance to see if they know anything, but given everything that's going on, I expect it will be a time before we hear much."

Valdesta stared off into the corner, considering all that she had invested and lost. *Gambled, more likely. How did I ever get in that deep?*

She scoffed at her own question. *You know how. Money . . . money and power, Val. You should have left well enough alone and settled for what the Aspect provided, and maybe you wouldn't be facing financial ruin.*

"Aunt Val," said Kyvan. "I've learned that there are still plenty of folks, those umm . . . associated with the breakers and favorable to the cause. Lots of them have been asking me if Tixon is going to . . . you know, start things up again."

"I don't know, Ky." She held up her broken wrist and rubbed the swollen fingers on her temple across the fading green pigments from the bruise she incurred two weeks ago.

"How many people are we talking about?" she asked.

Ky smiled. "Let's see . . . there's a textile guy, the one we had favorable contracts with, and he thinks he can see to looping you in on some lucrative work. There's actually a prospector interested in your land holdings, something about leasing mining rights. Then I've had inquiries from more people than I can count about when business will open. Lots of folks miss your girls . . . girls and the games. People . . . they need a little something to lift them from the troubles of the last two weeks."

"I suppose it's time to open the doors and see what the wind blows in. Send word that we're open to entertaining discerning clients and that the taverns and gaming halls are open for business."

Kyvan nodded and smacked his lips. "And the other thing?"

"What other thing?" she snapped.

"Well, the others I mentioned . . . they sort of want to meet you to see if the breakers are done or if we'll pick up."

Valdesta squinted at her nephew. She resisted the instinct to berate him and instead considered the proposition. *The Giver only smiles on a grifter once in a moon; better to seize the chance before the Taker spoils it.*

"How many people are we talking about exactly?" she asked.

"North of fifteen, and they're all folks we know, all loyal breakers," said Kyvan.

"Alright, Ky. After the close of business tonight, bring them to the private gaming room. It will be close quarters, but I can see who comes in first, and if I like what I see, I'll come down and listen to what they have to say."

Later that night, the crowds rolled in with a heavy rainstorm. While most of the patrons arrived soaked to their scanties, their collective emergence out of the storm and into a night of drinks and debauchery created a lively atmosphere. Patrons gambled with reckless abandon, and within the first hour, all the escorts found their company in high demand.

As the midnight hour approached, the crowds thinned, and Kyvan began to corral his contacts into the private gaming hall. Valdesta watched each of the breakers enter from the safety of a private room on the second floor. A peephole crafted years ago had given her an edge in more than one negotiation, and now she put it to good use.

Most of the Lacuna seemed familiar to her, though there were a few strangers in the mix. At least a third were women, a fact not lost on the brothel owner. She made mental notes of their builds, their . . . neediness. At least two looked like they could use the security of a job at the brothel.

Several merchant types dressed in clothing tailored to the seasonal style sat around a large circular table. A young woman, slight of frame, stood alone in one corner. One of the men, boldened by too much ale, walked over and traced a finger on her shoulder. When she stomped on his foot, more than a few giggled at his misfortune. The woman retreated to another corner of the room, just below the peephole and out of Valdesta's view.

That one, I could probably use. That hooded cloak is too shabby to cover anyone from the Delve. She's more likely one of the orphanage girls, all grown up. That kind of desperation makes for a loyal partner.

One of the men gave Valdesta pause. Something about his bearing looked stiff, unnatural. He tried to appear disinterested yet kept a strange vigilance, assessing the others in the room.

Kyvan climbed the stairs and knocked on her door. She closed the peephole and turned as he entered.

"Everything's all set, Aunt Val." Kyvan's bloodshot eyes and ruddy nose betrayed his use of resco. She thought of taking him to task, but the alcohol dimmed the twitchiness caused by the vivith, and he seemed in a proper state of mind, so she let it pass.

"I don't know. One of the men looks off to me," she said.

"Alright, what do you want me to do?" he asked.

"Go down there and thank them for their interest. Let them know that your employer, Tixon, will be late. Then engage them in conversation. Draw them out, gauge their intent, and whether or not they are serious in their desire to gather what's left of the Lacuna. I'll be watching from up here. If it looks promising, I'll make an appearance."

Kyvan bowed with unusual carefree agreement and descended the steps. *The boy must be more sauced than I realized. I wonder if he can even pull this off.*

She poured herself two fingers of resco and returned to the peephole just as Kyvan entered the room.

"Friends. The hour is late, so I'll get to the point. My employer, Tixon, is very interested in speaking with you, but will be delayed. Nonetheless, we are gathered by a common purpose and to defeat a common enemy." Kyvan stood on a wooden chair and held his hands in a circle, thumb to thumb and finger to finger . . . then sprang his fingers apart.

He turned to address each of the people in the room, waiting for them to repeat the salute. Valdesta studied not just their expressions but their posture and body language, trying to determine if their interest was genuine or merely speculative. When everyone had formed the gesture, Kyvan continued, nodding in appreciation.

"You see, I told Tixon that there were still free men and women of Aarindorn committed to breaking the circle. Our numbers took a hit in the Reckoning, but let's not forget what just a few of us accomplished. Some of our brothers and sisters died to make a statement that the nobles will not soon forget. Taker's grit, a few others took on the Outriders and put down Warden Reddevek! I know that if we regroup and rebuild in the shadows, one day, the Lacuna can rise up and break the chains of nobility once and for all. What I need to know is, are you committed to that end?"

Kyvan's voice squelched up in a strange pitch at the end of his sentence, and a sharp rasping noise, like the jab of an icepick, carried up through the peephole. Valdesta trained her gaze on her nephew, but her mind couldn't make sense of the details in the room.

A thin black spike erupted from Kyvan's chest, and blood fanned out onto his shirt. He stood a moment, gasping like a landed fish, a look of confused horror on his face as he examined the wound. Something like a black snake whipped back, retracting the spike with blinding speed, and Kyvan crumpled to the ground. The men around the table rose to their feet, chairs tumbling back, and everyone stared into the corner directly below the peephole.

Utter chaos and panic broke out. A mass of writhing onyx snakes tipped with spikes whipped about the room. The barbs lashed out, striking random targets: a thigh here, a hand there. One woman caught a hooked spine full in the face; a man turned only to be impaled in the back of the neck. In just seconds, half of the people in the room lay dead, blackened holes burned into their bodies.

Just as soon as the mayhem began, it stopped. The room fell silent save for the panted gasps of the living. Two men had drawn daggers, and another held a chair over his shoulder. More than a few whimpered with utter terror.

"Taker's sauce, where did she go?" asked one of them.

"Stop asking and get to the door!" said another.

The rasping sound lashed out again, and three tentacles struck from under the table. The crystal lamps on the walls broke apart, and the lone chandelier crashed down, dropping the room into darkness. Valdesta strained to see anything through the peephole, but only an occasional wispy shadow accompanied grunts of pain, the clamor of broken furniture, and the shuffle of footsteps. One by one, bodies thumped to the floor until . . . there was silence.

Valdesta pushed back, horrified by what she saw and heard, and fearful that whatever lay in the gaming hall might realize she'd born witness to the events. A flicker of light danced across the peephole, and she took a chance, leaning forward to see the most unusual thing yet.

It was the young woman, the one with the hooded cloak. She held the garment draped over one arm, her hair the most alluring tumble of tiny pale-yellow curls. She adjusted a ruby-hilted dagger on a belt sheath, threw the cloak over her shoulder, gathered her hair under the hood, and walked into the hallway.

Valdesta staggered to her feet and walked across the room. She made it to the second-floor balcony, hoping to see the young woman enter the taproom. But after several minutes, nobody emerged, and she began to wonder if she had imagined the entire scene.

A crack of thunder followed a gust of wind, and the front doors blew open. That had never happened before. For just a second, Valdesta saw a random scatter of rain in the threshold. The barman crossed the room, secured the floor bolts for the doors, and returned to polishing glasses. As the brothel owner stood to retreat into her chamber, she glimpsed a streak of yellow hair lifting out from under a dark hood as the young woman walked past the corner window and out into the rainy night.

Glossary of names, places, and terms

Aarin (AIR-in)—the name given to any unnamed patient at the Sanitorium in Aarindorn.

Aarindorn (AIR-in-dorn)—a kingdom in the Northlands, surrounded by the Great Crown Mountains.

Abrogator (AB-roh-gate-or)—a term used to describe one who wields the reductive force of nadir.

Ahben (AH-ben)—a Cloud Walker herb gatherer.

Amniah (am-NIGH-yuh)—a young female Outrider gifted with the ability to gust (shape wind) who hails from Stellance. An original member Karragin's quad.

Arca prime—the central rune of a zeniphile located on the center of the chest and determining the zeniphiles strongest affinity or ability.

Baellentrell (BAE-len-trell)—the last name of the current ruling family in Aarindorn.

- Bierden (BEER-den)—Kaellor's grandfather, capable of summoning rune fire.
- Bryndor (BRIN-dur)—oldest of two nephews to Kaellor. Older brother to Lluthean.
- Eldrek (EL-drek)—founder of the Baes line and first king of Aarindorn.
- Japheth (JAY-feth)—king of Aarindorn during the Abrogator's War. Father to Bryndor and Lluthean, brother to Kaellor.
- Kaellex (KAY-lex)—father to Kaellor and Japheth, grandfather to Bryndor and Lluthean.
- Kaellor (KAY-lore)—uncle to Bryndor and Lluthean.
- Lluthean (LOO-thee-in)—youngest of two nephews to Kaellor. Younger brother to Bryndor.
- Nebrine (neh-BREEN)—mother to Bryndor and Lluthean, wife to Japheth.
- Phethnem (FETH-nem)—mother to Kaellor and Japheth, wife to Kaellex.

Balladuren (bal-uh-DOO-ren)—family in Aarindorn famed for breeding Aarindin.

- Elbend (EL-bend)—father of the family, spouse to Madola, sits on the Aarindorian council. A gifted sympath.
- Madola (muh-DOLE-uh)—mother of the family, spouse to Elbend, sits on the Aarindorian council. A gifted sympath.
- Kervin (KURV-in)—fourth brother, senior only to Ksenia. As a sympath, he can communicate with animals.
- Kovle—Ksenia's great-uncle, a man whose arca prime was linguistics.
- Ksenia (keh-SEN-yuh)—youngest child of five and only daughter. Her runes enable her to channel zenith to empathically communicate with animals and decipher languages, among other talents.
- Rugen (ROO-gen)—oldest brother. Member of the city watch in Stone's Grasp.

Burl Fodensk (Burl FOE-densk)—this zeniphile led his forces from the deep south by ship to fight against the abrogators in the Great War. His forces were gifted in controlling the elements of wind and water.

Bashing Ram—a tavern and inn at Journey's Bend.

Beclure (beh-KLURE)—a duchy in west Aarindorn.

Benyon Garr (BEN-yun)—a wizened trainer of the gifted in Aarindorn, member of the Aarindorian military, and adviser to the Outriders.

Berwek (BURR-wek)—a prime in the Outriders.

Besken (BES-kin)—a kingdom in the western Northlands of Karsk.

Bekson's Fine Restoratives—a tavern and eatery in the Delve in Stone's Grasp.

Binta (BIN-tuh)—a serving maid at the Wolf's Maw in Midrock.

Boffle (BOFF-ul)—a minor lord from Dernegia taking residence in Sifter's Valley during the Winnowing of the Shades.

Bosulk (BO-sulk)—aka a greater driftian, a massive creature from the Drift.

Borsec (BORE-sek)—ruling monarch over the northwest region of the Southlands, including Riverton and Journey's Bend.

Braveska (bra-VES-kuh)—the royal family in Hammond and Malvress in the Southlands.

- Leland (LEE-land)—the duke in Malvress and youngest brother to Vendal.
- Lesand (leh-SAND)—niece to the king of Hammond and daughter to Duke Leland in Malvress.
- Shelland (SHELL-and)—queen in Hammond.
- Vendal (VEN-dull)—king in Hammond.

Cabe—owner of the King's Respite, a tavern in Sifter's Valley in the Torgrend Range northeast of Dernegia.

Callinora (cal-in-NORE-uh)—a city in northwest Aarindorn composed of erudites, scholars, and healers. The formal educational training of medics, healers, alchemists, and related fields takes place here. The city is a protectorate of Stone's Grasp with no specific familial loyalties but rather loyal to the welfare of Aarindorn. The kingdom's Sanitorium is located here.

Callish (CAL-ish)—port city along the northeast coast of the Southlands.

Cataclysm—the Great War in which the forces of abrogation caused a rent in the barrier between the world of the living and the Drift. The death toll was estimated at well over thirty thousand and led to the separation of Karsk into the Northlands and the Southlands. The timing of this event is used as the source of the dating system on Karsk, with dates being either before cataclysm (BC) or post cataclysm (PC).

Cloud Walkers—a tribe native to the valley deep in the center of the Korjinth Mountains. Formally called the Damadibo (dahm-uh-DEE-boe), meaning "the people."

Consort—the Consort are the group of umbral pulled from the Drift and acting on Tarkannen's direction.

Crush—a herd of six to ten grondle.

Damadibo (dahm-uh-DEE-boe)—the Cloud Walkers, the term means "the people."

Deadener—a zeniphile skill allowing one to ignore all pain.

DeChance

- Silvy—mother to Ranika.
- Ranika (RAN-ih-kuh)—found as a street urchin in Callish where she spent her childhood. One of the first innately gifted abrogators to walk Karsk since the Cataclysm.

Dedicant—the Dedicant is the title given to the leader of the ungifted, or the runeless, in Aarindorn.

Della—the proprietor at the Bashing Ram of Journey's Bend. She manages and owns the tavern with her brother Ingram.

Delve, the—a district in Stone's Grasp housing affluent merchant stores, shops, and wares.

Derrigand (DARE-ih-gand)—a family from Midrock, common people finding an uncommon place in Aarindorian history.

- Burl—owner of the Wolfs Maw, Savnah's father. A member of the Lacuna's inner circle.
- Kovesk (KOH-vesk)—brother to Savnah, a zeniphile gifted with forecasting the future when he dreams.
- Savnah (SAV-nuh)—a prime in the Outriders, known for her battle prowess with twin moonblade axes. A skilled deadener and minor nascent.

Drassle (DRASS-ul)—Lord Drassle was a customer at Felpinge House, where Silvy DeChance worked.

Dressla Rudang (DRESS-luh roo-DANG)—the queen of Voruden.

Drexn (DREK-sen)—the name for the sun god in the Southlands.

Dulesque (doo-LESK)—a duchy in west Aarindorn.

Eguma (eh-GOO-muh)—a lithe and small grotvonen possessing more-than-usual intelligence and the capacity for human speech.

Eidolon—prophesized in *The Book of Seven Prophets* as a person capable of wielding both zenith and nadir, and someone required to save the world.

Elcid—a bandit in Hammond.

Ellisina (el-eh-SEE-nuh)—a Cloud Walker child.

Elgruh—an adult female of the Cloud Walkers.

Endule (en-DUEL)—a family of nobles in Aarindorn related to and branching from the Lellendules. Currently, they rule the duchies of Dulesque and Beclure in Aarindorn.

- Alvric (ALV-rick)—former Outrider recruited into the city watch in Stone's Grasp.
- Alden—a zeniphile known as the Leech, a man who can siphon zenith and vitality from other living creatures. An assassin employed by the Lacuna.
- Berling (BURR-ling)—a young man gifted in the healing arts and a medic in the Outriders.
- Bextle (BEX-tul)—a member of the guard in Stone's Grasp, older brother to Craxton.
- Bexter (BEX-turr)—husband to Phelond, the matriarch of the family; he married into the family and assumed the Endule name.
- Craxton (CRAX-ton)—younger brother to Bextle and representative speaker for several guilds in Stone's Grasp. A sender who is a triplet.
- Dexxin (DEX-in)—an Outrider, sender, healer, and triplet to Craxton and Mullayne.
- Endera (en-DEER-uh)—the duchess of Beclure, mother to Velda.
- Mullayne (mull-AIN)—a member of the city watch in Aarindorn and sender triplet to Dexxin and Craxton.
- Phelond (feh-LOND)—the duchess of Dulesque, married to Bexter, mother to Berling.
- Velda (VEL-duh)—an Outrider skilled in archery. Daughter to Endera, from Beclure. Killed by misadventure (and the

warden's wrath) in book 1.

Exemplar Gre'Kanth (greh-KANTH)—the holy leader of the Immaculine, a sect founded in Caskayah in the deep south of the Southlands.

Fagle Hoff (FAY-gull)—the royal gardener in Stone's Grasp.

Feign—a shapeshifting creature from the Drift.

Festian Planes (FES-tee-un)—prairie and plains south of Callish in the Southlands.

Feth—a stableboy who works with his father, Steckle, at the Bashing Ram.

Firth—a name utilized by Lluthean while traveling anonymously.

fo'Vaeda (VAY-duh) and fo'Voshna (VOSH-nuh)—zeniphile sisters gifted in prophecy and prediction, both involved in a tangled relationship with Eldrek in the time of the Cataclysm.

Foden (FOE-den)—Southlander name for the god of the seas and wind.

Gauvin (go-VON)—a bard playing in the King's Respite.

Gavid Strictor (GAV-id STRIK-turr)—an official of the Immaculine.

Geddins (GEDD-ins)—a noble family in Aarindorn.

- Ashrof (ASH-rof)—the oldest son gifted with the ability to survey and measure distances.
- Marsona (mar-SAW-nuh)—younger sister to Ashrof.

Grasdok (GRAZ-dock)—the chieftan of the Brognaus, a clan of grotvonen in the Torgrend Range.

Griggs—a guard at the southern gate to Aarindorn. He is a sifter.

Grotvonen (GROT-voh-nen)—The "grot" are humanoid creatures who live in clans underground. Their senses evolved to survive in that environment. They possess only vestigial lips and utilize a language of nasal snorts, clicks, and a guttural speech pattern.

Guster—a zeniphile who controls and manipulates winds or air.

Gwillion (GWILL-ee-un)—the former alchemy master in Aarindorn, disgraced by his addiction to vivith.

Hawklin (HAWK-lin)—a family in Journey's Bend.

- Bruug (Broog)—the oldest brother.
- Heff—the middle brother.
- Rusn—the youngest brother.
- Gruus (Groos)—the father of the Hawklin family.

Hillen—a deceased Cloud Walker. When he died, a pregnant wolvryn bonded to him (Vencha), became feral and slipped from the misted valley, later to become the mother to Boru and Neska.

Homnibus (HOM-ni-bus)—the lead rector or abbot in service at the Abbey on the Mount in the Southlands.

Immaculine, the (im-MAC-u-you-leen)—a religious sect from Caskayah. They hunt and kill abrogators and zeniphiles alike.

Inasia Kell (in-AY-shuh)—a member of the inner circle of the Lacuna, planted in Callinora.

Ingram (ING-ram)—the proprietor and co-owner with sister Della of the Bashing Ram of Journey's Bend.

Jaspen Holling (JAS-pen HOLL-ing)—an entrepreneur and vineyard owner in Stellance.

Journey's Bend—a rural Southland town not far from Riverton, childhood home to the "Scrivson boys," Bryndor and Lluthean.

Jorund (YOUR-und)—a henchman working for Mallic and Volencia in Callish.

Kal'maldra—a zeniphile who rose in power and assumed the title of the Eidolon in the time before the Cataclysm.

Kaldera (kal-DEER-uh)—Overwarden in the Outriders, he serves at the pleasure of the regent and sets strategy for the group.

Karsk—the continent of the Northlands and Southlands, used interchangeably by the people there to describe the world.

Kemp—an alias name used by Bryndor during anonymous travel.

Keska—chambermaid in Stone's Grasp.

Kindred—the term used to describe the common speech known by most humans on Karsk.

Korjinth Mountains (CORE-jinth)—the mountainous peaks of this range erupted, and the central valley was formed, after the Great War when Eldrek Baellentrell marshaled the zeniphiles to wield their collective zenith in tandem with Mogdurian's abrogators. The colossal release of force, poorly synthesized, resulted in the formation of this range on the Plains of Jintha, and divided all of Karsk. Currently, warring currents of zenith and nadir make crossing the summit nearly impossible.

Krestus (CREST-us)—a fallen knight from Malvress.

Kunzie (KOON-see)—a member of the inner circle of the Lacuna.

Kyvon Murk (KAI-von)—nephew to Valdesta.

Lacuna (luh-COO-nuh)—a secret sect in Aarindorn seeking to replace the monarchy with a democracy. They seek to break the circle of recurrent or inherited familial leaders. Also known as the breakers.

Lawn Whirik (WHEER-ik)—constable in Journey's Bend.

Lefledge (leh-FLEJ)—a noble family in Aarindorn.

- Karragin (CARE-uh-gin)—an Outrider, sister to Nolan, daughter to Therek.
- Nolan (NO-lun)—an Outrider, son to Therek, brother to Karragin.
- Therek (THARE-ik)—the regent in Aarindorn.

Lellendule (lell-en-DOOL)—a noble family in Aarindorn.

- Aldrik—oldest brother of Volencia.
- Chancle (CHANS-ul)—the vice regent in Aarindorn, brother to Hestian, cousin to Laryn. He is a trusted friend to the regent and helped stabilize Aarindorn after the Abrogator's War.
- Charlest (char-LEST)—the last ruling Lellendule queen in Aarindorn and mother to Tarkannen.
- Elbare—Volencia's father, a disgraced drunkard.
- Evonda—Hestian's wife.
- Hestian (HES-tee-en)—older brother to Chancle. He is a

trusted friend to the regent, a strategist pressed into service in the offices of the regent.

- Kelledar (KELL-eh-dahr)—one of the first Lellendules, loyal friend to Eldrek Baellentrell.
- Larik (LARE-ik)—Hestian's son, a prime in the Outriders.
- Laryn (LARE-in)—a healer trained in Callinora; she married Kaellor in a secret ceremony and returns to Aarindorn as his wife and a prominent member of the Lellendule family.
- Maelos (MAY-lohs)—the last king in the Lellendule line, father to Tarkannen.
- Shalla (SHAHL-uh)—mother to Volencia.
- Tarkannen (tar-CAN-en)—the Usurper who reintroduced the utilization of nadir over zenith and resurrected the abrogators. In real life, the author's daughters argue about the best pronunciation. Some prefer "TARK-anon," others "tar-CANN-on." The author is perfectly content to let the reader decide which pronunciation suits their worldview for Karsk.
- Veldrek—Volencia's middle brother.
- Volencia—born gifted with affinities in water manipulation, she never sat for the trial to unlock her arca prime and instead embraced the path of the abrogator.

Lemm Sogle—a drunkard from Journey's Bend.

Lentrell (LEN-trell)—minor nobles in Aarindorn related by blood to the Baellentrells.

- Elbiona (el-bee-YOH-nuh)—an Outrider warden in Aarindorn. She is rumored to be exceptional with a bow.
- Venlith (VEN-lith)—a healer of the fourth circle (the highest rank) and referred to as docent. She is the leader overseeing the Sanitoruim in Callinora. A known master of the healing arts.
- Drevan and Bartoll—brothers who knew Volencia as a child.

Leveck (leh-VEK)—an officer of the court in Beclure in the employment of house Endule.

Luna Rova—see the Moonies.

Lutn Egaine (lutn eh-GAIN)—an abrogator and famed mathematician and tactician who sought a neutral relationship between zeniphiles and abrogators. Because he was seen by some as playing both sides, he was later remembered as the trickster and in the Southlands incorporated into the pantheon.

Lutney (LUT-nee)—Southland god of luck, tricks, and the unseen.

Maedra (MAY-druh)—Southland god of nature and healing.

Maedraness (may-druh-NESS)—in the time of the cataclysm, this zeniphile, known as the Shaman Queen, joined Eldrek and the other zeniphiles. Their natural talents lay in the healing arts and communicating and controlling plants and animals.

Mahkeel (mah-KEEL)—the wolvryn handler of the Cloud Walker tribe.

Malldra (MAHL-druh)—Southland term for the mother of the pantheon of gods, thought to have died birthing the other gods.

Margrave Rolsh—the ruler in Riverton and by default the territories in Journey's Bend, loyal to King Borsec.

Mawg—a Brognaus grotvonen.

Miljin (MILL-jin)—an elder shaman among the Cloud Walkers.

Mogdure (mog-DURE)—the Southland god of death, darkness, and illness.

Mogdurian (mog-DURE-ee-en)—in the time of the Great War, he led all the abrogators in his quest to bring order to Karsk.

Monk—affectionately, a Man of No Knowledge.

Moonies—nomadic clans who travel the Northlands following the cycles of the moons. They refer to themselves as the Luna Rova.

- Dev'advari clan—the clan that Reddevek grew up in. They hold to the mountains.
- Do'—proper title for a man.
- Rovinary clan (roe-vin-ARR-ee)—encountered in Aarindorn in book three. This clan roams the low country.
- Sintra—proper title for a woman.
- Movshka—speaker of the Rovinary clan.

Moorlok (MORE-lock)—a vast and ancient tract of timber in the Southlands bordering Journey's Bend.

Munts—stableman in the royal stables at Stone's Grasp in Aarindorn.

Nascent—a zeniphile skilled in projecting an image of him/herself.

Oren (ORE-en)—the captain of the city watch in Stone's Grasp.

Outriders—an elite paramilitary group excelling in spycraft, martial arts, woodcraft, and ranging.

- Argul—a munitions expert killed fighting an umbral.
- Boljer—a prime wounded trying to capture a grondle.
- Bacall—a prime.
- Feille—a medic.
- Kap—a munitions expert.

Ozhen (Oh-zhen)—a thug in the company of the Hawklin brothers in the Southlands.

Reacher—a term used by the Immaculine to describe anyone who "reaches into the Drift" to summon power, whether it be zenith or nadir (they make no exception in using the terminology). Also called a thrall with the implication that anyone using the power is enthralled or enslaved by a lust for power.

Reddevek (RED-eh-vek)—a warden in the Outriders. One of the few gifted with tracking. He rarely uses his last name, Taim.

Retta—Cabe's daughter.

Riverton—a city adjacent to Journey's Bend in the Southlands.

Rolsh—the margrave in Riverton.

Rona (ROE-nuh) Scrivson—the aunt to Bryndor and Lluthean in the Southlands.

Runefather/mother—an adult zeniphile in Aarindorn who assumes a semi-formal relationship with a gifted child to uphold the cultural norms of society. This person is often involved in training and rituals such as the Rite of Revealing.

Runeling—the gifted child who is the recipient of the mentoring relationship with a runefather/mother.

Runta—a mediocre healer among the Outriders in Savnah's quad.

Salveen (sal-VEEN)—the male leader of the Spicers, a gang running the vivith trade, gaming rackets, and brothels in the quarter known as the Sprawl in Aarindorn.

Sadeen Tunkle (suh-DEEN TUN-kull)—a townswoman in Journey's Bend.

Senda—a Cloud Walker herb gatherer.

Sender—a zeniphile who can telepathically communicate with another sender. In the entire history of Aarindorn, senders have always been born as twins, triplets, etc. As such they are rare.

Shass—the former servant to Volencia and Mallic at their estate in Callish.

Shaveen (shah-VEEN)—one of a set of five albino quintuplet zeniphile senders who lived in the time of the Cataclysm. Their arca prime gifted them with the ability to telepathically communicate with each other over any distance.

Shelwyn River (SHELL-win)—a river in the Southlands.

Sheshla (SHESH-luh)—a butterfly named in the Valley of the Cloud Walkers.

Sifter—a zeniphile who can recall people or events with an eidetic memory.

Skellig—a drug courier in the Sprawl.

Skoon Fepl—the resource administrator in Stellance.

Sprawl, the—the poor part of Aarindorn where houses are crammed into winding neighborhoods, overcrowded slums, and poorly maintained streets. The brothels, gaming houses, and taverns outnumber more reputable businesses.

Steckle (STEK-ul)—hired hand and handyman at the Bashing Ram in Journey's Bend.

Stone's Grasp—the castle and capital city of Aarindorn.

Suvi (SOO-vee)—an ungifted woman who manages several orphanages in the Sprawl.

Tellend (TELL-end)—a family of farmers in Journey's Bend.

- Emile (eh-MEEL)—wise matron of the family.

- Harland—son to Emile and Markum.
- Markum—Emile's husband.

Timson (TIM-son)—a stable boy at the Abbey on the Mount.

Tomlek (TOM-lek)—a rector in Journey's Bend.

Tovnik (TAHV-nik)—a medic among the Outriders.

Torgrend Range (TORE-gend)—a range of mountains in the far northwest finger of the Northlands.

Umbral—aka shadowmen, creatures wandering the Drift and wielders of nadir ruled by the forces there. Their origins are poorly understood, but they are likely abrogators who died while steeped in the frenze and are now enslaved by forces in the Drift.

Vaeda (VAY-duh)—Southland name for the goddess embodied as the red moon.

Valdesta (val-DEST-uh)—a member of the inner council of the Lacuna.

Vardell Becks—an assassin hired by the Lacuna from Aarindorn. He is gifted with gusting.

Veeble Hebben (VEE-bull HEH-ben)—an autistic savant who works in the archives of Stone's Grasp.

Vesta—servant to Mallic and Volencia in their estate in Callish.

Vinnedesta—a scribe in service to the regent in Aarindorn.

Voruden (voe-ROO-den)—a queendom in the Northlands on the north face of the Korjinth Mountains, ruled by Queen Dressla Rudang.

Voshna (VOSH-nuh)—Southland name of the goddess embodied as the blue moon.

Weckles—the deceased former steward of the archives and master linguist in Aarindorn.

Winter—Ksenia Balladuren's albino Aarindin.

The Animals, Elements, and Plants of Karsk

Aarindin (AIR-in-din)—a prized stock of horses bred for their combination of stamina, speed, and intelligence and preserved for use by the Outriders, a branch of the Aarindorian military and elite classes. The breed standard are a jet black or ebony color. They can use zenith to grip a chosen or preferred rider and are most often ridden bareback for this reason.

- Tacit—mount trained by Ksenia Balladuren with above average intelligence for the breed.
- Trinney—a spirited and loquacious young Aarindin ridden by Karragin.
- Winter—Ksenia's personal friend, an albino.
- Zippy—Reddevek's loyal steed.

Annan—a common horse in the royal stables in book 2.

Baellen's eclipse—a water flower that grows a dense purple-blue bloom that opens to reveal a tiny orange center.

Bandle root (BAND-ul)—aka stilben root in the Southlands or dreamsong among the Cloud Walkers. The herb can be steeped into tea or ingested raw. Low doses cause sedation, while concentrated dosing leads to dissociation or temporary paralysis and numbness. The herb smells and tastes like anise or black licorice.

Bartusk—a herd animal led by a matriarch, vaguely resembling the wild boar but with multiple sets of tusks and rivaling the size of a draft horse.

Bear claw leaf—used to treat minor pain and fever.

Billow tree—a common tree along riverbanks in the Southlands. The tree produces seed pods with a woody outer husk of smooth, marbled brown. After a time, once exposed to water, the husk splits to release wispy seeds of white fluff, which billow into the air.

Blue trumpet—a vine that grows in the Borderlands and can be used to aid breathing/wheezing.

Broga's beard—a flowering plant that lives on its ability to absorb concentrated strands of zenith. Broga was a fabled mountain god from the Cloud Walkers, the native region of this plant.

Cave lark—a large cave-dwelling herbivore cat that uses its underbite to chisel away plants and lichen from rocks. Normal cave larks live in the low lands. Greater cave larks dwell in the highlands of the Great Crown.

Crag-horned ram—a rare white ram native to the Torgrend Range in northwest Karsk. Believed by the locals to serve as vessels to house the spirits of the dead.

Darksun—a flowering plant that grows wild in the Borderlands and can treat the flux.

Eldrenol's solution—an oil that prevents abrogators from channeling nadir when ingested or inhaled.

Embertang—referred to as embertang in the Northlands and devil's tail in the Southlands, an antiseptic, hemostatic oil that, especially if undiluted, causes severe caustic pain even to casual skin contact. The less potent devil's tail is found as more of an oily resin. Both are harvested from varieties of redleaf.

Gellseed root—given with blackberry tincture to treat diarrhea.

Gendek—mountain relative to vestek, an elusive herd animal found only in the Valley of the Cloud Walkers.

Heh-gava—a powder used to treat a cough or wheezing.

Kaliphora—antiemetic.

Kevash—a juicy, tangy fruit that grows all year in the Valley of the Cloud Walkers.

Lammen—a bush that drops tart red berries in early winter, found in the Great Crown. The berries are restorative and tast a bit like kevash.

Maedra's pitchers—a plant that blooms south of the Korjinth Mountains and can be steeped into a tea that dulls pain and improves healing. Scholars suspect that the tea somehow enhances a body's ability to absorb zenith.

Moonstone—a drab round rock which, when fractured open, reveals a set of gemstones that collect, store, and emit the moon's light.

Moonwing—see riftwing.

Nettle tea—a diuretic.

Redleaf—a plant cultivated and distilled into embertang.

Resco—a distillate of wine akin to whiskey.

Riftwing—a nocturnal hawk that flies with its talons clutched together in the shape of a basket. Not much is actually known of the elusive creatures, but they have the capacity to fade into pure zenith. Folklore in Aarindorn indicates that the creatures ferry the spirits of the dead to the Drift.

Spiritwort—a tea that lessens pain without causing drowsiness. It can be distilled into a potent tincture with unpalatable qualities and a particularly astringent and desiccating effect on the tongue.

Sweetleaf—a tobacco smoked in Aarindorn.

Veramanth's decoction (VARE-uh-manth)—aka stillers powder, mixed as a tea that prevents zeniphiles from channeling zenith for two to three days. When 'ranthed, a zeniphile cannot channel zenith.

Vestek—agile plains herd animal in the Northlands.

Vivith—an illegal stimulant. Brewed as a tea or smoked, it is highly addictive and often leads to paranoia. The smoke smells like pine resin.

Weeping bark—used to treat minor pain and fever.

Winter night's asylum—a green leafy plant that has the unusual feature of dropping white flowers to the ground midwinter. Botanists believe the plant stores zenith, then uses it to create an exothermic reaction that releases heat, thereby thawing the ground and allowing the plant to spread uncontested by other foliage. The petals are quite fragrant and can be refined into an exotic perfume with sultry, sweet, and even musky qualities.

Wolvryn—creatures related to wolves but much larger, far more intelligent, and gifted with unique abilities to see and smell through a spectrum of zenith.

- Boru (bo-ROO)—male companion to Bryndor.
- Ghetti—matriarch of the pack in the Valley of the Cloud Walkers.
- Neska (NES-kuh)—crafty female companion to Lluthean.
- Vencha—mother to Boru and Neska.
- Voozsh—Reddevek's wolvryn as a young man.

Wolvryn eye—artifacts that petrify when a wolvryn dies and retain a unique ability to store zenith and release it as a blue light.

Don't miss out!

Visit the website below and you can sign up to receive emails whenever Lance VanGundy publishes a new book. There's no charge and no obligation.

https://books2read.com/r/B-A-LQHL-UIULC

BOOKS 2 READ

Connecting independent readers to independent writers.

About the Author

Lance grew up in central Iowa, the product of public education and good parents. He attended Cornell College in Mount Vernon, Iowa where he obtained a Bachelor of Special Studies with anthropology and biology majors. Then he attended medical school at the University of Iowa. He has lived in central Iowa with his wife of more than thirty years where they raised three daughters. There he continues to practice emergency medicine and the whimsical art of escapism with all things Scifi and fantasy for as much as his wife can tolerate... that is significant... He is, after all, a very lucky man.

Read more at https://www.lancevangundy.com/.